Contents

Penguin Books

In Case of Emergency &
The Little Saint

Georges Simenon was born at Liège in Belgium in 1903. At sixteen he began work as a journalist on the *Gazette de Liège*. He has published over 212 novels in his own name, many of which belong to the Inspector Maigret series, and his work has been published in thirty-two countries. He has had a great influence upon French cinema, and more than forty of his novels have been filmed.

Simenon's novels are largely psychological. He describes hidden fears, tensions and alliances beneath the surface of life's ordinary routine which suddenly explode into violence and crime. André Gide wrote to him: 'You are living on a false reputation – just like Baudelaire or Chopin. But nothing is more difficult than making the public go back on a too hasty first impression. You are still the slave of your first successes and the reader's idleness would like to put a stop to your triumphs there . . . You are much more important than is commonly supposed'; and François Mauriac wrote, 'I am afraid I may not have the courage to descend right to the depths of this nightmare which Simenon describes with such unendurable art.'

Simenon has travelled a great deal and once lived on a cutter, making long journeys of exploration round the coasts of northern Europe. A book of reminiscences, *Letter to My Mother*, was published in England in 1976. He is married and lives near Lausanne in Switzerland.

Many of Simenon's novels are published in Penguins together with several other omnibus editions.

Georges Simenon

In Case of Emergency &
The Little Saint

*Translated by Helen Sebba
and Bernard Frechtman*

Penguin Books

Penguin Books Ltd, Harmondsworth, Middlesex, England
Viking Penguin Inc., 40 West 23rd Street, New York, New York 10010, U.S.A.
Penguin Books Australia Ltd, Ringwood, Victoria, Australia
Penguin Books Canada Limited, 2801 John Street, Markham, Ontario, Canada L3R 1B4
Penguin Books (N.Z.) Ltd, 182–190 Wairau Road, Auckland 10, New Zealand

En Cas de malheur first published 1956
This translation first published by Hamish Hamilton 1960
Published in Penguin Books 1965
Copyright © Georges Simenon, 1956, 1958
Translation copyright © Hamish Hamilton, 1960

Le Petit Saint first published 1965
This translation first published by Hamish Hamilton 1966
Published in Penguin Books 1971
Copyright © Georges Simenon, 1965

First published in one volume as *In Case of Emergency & The Little Saint* 1986
All rights reserved

Printed and bound in Great Britain by
Cox & Wyman Ltd, Reading

In Case of Emergency

Translated from the French by
Helen Sebba

Chapter One

Sunday, 4 November

Scarcely two hours ago, after lunch, in the drawing-room where we had gone to drink our coffee, I was standing in front of the window, close enough to the glass to feel its cold dampness, when, behind me, I heard my wife say:

'Will you be going out this afternoon?'

And these words, so simple, so commonplace, seemed to me heavy with meaning, as if they concealed between their syllables thoughts which neither Viviane nor myself dared express. I did not reply at once, not because I wasn't sure of my intentions, but because for a moment I hung suspended in that rather terrifying universe, more real, essentially, than the everyday world, which gives you the feeling of discovering the underside of life.

In the end I must have stammered:

'No. Not today.'

She knows I have no reason to go out. She has guessed it, like everything else; maybe she checks up on my actions and movements as well. I don't blame her for it any more than she blames me for what is happening to me.

At the moment she asked her question, I was watching, through the cold, dismal rain which has been falling for three days, since All Hallows to be precise, a tramp walking up and down under the Pont-Marie, slapping his thighs to get warm. In particular I was staring at a heap of dark rags, up against the stone wall, wondering whether it was really moving or whether that was an illusion caused by the quivering of the air and the movement of the rain.

It was moving, I was sure of it a little later, when an arm emerged from the rags, then a woman's face, bloated and framed in tousled hair. The man stopped walking up and down, turned towards his companion for Lord knows what dialogue, then, while she was getting into a sitting position, went and pulled out, from between two stones, a bottle, half full, which he handed to her and from which she took a swig.

In the ten years we have been living on the Quai d'Anjou in the Île Saint-Louis, I have often watched the tramps. I've seen all kinds, women too, but this is the first time I've seen any of them acting like a real couple. Why did that touch me, making me think of a male animal and his female snug in their forest lair?

Some people talk about Viviane and me as a couple of wild creatures, I've been told, and no doubt they don't fail to stress that among wild beasts the female is the more ferocious.

Before turning round and going up to the tray on which the coffee was served, I had time to register another image: a very tall man with a ruddy face emerging from the hatch of a barge anchored just opposite our house. He had his black raincoat over his head to brave the dripping universe and, an empty quart bottle hanging from each arm, he started down the slippery gang-plank between the boat and the quay. At the moment, he and the two tramps, together with a yellowish dog squeezing up against a black tree, were the only living things in the landscape.

'Are you going down to the office?' my wife asked again, while I was finishing my cup of coffee, still standing.

I said yes. I have always detested Sundays, especially Sundays in Paris, which produce in me a restlessness which comes close to panic. The prospect of going and waiting in a queue, under an umbrella, outside some cinema, makes me sick; so does the prospect of strolling along the Champs-Elysées, for example, or in the Tuileries, or of going for a drive, in a line of cars, on the Fontainebleau road.

We got home late last night. After a dress rehearsal at the Théâtre de la Michodière, we went to Maxim's for supper and wound up, about three o'clock in the morning, in a basement bar somewhere near the Rond-Point, frequented by actors and film people.

I'm not as good at going without sleep as I was a few years ago. Viviane, though, never seems to feel tired.

How much longer did we stay in the drawing-room without saying anything? At least five minutes, I would swear, and five minutes of that silence seem long. I was looking at my wife as little as possible. For the last few weeks I have avoided looking her in the face and have cut short our private conversations. Did she perhaps want to talk? I thought she was going to when, as I had my back half turned, she opened her mouth, hesitating, and finally brought out, instead of the words she wanted to say:

'I'm going to Corine's soon. If you feel like it later in the afternoon, you can come and pick me up there.'

Corine de Langelle is a friend who causes quite a lot of talk and who owns one of the most beautiful town houses in Paris, in the Rue Saint-Dominique. Among her various original ideas, one is to keep open house on Sunday afternoons.

'It's not true that everyone goes to the races,' she will explain, 'and not many wives go shooting with their husbands. Why should one have to be bored just because it's Sunday?'

I walked round and round the drawing-room and finally muttered:

'See you later.'

I crossed the corridor and opened the door of the office. After all these years, it is still a queer feeling to enter it from the gallery. It was Viviane's idea. When the flat below ours came up for sale, she advised me to buy it and set up my chambers there, because we were beginning to be cramped, especially for entertaining. The ceiling of one of the rooms, the largest, was removed and replaced by a gallery at the level of the floor above.

This produces a very high room, with two rows of windows, lined with books top and bottom, which in fact looks a bit like a public library, and it took me some time to get used to working and receiving my clients there.

Still, I did fix myself up, in one of the original rooms, a more private retreat where I prepare my briefs and where a leather couch enables me to take a nap without undressing.

I took a nap today. Did I really sleep? I'm not sure. In the dusk I closed my eyes and I don't think I stopped hearing the water running down the rainpipe. I suppose Viviane took a rest too, in the red silk boudoir she fixed up for herself next to our bedroom.

It is a little after four o'clock. She must be dressing and she will probably drop in to kiss me good-bye before she goes to Corine's.

I feel that my eyes are swollen. For a long time I haven't been looking well, and the medicine Dr Pémal has prescribed does no good. All the same I keep on conscientiously swallowing the drops and pills which form a small arsenal in front of my place at table.

I have always had big eyes, a big head, so big that there are only two or three shops in Paris where I can find hats to fit me. At school they used to compare me to a toad.

Every now and then I hear a crack, because the wood of the gallery warps in damp weather, and each time I raise my head, as though caught doing something I shouldn't, expecting to see Viviane coming downstairs.

I have never hidden anything from her and yet I shall hide this from her and keep it locked up in the Renaissance cupboard in my den. Before beginning to write, I made sure that the key, which no one has ever used, hadn't been lost and that the lock works. I shall have to find a place for this key, too: behind certain books in the library, for instance; it is enormous and wouldn't fit into my pocket.

I have taken from my desk drawer a cream-coloured manila folder with my name and address stamped on it.

Lucien Gobillot
Avocat à la Cour d'Appel de Paris
17 bis, Quai d'Anjou – Paris

Hundreds of these dossiers, more or less stuffed with tragedy – those of my clients – fill a metal filing cabinet which Mademoiselle Bordenave keeps up to date, and I hesitated to write my name in the place where, on the others, the client's name stands. In the end, with an ironical smile, I traced one single word in red pencil: *Myself*.

It is, in fact, my own dossier that I am beginning, and it is not impossible that it may some day be put to use. I waited more than ten minutes, apprehensive, before writing the first sentence, tempted as I was to begin it like a will with:

I the undersigned, being sound in body and in mind ...

Because it is something like a will, too. To be more precise, I don't know yet what it will be like and I wonder if there will be, in the margin, the cabalistic signs I use for my clients.

It is, in fact, my practice to jot down, in their presence, while they are talking, the essence of what they say, the true and the false, the half-true and the half-false, the exaggerations and the lies, and, at the same time, I record my momentary impressions by means of signs which make sense only to me. Some of these signs are unexpected, baroque, like those little men or those shapeless doodles that some judges sketch on their blotters during long speeches by counsel.

I am trying to make fun of myself, not to treat myself as a tragic case. And yet, isn't it already a symptom that I need to explain myself in writing? For whom? Why? I have no idea. In case of emergency, in short, as those estimable characters say who lay money by. Against the possibility that things should turn out badly.

Can they turn out any other way? Even in Viviane I sense a feeling which has always been foreign to her and which looks the very image of pity. She doesn't know, either, what is in store for us. She understands, just the same, that things can't go on like this, that something is bound to happen, no matter what.

Pémal, too, who has been looking after me for fifteen years, suspects it, and when he gives me prescriptions I'm sure he does it without conviction. Besides, when he comes to see me, he puts on that free and easy, jaunty air, behind which he must hide when he visits someone who is seriously ill.

'What's the trouble today?'

Nothing. Nothing and everything. Then he talks about my being forty-five and about the terrific load of work I've always carried and keep on carrying. He makes a joke:

'There comes a time when the most powerful and the most perfect motor needs some minor repairs....'

Has he heard about Yvette? Pémal doesn't move in the same circles as we do, where my private life is no secret. He has doubtless read, in magazines, certain echoes which make real sense only to people in the know.

Besides, it's not only a matter of Yvette. It's the whole machine, to use his expression, which isn't running properly, and that doesn't date from today, or a few weeks or a few months ago.

Am I going to pretend that I have known for twenty years that it would end badly? That would be exaggerated, though no more so than to claim that it began a year ago with Yvette.

I want to ...

*

14

My wife has just come downstairs, dressed in a black suit under her mink coat, with a little veil which lends mystery to the upper part of her slightly faded face. When she came up to me, I could smell her scent.

'Do you think you'll join me?'

'I don't know.'

'We could have dinner out afterwards.'

'I'll ring you at Corine's.'

For the moment I want to stay by myself in my corner, in my own sweat.

She put her lips to my forehead and walked towards the door, her step brisk.

'See you later.'

She didn't ask what I am working on. I watched her go out and got up to press my forehead against the window-pane.

The tramp couple are still under the Pont-Marie. Just now the man and the woman are sitting side by side, leaning against the stone embankment and watching the water flowing under the arches. From this distance you can't see their lips move and it is impossible to know whether they are talking, the lower part of their bodies tucked up in the ragged covers. If they are talking, what do they find to say to each other?

The bargeman must have come back with his ration of wine, and one can make out, in the cabin, the reddish glow of a petroleum lamp.

It's still raining and it's almost dark.

Before beginning to write again, I picked out, on the telephone dial, the number of the flat in the Rue de Ponthieu, and it hurt me to hear the bell ringing there and not be there myself. This is a sensation I'm growing familiar with, a kind of cramp or spasm in the chest, which makes me press my hand to it like a heart patient.

The bell rang for a long time, as though in an empty apartment, and I was expecting it to stop when I heard a click. A sleepy, irritable voice muttered:

'What is it?'

I almost didn't answer. Without giving my name, I asked:

'Were you asleep?'

'It's you! Yes, I was asleep.'

There was a silence. Why ask what she did last night and what time she came home?

'You've not been drinking?'

She has had to get out of bed to answer the telephone, because the instrument isn't in her bedroom but in the sitting-room. She sleeps naked. Her skin, when she first wakes up, has a special smell, her woman's smell mixed with that of nicotine and alcohol. She is drinking much more just lately, as if she too had an intuition that something is in store.

I didn't dare ask her if he was there. What's the use? Why shouldn't he be, since I have, somehow, made way for him? He must be listening, propped on his elbow, fumbling for cigarettes in the half-light of the bedroom with the curtains drawn.

There are clothes scattered about on the carpet, on the chairs, glasses and bottles lying around, and, as soon as I hang up, she will go to the refrigerator to get some beer.

She makes an effort to ask, as if she were interested:

'Are you working?

'Is it still raining?' she adds – and this tells me that the curtains are drawn.

'Yes.'

That's all. I search for words to say and perhaps she searches too. All I find is a ridiculous:

'Be good.'

I think I can see her pose, on the arm of the green armchair, her pear-shaped breasts, her thin back like that of a scraggy teen-ager, the dark triangle of hair below her stomach which for some reason always looks pathetic to me.

'See you tomorrow.'

'All right: tomorrow.'

I have gone back to the window and already you can't see anything but the garlands of street lights along the Seine, their reflection in the water, and, in the blackness of the wet façades, here and there the rectangle of a lighted window.

I re-read the passage I was writing when my wife interrupted me.

*

'*I want to . . .*'

I can't remember what I had in mind. Besides, I think that if I want to go on with what I already call my dossier, it will be as well not to re-read anything: not even one sentence.

'*I want to . . .*'

Oh yes! That's probably it. To treat myself as I treat my clients. At the Palais de Justice they say I should have made a terrific examining magistrate, because I can get the truth out of the toughest customers. My attitude hardly ever varies and I admit that I take advantage of my physical appearance, my famous toad's face, my protruding eyes which, staring at people as if not seeing them, inspire them with awe. My ugliness is useful to me, giving me the mysterious look of a Chinese porcelain figure.

I let them talk for a time, taking notes myself with a relaxed hand, let them run through the rosary of phrases they prepared before knocking at my door, then, just when they are least expecting it, I interrupt, without moving, my chin still in my left hand:

'*No!*'

This little word, pronounced without raising my voice, as though in a void, hardly ever fails to disconcert them.

'*I assure you . . .*' they try to protest.

'*No.*'

'*You accuse me of lying?*'

'*Things did not* just *happen as you say.*'

With some people, especially women, that does it, and

17

they immediately smile confidentially. Others go on resisting.

'*But I swear* . . .'

With these people, I get up as if the consultation were over, and walk towards the door.

'*I'll tell you,*' they stammer, worried.

'*I don't need an explanation; I need the truth. It's up to me, not you, to find the explanations. As long as you prefer to tell lies* . . .'

Rarely do I have to press the buzzer.

Obviously I can't go through that act with myself. But if I write, for instance :

'*It began a year ago when* . . .'

I'm justified in interrupting myself, just as I do other people, with a simple, categorical :

'*No!*'

That 'no' confuses them even more than the ones before and now they don't understand.

'*And yet,*' they persist, '*it was when I met her that* . . .'

'*No.*'

'*Why do you insist it's not true?*'

'*Because you have to go further back.*'

'*Back where to?*'

'*I don't know. Try.*'

They try, and nearly always discover an earlier event to explain their tragedy. I've saved plenty of people that way, not, as they say at the Palais, by trick of procedure or by playing to the gallery for the benefit of juries, but because I have made them find the reason for their behaviour.

I myself, just like them, was about to write :

'*It began* . . .'

When ? With Yvette, that evening when, getting back from the Palais, I found her sitting all alone in my waiting-room ? That's the easy answer, what I'm tempted to call the romantic answer. If it hadn't been Yvette, it would probably have been someone else. Who knows even that the intrusion of a new element into my life was inevitable?

Unfortunately I haven't got, as my clients have when they sit down in what we call the confessional chair, someone facing me to help me find out my own truth, even if it were only by means of a commonplace:

'*No!*'

I won't allow them to begin at the end or in the middle, and yet that is what I am going to do, because the question of Yvette obsesses me and I need to get rid of it. Afterwards, if I still have the desire and the courage, I'll try to dig more deeply.

It was a Friday, just over a year ago, not much more because it was mid-October. I had just finished pleading a blackmail case in which the verdict had been deferred for a week and I remember that my wife and I were supposed to be having dinner in a restaurant on the Avenue du Président Roosevelt with the chief commissioner of police and various other important people. I had walked back from the Palais, just round the corner, and a fine rain was falling, almost warm, quite different from today's.

Mademoiselle Bordenave, my secretary, whom it has never occurred to me to call by her first name and whom I call Bordenave as everybody else does, and as I would call a man, was waiting for me to come back. But little Duret, who has been my assistant for more than four years, had already left.

'There's someone for you in the waiting-room,' announced Bordenave, raising her head beneath the green lampshade.

She is a blonde rather than a red-head, but her sweat smells unmistakably of red-heads.

'Who?'

'A young kid. She wouldn't tell me her name or what she wanted. She says she has to see you personally.'

'Which room?'

There are two waiting-rooms, the big one and the little

one, as we call them, and I knew my secretary was going to reply:

'The little one.'

She doesn't like women who insist on speaking to me personally.

I still had my brief-case under my arm, my hat on my head, my wet overcoat on my shoulders, when I pushed open the door and saw her leaning back in an armchair, legs crossed, reading a film magazine and smoking a cigarette.

Immediately she jumped to her feet and looked at me just as she would have looked, in flesh and blood, at the actor on the cover of the magazine.

'Come in here.'

I had noted her cheap coat, the run-down heels of her shoes and especially her hair done in a pony-tail like a dancer or one of the Left Bank girls.

In my office, I took off my things and sat down, motioning her to the armchair opposite me.

Then I asked, 'Did someone send you here?'

'No. I came on my own.'

'What made you come to me rather than to some other lawyer?'

I often ask this question, although the reply isn't always flattering to my self-esteem.

'Can't you guess?'

'I don't play guessing games.'

'Let's say because you usually get your clients off.'

A journalist put the same thing differently not long ago and since then it's gone from newspaper to newspaper:

'If you're innocent, take any good lawyer. If you're guilty, get in touch with Mâitre Gobillot.'

My visitor's face was harshly lighted by the lamp trained on the confessional chair, and I remember my distress when I analysed it, for it was a child's face and a very old face at the same time, a mixture of *naïveté* and deceit; of innocence and vice, I would like to add, except that I don't like those words, which I reserve for juries.

She was thin, physically run down, like girls of her age who live unhealthy lives in Paris. What made me think she probably had dirty feet?

'Is there a charge against you?'

'There's certainly going to be.'

She liked surprising me and I'm sure she purposely exposed her legs above the knees as she crossed them. Her make-up, which she had touched up while she was waiting for me, was exaggerated and clumsy, like that of fifth-rate prostitutes or those little servant girls who have just arrived in Paris.

'As soon as I get back to my hotel, if I go back, I shall be arrested, and probably all the police in the streets have my description by now.'

'You wanted to see me *first*?'

'Of course! It'll be too late afterwards.'

I didn't understand and I was beginning to be intrigued. No doubt that's what she wanted, and I caught a furtive smile on her thin lips.

I started in at random:

'I suppose you're innocent?'

She had read those items about me, because she retorted:

'If I was innocent, I wouldn't be here.'

'What are you wanted for?'

'Hold-up.'

She said it simply, dryly.

'You've committed armed assault?'

'That's what they call a hold-up, isn't it?'

Then I settled down in my armchair, assuming my familiar pose, chin in my left hand, my right hand tracing words and arabesques on a pad, my head slightly tilted, my big vague eyes fixed on her.

'Tell me.'

'What?'

21

'Everything.'

'I'm nineteen.'

'I would have said seventeen.'

I was provoking her deliberately, yet I don't know why. I might say that at our very first contact a kind of antagonism had sprung up between us. She was defying me and I was defying her. Maybe at that moment our chances still seemed even.

'I was born in Lyons.'

'Go on.'

'My mother is neither a housewife nor a factory worker nor a prostitute.'

'Why do you say that?'

'Because that's usually the case, isn't it?'

'Do you read trashy novels?'

'Only the newspapers. My father's a schoolteacher, and before she got married my mother worked in the Post Office.'

She seemed to be expecting a reply which didn't come, and this put her off for a moment.

'I went to school until I was sixteen, I got my school certificate and I worked as a typist for a year, in Lyons, with a road transport firm.'

I had decided on silence.

'One day I made up my mind to try my luck in Paris and I convinced my parents I had found a job by letter.'

I was still not speaking.

'Doesn't this interest you?'

'Go on.'

'I came here, without a job, and I got along, since I'm still alive. Don't you want to ask how I got along?'

'No.'

'I'll tell you just the same. Doing all kinds of things. Anything at all.'

I didn't move a muscle and she insisted:

'All kinds! Understand?'

'Go on.'

'I met Noémie, who's got herself pinched somewhere or other. They're probably interrogating her right now. Since they know there were two of us in the hold-up and they'll find out, if they haven't already, that we share a room together at the hotel, they'll be waiting for me. Do you know the Hôtel Alberti in the Rue Vavin?'

'No.'

'That's where it is.'

My attitude was beginning to get on her nerves and even to embarrass her. For my part, I was deliberately trying to look more stolid, more indifferent.

'Are you always like this?' she demanded resentfully. 'I thought your job was to help your clients.'

'Provided I know how I can help them.'

'To get the two of us off, damn it!'

'I'm listening.'

She hesitated, shrugged her shoulders, went on:

'All right. I'll try. In the end we got fed up, both of us.'

'What with?'

'Do you want me to spell it out for you? I don't mind, and if you enjoy dirty stories . . .'

There was scorn and disillusionment in her voice, and for the first time I encouraged her, feeling rather bad about having been even harsher than usual.

'Whose idea was the hold-up?'

'Mine. Noémie's too stupid to have an idea. She's a good kid but not very bright. While I was reading the papers I got the notion that with a bit of luck we could set ourselves up for weeks or maybe months with one single job. At night I'm often on the streets around the Gare Montparnasse and I'm getting to know that district pretty well. On the corner of the Rue de l'Abbé-Grégoire, I've noticed a watchmaker's shop that's open every night till nine or ten.

'It's a narrow shop, badly lighted. At the back you can

see a kitchen where an old woman knits or peels her vegetables while she listens to the radio.

'The watchmaker, who is as old as she is and baldheaded, works close to the shop window, with a blackrimmed magnifying-glass in his eye, and I took to walking past their shop often, on purpose, so as to watch them. That stretch of the street is badly lighted, with no shops near by ...'

'You were armed?'

'I bought one of those toy revolvers that look exactly like a real one.'

'This happened last night?'

'The night before last. Wednesday.'

'Go on.'

'A little after nine, the two of us went into the shop, and Noémie pretended her watch needed repairing. I was standing beside her and I got a bit worried when I didn't see the old woman in the kitchen. I almost gave the whole thing up on account of that, and then, just as the man was bending down to look at my friend's watch, I showed him the tip of the gun and said:

' "This is a hold-up. Don't call out. Give me your money and you won't get hurt."

'He could tell I wasn't fooling and opened the till, while Noémie, as we had planned, was grabbing the watches hanging beside his work-bench and stuffing them in her coat pockets.

'I was just about to stick out my hand to take the money, when I felt someone was behind me. It was the old woman, in her coat and hat, on her way back from Lord knows where, and she was standing on the doorstep and starting to scream for help.

'She didn't seem scared of my revolver and she was blocking the way, with her arms stretched out, and yelling:

' "Thief! Help! Murder!"

'That's when I noticed the handle they use to raise and

24

lower the iron shutter, and I grabbed it and threw myself on the old woman, shouting to Noémie:

' "Let's get out of here fast!"

'As I pushed the old woman aside, I hit her and she fell backwards on to the pavement and we had to step over her. We ran off in opposite directions.

'We had agreed to meet in a bar on the Rue de la Gaîté if we had to separate, but I doubled back on my tracks for more than an hour. I even took the underground all the way to the Châtelet before going to the bar. I asked Gaston:

' "Hasn't my girl friend been in?"

' "I haven't seen her this evening," he answered.

'I spent part of the night out and when it was getting light I went back to the Hôtel Alberti but I didn't find Noémie there. I haven't seen her since. In yesterday morning's paper there were a few lines about it, saying that the jeweller's wife had been taken to hospital with injuries to her forehead and one eye.

'They don't say anything else. They don't mention us, either last night or this morning. They don't say the job was done by two women either.

'I don't like it. I didn't go back to the Hôtel Alberti last night, and about noon, on my way to the bar in the Rue de la Gaîté, I spotted two plain-clothes cops just in time.

'I kept on walking, turning my head away. From a bistro in the Rue de Rennes, where they don't know me, I rang up Gaston.'

I was listening, still motionless, without letting her see the signs of interest she had counted on.

'Apparently they showed him a photo of Noémie, one of the kind they take of people who've been arrested, and asked him if he knew her. He said he did. Then they wanted to know if he knew her girl friend and he said he did, but that he didn't know where either of us lived. They must have done the same thing in all the bars around there and in the hotels too, no doubt. I asked Gaston, who's a pal, to do me a favour and he agreed.'

She looked at me as if all I had to do now was understand.

'I'm waiting,' I said, still coldly.

I don't know exactly what I resented in her, but I resented something.

'When they question him again, what's going to happen is that he'll say we were both in his bar on Thursday evening at the time of the hold-up and he'll find customers who'll identify us. Noémie doesn't know that, and she's simply got to be told. If I know her, she's probably kept her mouth shut and looked at them with her pig-headed expression. Now that you're our lawyer, you'll be allowed to go and see her and tell her what to say. You'll be able to straighten out the details with Gaston, too; you'll find him at his bar until two in the morning. I've told him on the phone. I can't offer you money just now, because I haven't got any, but I know you've sometimes taken cases free.'

I thought I knew everything, had seen everything, heard everything.

I felt that she was hesitant about finishing, that she hadn't come to the end yet, that she still had something to say or do which suddenly seemed difficult. Was she afraid of messing up this deal, which she must have planned as minutely as the hold-up?

I can see her now getting to her feet, trying to smile confidently and play her big scene sensationally. Her glance swept the room, stopped at the only corner of my desk that wasn't deep in papers, and then, pulling up her skirt to her waist, she lay back, whispering:

'As much as you want before they put me in jail.'

She wore no pants. That was the first time I saw her thin thighs, her rounded, childish belly, the dark triangle below it, and for no precise reason the blood rushed to my head.

I could see her face upside down, near the lamp and the vase of flowers which Bordenave renews every morning, and she was trying to see me, too; she was waiting, and, as she felt that I still hadn't moved, bit by bit losing confidence in her fate.

It took a little time for those eyes to fill with water, for her to sniff, then, at last, for her hand to fumble for the hem of her skirt which she still didn't pull down, asking in a disappointed, humiliated voice:

'It doesn't appeal to you?'

She got up slowly, turning her back to me, and it was still without showing her face that she asked, resignedly:

'Is it no to everything?'

I lit a cigarette. Now it was my turn to answer, looking away:

'Sit down.'

She didn't do so at once, and before turning towards me she blew her nose noisily, as children do.

It was she whom I telephoned just now in the Rue de Ponthieu, where there was a man in her bed, a man I know, whom I practically asked to become her lover.

*

The telephone bell rang just when I didn't know if I would go on writing today. I recognized my wife's voice.

'Still working?'

I hesitated.

'No.'

'Aren't you coming for me? Moriat's here. If you come, Corine wants us to stay for dinner with four or five friends.'

I agreed.

So I'm going to lock 'my' dossier up in the cupboard, and behind some books in the library I shall hide the key, then I'll go upstairs and dress.

Is the tramp couple still stretched out under the Pont-Marie?

Chapter Two

Tuesday, 6 November, evening

I went up to my room to change and I called Albert.

'Get the car out to take me to the Rue Saint-Dominique. I suppose Madame took the little car?'

'Yes, sir.'

We have two cars and chauffeur-manservant, but it's mostly the chauffeur that causes talk. He is put down to the slightly naïve vanity of a self-made man, when actually I engaged him for a rather silly reason.

If I had a client in front of me telling me all this, I would no doubt interrupt him with:

'*Stick to the facts.*'

And yet, while I'm at it, I want to explode a legend. Maître Andrieu, under whom I started, and, incidentally, the only man I ever devilled for, who was also Viviane's first husband, was one of the few Paris lawyers to be driven to the Palais by a liveried chauffeur. That suggests that I want to imitate him, that some complex or other compels me to prove to my wife ...

When we were getting started, while we were living on the Place Denfert-Rochereau, with the Lion de Belfort just under our windows, I used to take the métro. That didn't last long, about a year, and after that I could afford taxis. We lost no time in buying a second-hand car, and, while Viviane had a driver's licence, I wasn't capable of passing the test. I lack all mechanical sense, maybe the reflexes too. I'm so tense at the wheel, so sure of inevitable disaster, that the examiner advised me:

'It would be better to give up, Maître Gobillot. You're not the only man like this and they're nearly always people of more than average intelligence. If you take it over again two or three times, you'll finally get through, but sooner or later you'll have an accident. It's not your line.'

I remember the respect he put into these last words, for I was beginning to make a name for myself.

For several years, until we moved to the Île Saint-Louis, Viviane served as my chauffeur, driving me to the Palais and waiting for me in the evening, and it wasn't until Albert, the son of our gardener at Sully, was looking for a job, after his military service, that we thought of taking him on.

Our life had grown more complicated, and each of us had more obligations to meet.

People found it strange that we weren't inseparable any more, my wife and I, because it had become a sort of legend, and I'm sure that even now certain people think Viviane helps me prepare my briefs, if not my speeches in court.

I'm not proud in the sense my colleagues mean and if ...
'*Facts!*'

Why have I gone back to last Sunday evening, which wasn't singled out by any important event? Today's Tuesday. I didn't think I would want to immerse myself in my dossier again so soon.

So Albert drove me to the Rue Saint-Dominique, where I saw my wife's blue car in the courtyard, and I told Albert not to wait. At Corine de Langelle's I found about ten people in one of the drawing-rooms and three or four in the little circular room fixed up as a bar where the hostess was presiding in person.

'Scotch, Lucien?' she asked me before we exchanged a kiss.

She kisses everyone. In her house it's a ritual.

Then, almost immediately:

'What monster of cruelty is our eminent lawyer snatching from the clutches of Justice this time?'

Jean Moriat was there, in an enormous armchair, talking to Viviane, and I shook hands with the regular guests: Lannier, the owner of three or four newspapers, the deputy Druelle, a young man whose name I always forget and whose occupation I don't know except that he's always to be found where Corine is – *one of my protégés*, she calls him – two or three good-looking women over forty, which is normal for the Rue Saint-Dominique.

Nothing happened, as I've said, except what usually happens at this kind of party. We went on drinking and chatting until about eight-thirty, and by that time there was only a group of five or six left, as Viviane had said there would be, including Lannier and, of course, Jean Moriat.

It's on account of him that I come back to this, because on two or three separate occasions our eyes met and I got the impression, mistakenly perhaps, though I don't think so, that some kind of exchange took place between us.

Everyone knows Moriat, who has been a member of the cabinet ten times at least, and premier twice, and will be again. Photographs and caricatures of him appear on the front page of the papers as regularly as those of film stars.

He is a thick-set, stocky man, almost as ugly as I am, but he has the advantage of height, which I lack, and of a certain peasant toughness which gives him an air of nobility.

His life, too, is more or less an open secret, at least to those Parisians who call themselves insiders.

At forty-two, married and father of three children, he was still a veterinary surgeon at Niort and seemed to have no further ambitions when, after an electoral scandal, he ran for parliament and was elected.

He would probably have spent the rest of his life as a conscientious deputy, shuttling back and forth between a shabby apartment on the Left Bank and his constituency, if Corine hadn't met him. How old was she then? It's difficult to talk about Corine's age. Judging by the way she looks today, she must have been about thirty. Her husband, the old Comte de Langelle, had died two years earlier, and she was beginning to drift away from the Faubourg Saint-Germain, where she had lived with him, into a milieu of newspaper publishers and politicians.

They say that there was nothing casual about her choice of Moriat and that her emotions had nothing to do with it, that she had tried two or three other men first and discarded them, and that she had had her eye on the deputy for Niort for a long time before making him her choice.

Anyhow he was seen at her house more and more frequently, went back to Deux-Sèvres less regularly, and two years later was already a junior minister, being appointed to the cabinet shortly afterwards.

This is all more than fifteen years ago, almost twenty, I'm not bothering to check the dates which aren't important, and today their liaison is an accepted thing, semi-official since it's to the Rue Saint-Dominique that the prime minister, for example, or even the President, telephones when Moriat is needed.

He didn't break with his wife, who lives in Paris somewhere around the Champs-de-Mars. I've met her several times: she's still awkward, self-effacing, and she always seems to be apologizing for being so unworthy of the great man. Their children are married, and I think the eldest is in local government.

At Corine's, Moriat doesn't pose for the benefit of his constituents or posterity. He shows himself as he is, and he often looks to me like a man who is bored or more precisely a man who is trying to come up to expectations.

On Sunday, the first time our eyes met, he was watching me and wrinkling his brow as if he was discovering in me a new element, something I'm tempted to call a sign.

I wouldn't like to repeat aloud what I'm about to write,

out of shame and for fear of being ridiculous, but that Sunday I began to believe in the sign, an invisible mark that can only be discerned by the initiated, by those who bear it themselves.

Am I going to think this through to the end? Only special people can have that sign, people who have lived a lot, seen a lot, tried everything for themselves, above all, people who have made an abnormal effort, reached or almost reached their goal, and I don't think you can acquire it under a certain age, the middle forties, say.

I for my part was watching Moriat, first during dinner, while the women were telling stories, then in the drawing-room where the mistress of the newspaper proprietor had sat down on some cushions and was singing, accompanying herself on her guitar.

He wasn't enjoying himself any more than I was, that was obvious. As he looked about him, he must have been wondering what trick of fate had placed him in a setting which was in a way an insult to his personality.

He is supposed to be ambitious. He has his legend, just as I have mine, and he's said to be as formidable in politics as I am in court.

Yet I don't think he is ambitious, or else, if he once was, in a pretty childish way, he isn't any more. He submits to his fate, his personality, just as some actors are condemned to play the same role all their lives.

I watched him take drink after drink, without pleasure, without getting any kick out of them, and yet not like an alcoholic either, and I'm convinced that every time he asked for more liquor it was to nerve himself to stay.

Corine, who is almost fifteen years younger than he, looks after him like a baby, sees that everything he wants is right there.

Last Sunday, she, too, who knows him better than anyone else, must have been watching his lassitude, his apathy, increase as the evening advanced.

32

I haven't yet started drinking. I hardly ever do and never in that systematic way.

All the same Moriat had recognized the sign in me; it must lie in the eyes; perhaps it is nothing but a certain heaviness in the glance, a certain vacuity rather than any special facial expression.

We were talking politics, and he came out with a few sarcastic phrases, as one might throw crumbs to the birds. At that moment I left the drawing-room to go into a boudoir where I knew there was a telephone. I rang the Rue de Ponthieu first, where, as I expected, there was no reply. Then I dialled the number of Louis', the Italian restaurant where Yvette usually eats.

'Gobillot speaking. Is Yvette there, Louis?'

'She's just come in, Monsieur Gobillot. Do you want me to call her?'

I added, because I had to, and because Louis knows:

'Is she alone?'

'Yes. She's just started dinner at the small table in the back.'

'Tell her I'll drop in in half an hour, perhaps a little later.'

Has Moriat guessed this drama too? Neither of us is a vicious man, any more than we're ambitious, but who would admit this apart from the few who bear the sign themselves? He watched me again when I came back into the drawing-room, but his eyes were bleary and moist, as they always are after a certain number of drinks.

I suppose Corine made some signal to him, for there is the same understanding between them as between Viviane and me. The ex-premier, who one of these days will once again direct the destinies of the country, got up laboriously, made a gesture of benediction and murmured:

'You'll excuse me . . .'

He crossed the drawing-room with an unsteady, heavy tread, and through the glass door I caught sight of a footman waiting for him, no doubt to put him to bed.

'He works so hard!' sighed Corine. 'He carries such a load of responsibilities on his shoulders!'

Viviane, too, gave me a knowing look, and hers contained a question. She had understood that I had gone to make a phone call. She knew to whom, why, and she was aware that I would end up by going there; I think she was even silently advising me to.

. The evening would drag on for an hour or two before the good-bye kisses.

'I'll have to ask you to excuse me. I've got work waiting for me too. . . .'

Were they taken in? Probably not, any more than by Moriat. It doesn't matter.

'Did you keep the car?' Viviane asked.

'No. I'll take a taxi.'

'Wouldn't you like me to drop you?'

'Of course not. There's a cab rank just across the street.'

Once I'm out of sight, will she talk about my work and my responsibilities? I had to wait for a taxi in the rain for ten minutes, because it's Sunday, and when I got to Louis' Yvette was smoking a cigarette with her coffee, almost alone in the restaurant, looking vacant.

. She made room for me on the bench, offered me her cheek with a movement which has grown as familiar as Corine's kisses.

'Did you have dinner out?' she asked simply, as if our relationship were just like everybody else's.

'I had a bite at the Rue Saint-Dominque.'

'Was your wife there?'

'Yes.'

She isn't jealous of Viviane, doesn't want to take her place, doesn't want anything, in fact, being content to live in the present.

'What will you have, Maître?'

I looked at Yvette's cup and said:

'Coffee.'

She remarked :

'It'll keep you awake.'

That's right. In the end I'll have to take a sleeping-tablet, as I do almost every night. I have nothing to say to her, and we sit side by side on the bench, staring in front of us like an old couple.

Yet I do eventually ask :

'Tired ?'

She says no, without seeing any harm in the question, then it's her turn to ask :

'How did you spend your day ?'

'I worked.'

I don't say what exactly I worked on this afternoon, and she is far from suspecting that it was chiefly to do with her.

'Is your wife waiting for you ?'

This is an indirect way of finding out about my intentions.

'No.'

'Shall we go home ?'

I nod. I would like to be able to say no, to go away, but I gave up this losing battle long ago.

'Do you mind if I have a chartreuse ?'

'If you like. Louis ! One chartreuse.'

'Nothing for you, Monsieur Gobillot ?'

'Nothing, thanks.'

The cleaning-woman at the Rue de Ponthieu doesn't come on Sundays, and I'm sure Yvette hasn't bothered to tidy up the flat. Has she even made the bed ? Probably not. She drinks her chartreuse slowly, with long pauses between sips, as if putting off the moment for leaving. At last she whispers :

'Will you ask for the bill ?'

Louis is used to seeing us at this table and knows where we're going when we leave his place.

'Good night, mademoiselle. Good night, Maître.'

She takes my arm in the rain, and her heels, which are

too high, sometimes make her stumble. It's just round the corner.

*

It is imperative that I go back to our first meeting, that Friday night, just over a year ago, in my office. While she was sitting down again, intimidated, wondering what I had decided, I picked up the house telephone to speak to my wife.

'I'm in my office, where I've got some work that will take an hour or two. Go to dinner without me and make my excuses to the commissioner and our friends. Tell them, and I really mean it, that I hope to be there in time for coffee.'

Without looking at my visitor, I walked towards the door, telling her crossly:

'Stay there.'

I even added, perhaps to provoke her, as one might say to a naughty child:

'Don't touch anything.'

I went out to Bordenave in her office.

'I want you to go downstairs and make sure that the person in my office hasn't been followed.'

'The police?'

'Yes. You can tell me on the telephone.'

In my office, I walked back and forth, my hands behind my back, while Yvette watched me pacing up and down.

'This Gaston,' I finally asked, 'has he got a police record?'

'I don't think so. He's never mentioned one.'

'Do you know him well?'

'Pretty well.'

'You've slept together?'

'Occasionally.'

'Is your friend Noémie of age?'

'She's just turned twenty.'

'What does she do?'

'The same as me.'

'Has she never had a job?'

'She used to help her mother in the shop. Her mother sells vegetables in the Rue du Chemin-Vert.'

'She ran away from home?'

'She left, saying she'd had enough.'

'Long ago?'

'Two years.'

'Didn't her mother try to find her?'

'No. She doesn't care. Every now and then, when she's completely broke, Noémie goes to see her. They have a row, bawl each other out, but in the end her mother always gives her a little money.'

'She's never been arrested?'

'Noémie? Twice. Possibly more, but she told me twice.'

'What charge?'

'Soliciting. Both times they let her go the next day after giving her a medical check-up.'

'What about you?'

'Not so far.'

The telephone rang. It was Bordenave.

'I didn't see anyone, sir.'

'Thanks. I won't need you any more tonight.'

'You don't want me to wait?'

'No.'

'Good night.'

I simply must get down to the why and I'm all the more embarrassed because I would like to get at the absolute truth. Not two or three pieces of truth which form a whole that is satisfactory in appearance but inevitably false.

I felt no desire for Yvette that evening, nor pity for her. In my career I've come across too many specimens of her kind, and even if there was something excessive in her which made her slightly different, she was still no novelty to me.

Did I fall for the boost to my ego, flattered by the confidence she had placed in me even before she met me?

37

In all sincerity I don't think so. I believe it's more complicated, and that a Moriat, for instance, would have been capable of a decision of that sort.

Why not interpret my action as a protest and a challenge? I had already been forced to go far, much too far, in a direction foreign to my temperament and my tastes. My reputation was established, and I was trying to face up to it squarely, that reputation which accounted for this kid's visit and her cynical proposition.

On the professional level, I had never taken a risk on this scale, nor had I ever got involved in such a difficult, not to say impossible, case.

I took up the challenge. I am convinced that this is the truth, and for a year now I've had plenty of time to question myself on that point.

I wasn't concerned with Yvette Maudet, delinquent daughter of a Lyons school-teacher and a former Post Office employee, but with a problem which I was suddenly undertaking to solve.

I had sat down again and was taking notes, while asking precise questions.

'You went back to your hotel on the night of Wednesday to Thursday, but you didn't set foot there last night. The manager knows that and will notify the police.'

'It happens at least twice a week that I don't sleep at the Rue Vavin, because they won't let us take men upstairs.'

'They'll ask you where did you sleep?'

'I'll tell them.'

'Where?'

'In a hotel in the Rue de Berry, which only has rooms for that.'

'Do they know you there?'

'Yes. Noémie and I change our beat often. Sometimes we work as far down as Saint-Germain-des-Prés, other times we go to the Champs-Elysées, from time to time even Montmartre.'

'Did the jeweller see both of you ? '

'It wasn't very light in the shop and he looked at us the way you look at a customer; he bent over the watch right away.'

'Your pony-tail is noticeable.'

'He didn't see it, neither did his wife, for the good reason that I'd crammed it under a beret.'

'Ready for what happened ? '

'Just in case.'

I questioned her like this for almost an hour and I phoned the assistant of one of my friends at his home.

'Is the case of the jeweller in the Rue de l'Abbé-Grégoire in the hands of an examining magistrate ? '

'Are you interested in the girl ? Police Headquarters still have charge of her for some reason, I don't know why.'

'Thank you.'

I said to Yvette :

'You're to go back to the Rue Vavin as if nothing were wrong and you're to go with the police without protest, avoiding any mention of me.

I joined my wife and our friends about ten o'clock on the Avenue du Président Roosevelt, and they were only just starting on the pheasant. I talked about the case to the commissioner, giving him to understand that I would probably take it on, and the next morning I went over to the Quai des Orfèvres.

The case made quite a stir, far too much, and little Duret was more useful to me than ever. I don't know how he'll end up. He's a boy I can't quite fathom. His father, a big company director, suffered business setbacks. While still a law student, Duret used to hang around newspaper offices, placing an item here and there, getting to know some of the seamy sides of Paris life.

Before him I had a colleague called Auber who was beginning to feel that he could fly with his own wings. Duret got to know of it and applied for his job, even before being called to the Bar.

He's been with me for four years now, always respectful, yet, when I give him certain jobs, and even at other times, he has a look that's more amused than ironical.

It was he who went to see this famous Gaston in his bar on the Rue de la Gaîté and told me, when he got back, that he could be trusted. It was he, again, who, with the help of a reporter friend of his, discovered those details in the jeweller's life that gave unexpected colour to the trial.

The case could have been handled in the magistrate's court. I insisted on its being brought before a jury. The jeweller's wife, who hadn't died, was still wearing a black patch over one eye which they no longer had any hope of saving.

The hearing was stormy, with numerous threats on the part of the presiding judge to have the court cleared. None of my colleagues, not one single magistrate, had any illusions about it. For all of them Yvette Maudet and Noémie Brand were guilty of the unsuccessful hold-up in the Rue de l'Abbé-Grégoire. The question that arose, the one that made the headlines, was:

Will Maître Gobillot obtain an acquittal?

At the end of the second hearing, this appeared impossible, and even my wife had no confidence. She's never admitted it to me, but I know she thought I had gone too far and it embarrassed her.

A lot of dirt came up in the course of the arguments and occasionally one of the spectators would shout:

'That's enough!'

Some of my colleagues hesitated – a few still hesitate – to shake hands with me, and I have never been so close to expulsion from the Bar.

This trial, more than any other, made me understand the excitement of an election campaign or a big political manoeuvre, with all the limelight trained on you, the necessity of winning at any price, whatever the means.

My witnesses were dubious characters, but not one of them had a conviction against him; not one of them contradicted himself either or hesitated for a second.

I paraded before the court twenty Montparnasse prostitutes more or less resembling Yvette and Noémie, who testified under oath that the old jeweller, who had been presented by the public prosecutor as the prototype of the honest artisan, went in quite a bit for exhibitionism and used to entice girls into his shop in his wife's absence.

It was true. I owed the discovery to Duret, who himself had it from an informer who telephoned me repeatedly but wouldn't give his name. Not only did that put a new face on one of my opponents, but I was able to establish that the latter had on several occasions bought stolen jewels.

Was he aware that they were stolen? I don't know, and it's not my business.

Why, on that evening, when his wife happened to be out – she had gone to see her pregnant daughter-in-law in the Rue du Cherche-Midi – why, I say, shouldn't the jeweller have seized his chance of inviting in, as he had done before, two street girls, who had turned the situation to their own account?

I didn't try to draw a flattering picture of my clients. On the contrary, I made them out worse than they were, and that was my smartest trick.

I made them admit that they would perhaps have done the job if they had had the chance, but that they didn't since they were in Gaston's bar at the time.

I can see them now, during the three days the trial lasted, the bald-headed jeweller and his wife with the black patch over her eye, sitting side by side in the front row; I can see their growing mystification, their indignation, which reached such a paroxysm that in the end, dumbfounded, they didn't know where to turn their eyes any more.

Those two will never understand what happened to them, nor why I relentlessly set out, with such cruelty, to destroy the image they had of themselves. Even now, I'm sure that they haven't got over it, that they will never again feel the way they used to, and I wonder if the old woman, blind in one eye from now on, whose hair is growing again on the half of her skull laid bare by the blow, still dares to go and see her daughter-in-law in the Rue du Cherche-Midi.

We have never talked about it, Viviane and I. She was standing in the corridor at the moment of the verdict, which was greeted by boos, and when I came out of the court, my gown flying, not wanting to say anything to the press reporters crowding around me, she did nothing but follow me in silence.

She knows it is her fault. She has understood. I'm not sure that she wasn't frightened at seeing me go so far, but she admires me for it.

Did she also foresee how it would end? Probably. It is our habit, after trials which produce a high degree of nervous tension, to go and dine together in some cabaret and to stay out part of the night so as to relax.

That's what we did that evening, and everywhere we went we were looked at with curiosity; we were more than ever the couple of wild creatures in the legend.

Viviane really showed pluck. Never faltered for a second. She's three years older than I, which means she's approaching fifty, but, dressed up and ready for the fray, she's still prettier and attracts more attention than plenty of women of thirty. Her eyes, especially, have a brilliance, a vivacity, that I've seen only in her, and there is a mocking gaiety in her smile which makes her someone to be reckoned with.

People call her a bitch, and she isn't one. She's herself, goes her own way, as Corine goes hers, indifferent to rumours, not giving a damn whether she's liked or detested, trading smile for smile and blow for blow. The difference between her and Corine is that Corine is outwardly soft and sweet, while Viviane, all nerves, possesses an aggressive vitality which never fails.

'Where is she now?' she asked me, about two o'clock in the morning.

I noted that the 'she' was singular, so Viviane had never regarded Noémie as anything but an extra. At the Palais, no one was in any doubt either, for poor Noémie, with her big shapeless body, her bovine eyes, her obstinate forehead, can't fool anyone.

'In a little hotel on the Boulevard Saint-Michel. I wanted her to go back to the Rue Vavin to brazen it out, but the manager insists his place is full.'

Did it occur to her that the Boulevard Saint-Michel is just round the corner from us and quite close to the Palais? I have no doubt about it. And yet I didn't do it on purpose.

During the time which elapsed between Yvette's arrest and her acquittal, I realized that I would not get rid of her, nor of the image of her naked belly as I had seen it in my office.

Why? Even now I still haven't found the answer. I'm not a vicious man, nor a sexual maniac. Viviane's never shown jealousy and I've had the affairs I've wanted, almost all of them without future, many of them without pleasure.

Also, I've seen too many girls of all kinds to get sentimental, like some men of my age, about a kid who went wrong, and Yvette's cynicism doesn't impress me any more than what is left of her innocence.

During the preliminary investigation, I went to see her in the Petite Roquette without once departing from a strictly professional attitude.

Yet my wife knew even then.

Yvette too.

What surprises me most is that Yvette was clever enough not to show it. We were face to face as lawyer and client. We were preparing her replies to the magistrate. Even in what concerned her case, I wasn't telling her any more than necessary about my discoveries.

The night of the acquittal, about four in the morning, leaving the last cabaret and getting behind the wheel, my wife suggested naturally :

'Aren't you going to see her ?'

I had been thinking about it since the beginning of the evening, but I was refusing, out of pride, out of self-respect, to yield to the temptation. Wasn't it ridiculous, or hateful, to rush to her, the very first night, to claim my reward ?

Was the desire I felt for her so violent that it could be read in my face ?

I didn't answer. My wife drove down the Rue de Clichy, crossed the Grands Boulevards, and I knew she wasn't heading for the Île Saint-Louis but for the Boulevard Saint-Michel.

'What did you do with the other one ?' she asked again, sure that I'd got rid of her.

I had strongly advised Noémie, for a time at least, to go home and live with her mother.

I would like to avoid a misunderstanding. When I speak of my wife as I am doing at this moment, it might seem that there was in her attitude a certain provocation, that she pushed me, in some way, into Yvette's arms.

Nothing is further from the truth. I am certain, although she will never admit it, that Viviane is jealous, that my affairs made her suffer, or at least worried her. Only she's a good sport and looks truth in the face, accepting in advance what she is powerless to prevent.

We passed the dark mass of the Palais de Justice, and on the Boulevard Saint-Michel she murmured :

'Farther up ?'

'On the corner of the Rue Monsieur-le-Prince. The entrance is on the Rue Monsieur-le-Prince.'

I was still hesitating, humiliated, when she stopped the car.

'Good night,' she said, half under her breath.

And she kissed me, as she does every night.

Alone on the pavement, I found my eyes were wet and I began to wave to call her back, but the car was already turning the corner of the Rue Soufflot.

The hotel was dark, with nothing but a faint glow behind the frosted glass of the door. The night porter opened it for me, muttered that there were no vacancies and, slipping a tip into his hand, I stated that someone was expecting me in number 37.

It was true. Nothing had been agreed on. Yvette was asleep. But she wasn't surprised when I knocked at the door.

'Just a minute.'

I heard the click of the light switch, then her bare footsteps back and forth on the floor, and she opened the door, still pulling on a dressing-gown.

'What time is it?'

'Half-past four.'

That seemed to surprise her, as though she were wondering what had kept me so long.

'Give me your hat and coat.'

The room was narrow, the brass bed had been slept in, and some underclothes were trailing out of an open suitcase on the floor.

'Don't pay any attention to the mess. I went to bed as soon as I got in.'

Her breath smelled of alcohol, but she wasn't drunk. What did I look like, myself, fully dressed, in the middle of the room?

'Don't you want to come to bed?'

The most difficult thing was to undress. I didn't want to. I didn't want anything more, and I didn't have the courage to leave either.

'Come here,' I ordered.

She came to me, her face turned up, thinking I was

45

going to kiss her, but all I did was hold her to me without touching her lips, then, suddenly, I slipped off her dressing-gown, beneath which she was completely naked.

With a brutal movement, I threw her down on the edge of the bed and dropped on top of her while she stared at the ceiling. I had begun to take her, savagely, as though getting my revenge, when I saw her watching me with astonishment.

'What's the matter with you?' she whispered, using *tu* to me for the first time.

'Nothing!'

What was the matter with me was that I couldn't do anything, that I was getting up, ashamed, stammering:

'Forgive me.'

Then she said:

'You've thought about it too much.'

That could have been the explanation, but it wasn't. On the contrary, I had refused to think about it. I knew, but I wasn't thinking about it. Anyhow, it's happened with other women before her.

'Get undressed and come and lie down by me. I'm cold.'

Was I obliged to? Would the future have been different if I had said no, if I had gone away? I don't know.

Did she, for her part, know what she was doing, when, a little later, she stretched out her arm to put the light out and snuggled up against me? I could feel her, thin and alive against my body and, little by little, with hesitations and pauses, as if trying not to frighten me, taking possession of me.

We were still not asleep when an alarm clock went off in one of the rooms, nor when, later, some of the hotel residents began to move about behind the thin walls.

'It's too bad I haven't got any means of making coffee for you. I'll have to buy a spirit-lamp.'

Daylight was coming through the blind when I left at seven o'clock. I stopped in a bistro on the Boulevard Saint-

Michel to drink a cup of coffee and I looked at myself in the mirror behind the coffee machine.

At the Quai d'Anjou I didn't go up to the bedroom, but settled down in the office, where, by eight o'clock, the telephone began to ring, as it always does. Bordenave would be in soon, bringing me the morning papers, whose headlines could be summed up by:

Maître Gobillot Wins

As if it were a sports contest.

'Are you pleased?'

Did my secretary suspect that I wasn't proud of this victory? She is more devoted to me than anyone else in the world, including Viviane, and if I committed an act ignoble enough for everyone to reject me, she would probably be the only one who wouldn't abandon me.

She is thirty-five. She was nineteen when she began to work for me and she's never been known to have an affair. My various assistants unanimously maintain, as my wife does, that she's still a virgin.

Not only have I never flirted with her, but for no reason at all I'm more impatient, harsher, with her than with anyone else, often unjustly, and I've lost count of the times I've made her cry because she couldn't lay her hand fast enough on a file which I myself had misplaced.

Does she realize that I've come straight from Yvette's bed and that my skin is still impregnated with her acid smell? She will know one of these days, because, as my closest collaborator, there's nothing she doesn't know about my actions and movements.

Will she cry, alone in her office? Is she jealous? Is she in love with me and, if so, what kind of man does she think I am?

My first appointment was for ten o'clock and I had time to take a bath and change. I didn't wake Viviane, who was still asleep, and I didn't see her again until evening, because

I had to have lunch that day at the Café de Paris with a client whose case I was pleading in the afternoon.

This was a year ago.

I already knew Moriat at that time. We used to meet at Corine's, where we would often chat in a corner.

Before Yvette, why didn't Moriat look at me the way he looked at me last Sunday? Hadn't I got the sign then, or was it not yet visible enough?

Chapter Three

Saturday, 10 November

It is ten p.m. and I waited for my wife to go out before I went down to my office. She has gone with Corine and some women friends to the opening, in a gallery on the Rue Jacob, of the first exhibition of paintings by Marie-Lou, Lannier's mistress. There will be champagne, and the chances are that it will go on to the early hours of the morning. To get out of it, I argued that there will be a hundred people in a place hardly bigger than an ordinary dining-room and that the heat will be unbearable.

It appears that Marie-Lou has real talent. She began painting two years ago, during a visit to Saint-Paul-de-Vence. She and Lannier live together in the Rue de la Faisanderie, but they're both married, Lannier to a cousin of his who is said to be very ugly and from whom he's been separated for twenty years, Marie-Lou to an industrialist from Lyons, Morilleux, a friend of Lannier's with whom he still has business dealings. As far as anyone knows, it was all amicably settled to everyone's satisfaction.

She and Lannier were at our house for dinner yesterday, together with a Belgian politician temporarily in Paris, a member of the Academy whom we often invite, and a South American ambassador accompanied by his wife.

Every week we have one or two dinners like this for eight or ten people, and Viviane, an excellent hostess, never gets tired of entertaining. The ambassador was not at our house by chance. It was Lannier who brought him to me, and when the time came for coffee and liqueurs, he dropped a word or two about what he intends to discuss with me in my office: a more or less legal armament deal, if I understood certain hints correctly, in which he wants to engage for political reasons without getting into trouble with the French government.

He is a young man, thirty-five at the most, handsome and attractive, though with a tendency to fat, and his wife is one of the most beautiful creatures I have ever been privileged to admire. You can tell she is in love with her husband, she never takes her eyes off him, and she is so young, so fresh, that you would think she left her convent school last night.

What funny business is he going to get mixed up in? I'm still only guessing, but I have reason to think it's something to do with overthrowing the government of his own country, of which his father is one of the richest men. They have two children – they showed us photographs of them – and their embassy building is one of the most charming in the Bois de Boulogne.

I waited impatiently for them to leave, for I was anxious to get to the Rue de Ponthieu. I've spent three nights there this week and I'd go again today if Saturday were not 'his' day.

It is preferable not to think of it. When I came home in a taxi, at half-past six in the morning, when day had not yet completely broken, a violent storm was raging over the Paris region, where tiles have been blown off roofs, trees damaged, one in the Avenue des Champs-Elysées. Viviane told me later that one of our shutters had been banging all night. However, it didn't blow down, and about noon some workmen came to repair it.

On entering my office, where I always stop before going upstairs to take my bath, my first thought was to look if I could see my tramp couple under the Pont-Marie. Until almost nine o'clock, nothing moved under the rags which the wind stirred. When at last a man came out from under them, the one I'm used to seeing, who, with his jacket that's too wide and too long, his hirsute beard, his battered hat, looks like a circus clown, I was surprised to realize that two more figures were still lying there. Has he picked up a second partner? Has a friend joined them?

The wind is still blowing, but more gustily, and cold is predicted for tomorrow, possibly even frost.

I have thought a great deal, in the course of the week, about what I've written so far, and I have realized that up to now I've spoken only about the man I am at present. I have attacked the veracity of two or three legends, the most glaring ones. There are still some others I want to destroy, and for that I am obliged to go back much further.

For example, on account of my appearance it is generally believed, even by people who supposedly know me well, that I'm one of those men fresh from the country who, as they used to say in the last century, still have mud on their boots. That is the case with Jean Moriat, or almost so. It is, by the way, very advantageous in certain professions, including mine, because it inspires confidence, but I have to admit that so far as I'm concerned there is nothing in it.

I was born in Paris, in a maternity hospital in the Faubourg Saint-Jacques, and my father, who spent almost all his life in the Rue Visconti, behind the French Academy, came from one of the oldest families in Rennes. There were de Gobillots in the Crusades, later we find a Gobillot who was a captain of musketeers, and others, more numerous, were gentlemen of the robe, several of them more or less illustrious members of the Parliament of Brittany.

I don't take the slightest pride in it. As for my mother, who was called Louise Finot, she was the daughter of a laundress in the Rue des Tournelles, and when my father got her with child she was hanging around the taverns on the Boulevard Saint-Michel.

It is unlikely that these antecedents explain my character, still less the choice I made of a certain way of life, inasmuch as one can speak of choice.

My grandfather Gobillot, in Rennes, still lived an upper middle class life and would have ended up as a President of the Tribunal if a stroke hadn't carried him off before he was fifty.

As for my father, who had come to Paris to study law, he stayed there all his life, in the same flat in the Rue Visconti, where, until his death quite recently, he was taken care of by old Pauline, who saw him born but who was actually only twelve years older than he.

At that time it was still customary to have little girls to mind the babies, and this one, who was no more than a child when my grandparents engaged her, followed my father until his death, forming with him a curious household.

Did my father disclaim all interest in me at birth? I don't know. I have never asked him, or Pauline either, Pauline who is still alive, who is today eighty-two, and whom I sometimes go to see. Even though she still does her own housework, in the Rue Visconti as always, she has almost entirely lost her memory, except for the most distant events, the time when my father was a little boy in short trousers.

Perhaps he wasn't convinced that Louise Finot's child was his, or perhaps by then he had another mistress?

In any case, I spent my first two years in a foster home, out near Versailles, where, one fine day, my mother came for me to take me to the Rue Visconti.

'Here's your son, Blaise,' she must have announced.

She was pregnant again. She went on, as Pauline has often told me:

'I'm getting married next week. Prosper doesn't know a thing. If he found out I've already had a child, he might not marry me and I don't want to miss this chance because he's a good man, a hard worker who doesn't drink. I've come to give Lucien back to you.'

From that day on, I lived at the Rue Visconti, under the wing of Pauline, for whom, at the beginning, a child was such a mysterious creature that she hesitated to touch me.

My mother did in fact marry a salesman at Allez Frères; I caught a glimpse of him much later, wearing an ironmonger's grey apron, in the Châtelet stores, when I was buying some garden chairs for our house at Sully. They had five children, my half-sisters and half-brothers, whom I don't know and who must lead a hard-working, uneventful life.

Prosper died last year. My mother sent me an announcement. Even if I didn't go to the funeral, I did send flowers and since then I have paid two short visits to the little bungalow in Saint-Maur where my mother is living at present.

We have nothing to say to each other. There is no common ground between us. She looks at me like a stranger and just murmurs:

'You look successful. If you're happy, so much the better!'

My father was a member of the Bar and had his chambers in the flat in the Rue Visconti. Did he go on too long living the life of an ex-student? It is hard for me to judge. Physically, he didn't resemble me, for he was a handsome man, a thoroughbred, with an elegance I have admired in certain men of his generation. Cultured, he moved among poets, artists, dreamers and young women, and it was unusual to see him come home, unsteady on his feet, before two in the morning.

Sometimes he would bring a woman with him, who would stay with us for a night or a month, occasionally, like a certain Léontine, longer. Léontine entrenched herself in the house for so long that I expected her to get him to marry her in the end.

This didn't worry me, not by any means. I was rather proud of living in an atmosphere different from that of my school friends, still prouder when my father would give me

53

a conspiratorial wink, for example when Pauline discovered a new woman lodger in the house and looked like thunder.

I remember her putting one of them out of the door, bodily, with an astounding energy for such a little thing, while my father was absent of course (he must have been at the Palais), shouting at the girl that she was as dirty as a dish-rag and too foul-mouthed to stay another hour under a decent roof.

Was my father unhappy? I recall him nearly always smiling, although it was a smile devoid of gaiety. He was too reserved to complain and had the good taste to create around him a light-heartedness I have never known since.

When I was beginning to study law, he was, at fifty, still a handsome man, but he was growing less able to carry his liquor and he would sometimes spend whole days in bed.

He knew of my start with Maître Andrieu. He was present, two years later, at my marriage to Viviane. Although we lived at the Rue Visconti with the same liberty, the same independence, as guests in a boarding-house, even to the point where we would sometimes go three days without seeing each other, I'm sure he was upset by the void created by my leaving.

Pauline, as she got older, was losing her good humour and her indulgence, and treated him, not as her master any more, but as someone in her charge, inflicting on him a diet he abhorred, ferreting out his bottles, which he was obliged to hide, even going to look for him, at night, in the taverns of the neighbourhood.

My father and I never asked each other questions. Nor did we ever make any allusion to our private lives, still less to our ideas and opinions.

Even today I still don't know whether Pauline was anything more to him, at a certain time, than a governess.

He died at seventy-one, only a few minutes after I had been to see him, as if he had purposely waited in order to spare me the sight of his passing.

I have had to talk about all that, not out of filial piety, but because the Rue Visconti flat may have had a certain influence on my fundamental tastes. For me, it's true, my father's study, with its books lining the walls right up to the ceiling, its periodicals stacked on the floor, its small-paned windows looking out, beyond a medieval courtyard, on what was once Delacroix's studio, has remained the kind of place it's good to live in.

My ambition, when I entered law school, was not a rapid and brilliant career, but to live out my life in a lawyer's chambers, and I aspired to become an impecunious jurist far sooner than a barrister.

Is that still my dream today? I'd rather not ask the question. With my outsize head, I was the typical brilliant student, and when my father came home at night there was nearly always a light in my room, where I often studied until daybreak.

My idea of my future career was shared so fully by my tutors that, without telling me, they mentioned me to Maître Andrieu, at that time President of the French Bar, whose name is still cited today as one of the outstanding lawyers of the last half-century.

I can see now the visiting-card which I found one morning in my post, bearing, beneath the engraved words, one sentence written in very fine handwriting, very 'artistic', as was still the expression.

M. Robert Andrieu
would be obliged if you would call on him some
morning between ten o'clock and noon in his
chambers, 66, Boulevard Malesherbes.

I must have kept this card, which is probably in a cardboard box with some other souvenirs. I was twenty-five. Not only was Maître Andrieu one of the glories of the Bar, but he was one of the most elegant men at the Palais and reputedly led a life of great luxury. His flat impressed me; still more the huge office, austere yet tasteful, whose windows opened on the Parc Monceau.

Later, I was to make the ridiculous gesture of ordering a black velvet waistcoat, edged with silk braid, like the one he was wearing that morning. I hasten to add that I never put it on and that I gave it away before Viviane could catch sight of it.

The offer Maître Andrieu made me was to serve my apprenticeship with him, which was all the more unexpected since he had three assistants, lawyers already well-known on their own account.

I will not say that he resembled my father physically, and yet there were in the two men, who had experienced quite different fortunes, something like family traits, which were perhaps only traits of the period. The meticulous courtesy, for instance, which they affected in their slightest dealings with others, and also a certain respect for mankind which made them speak to a servant in the same tone as to a society lady. It was above all the similarity in their smile that struck me, a sadness – or nostalgia – well enough hidden to be barely suspected.

Not only did Maître Andrieu enjoy an exceptional reputation as a jurist, but he was a fashionable man and numbered artists, writers and Opera stars among his clients.

There were two of us working in the same office, a big, red-haired youth, who has since gone into politics, and myself, and all we knew about the society life of our head was from rumour. At the start, I went for a month without seeing him, receiving my briefs and instructions from a man named Mouchonnet, who was his right hand.

Often in the evening there was a big dinner or reception. Two or three times, in the lift, I saw Madame Andrieu, much younger than her husband, who was spoken of as one of the beauties of Paris and who was in my eyes an inaccessible being.

Shall I admit that my first recollection of Viviane is that

of her scent, one afternoon when I took the lift which she had just left? Another time, I caught sight of her in person, dressed in black, a little veil over her eyes, as she stepped into the long limousine whose chauffeur was holding the door open.

Nothing indicated that she was to become my wife, and yet that's what happened.

She didn't come, like many pretty women, from the demi-monde or the stage, but from a good bourgeois provincial family. Her father, son of a doctor in Perpignan, was at that time a captain in the *gendarmerie*, and lived with his family in various places in France, moving with every promotion, finally retiring to his native Pyrenees, where today he keeps bees.

We went to see him last spring. He also spends a few days in Paris from time to time, less often now that he's a widower.

I didn't know in the beginning that every two months or so Maître Andrieu gave a dinner for his staff, and it was at one of those dinners that I was introduced to Viviane for the first time. She was twenty-eight and she had been married for six years. As to the President of the Bar, he was over fifty and had lived alone for a long time after a first marriage which had given him a son.

This son, aged twenty-five, lived in a Swiss sanatorium and I think he has since died.

I am ugly, as I have said, and I don't underestimate my ugliness, which gives me the right to add that it is compensated for by the impression of power, or rather of intense life, which emanates from me. This, by the way, is one of my trump cards in court, and the newspapers have spoken of my magnetism often enough to justify my alluding to it.

This concentrated vitality is the only explanation I can find for the interest Viviane showed in me from the first day, an interest which sometimes bordered on fascination.

During the meal, as I was the youngest of the guests, I

found myself some distance away from her, but I felt her curious look resting on me and, when the time came for coffee, it was next to me that she sat down in the drawing-room.

Later, the two of us were to recall that evening, which we called 'the question evening', because, for almost an hour, she asked me questions, often indiscreet ones, which I, ill at ease, tried to answer.

The case of Corine and Jean Moriat might offer an explanation for what happened and it might not be entirely false, but I still think it wasn't considerations of that kind that came into play the first evening and that they wouldn't have come into play at all if there hadn't been a sort of involvement, right from the very first contact.

In keeping with his character, and on account of the difference in age, Andrieu had a tendency to treat his wife as a spoiled child rather than a partner or mistress. Later a few revealing words escaped Viviane, suggesting that with him she did not find the sexual satisfaction she urgently needed.

Did she seek it with other men? Did Andrieu suspect her of this?

I have heard a certain Philippe Savard smilingly mentioned, a young dilettante who was for a time a frequent visitor at the Boulevard Malesherbes and who suddenly stopped going there. During this period Viviane who, as a child, used to ride a great deal with her father, went riding every morning in the Bois with this Savard and, what's more, he used to accompany her to the theatre on the evenings when Maître Andrieu couldn't go.

In any case, after that first dinner our contacts became more frequent, though harmless. With the consent of her husband, Viviane used me, the junior member of the firm, for personal errands, little social duties, which every once in a while gave me access to her flat.

The theatre brought us even closer, or, more precisely, a concert which took place one evening when my master had to go to an official banquet. At Viviane's instigation, I suppose, he asked me to serve as her escort.

Did she study me, take my measure, as Corine did with the deputy for Deux-Sèvres? Was she already feeling a need to play a more active role than she could with her husband?

The idea didn't occur to me at the time. I was dazzled, carried away, incapable of believing that my dreams might be realized. For a week I even thought very sincerely of leaving Maître Andrieu's office to escape too cruel a disappointment.

A trip he made to Montreal, where he had just received an honorary degree from Laval University, was to precipitate events. His absence lasted two months, instead of the expected three weeks, because of an attack of bronchitis which he suffered over there. I didn't know that, as a young man, he had spent three years high in the mountains, as his son was doing now.

Viviane asked me several times to take her out in the evening. Not only did we go to the theatre, which she loved, but one night we had supper at a cabaret. She had sent the car home and it was on the way back in a taxi that, staking everything, I bent over her.

Two days later, on the maid's day off, I was admitted to her flat for an hour. Then, when Andrieu came home, we were forced to meet in a hotel, which, the first time, filled me with shame.

Did he find out the truth? Did he learn it only on the day when she decided to tell him what the situation was?

I, who so relentlessly demand precise facts from my clients, am having trouble establishing them in my own case. For years, I was convinced that Andrieu was unaware of anything. Later, I wasn't sure. For the last few months, I've been inclined to think the contrary.

I spoke about a sign just now. I suspected nothing at the time and I would no doubt have made fun of anyone who had spoken to me about one. Well, if anyone in the world ever bore that sign, it was certainly Maître Andrieu.

The day Viviane had fixed to tell him, I had submitted my resignation, surprised at the way he had accepted it, sad and resigned at the same time.

'I wish you the success you deserve,' he said, giving me his long, well-cared-for hand.

This was only a few hours before the confession.

I waited for word from Viviane for two long weeks. She had promised to telephone me at the Rue Visconti immediately after their talk. Her bags were packed. Mine too. We were to move into a hotel on the Quai des Grands-Augustins until we could get a flat, and I had already found a position with a commercial lawyer who has since come to a bad end.

The next day I didn't dare telephone the Boulevard Malesherbes and, leaving Pauline instructions in case there was a call, I went and stood watch outside her house.

It was not until three days later that I learned from my father, who had heard it at the Palais, that Andrieu had had a relapse and was confined to bed. On that point, too, my opinion isn't the same as I held twenty years ago. Today I think that a man for whom a woman has become the main reason for living is capable of anything, of cowardice, baseness, cruelty, to keep her, cost what it may.

A scribbled note finally told me :

'I'll be at the Quai des Grands-Augustins Thursday morning about ten.'

She arrived there at half past ten with her bags, in a cab, although Andrieu had insisted on her taking the car.

Our first days were joyless, and it was Viviane who recovered first, finding thousands of unexpected pleasures in her new life.

It was she, too, who found the flat in the Place Denfert-Rochereau and who dug up, among her former acquaintances, my first important client.

'You'll see, later, when you're the most prominent lawyer in Paris, how sentimental we'll get when we remember this flat!'

Andrieu had insisted on letting her divorce him as the guilty party. Weeks went by without our hearing anything about this when, one morning in March, the newspaper brought us the news:

'Andrieu, President of the Bar, victim of a climbing accident.'

It was reported that he had gone to visit his son in a Davos sanatorium and, taking the opportunity of doing a mountain climb alone, he had slipped into a crevasse. His body was not found until two days later by a guide.

That ending, too, like his long silky moustache, his courtesy, his half-tone smile, has for me the aroma of the period.

Is it clear now why, when people call us a couple of wild creatures, they are unwittingly touching on a hypersensitive point?

We had to cling to each other with all our strength so as not to be overwhelmed with remorse and disgust. Only a consuming passion could serve as our excuse, and we made love like two maniacs, we held one another tight as we looked stonily at a future which was going to be a revenge.

For a year I hardly saw my father, except from a distance, at the Palais, because I was working fourteen and fifteen hours a day, taking on any kind of case, soliciting them, while I waited for the one that would establish my reputation. It wasn't until the evening before our wedding that I went to the Rue Visconti.

'I'd like you to meet my future wife,' I said to my father.

He had certainly heard about our affair, which caused quite a lot of talk at the Palais, but he said nothing to me about it, just looked at me and asked:

'Are you happy?'

I said yes, and I thought I was. Perhaps I actually was.

We got married without any fuss at the town hall of the Fourteenth Arrondissement and we went for a few days' rest to an inn in the forest of Orléans, at Sully, where six years later we were to buy a country house.

It was there that a man came to see me who had obtained our address from our concierge and who, looking round the inn where a few customers were arguing at the bar, muttered as he motioned me to follow him:

'Let's go and talk by the canal.'

I couldn't place him socially. He didn't seem like what we then called a social outcast, nor what we today call a gangster. Rather shabbily dressed in dark clothes, untidy, his eyes defiant, his mouth bitter, he suggested one of those weary characters who go from door to door collecting payments on bills.

'My name won't mean anything to you,' he began, as soon as we had passed the few barges moored at the quay. 'As for me, I know all I need know about you and I think you're my man.'

He interrupted himself to ask:

'Is that your legal wife staying with you at the inn?'

And, when I said yes:

'I don't trust people in irregular situations. I go straight to the point. I'm not in any trouble with the law and I don't want to be. All the same, I still need the best lawyer I can afford and you may be the man. I don't own any shops or offices, I haven't got any factories or patents, but I deal in very big business, much bigger than most men who think they're somebody.'

He put a certain aggressiveness into it, as if in protest against the modesty of his appearance and dress.

'As a lawyer, you have no right to repeat what I'm going to tell you in confidence and I can show my own hand. You've heard of the gold traffic. Since rates of exchange vary almost every day and currencies, in most countries, are pegged at an official rate, there's a big profit in moving gold from one place to another, and the frontiers to be crossed change with the market. From time to time the papers report that an agent has been caught at Modane, at Aulnoye, getting off the Dover boat, or somewhere else. They hardly ever follow the chain much further back, but it might happen. Well, the end of the chain is me.'

He lit a cigarette and stopped to look at the circles made by insects on the surface of the canal.

'I've studied the question, not as a smart lawyer might, but enough to realize that there are legal ways to keep out of trouble. I have at my disposal two export-import companies and as many agencies abroad as I need. I'll buy your services by the year. I'll only take up a small part of your time and you're free to defend anyone you like in court. Before every deal I'll consult you and it's up to you to make it safe.'

He turned towards me for the first time since we had left the inn and, looking me in the face, he said casually :

'That's all.'

I had grown red and my fists were clenched in anger. I was going to open my mouth – and without doubt my protest would have been violent – when, seeing my reaction, he murmured :

'I'll see you tonight after dinner. Talk to your wife.'

I didn't go back immediately, because I wanted some exercise to calm my nerves. At the hotel it was apéritif time and there were too many people at the bar for us to be able to talk.

'All alone ? ' Viviane asked, surprised.

It was beginning to get cool outside, a damp coolness. I took her up to our bedroom, with its flowered wallpaper, smelling of the countryside. I spoke quietly, because we heard the voices of the people in the bar and they could have heard us.

'He left me on the tow-path and told me he'd come for my reply this evening after I'd talked it over with you.'

'What reply?'

I repeated what he had said to me and I saw her listen without reacting.

'It's unhoped for, isn't it?'

'Don't you understand what he wants of me?'

'Advice. Isn't it your job as a lawyer to give it?'

'Advice in getting round the law.'

'That's true of most of the advice people want from a lawyer, if I'm not entirely mistaken.'

I thought she didn't comprehend, I made an effort to dot all the i's, but she remained calm.

'How much did he offer you?'

'He didn't mention any figure.'

'And yet it all depends on the figure. Do you realize, Lucien, that this means the end of our difficulties and that a lawyer for a big company does exactly the same work?'

She was forgetting to speak quietly.

'Ssh!'

'You didn't say anything that might prevent him coming back?'

'I didn't open my mouth.'

'What's his name?'

'I don't know.'

I know it well enough today. He's called Joseph Bocca, although even after so many years I'm not sure that that's his real name, any more than I would swear to his nationality. Besides his town house in Paris and farms all over France, he has bought a magnificent estate on the Riviera, at Mentone, where he lives for part of the year and where he has invited us, my wife and me, to spend as much time as we like.

He is a well-known man now, because, with the fortune he made in the gold traffic, he set up a textile business which has branches in Italy and Greece and he has interests in various companies. I wouldn't be surprised, on Monday, when the South American ambassador comes to see me, to discover that Bocca is mixed up in this arms business.

I was still dreaming of becoming a distinguished jurist.

'All I ask of you, tonight, is not to put him off with a ruthless no.'

When he returned, about half-past eight, just as we were finishing dinner, we went for a walk in the dark and I said yes, straight away, to get it over with, and also because he left me no choice.

'It's all or nothing.'

He named his figure.

'Next week I'll send one of my men to you; he's called Coutelle and he'll explain the actual set-up of the operations. You are to study the question at your leisure and, when you've found a solution, you're to telephone me.'

He handed me not a visiting-card but a scrap of paper on which was written the name Joseph Bocca, a telephone number somewhere near the Louvre and an address in the Rue Coquilière.

Out of curiosity, I went and took a look at the building with its dingy staircase and corridors, where I found, as enamel plates on the street door indicated, a queer sampling of the most unexpected professions: a masseuse, a typing school, a firm dealing in artificial flowers, a private detective, an employment agency and a butchers' trade paper.

And, in addition, the 'I.P.F.' export company.

I preferred not to show my face and to wait for this man Coutelle's call at my office. He came back often over the years and, last time, it was to tell me that he was retiring to a house he had just built on the cliffs at Fécamp.

Viviane did not force my hand. I acted of my own free will. What I regret now is having gone so far back in my life, for it is not the past but the present that I had promised myself to deal with in this dossier.

They say that one explains the other and I'm reluctant to believe it.

It is two o'clock in the morning. In spite of the weather

forecast, the wind has begun to blow at gale force once more and I can hear the shutter on the floor below beginning to bang again. In the Rue Jacob the heat must be stifling, and half the people crowding in there already meet ten times a week at dress rehearsals, cocktail parties, charity bazaars or more or less official ceremonies.

It is possible that Marie-Lou has talent, although I don't believe in belated vocations. She told me yesterday at dinner that she would like to do a portrait of me because I have a 'powerful mask', and Lannier, who heard it, smiled and slowly exhaled the smoke of his cigarette.

He's an important man, and every time his newspapers are sued for libel, he appeals to me. On the other hand, he's never asked me to represent him in a civil suit, of which he always has one or two on hand. No doubt he, and he's not the only one, considers me a show-off, capable of getting a verdict by the brilliance and fire of a speech to the court, by the violence and astuteness of attacks and counter-attacks, but he wouldn't let me appear before the cold judges of the civil courts.

Does he too have dealings with Bocca? Probably. You don't stay long in my business without realizing that at a certain level in the pyramid there are just a few men left who share the power, the money, and the women.

I'm trying not to think of Yvette and every five minutes I'm wondering what 'they' are doing. Have they gone to one of those cheap night-clubs she likes where, in spite of everything, I would be out of place? Or did they choose one of those popular dance-halls in Montmartre full of typists and sales-girls from the big shops?

She'll tell me tomorrow if I ask her. Are they eating *choucroute* in a bar?

Perhaps they've gone home already?

I'm getting impatient, wishing my wife would come in, so I can go to bed. I think of Maître Andrieu; perhaps he, too, used to wait in his office, where, as soon as it was autumn, he loved to plant himself with his back to the log fire.

I have no intention of going to Switzerland or doing any mountain climbing. The case is different. Everything is different. Two lives, two situations, are never alike and I'm wrong to pay any attention to this business of signs, which is beginning to haunt me.

It's a long time since I had a holiday. I'm tired. Older than I though she is, Viviane sets a pace I can't keep up without getting out of breath.

I'll ask Pémal to come to see me. He'll prescribe new medicine, advise me again not to drive the engine too hard and he'll repeat that men, like women, have their change of life.

According to him, I'm in the middle of the change of life!

'Wait till you're fifty and you'll be surprised how much younger and more vigorous you feel than today.'

He, at sixty, begins his calls at eight in the morning, if not earlier, and finishes them at ten at night and he doesn't hesitate to answer night calls.

I've always known him even-tempered, a mischievous smile on his lips, as if he found it amusing to watch people worry about their health.

The lift is coming up, stops at the floor below.

It's my wife coming home.

Chapter Four

Sunday, 11 November, 10 a.m.

When I got home this morning about half-past eight, I took two pheno-barbitones and lay down, but the drug had no effect and in the end I thought I might as well get up. After a cold shower, I went down to my office and, before sitting down, I made sure that 'he' isn't keeping watch on the sidewalk.

The weather forecast was right, after all. The wind has dropped, the sky is like new and there's a nip in the air; the people you see going to Mass have their hands stuck in their pockets and their heels ring out on the pavement. My tramps aren't under the Pont-Marie; I wonder if they've moved on or if it's their turn to sleep aboard the Salvation Army barge.

Last night, when I heard Viviane come home, I closed my dossier and, when I was almost at the top of the stairs, the telephone bell startled me, because I immediately thought of bad news.

'Is that you?' said Yvette's voice at the other end.

It wasn't her normal voice, but her voice when she's been drinking or is over-excited.

'You weren't in bed?'

'I was just going up.'

'You told me you hardly ever go to bed before two, especially on Sa ...'

She bit her tongue without finishing the word Saturday. It was I who asked:

'Where are you?'

'Rue Caulaincourt, at Manière's.'

There was a silence. For her to call me on a Saturday night meant there had been trouble.

'Alone?'

'Yes.'

'For long?'

'Half an hour. Look, Lucien, would you mind coming for me?'

'You're worried? What's going on?'

'Nothing. I'll tell you. Are you coming straight away?'

I found my wife undressing.

'Aren't you in bed?' she said.

'I was going upstairs when I got a phone call. I've got to go out.'

She threw me an inquisitive glance.

'Something wrong?'

'I don't know. She wouldn't tell me.'

'You'd better wake Albert to drive you. He'll be ready in a few minutes.'

'I'd rather take a taxi. Was it a good party at the Rue Jacob?'

'We were twice as many as expected and some friends had to volunteer to go and get some extra cases of champagne in their car. You look annoyed.'

I was. Outside, surprised by the cold, I had to walk all the way to the Châtelet to find a taxi. I know Manière's restaurant, in Montmartre, but I didn't know that Yvette was going there nowadays, too. For my wife and myself, it represents a period, a phase. The second year of our marriage, we were crazy about canoeing for a time, and we used to go out on Sundays on the Marne, between Chelles and Lagny. The same group used to get together there, mostly young couples, especially doctors and lawyers, and we got into the habit of meeting during the week at Manière's.

From one day to the next, for no reason that I can

remember, that period came to an end and another began; we belonged to several groups, one after another, before ending up in our present circle. I have sometimes envied people who stay in the same milieu all their lives. Not long ago we went through Chelles, one Sunday morning, on our way to friends who have a place near there, and I was surprised to recognize on the water, in the same canoes, a certain number of couples of those days, old now, with grown-up children.

I don't know how many years it is since I set foot in Manière's, but as I pushed open the door, I got a whiff of a familiar smell and I don't think the atmosphere has changed much. I caught sight of Yvette with a glass of whisky and her selection of that drink told me what I needed to know about her state of mind.

'Take off your coat and sit down,' she said, with the important air of someone who has serious news to announce.

The waiter came forward and I ordered whisky too. I drank several more later and that is what prevented me from sleeping this morning, for a certain amount of alcohol makes me restless rather than drowsy.

'You didn't notice anyone on the pavement?'

'No. Why?'

'I was wondering if he hadn't come back to spy on me. He's that type of man. In the state he's in, he's capable of anything.'

'You've had a row?'

When she has had two or three drinks, things are never that simple. She looked me in the eyes, tragically, to declare:

'Forgive me, Lucien. I ought to make you happy. I try with all my might and I only manage to make trouble for you and hurt you. You should have thrown me out the first day I came to see you, and at this moment I'd be in my right place, in prison.'

'Don't speak so loud.'

'Excuse me. It's true that I've been drinking, but I'm not drunk. I swear to you I'm not drunk. It's important that you believe me. If you see me in this state, it's because I'm afraid, especially for you.'

'Tell me what's happened.'

'We went to a cinema where they were showing a picture he'd been wanting to see for ages and, when we came out, I wanted to have a snack in the Place du Tertre.'

Her taste runs to noisy, brightly-coloured places, vulgar, strident settings.

'He didn't speak to me immediately. I could tell he wasn't his usual self, but I didn't think it was that serious. All of a sudden, when we'd been dancing and were going back to our seats, he stopped me just as I was sitting down and said, knitting his brows:

' "Do you know what we're going to do?"

'And I – forgive me – said:

' "For heaven's sake!"

' "That's not what I'm talking about. We are going to the Rue de Ponthieu, but it's to get your things and you're coming to my place. I've finally got the room they've been promising me for so long. It's big enough for two and it overlooks the street."

'Thinking he was just talking, I answered:

' "You know that's quite impossible, Léonard."

' "No. I've thought about it. It's too stupid to live the way we do. You've often told me you don't care about a big flat or a luxurious life. You've known worse than the Quai de Javel, haven't you?" '

While she was talking with animation, I sat quite still on the bench, my eyes fixed on a couple drinking champagne and kissing between swallows. At one point, they were diverting themselves by transferring the champagne from mouth to mouth, by kissing.

'I'm listening,' I sighed, after Yvette had been silent for a few moments.

'I can't tell you everything. It would take too long. He's never said as much as he said today. He maintains that he's finally sure he loves me and that nothing will make him give me up.'

'Did he talk about me?'

She didn't answer.

'What did he say?'

'That I don't owe you any gratitude, that you are nothing but an egoist, a ...'

'A what?'

'Well then, since you insist, a pervert. He hasn't understood anything, says you're acting just like a man of your class, and so on ... I told him that was untrue, that he didn't know you and that I refused to leave you. There were a lot of people around us. A singer made us be quiet for a time and that gave me a chance to observe him and to realize that he's acquired an evil look. When the singer shut up, he said:

'"If you want to do it, call him right now on the phone and tell him our decision."

'I refused, repeating that I wouldn't go with him.

'"In that case, I do the telephoning and speak to him myself. I bet you he'll understand."

'I clung to him and to gain time I suggested:

'"Let's go somewhere else. Everyone's looking at us and thinking we're having a row."

'We walked in the darkness of the little streets up there, with long silences. You've asked me to tell you everything, Lucien. I swear to you that I didn't hesitate in making my decision, that I was only looking for a way to get rid of him. When I saw the lights in Manière's, I pretended I was thirsty, we came in and I ordered a whisky, which I badly needed, because the scene was beginning over again.

'"What would you have that you haven't got now," I asked him, "if I came to live with you at Javel?"'

' "You'd be my wife." '

' "What do you mean?" '

' "What I say. I'd marry you." ' '

She emptied her glass, laughed scornfully:

'Do you realize? I burst out laughing, but it was a queer feeling all the same, because that's the first time a man has made me that proposal.

' "Within a month," I replied, "you'd regret it, or else I'd have had enough of you."

' "No." '

' "I'm not made to live with a man." '

' "All women are made for that." '

' "Not me." '

' "That's my business." '

' "That's my business too." '

' "Admit that it's because of him that you're refusing." '

'I admitted nothing, I kept silent and he went on:

' "You're afraid of him?" '

' "No." '

' "Then you love him?" ' '

She fell silent again, signalled to the waiter.

'Same again.'

'For both?'

I said yes without thinking.

'He repeated:

' "You love him? Admit it. Tell me the truth." '

'I don't know any more what I finally replied, and, in great anger, he got up, snapping at me:

' "I'll settle the matter with him and no one else." '

'He left, furious and pale, after throwing some money on the table for our drinks.'

'Had he been drinking?'

'A few. Not enough to have that much effect. I expected him to calm down when he got outside and come back and apologize. Before I rang you, I sat here all alone in my corner for half an hour, cooling my heels and jumping every time the door opened. Suddenly it dawned on me that he might have gone to find you at home.'

'I didn't see anyone.'

'He'll do it, I'm sure, because he wasn't just talking. He's not the type of boy to reach a decision lightly, and when he has an idea in his head, he carries it out at any price. Like in his studies! I'm frightened, Lucien. I'm so afraid something may happen to you.'

'Let's go.'

'Let me have another drink.'

It was the one too many; I knew it when her speech got thick and her eyes glassy, and also from the tone of what she said:

'You are sure I wouldn't leave you for anything in the world, aren't you? You must know it, you must know that you mean everything to me, that before you I didn't exist and that, if you weren't there any more ...'

I called the waiter to pay and she succeeded in finishing my drink as well. When we left, she begged me to make sure no one was watching for us outside. We were lucky enough to find a taxi without waiting and told him to take us to the Rue de Ponthieu. In the car she huddled against me, sniffling, shaken from time to time by a sob.

Her story isn't necessarily accurate and I shall never know what she said to Mazetti. Even without any reason to lie, she feels a need to tell stories and ends by believing them.

When it started, didn't she swear to Mazetti that I was no more than her lawyer, that she was innocent in the Rue de l'Abbé-Grégoire affair and that she owed me eternal gratitude for having saved her from an unjust conviction?

This leads me back to July, one week-day, I don't remember which, when I had taken her to Saint-Cloud for lunch in an outdoor restaurant of the kind she likes. The terrace where we were eating was crowded and I paid only slight attention to two young men in shirt-sleeves, one with very dark curly hair, who were sitting at the next table and never stopped looking in our direction. I had an important appointment at half past two and at a quarter past we hadn't even reached the dessert. I told Yvette I would have to go.

'May I stay?' she asked.

She didn't tell me anything the next day, nor the day after, not until three days later, when the lights were out and we were going to sleep.

'Are you asleep, Lucien?'

'No.'

'Can I talk to you?'

'Of course you can talk to me. Do you want me to put the light on?'

'No. I think I've done something bad again.'

I've often wondered if her honesty and her mania for confession come from her conscience or from a natural cruelty, perhaps from a need to give her life interest by colouring it with drama.

'Didn't you notice the two young men, the other day, at Saint-Cloud?'

'Which ones?'

'They were at the next table. One of them was dark and very muscular.'

'Yes.'

'When you left, I realized he was going to speak to me when I saw him getting rid of his friend, and, as a matter of fact, a little later he asked me if he might have his coffee at my table.'

She's had other affairs since we've known each other and I think she is honest when she claims that I know about all of them. The first, a fortnight after her acquittal, while she was still living on the Boulevard Saint-Michel, was with a jazz-player in a night-club near Saint-Germain-des-Prés. She confessed to me that she used to sit the whole evening near the band and that the second night he took her home with him.

'Are you jealous, Lucien?'

'Yes.'

'Does this hurt you very much?'

'Yes. Never mind.'

'Do you think I'm capable of controlling myself?'

'No.'

It's true. It's not only the senses that are responsible. It's deeper, a need to live a different life, to be the centre of something, to feel attention on herself. I had been convinced of it at the assizes, when she probably spent the most intoxicating hours of her life in that court.

'You still want me to tell you everything?'

'Yes.'

'Even if it hurts you?'

'That's my problem.'

'Are you angry with me?'

'It's not your fault.'

'Do you think I'm made differently from other women?'

'No.'

'Well then, how do the others manage?'

At these moments, when we reach a certain point of absurdity, I turn my back on her, because I know what she wants: for us to discuss her case endlessly, analyse her personality, her instincts, her behaviour.

She realizes it too.

'I don't interest you any more?'

Whereupon she sulks, or cries, then she watches me for a moment like a little girl who's been disobedient and decides to come and apologize.

'I don't understand how you put up with me. But have you ever thought, Lucien, how exasperating it can be for a woman to find herself confronted by a man who knows everything, who guesses everything?'

With the jazz-musician, it only lasted five days. One

evening I found her strange, feverish, her eyes dilated and, by asking her the necessary questions, I obtained the admission that he had persuaded her to take heroin. I got angry and when, next day, I realized that she had seen him again although I had forbidden it, I slapped her in the face for the first time, so hard that she bore a mark under her left eye for several days.

I can't watch her day and night, or demand that she spend all her time waiting for me. I know I don't satisfy her and I'm obliged to let her seek the rest elsewhere. If I suffer for it, that's too bad.

During the early months, anxiety predominated, for I wondered if she would come back to me or if she would charge headlong into some sordid affair.

Since Saint-Cloud my worries have taken on a different form.

'He's a boy of Italian origin, but he was born in France and he's a French citizen. Do you know what he does? He's both a medical student and a worker on the night-shift at Citroën's. Don't you think that shows guts?'

'Where did he take you?'

'Nowhere. That's not his line. We walked back through the Bois de Boulogne and I don't think I ever walked as far in my life. Are you angry?'

'Why should I be angry?'

'Because I didn't tell you before.'

'Have you seen him again?'

'Yes.'

'When?'

'Yesterday.'

'Where?'

'On the terrace of the Normandie, on the Champs-Elysées, where he'd made a date with me.'

'By telephone?'

So he already knew her number.

'You're always afraid I'll get mixed up with some

hoodlum, so I thought you'd be glad. His father's a brick-layer at Villefranche-sur-Saône, not far from Lyons where I was born, and his mother washes dishes in a restaurant. He has seven brothers and sisters. Since he was fifteen he's been working to pay for his studies. At present he lives in a little room, at Javel, near the factory, and doesn't sleep more than five hours a day.'

'When are you seeing him again?'

I knew she had an idea in the back of her mind.

'That depends on you.'

'What do you mean?'

'If you don't want me to, I won't see him again at all.'

'When did he ask you to see him again?'

'On Saturday evenings he doesn't work at the factory.'

'Do you want to meet him next Saturday?'

She didn't answer. On Sunday morning, telephoning the Rue de Ponthieu, I realized from her embarrassment that she wasn't alone. That was the first time, to my knowledge, that she had taken someone else to a flat which is, after all, ours.

'Is he there?'

'Yes.'

'Shall I meet you at Louis'?'

'If you like.'

The night of Saturday to Sunday has become 'their' night, and, for some time, Mazetti believed the story of the big-hearted lawyer. Yvette confessed to me that, occasion-ally, during the day, she would go over to the Quai de Javel to give him a kiss while he was studying.

'Just to cheer him up. The room is tiny and there's nothing but factory hands in the hotel, mostly Arabs and Poles. On the stairs, I'm scared of those men who don't stand aside to let me pass and look at me with shining eyes.'

He has been to the Rue de Ponthieu on other days besides Saturday, because one afternoon I passed him in the entrance. We recognized each other. He hesitated, nodded to me with some embarrassment, and I returned his courtesy.

Possibly just to add piquancy to the affair, Yvette, as I was expecting, finally admitted to him that I am not only her benefactor, but her lover.

She also told him about the hold-up in the Rue de l'Abbé-Grégoire, the true version this time, adding that, for her sake, I risked my honour and my position.

'That man – he's sacred. Understand?'

What does it matter whether she said it or not? The fact remains that he didn't protest and that another time we met in the street he nodded to me again, looking at me curiously.

I wonder if she hasn't made out that I'm impotent, that I confine myself to intimacies which he has no need to resent? It's not true, but she's told me less plausible fairy tales.

Neither of them understands a thing, of course. And now what was bound to happen is happening.

'What else did he say?' I asked, once we were inside the flat.

'I forget. I'd rather not repeat it. All those things that young men say about men of your age who act as if they were in love.'

She had opened a cupboard and I saw her drinking out of a bottle.

'Stop that!'

Looking at me, she took the time to swallow one last gulp. Then, her speech thick, she asks:

'Can't you have him arrested, with your connexions?'

'On what pretext?'

'He has threatened you.'

'What threats?'

'Maybe it wasn't very definite, but he hinted that he'd find a way to get rid of you.'

'In what terms?'

Here I know she is lying, or at least embroidering.

'Even if that were true, it wouldn't be sufficient reason to arrest him. Would you like to see him in prison?'

'I don't want anything awful to happen to you. You're all I have, you know it.'

She thinks so and it's more serious than she believes. She would be totally lost, and unhappy, if she found herself on her own again; it wouldn't take her long to come to a bad end.

'I'm sick, Lucien.'

I can see it. She's drunk too much and it won't be long before she vomits.

'I hadn't the vaguest idea that it would turn out like this! I thought it was convenient. I knew you were pleased. . . .'

She realizes that the word is a bit strong.

'Forgive me. You see! It's always the same with me. I make every effort to do what's right and everything I try turns out wrong. What I do swear to you, on your life, is that I won't see him again. Take a look in the street, will you?'

I opened the curtains a crack and saw no one in the lamp-light.

'What I'm afraid of is that he may be getting drunk, because he doesn't carry his liquor very well. It makes him mean; and he's usually so calm and so easy to get along with. Once, when he'd had one glass too many . . .'

She doesn't finish her sentence and rushes into the bathroom where I can hear her retching.

'I'm ashamed of myself, Lucien . . .' she mumbles, between two bouts of sickness. 'If you knew how I hate myself! . . . I wonder how you can . . .'

I undressed her and put her to bed. I got undressed myself and lay down beside her. Two or three times, in her restless sleep, she uttered words I couldn't distinguish.

It's possible that Mazetti is getting drunk in an all-night

bar of which there are a few in Paris, or perhaps he is walking about the deserted avenues with long strides, exuding his grievances. It is also possible that he may come hanging around the Rue de Ponthieu, just as I myself, one day, hung around under the windows of the Boulevard Malesherbes.

If the account Yvette has given me of their evening and his attitude is not too romanticized, he will not let her go easily and it won't be long before he goes to work on her again.

Has she really told him all about her past and has she been as honest with him as with me? It didn't stop him from offering to marry her.

I must have dozed for a time because the telephone bell made me jump out of bed and I hurried into the sitting-room to take off the receiver, hurting my foot badly when I bumped into a piece of furniture on the way. My first thought was that my wife was telephoning me, as has happened before, about something urgent. I didn't know what time it was. The bedroom was dark, but in the sitting-room I saw the whiteness of daylight through the crack in the curtains.

'Hello.'

Not hearing anything, I repeated:

'Hello.'

I understand. It is he who has rung up, not expecting me to be here. Now that he has recognized my voice, he hasn't hung up and I can hear him breathing at the other end. It is rather impressive, especially as Yvette, who has woken up, has just appeared, naked and deathly pale in the half-light, and is staring at me with her wide-open eyes.

'Who is it?' she asks in a low voice.

I hang up and say:

'Wrong number.'

'Was it him?'

'I have no idea.'

'I'm certain it was. Now that he knows you're here, he'll come over. Put the light on, Lucien.'

That ray of daylight between the curtains gives her the shivers.

'I wonder where he's telephoning from. Maybe he's in the neighbourhood.'

I admit that I was uneasy myself. I have no desire to hear him knocking at the door of the flat, because, if he has gone on drinking, he is capable of making a scene.

I'm not answerable to him for anything, owe him no explanation. A three-way discussion would be ridiculous, odious.

'You'd better go.'

I don't want to seem to be running away, either.

'Would you rather be alone ?'

'Yes. I can always find some way out.'

'Do you intend to let him in ?'

'I don't know. I'll see. Get dressed.'

And another idea passes through her mind.

'Why not telephone the police ?'

I dressed, humiliated, furious with myself. All this time, still naked, she was looking out of the window, her face pressed against the glass.

'You're sure you'd rather be alone ?'

'Yes. Be quick !'

'I'll ring you when I get to the Quai d'Anjou.'

'All right. I'll be here all day.'

'I'll drop in and see you later.'

'Yes. Go along !'

She accompanied me on to the landing and kissed me, still with nothing on, leaning over the banisters to remind me :

'Be careful !'

I wasn't afraid, although I don't pride myself on physical courage and I hate violence. All the same I was anxious to avoid an encounter, which could have been unpleasant, with an infuriated young man. All the more since I have

82

nothing against him, nothing to reproach him with, and since I understand his state of mind.

The Rue de Ponthieu was deserted and only my footsteps were to be heard as I walked as far as the Rue de Berry to get a taxi. On the Champs Elysées a couple in evening dress, foreigners, were going into Claridge's arm in arm, and the woman still had scraps of paper streamers in her hair.

'Quai d'Anjou. I'll tell you where.'

I was still worried for Yvette. If I know her, she hasn't gone back to bed and she's on watch at the window without thinking of getting dressed. Sometimes she spends most of the day with nothing on, even in summer, when all the windows are open.

'You do it on purpose,' I once declared.

'What?'

'Show yourself naked to the people across the street.'

She looked at me the way she looks at me when I've guessed right, with a smile which she tries to hide.

'It's fun, isn't it?'

Perhaps it would be fun for her, too, if Mazetti comes hounding her again? I'm not sure that if she knew where to get hold of him she wouldn't ring him up. This perpetual need of hers to get out of her own life, to create a character for herself.

I'm afraid that if she sees him in the street she may telephone the police, just for the excitement.

I'm the one who rings her up, the moment I'm in my office.

'This is Lucien.'

'Did you get home all right?'

'He hasn't come?'

'No.'

'Were you still at the window?'

'Yes.'

'Go back to bed.'

'You don't think he'll come?'

'I'm sure he won't. I'll ring you again soon.'

'I hope you're going to sleep too?'

'Yes.'

'I'm sorry for the bad night I've given you. I'm ashamed of getting tight, but I didn't realize I was drinking.'

'Go to bed.'

'Are you going to tell your wife?'

'I don't know.'

'Don't tell her I was sick.'

She knows that Viviane is fully informed and this bothers her, because, where Viviane is concerned, she would like to play a role that is not too humiliating. Suddenly she asks me about her.

'What exactly do you tell her? Everything we do?'

Occasionally, when she asks that question, she has added with an excited laugh:

'Even what I'm doing to you now?'

I looked out of my office window, as I've already written, and didn't see anyone on the quay. Probably Mazetti has gone home and is fast asleep.

I went up without a sound. All the same my wife half opened her eyelids just as I was swallowing my two tablets.

'Nothing serious?'

'No. Go to sleep.'

She couldn't have been quite awake, because she drifted back into sleep immediately. I tried to sleep too. I couldn't. My nerves were on edge, still are; I only need to see my writing to be convinced of it. Perhaps a graphologist would conclude that it is the writing of a madman or a drunk.

For some time I've been expecting something disagreeable, but I never imagined anything more disagreeable or more humiliating than the night I have just been through.

My eyes closed; in the warmth of my bed, I asked myself if Mazetti were not capable of doing violence to me. In the course of my career I've known more senseless gestures. I've never spoken to him. I've done no more than catch sight of him and he gave me the impression of a serious, reserved boy, who follows fanatically the line of conduct he has laid down for himself.

Does he realize that his affair with Yvette threatens the whole future he has prepared with such difficulty? If she has told him everything, if he knows her as I know her, is he naïve enough to hope that he will suddenly change her by making her the wife of an ambitious young doctor?

He is in the middle of a crisis, incapable of reasoning. Tomorrow, or in a few days, he will see reality clearly and will be happy that I exist.

The trouble is that I'm not so sure of it. Why should he react differently from me? Because he's too young to understand, to feel what I have felt?

I would like to believe that. I have looked for so many explanations of my attachment to Yvette! I have rejected them, one after another, taken them up again, combined them, mixed them up together without getting any satisfactory result and this morning I feel old and stupid. When I came down to my office just now, my head empty, my eyes stinging for lack of sleep, I looked at the books covering the walls and I shrugged my shoulders.

Did Andrieu in those days ever look at himself with contemptuous pity?

Today I envy those people who still go canoeing between Chelles and Lagny and all the others I dropped on the way because they couldn't keep up with me.

I'm busy watching through the window for a young lunatic who, it appears, has threatened to demand an explanation from me! I say it appears, because I'm not even sure that all this is true, that tonight or tomorrow Yvette won't confess to me that she exaggerated, if she didn't invent, a large part of what she told me.

I can't hold it against her, because that's her nature and because in the long run we all do it to some extent. The difference is that she has all the faults, all the vices, all the weaknesses. Not even that! She'd like to have them. It's a game she plays, her way of filling the void.

I'm not in a fit state, this morning, to analyse myself. What's the use, anyhow, and what's the use of knowing why, on account of her, I've reached the point I'm at?

It's not even certain that it's on account of her. The authors of musical comedies, the amusing authors who succeed in making life funny, call it the Indian summer and it becomes a subject for jokes.

I've never taken life tragically. I still try not to. I try to remain objective, to judge myself and to judge other people coldly. Above all I try to understand. When I began this dossier, I kind of winked at myself once, as if I were going in for some solitary game.

Well, I haven't laughed yet. This morning, I feel less like laughing than ever and I wonder if I wouldn't rather be inside the skin of one of those little bourgeois dressed up in their Sunday best hurrying to High Mass.

*

I've just rung Yvette for the second time, and she took a little while to come to the phone. From the way she says 'Hello' I sense something new.

'Are you alone?'

'No.'

'Is he there?'

'Yes.'

So that she won't have to talk in front of him, I ask precise questions.

'Furious?'

'No.'

'Has he apologized?'

'Yes.'

'Are his intentions still the same?'

'Well ...'

Mazetti must have snatched the receiver from her hands, because it was abruptly hung up.

Old fool!

Chapter Five

Saturday, 24 November

For two weeks now I haven't had a minute to open this
dossier and I've been living on my own momentum, convinced that the time will come when I shall collapse of
exhaustion, incapable of one further step or word. Never
before have I foreseen the possibility that talking may be
beyond my strength, and it is a fact that I'm already beginning to talk less, from tiredness.

I'm not the only one to think of this eventual breakdown
of my nerves. I read the same uneasiness in the expressions
of the people around me and they are beginning to watch
me surreptitiously like someone who's seriously ill. What
do they know at the Palais about my intimate life? I have
no idea, but there's a certain firmness in some handshakes,
and there's the way they say, without insisting:

'Don't overdo it!'

Pémal, usually optimistic, raised his eyebrows as he took
my blood-pressure the other day, in the den where I had
to receive him hurriedly because I had a client in my office
and two more in the waiting-room.

'I suppose it's useless to ask you to rest?'

'Impossible for the moment. It's up to you to see to it
that I keep going.'

He gave me some vitamins or other, by injection, and
since then a nurse comes every morning to give me another,
between one door and the other, in the time it takes me
to go into my den and let down my trousers. Pémal doesn't
really have much faith in them.

'A time comes when you can't stretch the spring any tighter.'

That's the impression I have – of a spring which is beginning to quiver and which is about to snap. I feel all over my body something like a tremor which I'm powerless to stop and which is sometimes agonizing. I hardly sleep. I haven't got time. I don't even dare to sit down in an easy-chair after meals, because I'm like those ailing horses which avoid lying down for fear of not being able to get up again.

I am making an effort to meet my obligations on all fronts and it's a matter of vanity to me to accompany Viviane to fashionable occasions, to cocktail parties, to dress rehearsals, to dinner at Corine's and anywhere else where I know it would be embarrassing for her to be seen alone.

She's grateful for it, although she doesn't mention it to me, but she is worried. As if it had been deliberately arranged, I've never had so many cases, at the Palais, nor such important ones, which I can't delegate to anyone else.

The South American ambassador, for instance, came to see me on Monday as arranged and, even though I hadn't been altogether wrong about the nature of his problems, I hadn't guessed the truth. They've got the arms. It's his father who intends to seize power by means of a *coup d'état* which is supposed to be brief and not too bloody. According to my informant, whose voice had become passionate, his father is staking his life and his fortune, which is immense, for the sole good of his country, now in the hands of a gang of politicians who are ruining it for their own gain.

So the arms, including three four-engined aircraft on which the conspirators' plan rests, are aboard a ship flying the Panamanian flag, which, having sustained some damage, has had the bad luck to have to seek temporary shelter at Martinique.

The damage wasn't serious. It was a question of two or three days. As luck would have it, a customs official, an eager beaver, inspects the cargo and finds that it doesn't correspond to the bill of lading. The captain, for his part, was tactless enough to offer him money, and the customs man has set the clumsy administrative machinery going, immobilizing the ship in port.

Without him, everything would have been easy, because the French government asks only to keep its eyes shut. But now, with official reports on the way, it becomes an extremely touchy affair and I've had an interview with the premier himself, who is full of goodwill but almost defenceless against the customs official. Cases do exist, as I know from experience, in which the most insignificant civil servant can hold cabinet ministers in check like this.

In a few days I am pleading the Neveu case, which for months has demanded an enormous amount of work and caused a lot of talk. The mistress of a man in the consular service fired six shots at her lover, at the moment when the latter, in order to get rid of her after giving her two children, was leaving for the Far East, where he'd had himself transferred. She made the mistake of behaving quite coldbloodedly in the presence of the authorities and the press, telling the latter, with the smoking gun still in her hand, that she dared the courts to condemn her. A reverse, in my present situation, would do me a lot of harm and would be regarded as the beginning of my decline.

I had a bit of luck this week with young Delrieu, who killed his father for reasons which remain rather mysterious and whom I got off with confinement to a mental hospital.

New clients turn up every day. If I listened to Bordenave, I wouldn't receive them. She sits around in her office like a watchdog who's not allowed to bark at the approach of prowlers, and I often see her with red eyes.

I have sometimes thought, in moments of discouragement, that if all the world turned against me I'd still have my secretary to end my days with. Isn't it ironical that towards her I feel a physical antipathy, almost a repulsion, which would prevent me from taking her in my arms or looking at her naked body? I suspect that she has guessed this and is hurt by it, and that because of me she will never belong to any man.

The hardest thing was not so much taking my decision as telling Viviane, because, this time, I was conscious of going a bit too far and venturing on to slippery ground. Whatever happens, I shall be lucid to the end and I assume complete responsibility for my actions, for *all* my actions.

The week following the night at Manière's was one of the most painful and perhaps the most ridiculous of my life. I wonder how I found time to plead cases, to study my clients' affairs and, into the bargain, to be seen with Viviane at a certain number of Paris functions.

It came about, as I expected, through Mazetti and his new tactics. In fact, I can't get rid of the notion that he did it on purpose, and that's obviously not so foolish since it almost came off.

On Sunday evening I had a serious conversation with Yvette and I was sincere, or almost, when I gave her a choice.

'If you decide to marry him, ring him up.'

'No, Lucien. I don't want to.'

'Would you be unhappy with him?'

'I can't be happy without you.'

'Are you sure?'

She was so tired that she looked almost ghost-like and she asked me if she might have a drink to pick her up.

'What did he say to you?'

'That he would wait as long as necessary, certain that I will marry him some day.'

'Is he coming back?'

She didn't need to reply.

'In that case, if you've really made up your mind, you must write him a letter which will leave him no hope.'

'What shall I say to him?'

'That you won't see him again.'

She had been making love with him for part of the day and still bore the marks; her bruised lips looked somehow diluted and seemed to swallow up her face.

I partly dictated the letter to her and posted it myself.

'Promise, if he rings you up or comes knocking at the door, that you won't answer.'

'I promise.'

He didn't telephone or try to get into the flat. By the next morning, however, she was on the phone.

'He's there.'

'On the pavement.'

'He hasn't rung your bell?'

'No.'

'What's he doing?'

'Nothing. He's leaning against the house opposite and staring at my windows. What do you advise me to do?'

'I'll come and take you out to lunch.'

I went over. I saw Mazetti standing in the street, unshaven, dirty, as though he had hurried straight from the factory without changing.

He didn't approach us, satisfied to look at Yvette with the eyes of a whipped dog.

When I brought her home an hour later, he wasn't there any more, but he came back the next day, then the day after, his beard longer every time, his eyes feverish, and he was beginning to look like a beggar.

I don't know how much sincerity there is in his attitude. He's in the middle of a crisis, too. From one day to the next, he seems to have renounced the career for which he has made so many sacrifices, as though only Yvette still mattered in his eyes.

In the course of the week, our glances have crossed several times and I have read a scornful reproach in his eyes.

I have contemplated all imaginable solutions, including impossible ones, like installing Yvette in the lower flat, the one where my chambers and offices are. We've kept a bedroom and bath there which Bordenave uses when she works late.

For hours, this plan excited me. I was intrigued by the prospect of having Yvette within reach day and night, until finally my reason regained the upper hand. It is impractical, obviously, if only because of Viviane. She has accepted a great deal up to now. She is ready to accept plenty more, but she wouldn't go as far as that.

I felt this when I informed her of the decision I have finally reached. It was after luncheon. I had chosen the time purposely, because I was due at the Palais and had only a quarter of an hour to spare, which prevented the conversation from being dangerously prolonged.

As we went into the drawing-room for coffee, I murmured:

'I want to talk to you.'

The strained look that appeared on her features showed me that there wasn't much left to tell her. Was she perhaps expecting a decision even more serious than the one at which I had stopped? In any case I felt the shock and, from one minute to the next she looked her age.

My heart contracted, rather as it does when you are obliged to put away an animal which has long been faithful to you.

'Sit down. Don't talk. It's nothing bad.'

She managed to smile and her smile was hard, defensive; when I told her which flat I had in mind, I knew that it wasn't for sentimental reasons that she stiffened. I even thought for a moment that the fight was on, and I'm not sure I didn't hope so. The two of us would have got it done with once and for all, instead of proceeding by stages. I was determined not to yield.

'For reasons too long to explain to you, which I suppose you are aware of anyhow, it is impossible for her to go on living in a hotel room.'

We always say 'she'; I do it out of tact, my wife out of contempt.

'I know.'

'In that case, it will be easy. It is essential that as soon as possible I settle her in a place unknown to a certain person who is harassing her.'

'I understand. Go ahead.'

'It happens that there is a flat vacant.'

Did she already know, through the agency, for instance?

When we were living in the Place Denfert-Rochereau, the second year if I remember correctly, we were already beginning to find our apartment inconvenient and had dreams of moving closer to the Palais. Several times we had been for walks in the Île Saint-Louis, which attracted us both.

There was a vacant flat there at the time, at the extreme tip of the island, on the spur that faces the Cité and Notre-Dame, and we went to look at it together, exchanging covetous glances. The rent, controlled by law, was not outrageously high, but it was tied in with buying some furnishings, which the state of our finances did not permit us to consider, and we left with heavy hearts.

Later, we were to meet, at a friend's house, an American woman, Miss Wilson, who had not just rented our dream flat but bought it, and I think Viviane later went to tea with her. She was a writer, was always at the Louvre and with artists, and, like certain expatriate American intellectuals, considered her own country barbaric and swore she would end her days in Paris. Everything there enchanted her, the bistros, Les Halles, the little more or less slummy streets, the tramps, the morning *croissants*, the cheap red wine and the *bals musettes*.

Well, two months ago, at forty-five, she married a visiting American, a man younger than herself, a Harvard professor, and followed him to the United States.

She broke completely with her past, with Paris, and

commissioned an estate agency to sell her apartment, furniture and furnishings as quickly as possible.

It's two minutes' walk from our house and when I go to see Yvette I won't need to take taxis any more or bother Albert.

'I've thought about it a lot. At first sight it seems crazy, but . . .'

'Have you bought it?'

'Not yet. I'm seeing the agency man tonight.'

From now on I had before me a woman defending, no longer her happiness, but her interests.

'I suppose you don't intend to take the flat in her name?'

I was expecting that. It was, in fact, my original intention to make Yvette that present, so that whatever may happen to me, she won't find herself out on the street again. Viviane, for her part, will be well provided for when I die, will practically be able to keep up our standard of living, thanks to heavy insurance policies I have taken out for her benefit.

I hesitated. Then, lacking courage, I retreated. I'm furious with myself for that cowardice, for having stammered, blushing:

'Of course not.'

I'm all the more annoyed because she guessed that my original intention was different and this meant a victory for her.

'When are you signing?'

'This evening, if the deed of sale is in order.'

'She's moving in tomorrow?'

'The day after tomorrow.'

She gave a bitter smile, probably remembering our visit years ago, our dismay when we were told how much they wanted for the purchase of a few worthless carpets.

'You haven't got anything else to tell me?'

'No.'

'Are you happy?'

I nodded and she came up to me and put her hand on my shoulder in a gesture that was both protective and affectionate. Because of that gesture, which I had never seen her use, I understood her attitude to me better. For a long time, perhaps always, she has considered me her own creation. Before I knew her, I didn't exist as far as she's concerned. She chose me as Corine chose Jean Moriat, except that I wasn't even a member of parliament, and for me she gave up a luxurious, easy life.

She has helped me rise in my career, certainly – I should be ungrateful if I denied it – by her social activity which has opened plenty of doors to me and brought me a lot of clients. Also she is partly responsible for my name being constantly in the papers, and not only in the legal section, for she has made me a Paris celebrity.

She didn't tell me so that day, didn't reproach me with anything, but I felt that I mustn't risk one step further, that the flat on the Quai d'Orléans, *on condition that it remain in my name*, was the final limit which she would not permit me to pass.

I wonder whether they talk about me, Corine and she, whether they form a sort of clan, for there are a certain number of them in the same situation, or if, on the contrary, they are jealous of each other and exchange false confidences and smiles.

That whole week I was fighting time, for my great fear was that Yvette would break down, that at her window she would make the gesture Mazetti was waiting for to hurl himself into her arms. I telephoned her every hour, even during court recesses, and as soon as I had a moment I would rush to the Rue de Ponthieu where, for safety's sake I spent every night.

'If I take you away from here, do you promise me not to write to him, never to let him know your new address, not to go, for the time being, to places where he might find you?'

I didn't immediately understand the terror I read in her eyes. Yet she replied, docile:

'I promise.'

I could tell she was frightened.

'Where is it?'

'Just near my house.'

Then, only, she was relieved and admitted:

'I thought you wanted to send me to the country.'

Because she's scared of the country. A sunset behind trees, even the trees of a Paris square, is enough to plunge her into black melancholy.

'When?'

'Tomorrow.'

'Shall I pack?'

She has enough now to fill a trunk and two suitcases.

'We'll move at night, when we're sure the coast is clear.'

At eleven-thirty, after a banquet given by the President of the Bar, I called for her in the car with Albert. It was Albert who carried down her luggage, while I kept watch, and slushy snow was falling. Two girls walking the pavement in the Rue do Ponthieu first tried to pick me up, then watched, curiously, the elopement.

For months I have been living on the promise, for tomorrow or for next week, of a calmer, more peaceful existence. When I bought the apartment on the Quai d'Orléans, I was convinced that it would solve everything and that from then on I would go and see Yvette while taking a walk, as others walk their dog, morning and evening, around the island.

It's not worth continuing this dossier unless I tell everything. I was seized by an almost adolescent fever. The flat is stylish, feminine, tasteful.

The room on the Boulevard Saint-Michel was like a cheap whorehouse, the one in the Rue de Ponthieu like that of a little Champs-Elysées tart.

Here, it was a new world, almost a leap into the ideal,

and, so that Yvette shouldn't feel too much out of place, I dashed over to the Rue Saint-Honoré and bought her underclothes, négligées and housecoats to match the surroundings.

Also, so that she wouldn't think of going out, at least in the beginning, I bought her a gramophone and records and finally a television set, and I filled the bookshelves with fairly spicy books, as she likes them, without going so far as to bring her trashy novels.

Without telling her, I engaged a maid, Jeanine, quite a pretty girl, attractive and talkative, who will keep her company.

I have made no allusion to these arrangements in front of Viviane, but I have reason to think she is informed. During the three days I spent chasing about like this, she took to looking at me with a maternal, rather sympathetic tenderness, as one looks at a boy who is going through the awkward age.

The third night we spent in the new flat, I woke up with the impression that Yvette beside me was terribly hot. I was not mistaken. When I took her temperature, about four in the morning, it was a hundred and three and at seven o'clock the thermometer was close to a hundred and four. I phoned Pémal. He hurried over.

'Quai d'Orléans, you say?' he asked in surprise.

I gave him no explanation. He didn't need any when he found me in the bedroom with Yvette naked in bed.

It isn't anything serious, a bad case of tonsilitis, which lasted a week, with ups and downs. I shuttled between the two houses and between them and the Palais.

This indisposition revealed to me that Yvette has a mortal terror of death. Every time her temperature began to go up again, she would cling to me like an animal in distress, begging me to call the doctor whom I sometimes had to disturb three times in one day.

'Don't let me die, Lucien!'

Often she cried to me for help like this, her eyes staring as if she had caught a glimpse of Lord knows what terrifying beyond.

'I don't want to. Never! Stay with me!'

One of her hands in mine, I would telephone to put off appointments, to apologize for missing others, and I had to call Bordenave over so that I could dictate, beside Yvette's bed, letters which couldn't wait.

Nevertheless, I appeared, in formal dress, at the Nuit des Étoiles, and Viviane kept her eye on me, wondering if I would hold out to the end, if I wasn't going to drop everything to rush over to the Quai d'Orléans.

To make the situation still more complicated, all I needed, next day, was to find Mazetti, who is still letting his beard grow, on sentry duty outside the house on the Quai d'Anjou. He must have figured that I would sooner or later lead him to Yvette and maybe he thinks she is at my home.

I had to use Albert, take the car and make a tour of the island every time I visited the Quai d'Orléans and not leave Yvette's flat until I was sure the coast was clear.

If I note these sordid details, it is because they have their importance and help to explain this stupor in which I am living at present.

Fortunately Mazetti didn't persevere. He came three times. I was expecting him to come up, ask to see me, and I had given instructions. I had also thought of the possibility that he might be armed and I kept my revolver in my drawer.

Well, he disappeared from one day to the next, just about the time Yvette was beginning to feel better.

She is up, almost well again, but she is weak and Pémal gives her the same injections he gives me; he gives us them one after the other, with the same hypodermic, which seems to amuse him.

I don't know whether he has recognized Yvette, whose

photograph appeared in the papers at the time of the trial. He must harbour a certain pity for me and maybe he, too, thinks it's the Indian summer.

That expression irritates me. I've always detested simplifications. One of my colleagues, who is talked about nearly as much as I am, on account of his clever remarks, and is reckoned one of the wittiest men in Paris, has an explanation of that sort for every case, an explanation which is both penetrating and over-simple.

For him the world can be reduced to a few human types, life to a certain number of more or less acute crises through which men sooner or later pass, sometimes without noticing it, as they passed through childhood diseases in their youth.

It's attractive, and he has managed to disarm judges by making them laugh at a flash of wit. He must joke about me, and his witticisms make the rounds of the Palais and the drawing-rooms Isn't it funny, a man of my age, my position – does he perhaps add, of my intelligence? – who is wrecking his whole life and his wife's because one evening a young slut came to ask him to defend her and lifted her skirt to her waist?

What surprises me personally, and I admit it, is that Mazetti should be in love with Yvette and I'm inclined to believe that, if it hadn't been for me, he would hardly have given her a thought.

If some day someone reads the pages of this dossier, he will note that up to now I've never written the word love, and this is not accidental. I don't believe in it. More exactly, I don't believe in what is generally called by that name. I have never loved Viviane, for example, infatuated with her as I was at the time of the Boulevard Malesherbes.

She was the wife of my chief, of a man whom I admired and who was famous. She lived in a world well equipped to dazzle the poor, unsophisticated student that I still was the day before. She was beautiful and I was ugly. To see her yield to me was a miracle which suddenly made me swell with confidence in myself and my destiny.

For I already understood what attracted her in me: a certain power, an inflexible will in which she put her trust.

She was my mistress. She became my wife. Her body gave me pleasure but never haunted my dreams, was never anything but a woman's body, and Viviane played no role in what I believe to be the most important part of my sexual life.

I was grateful to her for having singled me out, for having accepted, for my sake, what I still regarded as a sacrifice, and it was not until much later that I suspected the truth about what she, for her part, called her love.

Wasn't it above all a need to assert herself, to prove to herself and others that she was more than just a pretty woman to be dressed, protected and taken out?

And wasn't there, more than anything else, a craving in her for domination?

Well, she dominated me for twenty years and she's trying to keep on dominating me. Up until the matter of the flat on the Quai d'Orléans she lived without much to worry about, giving me plenty of rope, sure of herself, sure that I would come back to her after a more or less stormy crisis which offered no threat to her.

What her face revealed to me, during the conversation after lunch, was her sudden discovery of a real threat. For the first time she had the impression that I was getting away from her and that it might be for good.

She reacted as best she could. She continued to play the game, watching me more closely. She is suffering, I know; I see her growing older day by day and she is using more make-up. But it is not on my account that she is suffering. It is on her own, not only because of the situation she has created with me, but because of the idea she has formed of herself and her power.

I am sorry for her and, in spite of the alarmed glances

she darts at me, she is not sorry for me. Her solicitude is selfish; what she is waiting for is not for me to regain my serenity but to come back to her. Even if I should come back to her mortally wounded. Even if in future I am to be nothing but an empty body at her side.

How does she explain my passion for Yvette? The others, the women I had before her, she puts down to curiosity and also to masculine conceit, to the need every man feels, especially if he's ugly, to prove to himself that he can reduce a woman to his mercy.

But in most cases it wasn't like that, and I think I am lucid enough in what concerns myself not to be mistaken. If she were right, I should have had gratifying affairs with, among others, some of our women friends whom I could have had without any trouble. And occasionally, rarely, this has happened, always at times of doubt or discouragement.

More often I've slept with girls, professional or non-professional, and when I think about it, I realize that they all had certain things in common with Yvette, which had escaped me until now.

My strongest impulse was probably a craving for pure sex, if I can use that expression without raising a smile, I mean sex without any considerations of emotion or passion. Let's say sex in its raw state. Or its cynical state.

I've listened, sometimes unwillingly, to the confidences of hundreds of clients, men and women, and I've been able to convince myself that I'm not an exception, that a need does exist in the human being to behave at times like an animal.

Perhaps I was wrong to have been afraid to show myself to Viviane in this light, but the idea would never have occurred to me. Who knows if she, for her part, doesn't hold it against me, if she hasn't sought that particular satisfaction elsewhere?

That's the case with several of our women friends and

with almost all the men and, if this instinct were not practically universal, prostitution wouldn't have existed since
time immemorial, in all latitudes.

It's a long time since I have had any pleasure with Viviane
and she puts my frigidity down to worry and work, and
no doubt also to my age.

But I can't be with Yvette for an hour without feeling
an urge to see her nakedness, to touch her, to ask her to
caress me.

It's not only because I'm not overawed by her, because
she's a kid of no importance, nor because I have no inhibitions with her.

Tomorrow it's possible that I may think and write the
opposite, but I doubt it. For me Yvette, like most of the
girls who have meant anything to me, personifies the
female, with her weaknesses, her cowardice, and also with
her instinct to cling to the male and make herself his slave.

I remember her surprise and pride the day I slapped her
face, and since then she has sometimes driven me to the
breaking-point just to see me do it again.

I don't claim that she loves me. I don't want anything to
do with that word.

But she has renounced being herself. She has placed her
fate in my hands. No matter if it is out of laziness or lack
of initiative. It's her role, and I see, perhaps naïvely, a
symbol in the way she once spread her thighs apart on the
corner of my desk, after asking me to defend her.

If tomorrow I abandon her, she will turn back, on the
streets, into a little bitch wandering about in search of a
master.

That, Mazetti cannot have understood. He's got the
wrong woman. He hasn't noticed that he had a female to
deal with.

She tells lies. She's deceitful. She puts on acts. She makes
up stories to worry me and, now that she's sure of her
daily bread, she wallows in laziness; there are days when

103

she hardly gets out of bed, keeping the television switched on at the foot of it.

At the sight of a passing male she's on heat and, in the street, she stares at men's trousers, at one definite place, as intensely as men stare at the bottoms of women walking past. More than once it's taken no more to excite her than a picture of underpants or swimming-trunks in a magazine advertisement.

She's done everything with Mazetti that she does with me. She's done it with other men too, ever since she reached puberty. No part of male, none of his demands, arouses her disgust.

I suffer when I know she is in someone else's arms, I can't help imagining every one of their movements, and yet she wouldn't be herself if she didn't act that way.

Would I have chosen her?

I've just written that word deliberately because, when she came to see me, anyone would have said I was waiting for her; it was that night that I made my decision.

On account of my age?

Perhaps. But it's nothing to do with the Indian summer they talk about. Nor is it anything to do with the change of life or impotence, still less with the need for a younger partner.

I know I'm touching on a complex problem which is most often treated jokingly because that's easier and more reassuring. Usually we only joke about what we're afraid of.

Why, at a certain degree of maturity, shouldn't a man discover that . . .

No! I can't manage to express my meaning exactly, and all the approximations irritate me.

The facts!

The essential fact is that I can't do without her, that I suffer physically when I'm separated from her. The fact is that I need to feel her near me, to watch her live, to breathe her odour, to indulge her and to know she is satisfied.

There still remains an explanation, but no one will believe it : the will to make someone happy, to take charge of someone, completely, someone who owes everything to you, whom you pull out of the abyss knowing that he will fall back into it if you fail him.

Isn't it for the same reason that so many people have a dog or a cat, canaries or goldfish, and that parents can't resign themselves to seeing their children living their own lives ?

Is that what's happened with Viviane and is that why she suffers as she sees me getting away from her ? Haven't I, too, suffered every Saturday, imagining Mazetti at the Rue de Ponthieu ?

And, in days gone by, Andrieu, the President of the Bar ?

Today's Saturday and tonight I can go and see her. There won't be any more damned Saturdays, cruel Saturdays. I'm tired ; at the end of my strength, I keep going like a machine with a faulty brake, but she lives two minutes away from me and I'm not in any pain.

That doesn't mean that I'm happy, but I'm not in any pain.

Other troubles are waiting for me ; I can feel them ready to descend on me as soon as I think I'm justified in relaxing. My first worry is that my carcass may not hold out. Those people who look at me with a worried or sympathetic eye are beginning to frighten me. What would happen if I became ill and had to stay in bed ?

If I have an attack in the office I could hardly demand to be taken to the Quai d'Orléans. Would I be capable of expressing any wish at all ?

And if I fall ill there, won't Viviane come and take me home ?

But I don't want to be separated from Yvette at any

price. So I simply have to hold out and tomorrow I'll ask Pémal if it wouldn't be a good idea for me to consult a really big man.

We're going out in an hour, Viviane and I, to dine with the South American ambassador. My wife, who's changing already, will wear something new she has had made for the occasion, for they'll all be dressed up to the nines. I've got to wear tails, which will force me to come home after the party and change before going to the Quai d' Orléans.

Yvette's convalescence, her present weakness, won't last for ever. For the moment her hermit's existence, new to her, still delights her. Yesterday, when Jeanine, the maid, was bringing us tea, she said to me :

'You ought to make love to her too. It would be rather like a harem.'

Jeanine, who had her back to her, didn't protest, and I'm convinced she would enjoy it too.

'You wait till you see her with her clothes off !'

Will playing harem keep her quiet for long ? When she goes out again, I shall live in torture, not only for fear of Mazetti, whom she might meet by accident, but for fear she may start all over again with someone else.

In spite of her promise, isn't she capable, as soon as she gets out, of making straight for the Quai de Javel ?

I can't deliver lovers to her door and she'll be hungry for them some day, even if it's only from having seen a man of a certain type passing in the street.

Jeanine, in fact, is the only one who takes our situation for natural. I don't know where she's worked until now; I think the director of the employment agency told me something about a hotel in Vichy or some other spa.

There's a knock at the door. Albert appears up there, at the top of the stairs, and when he opens his mouth I've already understood.

'Tell Madame I'm coming up.'

It's time for me to dress and before that I must go and give some instructions to Bordenave, who hasn't finished dealing with the post. Little Duret is with her, straddling a chair, watching her work, knowing that she hates it and that she doesn't like him. He does it on purpose, to make her angry.

He doesn't look at me either with pity or with irony. Everything in life still amuses him, like exasperating Bordenave until she's reduced to tears, and also no doubt whatever he knows about my affair.

'Have you finished the palut-Rinfret letter?'

'Here it is. In ten minutes the post will be ready to sign. Shall I bring it up to you?'

'Please.'

It would take so little to make her happy. If I could give her a hundredth, a thousandth part of what I offer Yvette. Bordenave would be satisfied with crumbs, would melt with gratitude. Then why is this beyond my power?

During Yvette's illness I thought once that my secretary was going to faint, she was so hurt by our intimacy. Besides, Yvette would deliberately call me Lucien, ask me to do little services for her, just as she would deliberately get out of bed, naked as usual, to go to the bathroom.

I shall find my wife in her slip in front of her dressing-table, for she always waits till I'm ready before putting on her dress.

'We've got a quarter of an hour,' she'll tell me.

'That's plenty.'

'Were you working?'

'Yes.'

Although she doesn't exactly concern herself with what goes on in the office, she suspects the truth about this dossier, which she saw me putting away one day when she dropped in to say good-bye to me. She has antennae for everything that concerns me, which can be irritating. I don't like to be seen through, especially, as is often the case, when it's a matter of petty weaknesses which one would rather hide from oneself.

I ought to go up and can't make up my mind to. I have the feeling that after having searched so hard for the truth I'm as far away from it as before, if not farther. There will be a lot of people at the ambassador's and I shall find myself seated on the right of his young wife who will have eyes for no one but her husband.

Does that couple invalidate my theories – if they can be called theories – or do we have to wait ten or twenty years to find out?

Viviane must be getting impatient and I know why I'm dawdling, why I hesitate. I foresaw that this would happen when I installed Yvette on the Quai d'Orléans.

It was the most dangerous stage, because in order to keep moving forward there is only one possible step left now.

This reluctance to go upstairs, to face Viviane, is in a way a kind of alarm signal.

Let's go! I cause her enough trouble without annoying her by being late.

I must just lock up my dossier and slip the key behind the complete works of Saint-Simon.

Chapter Six

Wednesday, 28 November

He's come, choosing his day and time as inconveniently as possible.

On Sunday evening Yvette had gone out for the first time since she's been living on the Quai d'Orléans. First I had made sure that no one was prowling about in the neighbourhood. She took my arm and all the time we were walking she seemed to be hanging on it, in a pose I've often envied in loving couples. There were couples on the benches, in the Square Notre-Dame, in spite of the cold, and that reminded me of my Pont-Marie tramps. I talked to Yvette about them.

'They had been gone for some time,' I told her, 'and this morning there they were again, the two of them, under the blankets.'

It surprised her that a man of my type should be interested in such people; I could tell from the look she gave me, as if that brought me a bit closer to her.

'Do you watch them through binoculars?'

'I never thought of that.'

'I would.'

'Wait. Well, this morning, the woman got up first and made a fire between two stones. When the man crawled out of the heap of rags, I saw that he had red hair, that it wasn't the same man. This one is taller, younger.'

'Maybe they put the other one in prison.'

'Maybe.'

We had dinner at the Rôtisserie Périgourdine, where she

chose the most elaborate dishes, then we went to a cinema on the Boulevard Saint-Michel. It seemed to me that when she glimpsed from a distance the hotel I had taken her to after the trial she became gloomy. It would be hard for her already to go back to poverty, even to a certain kind of mediocrity. Miss Wilson's flat has had its effect. Even the street, through which a cold wind was blowing and where the people were walking quickly, frightened her a bit.

A sad film was being shown, and several times, in the dark, her hand groped for mine. Coming out, I asked her what she wanted to do and she replied without hesitating:

'Go home.'

This is all the more unexpected as, even at the Rue de Ponthieu, she always put off that moment. For the first time she feels sheltered, feels she has a home. I left her early, because Monday morning was a heavy one for me, like almost all my mornings. For a month it's been stormy or raining, and we haven't had more than half a day of sunshine. People all have colds and are irritable. At the Palais several cases have had to be adjourned because one party or the other had 'flu.

In the evening my wife and I were to dine with Corine, where you rarely get to table before half past nine and where, the last few days, there's been considerable excitement. The country is without a government. The various candidates for premier have been considered and they say that Moriat will be the last-minute choice, that he already has his cabinet in his pocket. According to Viviane, he wants to set up, as appears to be advisable when the public loses confidence, a government of specialists selected from people unconnected with politics.

'If it hadn't been for the two or three rather too sensational cases you've handled, he would have insisted on you for Garde des Sceaux,' my wife added.

That would never have occurred to me. She thought of it. The funny thing is that it has been she who has expressed an implicit reproach for my having accepted certain briefs; she must have forgotten the incident at Sully.

I left the Palais fairly early, a few minutes before six, and went to the Quai d'Orléans where I found Yvette in a new négligée in front of the log fire.

'You're so cold,' she remarked when I kissed her. 'Hurry up and get warm.'

At first I thought it was the flames in the fireplace that were giving her eyes an unusual sparkle, a sort of mischievous look. Then I assumed she had a surprise in store for me, because she set about making martinis with feverish haste while I was warming myself, sitting on a hassock.

'Remember what I told you the other day?'

I still didn't know what she was referring to.

'We were talking about it, the two of us, this afternoon. I'm not joking. Jeanine would like to. She told me she hasn't had a boy friend for two months.'

She had emptied her glass and was watching me.

'Shall I call her?'

I didn't dare to say no. She went to the door.

'Jeanine! Come here.'

*

Suddenly the telephone bell filled the room and, although telephone bells are impersonal, I knew it was my wife ringing. She spoke only one sentence:

'It's nine o'clock, Lucien.'

I answered, as though caught out:

'I'm coming straight away.'

I found out afterwards, when I got back from the Rue Saint-Dominique, where we didn't see Moriat, that Yvette and Jeanine didn't get dressed after I left, that they went on drinking martinis and swapping stories. They didn't have any dinner, just snacks from the refrigerator.

'It's a shame you had to leave. You can't imagine how funny Jeanine is when she cuts loose. You'd think she was

111

made of rubber. She can hold the most difficult poses just like a circus acrobat.'

This morning I was empty. I won't go so far as to claim that I had a guilty conscience or that I was ashamed, but this experience left me with a queer taste in my mouth and a certain uneasiness.

Perhaps this is due to the fact that for some time now I've been catching glimpses of the stage ahead. I try not to think about it, to persuade myself that we're all right as we are, that there's no longer any reason to change.

I was following the same reasoning when I took the room on the Boulevard Saint-Michel for Yvette, and again when I installed her in the Rue de Ponthieu. Ever since I've known her, an obscure force is pushing me forward, independent of my will.

It embarrasses me more and more to be alone with Viviane, to take her around town, to be, in the eyes of the world, her husband, her companion, while Yvette mopes around waiting for me.

Does she really mope around? I come close to believing it. As far as I'm concerned, I always feel the same 'something missing', the same agonizing unsteadiness, as soon as I'm separated from her.

A time will come when I shall face the only acceptable solution : that she share my life completely. I'm not blind to what that means, nor to the inevitable consequences. That still seems to me an impossibility, but I've seen so many other impossibilities realized in time !

A year ago the Quai d'Orléans would have looked like an impossibility too, even three months ago.

Viviane, who senses it, is getting ready for the fray. Because she won't give it up without defending herself ferociously. I shall have not only her against me, but the whole world, the Palais, the press, our friends, who are her friends more than mine.

It won't happen tomorrow. It's still in the sphere of

dreams. I'm keeping a grip on the present, trying to take pleasure in it and find it acceptable. All the same I'm still clear-sighted enough to realize that it's not the end.

Precisely because of this state of mind, our threesome of the day before yesterday bothers me. Since it's happened once, it will happen again. Perhaps that's the way to prevent Yvette seeking pleasure elsewhere, but it's possible that it won't end there and that what has taken place at the Quai d'Orléans will inexorably take place later at the Quai d'Anjou.

After a cold shower, I was in my office by a quarter past eight on Wednesday morning, making a few telephone calls and catching up on current business before the conference set for nine o'clock.

The three men were punctual for the appointment and we went to work, Bordenave seeing to it that we weren't disturbed.

A very big deal is involved: the purchase by Joseph Bocca, and no doubt by people behind him, of a chain of big hotels. One of the men at the conference was the successor of Coutelle, who has retired to Fécamp, a younger fellow who has the title of count and is a regular habitué of Fouquet's and Maxim's, where I've often seen him.

Facing us we had one of my colleagues, with whom I'm on excellent terms, representing the sellers, accompanied by a fat, shy gentleman carrying a heavy brief-case, who proved to be the top expert on company law.

The deal is completely above-board. It's simply a matter of working out the terms so as to avoid taxes to the greatest possible extent.

The fat gentleman passed out cigars, and by ten o'clock the air in my office was blueish and it smelt like a smoking-room after dinner. From time to time I heard the telephone bell in the adjoining office and I knew Bordenave was there to answer it. I wasn't worried. For a long time she's had orders to interrupt me in the middle of any work at

113

all, any conversation at all, as soon as Yvette telephones, and this has occurred several times. I can imagine what it costs my secretary to obey my orders.

It was just after half-past ten, and our conference was still going on, when there was a light knock at the door. Bordenave came in without waiting for an answer, as I've told her to, and approached the desk on which she put down an appointment slip, and stood there waiting for the reply.

There was just one word, written with a ballpoint pen, a name: Mazetti.

'He's here?'

'For the last half-hour.'

Bordenave had a serious worried face, which implies to me that she knows what's up.

'Did you tell him I'm in conference?'

'Yes.'

'Didn't you ask him to come back another time?'

'He said he'd rather wait. Just a minute ago he asked me to bring you this slip and I didn't dare to annoy him.'

My colleague and the two other men were talking in undertones in order to appear not to be listening.

'What's he like?'

'More impatient than when he got here.'

'Tell him again that I'm busy and that I'm sorry I can't see him at once. He can wait or call again, whichever he likes.'

Then I understood why she had disturbed me.

'You don't want me to take any action?'

I suppose she was thinking of the police. I shook my head negatively, less confident than I wanted to appear. This visit would have worried me less a fortnight ago, when Mazetti used to keep watch under my windows, because then it would have been a natural reaction. I don't like him reappearing like this after going two weeks with-

114

out showing a sign of life. This doesn't fit in with my expectations. I sense something wrong.

'I apologize for the interruption, gentlemen. Where were we?'

'If it's a matter of importance, perhaps we could meet again tomorrow.'

'Not at all.'

I was well enough in control of myself to continue the discussion for three quarters of an hour, and I don't think my attention wandered once. At the Palais they claim that I'm capable of writing the text of a tricky appeal while dictating letters simultaneously and making telephone calls on the side. That's exaggerated, but it's true that I can follow two ideas at once without losing track of either one of them.

At a quarter past eleven, my callers got up, the stout little man put away his documents in his brief-case, offered another round of cigars, as if to reward us, and we shook hands at the door.

Alone again, I barely had time to come back to my chair when Bordenave came in.

'Will you see him now?'

'Is he still upset?'

'I don't know if you can call it upset. What I don't like is his fixed stare and the fact that he's talking to himself in the waiting-room. Do you think it's all right for you to ...'

'Bring him in as soon as I ring.'

I took a few steps back and forth, without any definite reason, as athletes loosen up their muscles before an event. I glanced at the Seine, then, sitting down, opened the drawer where the revolver lies within reach of my hand. I laid a sheet of paper over it, so that with the drawer open the gun wouldn't show and it wouldn't look like a provocation. I know it's loaded. I don't carry forethought so far as to release the safety-catch.

I press the buzzer and wait. Bordenave must be going to fetch my visitor from the waiting-room, the small one, I suppose, the one where, just over a year ago, Yvette, too, waited a long time for me. I hear the steps of two people approaching, a quick knock, and the door swings open.

Mazetti comes forward two or three feet and looks smaller than I remember him, more awkward too, more like a factory-hand than a student.

'You want to talk to me?'

I motion him to the chair on the other side of my desk, but he waits, standing up, until my secretary has closed the door behind her, listens to be sure she is going away.

He has seen my three callers leave. The air is still opaque with smoke and there are cigar-stubs in the ashtray. He has noted all that. So he knows that Bordenave hasn't been lying to him.

He is freshly shaved, cleanly dressed. He doesn't wear an overcoat but a leather jacket, because he usually gets around by motor cycle. He seems thinner, and his eyes are sunken in their sockets. I thought he was handsome. He isn't. His eyes are too close together; his nose, which must have been broken, is still crooked. He doesn't alarm me. Instead, I'm sorry for him and for a moment I imagine that he's come here to confide in me.

'Sit down.'

He refuses. He doesn't want to sit down. Standing up, his arms dangling, he hesitates, opens his mouth two or three times before coming out with:

'I need to know where she is.'

His voice is hoarse. He hasn't had time to get it in pitch or to familiarize himself with the rather solemn atmosphere of my office, with its gallery. Others besides him have been intimidated by it.

I wasn't expecting such a simple, direct question straight off, and I spend a few moments looking for an answer.

'First, let me inform you that you have no proof that I know where she is.'

Both of us have said 'she', as if there were no need to mention any name.

His lip has twisted slightly into a bitter smile. Without giving him time to retort, I went on :

'Supposing I do know it and she doesn't want her address given out, I have no right to reveal it to you.'

He stares at the half-open drawer, repeats :

'I need to see her.'

It disturbs me that he remains standing while I am seated, and I don't dare to get up because I want to stay within reach of the revolver. The situation is ridiculous and I wouldn't have our interview recorded by a film camera or a tape-recorder for anything in the world.

How old is he ? Twenty-two ? Twenty-three ? Till now I've thought of him as a man : he was the male who was pursuing Yvette, and now suddenly he looks to me like a little boy.

'Listen to me, Mazetti . . . '

That's not my voice either. I'm looking for the right tone without finding it, and I'm not proud of the result.

'The person you are speaking of has made a decision and informed you of it honestly. . . .'

'It was you who dictated the letter.'

I blushed. I can't help it.

'Even if I did dictate it, she wrote it, knowing what she was doing. So she decided her future with her eyes wide open.'

He raised his eyes to give me a look which is both sad and callous at the same time. I begin to understand what Bordenave meant.

Perhaps because of his thick eyebrows which meet, his face has a shifty expression ; you sense a restrained violence in him which might break out at any minute.

Why doesn't it break out ? What keeps him from raising

his voice in an outburst of threats and accusations against me? Isn't it more than anything else the fact that I'm an important, famous man and that I'm receiving him in a setting whose opulence overawes him?

He's the child of a bricklayer and a dish-washer, has been brought up with his brothers and sisters in a poor neighbourhood and has heard the bosses spoken of as inaccessible people. For him, men above a certain social level are made of different stuff from him. I've almost been through that myself, when I started out at the Boulevard Malesherbes, and yet I had no such heavy heritage of humility.

'I want to see her,' he repeats. 'I've got some things to tell her.'

'I regret that I'm not in a position to oblige you.'

'You refuse to give me her address?'

'I'm extremely sorry.'

'Is she still in Paris?'

He tried to bluff, to trick me, as Yvette would have done. I look at him without saying anything and he goes on in a lower voice, head down, without looking at me:

'You have no right to act like this. You know I love her.'

Isn't it wrong of me to reply:

'She doesn't love you.'

Am I going to begin to discuss love with a young man, to try to prove to him that it is to me that Yvette belongs, to argue over our respective claims to ownership?

'Give me her address,' he repeats, his forehead obstinate.

And as he moves his hand towards his pocket I make a slight gesture towards the open drawer. This he immediately understands. It was his handkerchief he wanted, because he has a cold, and he mutters:

'Don't be afraid. I'm not armed.'

'I'm not afraid.'

'Then tell me where she is.'

What direction have his thoughts taken during the

fortnight since he showed any sign of life? I don't know. A wall stands between him and me. I was expecting violence and find myself confronted by something muted, morbid, disquieting. The idea even occurred to me that he had made his way into my office with the intention of committing suicide there.

'Tell me. I promise you that she will decide for herself.'

He adds, to goad me:

'What have you got to be afraid of?'

'She doesn't want to see you again.'

'Why?'

What am I to reply to that question?

'I'm sorry, Mazetti. Let me ask you not to insist, because my position will not change. You will soon have forgotten her, believe me, and then ...'

I stopped in time. After all I couldn't go so far as to say to him:

'... and then you'll be grateful to me.'

At that moment my cheeks flushed hotly, because a memory of the previous evening came back to me: our three naked bodies in the cloudy water of a mirror.

'I ask you once more ...'

'It's no.'

'Do you realize what you are doing?'

'I've been in the habit of taking the responsibility for my actions for a long time.'

I felt as if I were reading a bad part in a worse play.

'You'll regret it some day.'

'That's nobody's business but mine.'

'You're cruel. You are doing a wicked thing.'

Why did he use words to me which I wasn't expecting, in an attitude which didn't go with his young tough's body? The climax would have been for him to burst into tears, and perhaps it almost came to that, for I saw his lip tremble. Wasn't it suppressed rage?

'A wicked thing and a cowardly one, Monsieur Gobillot.'

Hearing him pronounce my name startled me, and the 'Monsieur' suddenly introduced a curious note of formality into our interview.

'Once again, I'm sorry to disappoint you.'

'How is she?'

'All right.'

'She hasn't spoken of me?'

'No.'

'She ...'

He saw that, my patience exhausted, I was pressing the buzzer.

'You'll regret it.'

Bordenave, on the alert, opened the door.

'Show Monsieur Mazetti out.'

Then, standing in the middle of the office, he looked at us in turn with his heavy eyes, and this lasted an eternity. He opened his mouth, didn't say anything, merely dropped his head and walked towards the door. I remained motionless for a while and when I heard the engine of his motorcycle start up I rushed to the window. I saw him in his leather jacket, bare-headed, his hair tousled by the November wind, disappearing down the Rue des Deux-Ponts.

If I had any liquor in my office, I would have poured myself a drink, to get rid of the bad taste in my mouth, which seemed to me the bad taste of life.

He has upset me more than he has worried me. I feel that he's going to bring up new questions which won't be easy to answer.

*

I had to interrupt myself to take a telephone call from an opposing counsel who asked me if I would agree to an adjournment. I said yes without arguing and this surprised him. Then I called Bordenave in and, without referring to the visit I had received, I dictated for an hour and a half, after which I went upstairs for lunch.

An old question is bothering me, which has often bothered me and which I always end by putting aside, unless I make do with a half-satisfactory explanation. Since my adolescence, I might say since my childhood in the Rue Visconti, I've never believed in conventional morality, the morality you learn from textbooks and meet again later in official speeches and in articles in orthodox newspapers.

Twenty years in my profession and association with what is called Paris society, which includes the Corines and the Moriats, haven't done anything to change my opinion.

When I took Viviane away from Maître Andrieu I didn't consider myself a dishonourable man or feel guilty, any more than I had any feeling of guilt about installing Yvette on the Boulevard Saint-Michel.

I wasn't guilty of anything yesterday either, when Jeanine joined in the fun in front of the big mirror in which Yvette found it amusing to watch us. I was more dissatisfied with myself on the canal bank at Sully, the evening I accepted Joseph Bocca's proposition, because that was a question of principle, because it didn't correspond to my idea of my career.

It happened again later, it happened often, especially in the professional field, just as the reputation for integrity of certain colleagues sometimes makes me envious, or the serenity of good women on their way out from Mass.

I don't repent of anything. I don't believe in anything. I've never felt remorse, but what troubles me from time to time is being seized with a longing for a different life, in fact a life which would have more in common with prize-giving speeches and picture-books.

Have I been wrong about myself since the beginning of my existence? Did my father know these same tortures and did he regret that he wasn't a husband and family man like the others?

Like what others? I've been able to satisfy myself from experience that 'families like others' don't exist, that all

121

you have to do is to scratch the surface and get to the bottom of things to find the same men, the same women, the same temptations and the same failings. Only the front changes, the greater or lesser degree of candour or discretion – or illusions?

In that case, then, how is it that I am periodically restless, as if it were possible to behave in a different fashion?

Does a being like Viviane know these same disturbing thoughts?

I find her, unstairs, tall and neat in a dark woollen dress relieved only by a diamond clip.

'Are you forgetting that it's the Sauget auction at the Hôtel Drouot today?'

Since I bought the flat on the Quai d'Orléans, she has developed a mania for spending, especially on personal things, particularly jewellery, as if she were getting her own back or making things even. The Sauget auction is a sale of jewellery.

'Tired?'

'Not too.'

'Are you pleading a case?'

'Two uninteresting ones. In the third, which is harder, the other side wants an adjournment.'

If only she could get out of the habit of examining me as though to discern my secrets or a moment of weakness in my face! It's become an obsession. Perhaps she's always had it, but I never noticed it before.

It's Albert who waits on us at table, busy and silent.

'Did you read the news about Moriat?'

'I haven't read the papers.'

'He's making up his cabinet now.'

'The list Corine read us yesterday?'

'With a few insignificant changes. One of your colleagues will be Garde des Sceaux in the new cabinet.'

'Who?'

'Guess.'

122

'I haven't the slightest idea and it doesn't interest me.'

'Riboulet.'

What I might call an honest ambitious man, I mean a man who uses his reputation for honesty to get to the top or, if you prefer, who has chosen honesty because it is sometimes the easiest way. He has five children whom he is bringing up according to rigid principles, and they say he belongs to the Third Order of Oblates. It wouldn't be surprising, because he gets nearly all the ecclesiastical cases and he's the man rich people turn to when they want their marriage annulled by Rome.

'Did you see Pémal?'

'Not this morning. I had a conference.'

'Is he still giving you injections?'

To make me admit that now he gives me them at the Quai d'Orléans. This is becoming embarrassing. We are not yet enemies, but we can find nothing to say to each other, and mealtimes are growing increasingly unpleasant.

She thinks of nothing but getting me back or, to put it differently, of my break with Yvette, out of weariness or for any other reason, while I, for my part, am obsessed with the desire to see Yvette in her place.

How can we look each other in the face under these conditions? I'm sure, for instance – the idea suddenly came to me at table – that if she found out about this morning's visit and knew Mazetti's address Viviane would not hesitate to inform him somehow or other where Yvette is to be found.

The more I think about it the more it frightens me. In Mazetti's place, I wonder if I wouldn't telephone Viviane to ask her the question which he repeatedly asked me this morning. With her, he would get somewhere!

It's time I regained my balance. Most of my troubles arise from my fatigue, and this gives me a new idea which is enough to dispel the others. Since I'm always being told that I ought to take a holiday, why not take advantage of the Christmas recess and go away somewhere, to the mountains or the Riviera, with Yvette? It would be the first time we'd travelled together, and the first time she'd seen any scenery apart from Lyons and Paris.

How will Viviane react? I foresee friction. She will defend herself, talk about the harm it would do me from a professional point of view.

Here I am, all excited at the prospect. I was talking about a new stage. I was trying to guess what it would be. Well, here it is: a journey, together, like a real couple!

Just the word 'couple' alone seems to me marvellous. We've never made a couple, Yvette and I. For a few days at least we'll be one, and at the hotel the servants will call her Madame.

How could my mood change so much, within a few minutes?

'What's the matter with you?'

'With me?'

'Yes. You've just thought of something.'

'It was you who mentioned my health.'

'Well?'

'Nothing. The idea occurred to me that Christmas isn't far off and that I might give myself a break.'

'At last!'

She doesn't suspect the truth or she wouldn't have sighed with relief:

'*At last!*'

I simply must drop in at Yvette's for a moment on my way to the Palais, to tell her the big news. How my plan is to be worked out, I don't know yet, but I know it will be.

'Where are you planning to go?'

'I haven't the least idea.'

'To Sully?'

'Certainly not.'

I don't know what aberration made us buy a country house near Sully. Even the first year I found the forest of

124

Orléans gloomy, oppressive, and I can't stand people who talk about nothing but wild boar, guns and dogs.

'For ages Bocca's been inviting you to come to his place at Mentone, even if he's not there. They say it's unique.'

'I'll see.'

She is beginning to be worried, because I said 'I' and because I'm not asking her advice. Am I getting wild? I feel bad about it and yet I can't restrain myself. I'm light-hearted. I have no problems any more. Yvette and I are going away on holiday to act as Monsieur and Madame. This title will touch her. It hadn't occurred to me before. When we go out in Paris, she's always called Mademoiselle. In a hotel in the mountains or on the Riviera, it will be different.

'Are you in a hurry?'

'Yes.'

It's a pity there are still three weeks to wait. It seems an eternity to me and, as I know myself, I'm going to start being afraid of all kinds of hindrances. To be all right, we ought to leave today and from then on I wouldn't give another thought to Mazetti or to our disgusting interview. It wouldn't take much to make me drop everything and go away without telling Viviane.

I can imagine her face when she received a telegram or a telephone call from Chamonix or Cannes!

'Has anything happened this morning?' she asks, casually.

There it is? She's guessed, again, and it exasperates me.

'What should have happened?'

'I don't know. You don't seem your usual self.'

'How do I seem?'

'As if you wanted at any price to avoid thinking about an annoying subject.'

I hesitate to get angry, because this hits home. Perhaps it would relieve me to lose my temper, even if it were only, as she says, to forget Mazetti, but I still have enough self-possession to see that if I start it will be hard for me to stop.

How far would I go? I have too much on my mind and I'm not prepared for a break today. I want to avoid an explosion. Besides, they're waiting for me at the Palais, in two different courts.

'You're very subtle, aren't you?'

'I'm beginning to know you.'

'Are you so sure?'

She has the inward smile of someone who has never doubted herself.

'A lot better than you think!' she declares.

I get up from table without waiting for her to finish her dessert.

'Excuse me.'

'Of course.'

At the door I hesitate. It's hard for me to leave her like this.

'See you soon.'

'I suppose we'll meet at Gaby's for cocktails, won't we?'

'I hope I can get there.'

'You promised her husband.'

'I'll do my best.'

As I leave the building, it occurs to me to make sure that Mazetti isn't in the neighbourhood. No! I don't see anything. Life is beautiful. I walk along the quay. There is a white dust suspended in the air, but it can't be called snow yet. The couple of tramps, under the bridge, are busy going through some old papers.

The staircase is familiar to me. It's the same, or almost the same, as the one at the Quai d'Anjou, with a wrought-iron banister which is always cold to your hand and stone steps as far as the first floor.

The flat is on the third floor. I have a key. It is a pleasure to me to use it and yet, every time, I'm overcome with anxiety because I wonder what is in store for me.

In the hall, I open my mouth to tell her the news, to call out in a triumphant voice:

'Guess where the two of us are going to spend Christmas.'

But Jeanine appears, in a black dress and a white apron, an embroidered cap on her head, very much the theatrical maidservant, and puts a finger to her lips.

'Ssh!'

My glance, already anxious, questions her, although Jeanine is smiling.

'What is it?'

'Nothing,' she whispers, bending forward. 'She's sound asleep.'

With affectionate complicity she takes my hand and leads me to the bedroom door which she opens a crack, and in the semi-darkness I can distinguish Yvette's hair on the pillow, the outline of her body under the bed-clothes, a bare foot sticking out.

Jeanine goes and covers it up soundlessly, comes back to me and closes the door again.

'Do you want me to give her a message?'

'No. I'll come back this evening.'

Her eyes are twinkling. She must be thinking of what happened yesterday, and it amuses her; she stands nearer to me than usual, brushing me with her breasts.

On my way out, I ask:

'Nobody's been here?'

'No. Who should have been here?'

She must know all about it. Yvette has certainly told her the story of her life, and it was wrong of me to ask that question.

'Did you get any rest?' she asks in turn.

'Yes, a bit. Thanks.'

*

I just had time to hurry into the robing-room and put on my gown. Judge Vigernon, a martinet who doesn't like

127

me and has a nervous habit of stroking his beard, was looking around for me as I dashed into court.

'The case of Guillaume Dandé versus Alexandrine Bretonneau,' declaimed the clerk. 'Guillaume Dandé? Stand up when your name is called and answer: "Present".'

'Present.'

'Alexandrine Bretonneau?'

Impatient, he repeats:

'Alexandrine Bretonneau!'

The judge searches the rows of faces as if he were about to discover her in the anonymous crowd, and finally the woman appears, fat, out of breath, having waited for an hour in another court to which she had been directed by mistake.

From the far end of the room she calls:

'Here I am, your Honour! I beg your pardon....'

There is a pervading smell of official building and un-washed humanity, which is to some extent the smell of my own stable.

Am I not at home here?

Chapter Seven

I was about to write that just lately my life has been too busy to leave me any leisure to open the dossier cupboard. It was no less busy in the weeks before this. Tiredness? Or haven't I felt the same need to reassure myself?

From time to time, however, I have scribbled words on my note-pad, sort of memory-joggers which I go over and explain.

Thursday, 29 November

'Ski-ing trousers. Pémal.'

It was on Tuesday evening, two days before this note, that I mentioned a holiday to Yvette, and her reaction was unexpected. She looked at me suspiciously and said:

'Do you want to send me away somewhere to get rid of me?'

I don't remember the phrase I had used, something like:

'Get ready to spend Christmas in the mountains or on the Riviera.'

The idea never occurred to her that I might be going with her. I reassured her, but for a while she was still worried, finding it too wonderful.

'Will your wife let you go?'

I lied so that she wouldn't worry about it.

'She's been told.'

'What did she say?'

'Nothing.'

Only then did she call Jeanine in, needing an audience.

'Do you know what he's just told me? We're going to spend Christmas in the snow.'

It was my turn to frown, because I'm not planning to take

Jeanine. Fortunately that wasn't what 'we' had meant to Yvette.

'Or on the Riviera,' I added.

'If I'm to choose, I'd prefer the mountains. They say there's nothing but old people on the Riviera in winter. What is there to do there anyhow, if you can't swim or sunbathe? I've always dreamed of ski-ing. Do you know how?'

'A bit.'

I took a few lessons, a long time ago.

The next day, when I went to see her, she was wearing black gaberdine ski-ing trousers, partly to show them off to me, partly because she liked them herself; they were very tight and outlined her little round behind.

'Like them?'

Pémal, who came to give us our injections, found her in them and she pulled her trousers down like a man. In the hall, he couldn't help pausing in front of the skis she has also bought and looking at me with an inquisitive glance. I said:

'Yes indeed! I've finally decided to take a holiday.'

I went out on to the landing with him and whispered:

'Don't mention it at the Quai d'Anjou.'

Yvette has also bought a bulky Norwegian woollen sweater with a design of reindeer. I'll have to see about booking rooms at the hotel, because for the Christmas season everything in the mountains is full; I found that out years ago.

Saturday, 1 December

'Prime Minister's dinner. Viviane – Mme Moriat.'

Jean Moriat, who is Premier as was expected, has taken up residence in the Hôtel Matignon with his wife, his legal one, but he still spends almost every night at the Rue Saint-Dominique. That Saturday he was giving a semi-official dinner to which, in addition to his closest collaborators, he had invited a few friends. We were included, and Corine too, of course. Madame Moriat, who is hardly known, was hostess and went about it so awkwardly, with such an obvious dread of making gaffes, that one felt a desire to go to her rescue.

I don't think she minds about her husband's liaison. She doesn't hold it against him and if she thinks that either one of them is to blame, she takes it upon herself. During the whole reception, then during the dinner, she seemed to be apologizing for being there, ill at ease in a high-style dress which didn't suit her, and at embarrassing moments I saw her turn to Corine to ask her advice.

She is so basically humble that you reach the point of not wanting to look at her or speak to her, because you feel so strongly that it embarrasses her. She can breathe easily only when she's forgotten in her corner, which did happen several times, especially after dinner.

In the car coming home, Viviane murmured:

'Poor man!'

'Who?'

'Moriat.'

'Why?'

'It's awful for him, in his position, to be saddled with a wife like that. If she had the least bit of dignity she would have given him his freedom long ago.'

'Has he suggested a divorce?'

'I don't think he's ever dared to.'

'If he were free, would Corine marry him?'

'It's almost impossible for them to get married. It would be political suicide, because Corine's too rich and he'd be accused of having married for money. If you ask me, they both want to keep the poor woman as a front.'

I was struck by this reflection, if only because it emphasizes Viviane's cruelty towards the weak and shows what she must think of Yvette in her heart of hearts, the tone she must use in talking to her friends about her.

'Are you serious about your holiday plans?'

131

'Yes.'

'Where?'

'I don't know yet.'

Not only does she still think she's going with me, but she's sure I'll choose the sea because, the few times we have been to the mountains, I've complained of feeling as though I were in a hostile climate there. I bet she'll lose no time ordering clothes for the Riviera and I swear to myself not to say a word until the last minute.

Sunday, 2 December

'Pants, Jeanine.'

I wonder what Bordenave thought if she saw that note on my pad. This Sunday, like most other Sundays, I spent the afternoon at the Quai d'Orléans. I was freezing. The people in the street were walking quickly and in the flat the log fire gave off a pleasant smell.

Yvette asked me:

'Are you sure you don't want to go out?'

She is acquiring a taste for curling up cosily, purring, in the overheated atmosphere of the sitting-room or the bed-room, and Jeanine, as was to be expected, is occupying a larger and larger place in her personal life, in ours too, which sometimes bothers me. I realize that for Yvette it's a good thing. She has never been so relaxed, nearly always gay, with a gaiety which doesn't seem forced as it used to. I'm pretty sure she doesn't think about Mazetti much.

I got there in time for coffee, and, as Jeanine was serving us, Yvette suggested:

'Feel her buttocks.'

Without knowing why she should tell me to do this, I passed my hand over her behind, while Yvette went on:

'Don't you notice anything?'

Oh yes. Under her dress there were no petticoats, no

132

underclothes, nothing but her skin, over which the black fabric slid easily.

'We've decided that she shouldn't wear pants any more at home. It's more fun.'

The mood of both girls, when they're together, is charmingly light-hearted, and often, when I come in, I hear them whispering, bursting into laughter, and occasionally, too, they exchange knowing looks over my shoulder. Jeanine, who seems to be flourishing here, is blossoming forth and makes a great fuss of Yvette and of me. Sometimes, showing me out, she asks me in a low voice:

'What do you think of her? She seems happy, doesn't she?'

It's true, but I've seen her acting too many parts not to be on the defensive. As we were lying there, watching the flames dancing, Yvette began to talk about her experiences in a joking, ironical way, not always in harmony with the images she provoked, because she revealed certain perversions which I hadn't suspected, some of which distressed me. She's making a game of this at present, addressing herself mainly to Jeanine, who laps up her words, quivering.

That Sunday I discovered that Yvette isn't as unconscious of how things are as she is trying to appear. When we were alone together with the light out, she huddled herself in my arms. I could feel her trembling from time to time and at last I asked her:

'What are you thinking about?'

She shook her head, rubbing her hair against my cheek, and it wasn't until a tear fell on my chest that I knew she was crying. She was incapable of speaking right away. Touched, I embraced her tenderly.

'Tell me now, child.'

'I was thinking about what would happen.'

She began to cry again, continuing in jerky sentences:

'I couldn't bear it any more. I put up a brave front, I've always put up a brave front, but ...'

133

She sniffed; I knew she was wiping her nose on the sheet.

'If you left me, I think I'd go and throw myself into the Seine.'

I knew she wouldn't do it, because death terrifies her, but perhaps she would try, changing her mind at the last minute, perhaps to arouse the pity of spectators. But there's no doubt either that she would be unhappy.

'You're the first man who's given me a chance to live decently and I still wonder why. I'm no good. I've hurt you and I'll go on hurting you.'

'Ssh.'

'Do you mind about Jeanine?'

'No.'

'She has to have some fun too. She's nice to me. She thinks up all kinds of things to make life pleasant for me, and when you're not there I'm not always exactly cheerful.'

I make allowances for her play-acting. It's always present, mixed up with her sincerity. The last phrase, for example, is too much, and I wondered if, on the contrary, it isn't when she's alone with Jeanine that she's at her liveliest.

It's the same with her as with Mazetti. No matter if she does see me in the crudest, least-flattering light, I'm still the great lawyer who saved her and besides, to her, I'm a rich man. I would swear that she entertains respect and admiration for Viviane and that she would be frightened at the idea of taking her place.

'When you're tired of me, will you tell me?'

'I'll never be tired of you.'

The logs crackle, the darkness is tinged with deep pink, we can hear Jeanine, on the other side of the wall, moving about in her room, then dropping heavily on her bed.

'Did you know she's had a child?'

'When?'

'When she was nineteen. She's twenty-five now. She put it out to nurse in the country, and they neglected it so

134

badly that it died of digestive trouble. They said its stomach was all swollen.'

My mother, too, turned me over to some people in the country.

'Are you happy, Lucien?'

'Yes.'

'In spite of all the trouble I bring you?'

Fortunately she finally goes to sleep, and I think for a time about Mazetti. He hasn't returned to hang around the Quai d'Anjou and that worries me, irritates me, as anything I don't understand always does. I promise myself to think about him tomorrow and at last it's my turn to fall asleep, on the very edge of the bed, because Yvette's curled up in the middle and I don't want to wake her.

Tuesday, 4 December

'Grégoire – Javel.'

I couldn't do it on Monday after all, because that's a big day for me, taken up mostly with telephone calls, for, when people come back from week-ends, they seem to be seized with remorse and throw themselves frantically into serious business.

I could set up a kind of barometer for people's moods during the week. On Tuesday they get back to normal, but the temperature goes up again on Thursday afternoon so that they can get through faster and leave for the country by noon on Friday, Friday morning if possible.

So it was on Tuesday, according to my note-pad, that I telephoned Grégoire, whom I used to know in the Latin Quarter and who has become a professor in the Faculty of Medicine. We don't meet once in five years, but from habit we still say 'tu' to each other.

'And you? Your wife?'

'Very well, thank you. I wanted to ask you a favour because I don't know who else to ask.'

'I'll be glad to help you if I can.'

'It's about a student named Léonard Mazetti.'

'It's not a matter of his exams, I hope.'

His voice suddenly became colder.

'No. I'd like to know if he is really registered in the School of Medicine and if he's been attending classes regularly lately.'

'What year is he in?'

'I don't know. He must be twenty-two or twenty-three.'

'I'll have to ask the registrar's office. I'll ring you back.'

'Can it be handled discreetly?'

'Of course.'

He is wondering why I'm concerned about this young man. I wonder myself why I'm going to so much trouble. Because that isn't the end. Now I ring the Citroen office, on the Quai de Javel. A few years ago I happened to plead a case for the company and thus got to know one of the directors.

'Is Monsieur Jeambin still with you?'

'Yes, sir. What name, please?'

'Maître Gobillot.'

'Just a minute. I'll see if he's in his office.'

A little later, a different voice, that of a busy man.

'Yes.'

'I'd like to ask you a small favour, Monsieur Jeambin . . .'

'Excuse me, who is that speaking? The operator didn't catch the name.'

'Gobillot, the lawyer.'

'How are you?'

'Very well, thank you. I'd like to know whether a man named Mazetti is working for you as a factory-hand, and if so, if he hasn't had an unusual absentee record recently.'

'That's easy, but it will take a little while. Will you ring me back in an hour?'

'I'd rather he didn't know about it.'

'Is he in trouble?'

136

'Not at all. Don't worry.'

'I'll take care of it.'

I got the two replies. Mazetti wasn't lying. He's been working for three years at the Quai de Javel where his absences are rare and nearly always coincide with examination periods, except for the last two, which go back to the time when he was watching Yvette from the pavement of the Rue de Ponthieu. And this week he's been out only twice.

It's the same thing at the Medical School, where he is in his fourth year and where he cut classes for a week at the same period.

'I made inquiries about this boy,' Grégoire added, 'not knowing exactly what you want. He's not a brilliant student, but he is such a hard worker that he does well in his exams and he'll go through all right. It looks as though he'd make an excellent country doctor.'

So Mazetti has taken up again the regular rhythm of his existence working by night at the Quai de Javel and attending lectures or in the operating-theatre during the day.

Does this mean that he has calmed down and is beginning to get over it? I'd like to believe it. I think of him as little as possible.

Except for him, the present period would be the best I've known for a long time.

Thursday, 6 December

'Saint-Moritz.'

This time it's snowing in big soft flakes which still won't lie on the ground but are already leaving white streaks on the roofs. This reminds me that I ought to book our hotel room if we want to go away for Christmas. I couldn't make up my mind, thinking first of Mégève or Chamonix, where Viviane and I went years ago. I read in the paper that everything is full for the holidays. That doesn't mean there's no more room, I know how newspapers are, but it did remind me that a lot of my young colleagues, crazy about ski-ing, go to those two resorts.

I have no intention of hiding Yvette. I'm not ashamed of her. Anyhow, I have good reason to think that everyone knows.

Still, it would be unpleasant to find ourselves in the same hotel as lawyers whom I meet every day at the Palais, especially if they are with their wives. I don't give a damn about making myself ridiculous. I'll be ridiculous on skis all right anyhow. But I want to spare Yvette any incident which might spoil our holiday, and, with certain wives, that might happen.

That's why I finally decided on Saint-Moritz. The people there are different, more international, less familiar. The luxurious style of the Palace Hotel will make her feel strange at first, but it will be easier for us to maintain a certain anonymity.

So I telephoned. I got the reception manager on the line and he seemed to know my name, although I've never stayed there. Almost full, he told me, putting me down just the same for a room with a bath and a small sitting-room.

'Overlooking the skating rink,' he specified.

That same day, after dinner, Viviane opened the latest issue of *Vogue* and showed me a white dress with heavy pleats which is by no means unattractive.

'Like it?'

'Very much.'

'I ordered it this afternoon.'

For Cannes, I've no doubt. The dress is called 'Riviera' but I didn't smile; I had no desire to, because, as the time for explanations approaches, I realize more fully that it's going to be hard.

All the harder since my attitude recently is reassuring to her. It's the first time, to my knowledge, that she's been

138

grossly mistaken. At first she worried when she saw that I was in a more easy-going, almost relaxed state. She may even have mentioned it to Pémal, who sees her quite often, and I don't know what he would have said.

'It looks to me as though your vitamins are doing you good.'

'Why shouldn't they?'

'Don't you feel better than you did a fortnight ago?'

'Yes, I think I do.'

Perhaps she also thinks that having Yvette so handy, just a stone's throw from home, is beginning to produce a certain satiety. She doesn't suspect that the very opposite is true and that now it seems to me a monstrosity to leave the Quai d'Orléans for a few hours.

So let her order her dresses for the Riviera. There'll be nothing to stop her going there alone while Yvette and I are at Saint-Moritz.

For a long time I had a tendency to feel pity for Viviane. That's over. I observe her coldly, like a stranger. Her reflections on poor Madame Moriat, when we left the Hôtel Matignon, are part of the reason. In rehashing the past, I have discovered that Viviane herself has never pitied anyone.

When she left, did she pity Andrieu? Of course, it would be improper for me to blame her for it. Nevertheless it's a fact and if she were thirty today or even forty, she wouldn't hesitate to sacrifice me as she sacrificed her first husband.

This has reminded me of the way he died and I'm embarrassed by it, just when I'm going to Saint-Moritz, which isn't far from Davos.

Sunday, 9 December

'Jeanine.'

I wonder why I wrote that name on my note-pad when I came home. I must have had a reason. Did I have some

139

precise thought or did I only have her vaguely in mind?

Since it was Sunday, I spent the afternoon at the Quai d'Orléans and, I remember now, part of the evening but not the night, because we were to meet Moriat, who had a political dinner, at the Rue Saint-Dominique at about half-past ten. That was the evening when Viviane announced that we were spending the Christmas holidays in the Midi, at Cannes she specified without consulting me, and Corine gave me a glance which makes me think she has an inkling of my plans.

What happened with Jeanine that hasn't happened on other Sundays and some week nights? She is increasingly at her ease with us, free of any inhibitions, and once Yvette remarked:

'Even when I was a little girl, I used to dream of living in a place where everyone would be naked and spend their time petting and doing anything they liked with each other.'

She smiled at her memories.

'I used to call it playing Earthly Paradise, and I was eleven when my mother caught me playing Earthly Paradise with a little boy called Jacques.'

It wasn't on account of that phrase that I wrote down Jeanine's name. Nor, I suppose, because of another reflection of Yvette's, who was gravely watching us, Jeanine and me, in an embrace.

'That's wonderful!' she suddenly exclaimed with a laugh which immobilized us.

'What's wonderful?'

'Didn't you hear what she just said to you?'

'That I was hurting her a bit?'

'Not exactly. She said:

'"Monsieur, you're hurting me a bit!"'

'I think that's funny. It's as if she spoke to you in the third person to ask your permission to . . .'

The end of the sentence was crude, the image comical.

In these circumstances, she likes to use precise, vulgar words.

Oh yes! I remember. It's a thought which came to me and which I wanted to remember, although it's not specially important. Jeanine seems to have taken Yvette under her wing, not against me but against the rest of the world. She seems to have grasped the bond between us, which I find extraordinary, and she's doing her utmost to build up a sort of zone of security around us.

I can't explain myself precisely. After the episode I've just mentioned, it would be ridiculous to speak of a maternal feeling, and yet that's what I have in mind. Making Yvette happy has become a game for her, and a reason for living, too. She's grateful to me for having gone in for it before she did; she approves of everything I do to this end.

It's rather as if she were taking me under her wing too, although, if I stopped behaving in the same way, if a quarrel, for instance, or a difference of opinion broke out between Yvette and me, I would be faced with an enemy.

She isn't a lesbian, mentally or physically. Unlike Yvette, before she came to the Quai d'Orléans, she had never had anything to do with women.

It doesn't matter. I don't remember why I thought of that when I came home. More exactly, I didn't suspect that it would be connected with a subsequent event.

It's only now that I know the reason why she advised me, that Sunday:

'Don't let her get too tired today.'

Tuesday, 11 December

'Caillard.'

An exhausting appearance in court, three hours spent working on the jury in order to obtain a sentence of ten years' penal servitude when, without the mitigating circumstances that by some unknown miracle I managed to disclose, my client would have seen himself condemned to hard labour for life.

Instead of being grateful, he looked at me stonily, muttering:

'A lot of good all that fancy talk did!'

On the strength of my reputation he was counting on an acquittal. His name is Caillard and I'm beginning to regret – because he deserves it – that they didn't take him out of circulation for good.

I found Yvette already in bed by nine o'clock that evening.

'You'd better let her sleep,' Jeanine advised me.

I don't know what came over me. As a matter of fact, I do know. After the nervous effort of an important speech in court, after the strain of waiting for the verdict, I nearly always feel the need to let off steam violently, and for years I used to go straight to a brothel on the Rue Duphot. I'm not unique in this.

Through the half-open door I had just seen Yvette asleep. I hesitated, looking inquiringly at Jeanine, who blushed slightly.

'Here?' she whispered, in reply to my unspoken question.

I nodded. I didn't want anything more than a quick tumble. A little later, I heard Yvette's voice saying:

'Are you having a good time, you two? Why don't you open the door so I can see you?'

She wasn't jealous. When I went to kiss her, she asked me:

'Did she do all right?'

And she turned over on her side to go to sleep again.

Wednesday, 12 December

'? ? ? ?'

Jeanine finally talked to me, on the stairs, as she was

showing me out. At eleven in the morning Yvette was still in bed, looking sickly, and I had noticed her breakfast untouched on a tray.

'Don't worry. It's nothing. Have you got the railway tickets?'

'I got them yesterday. They're in my pocket.'

'Don't lose them. Do you know it'll be the first time I've travelled in a sleeper?'

Because she had looked troubled, a bit washed-out, as if I had seen her through a veil, I asked Jeanine in the hall:

'It's not because of yesterday, is it?'

'No ... Hush! ...'

It was then that she followed me out to the stairs.

'I'd better tell you now. What's worrying her is that she thinks she's pregnant and she's wondering how you'll take it.'

I stood still, one hand on the banister, my eyes staring. I didn't analyse my emotion and I'm still incapable of doing so; I only know that it was one of the most unexpected and one of the most violent ones of my life.

It took quite a while for me to get control of myself and I pushed Jeanine aside to go back up the few stairs. I rushed to the bedroom and cried:

'Yvette!'

I don't know what my voice was like or the expression on my face as she sat upright.

'Is it true?'

'What?'

'What Jeanine's just told me.'

'What did she tell you?'

I wondered how she failed to understand at a glance that my reaction was one of joy.

'Are you angry?'

'No, darling! Anything but! And last night, I ...'

Exactly!

And it was for the same reason that on Sunday Jeanine had advised me not to tire Yvette!

For my wife and myself there was never any question of children. That's a subject she never brought up and I concluded from that and also from the precautions she has always taken that she didn't want any. Besides, I've never seen her look at a child in the street, on a beach or in other people's houses. For her they are a strange, vulgar, almost indecent world.

I remember the tone in which she said, when someone told us that the wife of one of my colleagues was pregnant for the fourth time:

'Some women are born to be rabbits. Some of them even like it!'

You would think maternity disgusted her; maybe she considers it a humiliation?

Yvette, for her part, was sitting there in her bed, scared, ashamed, but not for the same reason.

'You know, if you'd rather I got rid of it . . .'

'Has this ever happened to you before me?'

'Five times. I didn't dare to tell you. I was wondering what I ought to do. With all the complications I've involved you in already . . .'

My eyes were misty and I didn't grab her in my arms. I was afraid of being theatrical. I just took her hand and kissed it for the first time. Jeanine was tactful enough to leave us alone.

'Are you sure?'

'You can't be sure so soon, but it's ten days already.'

She saw me turn pale, and understanding why, she hastened to add:

'I've counted. If it's true, it can only be yours.'

My throat was tight.

'It would be funny, wouldn't it? You know, this doesn't stop us going to Switzerland. I'm staying in bed because

144

Jeanine won't let me get up. She says if I want to keep it I've got to rest for a few days.'

Funny girl! Funny girls, both of them!

'Would you really be pleased?'

Naturally! I haven't thought about it yet. She's right in saying that it will mean complications. And yet I'm happy, touched, affected as I can't remember ever being before.

'In two or three days, if nothing happens, I'll see the doctor and have a test.'

'Why not straight away?'

'You want to? Are you in a hurry?'

'Yes.'

'In that case, I'll send a specimen to the lab tomorrow morning. Jeanine can take it. Call her.'

And to Jeanine:

'Do you know? He wants me to keep it!'

'I know.'

'What did he say when you told him?'

'Nothing. He stood quite still and I was afraid he was going to fall downstairs, then he nearly knocked me over as he rushed up here.'

She's making fun of me.

'He insists you're to take a specimen to the lab tomorrow morning.'

'Then I'll have to go and buy a sterilized bottle.'

All this is familiar routine to both of them.

I'm due in my office. Bordenave telephones for instructions. It is Jeanine who answers.

'What shall I say?'

'That I'll be there in a few minutes.'

It's better for me to leave, because there's nothing more I can do here just at present.

Thursday, 13 December

'Specimen sent off. Dinner Embassy.'

That means my South American ambassador, who gave an intimate but extremely elegant dinner to celebrate our success. Thanks to Moriat, the arms are under way unmolested to some port or other where they are feverishly awaited, and the *coup d'état* is planned for January.

In addition to my fee, I received a gold cigarette-case.

Friday, 14 December

'Waiting. Viviane.'

Waiting for the result of the test, which we won't know until tomorrow. Viviane's impatience.

'Have you booked a suite for us at the hotel?'

'Not yet.'

'The Bernards are going to Monte Carlo.'

'Oh.'

'Are you listening?'

'You said the Bernards are going to Monte Carlo and since that doesn't interest me I said "Oh".'

'Monte Carlo doesn't interest you?'

I shrug my shoulders.

'I prefer Cannes myself. What about you?'

'I don't mind.'

There'll be a change in a few days, but for the moment in dealing with her I'm almost jaunty. My smile baffles her, because she doesn't know what to think any more, and suddenly she gets angry.

'When do you intend to do something about it?'

'About what?'

'About Cannes.'

'We have time.'

'Not if we want a suite at the Carlton.'

'Why the Carlton?'

'We've always stayed there.'
To get it over with, I retorted:
'Why don't you telephone yourself?'
'May I tell your secretary to?'
'Why not?'
Bordenave heard me speaking to Saint-Moritz. She will understand, won't say anything, and will have red eyes again.

Saturday, 15 December

'Positive.'

Chapter Eight

Monday, 17 December

I don't know what happened about the flowers, and this will remain one of those irritating little mysteries. On Saturday, before going to the Palais, I stopped in at Lachaume's to send six bunches of roses to the Quai d'Orléans. I had taken a taxi and kept it while I dropped into the shop. I can still see myself pointing out the dark red roses to the sales-girl. She knows me and she asked:

'No card, Maître?'

'It's not necessary.'

I'm sure I gave Yvette's name and address, or else I'm forced to believe that I'm subject to lapses. Outside, the driver was arguing with a policeman who was telling him to keep moving and who exclaimed when he, too, recognized me:

'Excuse me, Maître. I didn't know he was with you.'

When I called at the Quai d'Orléans before dinner, I wasn't thinking about the flowers any more and I didn't notice anything. I didn't stay long, telling Yvette I had to dine out and would see her about eleven.

At the Quai d'Anjou I went straight up to the bedroom to change, and Viviane's sardonic smile, as she went on dressing, made me wrinkle my brows.

'It's nice of you!' she said after I'd taken off my tie and coat and was looking at her in the glass.

'What?'

'Sending me flowers. As there wasn't a card, I assumed they were from you. Was I wrong?'

148

That very moment I caught sight of my roses in a big vase on a little table. This reminded me that Yvette hadn't mentioned them and that I hadn't noticed any flowers in the flat.

'I hope they didn't come to the wrong address?' Viviane went on.

She's convinced they did. I had no reason at all to send her flowers today. I don't understand how the mistake occurred. I've thought about it more than I wanted to because these mysteries plague me until I find a plausible explanation for them. At Lachaume's I gave Yvette's name, I'm certain: *Yvette Maudet*, and I can still see the young woman writing it on an envelope. Did I then automatically dictate the Quai d'Anjou address instead of that on the Quai d'Orléans?

In that case, Albert, unsuspecting, unpacked the flowers in the butler's pantry without reading what was written on the envelope and, seeing nothing in it, threw it in the waste-paper basket. Viviane, who must have reached the same conclusions as I have, no doubt went and rummaged there.

It was too late to send more flowers and, the next day being Sunday, the shops were closed; it didn't occur to me that I could have gone to the flower market, which is no distance away. I didn't go to Yvette's until after luncheon, because I worked all morning, and she told me she had given Jeanine permission to go and see her sister, who keeps a little restaurant with her husband at Fontenay-sous-Bois.

The weather was ideal, cold but sunny.

'What do you say to going out for a breath of air?' she proposed.

She put on her beaver coat, which I bought her at the beginning of the season, while she was still living at the Rue de Ponthieu, and which means more to her than any of her other possessions, because it's her first fur coat. Perhaps she only wanted to go out in order to wear it?

'Where do you want to go?'

A lot of couples and families had had the same idea, and from the Rue de Rivoli on we were caught up, on the pavements, in a sort of procession which made a characteristic noise of feet dragging on the stones, a Sunday noise, because people walk more slowly, not going anywhere, stopping in front of all the shop windows. Christmas isn't far away and there are spectacular displays everywhere.

In front of the Magasins du Louvre the crowd was channelled by barriers, and we were content with admiring, from the ramparts, the brilliant fairyland which illuminates the whole façade.

'Suppose we go and see what they've done this year at the Galeries and the Printemps?'

Night had fallen. Tired families were sitting around the braziers on café terraces. I don't know if this is a new part she is acting. You would have said she was enjoying imitating the middle-class couples we were following, and the only thing lacking was some children to hold by the hand.

She hardly talks about her coming motherhood at all and, when she does refer to it, it is unemotionally, as though she already took it for granted. In her eyes it holds nothing mysterious or frightening as it does in a man's. She is pregnant, and for the first time she is going to keep her baby. That's all. What upset her for a moment was that I should make her keep it. She wasn't expecting that.

I wonder if it wasn't to thank me and, at the same time, to show herself in the reassuring role she's about to play, that she proposed this walk, so foreign to her habits and mine.

We stopped in front of the same displays as the crowd, moving forward, then stopping again a few yards farther on, and whiffs of various scents, on the pavements, mingled with the smell of dust.

'Where would you like to have dinner?'

'Shall we go and have some *choucroute*?'

It was too early and we went into a café near the Opéra.

'You're not tired?'

'No. Are you?'

I felt a certain lassitude, but I'm not sure that it was purely physical. Anyhow it had nothing directly to do with Yvette. It was what I'd call a cosmic melancholy, aroused no doubt by the depressing tramping of the crowd.

We dined at the Alsatian brasserie in the Rue d'Enghien, where we've often eaten *choucroute*, and although I suggested a cinema afterwards, she preferred to go home.

About ten o'clock, while we were watching television, we heard the key turn in the lock and for the first time I saw Jeanine in her Sunday best, very respectable in a navy-blue skirt, a white blouse and a blue coat, with a little red hat on her head. Her make-up was different, so was her scent.

We went on watching television. Yvette, who had yawned two or three times, suggested a hot toddy, and at half-past eleven everyone in the flat was asleep.

It's been one of the calmest, slowest days I have lived through for a long time. Shall I admit that it has left an after-taste which I'd rather not analyse?

Chapter Nine

Cannes, Tuesday, 25 December

The sun is shining, people without coats are walking on the Croisette whose palm-trees are outlined against the blue of the sea, against the purplish blue of the Esterel, while little white boats seem to hang suspended in the universe.

I have insisted that my wife go out with Géraldine Philipeau, the friend she met in the foyer of the Carlton when we arrived and whom she hadn't seen for years. She dates back before my time, and they fell right into each other's arms.

I'm going to make an attempt to put down everything in order, although it seems useless. There's a calendar in front of me, but I don't need it to remember by. These pages aren't the same size as the others, because I'm using hotel paper.

I've just re-read what I wrote in my office on the morning of 17 December, a Monday, as though that had happened in another universe, or anyhow a long time ago, and it takes an effort to convince myself that the Christmas I am now living through is the same Christmas for which Yvette and I watched the preparations that Sunday, in the streets of Paris.

On the Monday morning, I sent her flowers, making sure this time that they should reach her and no one else, and when I went up to give her a kiss at noon, she was obviously touched by them. Through not having thought of it, I had never given her flowers, except in a café or on a terrace, and then nearly always violets.

'You know, you treat me like a lady,' she remarked. 'Come and see how beautiful they are.'

I spent the afternoon at the Palais. I had promised Viviane to be home early, because that evening we were giving what we call the President's dinner, a dinner we give every year for all the old greybeards of the Bar.

My intention, in returning by way of the Quai d'Orléans, was just to go up for a few seconds. It happened that, as I crossed the footbridge which joins the Cité to the Île Saint-Louis, I glanced at the windows of the flat. This isn't my usual habit. The pink windows stood out, and I remember noticing that one got the impression of a comfortable, downy nest, of a good place to live à deux. The young couples who stroll along the quays, not able to walk straight because they have their arms around each other's waists, must sometimes glance at our windows sighing:

'Later on, when we ...'

I didn't need to use my key, because, recognizing my step on the stairs, Jeanine opened the door, and I realized that something was wrong.

'Is she ill?'

Jeanine, following me through the entrance hall, asked:

'Haven't you seen her?'

'No. Has she gone out?'

She didn't know what kind of face to put on it.

'About three o'clock.'

'Without saying where she was going?'

'Only that she wanted to go out for a walk.'

It was half-past seven. Since she had been living at the Quai d'Orléans, Yvette had never come home so late.

'Perhaps she's gone to buy some things,' Jeanine went on.

'Did she say anything about it?'

'Not directly, but she told me about everything she'd seen yesterday in the shop windows. She'll surely be back any minute.'

I realized that she didn't believe it. I didn't believe it either.

'Did she suddenly get the idea of going out?'

'Yes.'

'She hadn't received any phone call?'

'No. The phone hasn't rung all day.'

'What state was she in?'

This is what Jeanine doesn't want to tell me, for fear of betraying Yvette.

'Wouldn't you like me to bring you something to drink?'

'No.'

I sank into an armchair in the living-room, but I didn't stay there long, not being able to keep still.

'Would you rather I stayed here or left you?'

'She didn't mention Mazetti?'

'No.'

'Never?'

'Not for several days.'

'Did she speak of him fondly?'

She says no, and I feel that this isn't entirely true.

'Don't think about it, Monsieur. She'll come back and ...'

At eight o'clock she had not come back, nor at half-past eight either, and, when the telephone rang, I snatched it up. It was Viviane.

'Have you forgotten that we have fourteen people for dinner?'

'I won't be there.'

'What?'

'I won't be there.'

'What's going on?'

'Nothing.'

I can't go and get dressed to dine with the President of the Bar, my colleagues and their wives.

'Something wrong?'

'No.'

'You won't tell me?'

'No. Make my excuses to them. Invent what you like and tell them I may get there later in the evening.'

I have thought of all eventualities, and with Yvette everything is possible, even that she is at this moment in a disreputable hotel with a man she didn't know at noon. That happened during the Rue de Ponthieu period. Lately she has changed, seemed like a different girl, but her metamorphoses are brief.

Is that what Jeanine thinks? She is trying, half-heartedly, to take my mind off it. In the end she persuaded me to drink a whisky and she was right.

'You mustn't be cross with her.'

'I'm not cross with her.'

'It's not her fault.'

It's Mazetti she has in mind, too. Has Yvette ever forgotten him? And even if, for a time, he did lose all interest for her, isn't it possible that the approach of the holidays, for example, should have brought back memories?

It's not likely that we met him yesterday in the Sunday crowds and that she didn't tell me. But we passed hundreds of other couples, other men, one of whom perhaps looked like him, and that might have been enough.

I don't know. I'm all at sea.

Even her motherhood ... Maybe she rushed over to Javel to tell him?

We both tremble every time we hear steps on the stairs. It's never for our floor, and we've never heard the sounds of the building so clearly as today.

'Why don't you go to your dinner party?'

'It's impossible.'

'It would stop you thinking. You're driving yourself crazy here. I promise to phone you as soon as she gets in.'

It's my wife who phones, about ten o'clock.

'They're in the drawing-room. I got away for a moment. You'd better tell me the truth.'

155

'I don't know it.'

'She's not ill?'

'No.'

'An accident?'

'I don't know.'

'You mean she's disappeared?'

There was a silence, then she brought out in a strained voice:

'I hope it's nothing serious.'

Eleven o'clock. Jeanine has tried in vain to get me to eat. I couldn't. I've drunk two or three glasses of liquor; I didn't count them. I don't dare to call the police for fear of setting all the machinery in motion when the truth is perhaps too simple.

'She never told you his address?'

'Mazetti's? No. I only know it's somewhere near the Quai de Javel.'

'Or the name of his hotel?'

'No.'

It occurs to me to try to find Mazetti's hotel, but I realize that it won't work. I know the district and if I went from one cheap hotel to another asking for him, they wouldn't even answer me.

At ten past twelve, Viviane rings me again and I'm annoyed with her for raising false hopes each time.

'No news?'

'No.'

'They've just left.'

I hang up and suddenly I seize my coat and hat.

'Where are you going?'

'To make sure nothing has happened to her.'

This isn't the same as telephoning the police. I cross the Parvis Notre-Dame and enter the courtyard of the Prefecture of Police by the back entrance, where there are only a few lighted windows. The deserted corridors, where my

156

steps echo, are familiar to me. Two men turn round as I pass and I push the door of the Emergency Squad, where a voice exclaims good-naturedly :

'Well; Maître Gobillot's come to see us. You can bet some crime or other's just being committed.'

It's Griset, an inspector I've known for a long time. He gets up and shakes hands. There are three of them in the vast room, where the telephone switchboard contains hundreds of holes and where, from time to time, a light flashes on a map of Paris on the wall.

Then one of the men sticks a plug in one of the holes.

'Quartier Saint-Victor ? That you, Colombani ? Your van's just gone out. Serious ? No ? Street fight ? All right.'

All the small news items of Paris converge here, where the three men smoke their pipes or their cigarettes and one of them is preparing coffee on a spirit-lamp.

This reminds me that Yvette spoke of buying a spirit-lamp one morning a long time ago, while I was dressing, so tired that I was dizzy.

'Will you have a cup, Maître ?'

They are wondering what I've come for, although it's not the first time I've been to see them.

'May I use your telephone ?'

'Use this one. It's an outside line.'

I dial the number of the Quai d'Orléans.

'It's me. No news ?'

Of course not. I go up to Griset, who has a toothbrush moustache in which his cigarette has in course of time outlined a dark circle.

'You haven't been informed of an accident or anything involving a young girl ?'

'Not since I came on duty. Wait.'

He consults a ledger with a black cover.

'What name ?'

'Yvette Maudet.'

'No. I see a Bertha Costermans, taken ill in the street, who's been moved to hospital, but she's a Belgian and she's thirty-nine.'

He doesn't ask me any questions. I watch the little lights flashing on the map of Paris, particularly those of the Fifteenth Arrondissement, the Javel district. I thought of calling Citroen's but the offices are closed and the workshops wouldn't give me any information. Even if they told me Mazetti is at work, would my mind be entirely at rest? What would that mean?

'Hello, Grandes-Carrières, what's happened over there? ... What? ... Yes ... I'll send you the ambulance ...'

He turns to me.

'It's not a woman, but a North African who's been stabbed.'

Sitting on the edge of a table, my legs dangling, my hat pushed back, I drink the coffee someone has handed me, then, incapable of sitting still, I begin to walk about.

'What kind of girl?' asks Griset, not out of curiosity but in the hope of helping me.

What am I to tell him? How am I to describe Yvette?

'She's twenty and doesn't look it. She's small, slim, wearing a beaver coat and her hair in a pony-tail.'

I ring Jeanine once more.

'It's me again.'

'Still nothing.'

'I'm on my way.'

I don't want to make an exhibition of my impatience, and it's worse here, watching a light flash on every five minutes, than at the Quai d'Orléans. They've understood me. Griset promises:

'If anything comes up, I'll give you a ring. Are you at home?'

'No.'

I write down the Quai d'Orléans address and telephone number for him.

What's the good of going into detail about that night? Jeanine opened the door to me. Neither of us went to bed, we didn't undress, we stayed in the sitting-room, both in armchairs, watching the telephone and jumping every time a taxi passed beneath the windows.

How did I leave Yvette at noon? I try to remember and already I can't any more. I would like to recapture her last glance, as if it were capable of providing a clue.

We saw the day break, and before that Jeanine had dropped off a couple of times; possibly I did, too, without realizing it. At eight o'clock, while she was making coffee, I caught sight from the window of a boy on a bicycle with a bundle of newspapers under his arm, and that gave me the idea of buying a paper. Wouldn't I find news of Yvette there?

Jeanine was looking at the pages over my shoulder.

'Nothing.'

Bordenave telephoned me.

'You're not forgetting that you've got an appointment at ten with the Minister of Public Works?'

'I won't be there.'

'And the other appointments?'

'Do something about them.'

Through some kind of irony, I wasn't the one to answer the real telephone call; it was Jeanine.

'Just a minute. Yes, he's here. Here he is.'

I questioned her with my eyes and understood that she preferred not to tell me anything. I had hardly grasped the phone when I heard her burst into sobs behind me.

'Gobillot speaking.'

'Inspector Tichauer, Maître. My night colleague left me a message to get in touch with you if . . .'

'Yes. What's happened?'

'You did say Yvette Maudet, didn't you? Aged twenty, born at Lyons. The girl who last year . . .'

'Yes . . .'

I stood motionless, not breathing.

'She was stabbed to death tonight at the Hôtel de Vilna on the Quai de Javel. The murderer, after wandering about the neighbourhood for several hours, has just given himself up at the Rue Lacordarie police station. The police van went to the scene, and the victim was found in the room he had stated. The man is a factory worker named Mazetti, who has made a complete confession.'

Wednesday, 26 December

The rest I learned later, and the papers are still talking about it with my name in big type. I could have avoided it. My colleague Luciani telephoned me as soon as he had been instructed to defend Mazetti. The latter, indifferent to what becomes of him, simply pointed to the first Italian-sounding name on the list which the examining magistrate handed him. Luciani wanted to know if he was to try to keep my name out of it. I said no.

Yvette was naked when they found her body, with a wound in the left breast, on the narrow iron bed. I went over there. I saw her before they took her away. I saw the room. I saw the hotel where the stairs were crowded with the men who frightened her.

I saw Mazetti, and we looked at each other; I was the one who looked away; there was no trace of remorse on his face.

To the police, to the examining magistrate, to his lawyer, he would only repeat:

'She came. I begged her to stay, and when she wanted to leave, I stopped her.'

So she did try to return to the Quai d'Orléans.

She had been determined to go over there first, and in the room was found a thick Norwegian knitted woollen sweater, a man's sweater, just like her own, which must have been intended as her Christmas present. The cardboard box, with the name of the shop, was under the bed.

We buried her, Jeanine and I, because her family, notified by telegram, put in no appearance.

'What shall I do with her things?'

I told her I had no idea, that she could keep them if she liked.

I had a talk with the examining magistrate and told him that since I couldn't undertake the defence of Mazetti, as I wanted to, I would testify in court. This surprised him. People look at me as if they couldn't understand me, Viviane too.

On my return from the funeral, she asked me without any hope:

'Don't you think it would do you good to get away from Paris for a few days?'

I agreed.

'Where do you want to go?' she went on, astonished at so easy a victory.

'Didn't you reserve a suite at Cannes?'

'When do you intend to leave?'

'As soon as there's a train.'

'This evening?'

'All right.'

I don't even hate her. It doesn't matter whether she's there or not, whether she speaks or keeps silent, whether she imagines she's still controlling our destiny. For me she has ceased to exist.

'In case of emergency ...' I wrote somewhere.

My colleague Luciani, to whom I'm going to send this dossier, will perhaps find in it what he needs to get Mazetti acquitted, or anyhow to spare him too stiff a sentence.

As for me, I'll go on defending the real scum.

'Golden Gate'
Cannes, 8 September, 1955

The Little Saint

Translated from the French by
Bernard Frechtman

Part One

The Little Boy in the Rue Mouffetard

Chapter One

He was between four and five when the world came to life around him, when he grew aware of a real scene involving human beings and was able to distinguish them from each other, to locate them in space, in a particular setting. Later on, he could not tell whether it had been in summer or winter, though he already had a sense of the seasons. Probably in autumn, for the curtainless window was dimmed by a slight blur, and the yellowish gaslight that came from the lamp-post outside, which was the only light in the room, seemed humid.

Had he been sleeping? His body was warm beneath the blanket. He had not been abruptly awakened by any particular sound, he had merely heard behind the curtain, which was only an old sheet that hung from a rod, a familiar panting broken by moans, and from time to time the creaking of the bedspring. It was his mother who slept in that bed, almost always with some-one. On his side of the hanging sheet were Vladimir, then Alice, then the twins, then he himself, each on his straw mattress, and, against the wall, the baby on her iron folding-cot.

Vladimir was a big boy, at least eleven and a half, if not more. Alice must have been nine, and the red-haired twins, who had freckles under their eyes, about seven.

The mattresses lay side by side on the floor and smelled of mildewed hay. The room was filled with other odours which were those of their home, of their universe, and there were also the odours of the whole house and, when the window was open, those from outside.

He had opened his eyes, not out of curiosity, but because he was awake. He had recognized the gleam of the gaslight on the ceiling and through the cloth partition. He had listened vaguely to the panting, then had gradually made out the figure of

Vladimir, in a shirt, kneeling on his mattress and peeping through a hole in the sheet.

Louis was neither surprised nor curious. It was all familiar to him, as if he had often been through the scene without realizing it. But it was the first time that the images and sounds had ever merged into a significant whole.

'Alice!' whispered Vladimir, turning to his sister.

'What?'

'Are you asleep?'

'Almost.'

'Look ...'

She too was in a shirt. None of them wore night clothes, and they slept in shirts.

'What?'

Vladimir motioned to her to come to his mattress, and she in turn got on her knees and looked.

The twins were breathing evenly and did not stir. Emilie, the six-month-old baby on the cot that had been used by all of them, each in turn, did not yet matter.

Again he heard the muted though distinct voice of Vladimir, who ordered:

'Do it to me.'

'Will you do it to me afterwards?'

Vladimir had lain down with his shirt pulled up above his belly.

'Be careful with your teeth.'

Louis was so unmoved, so uninterested, that he dozed off. When he opened his eyes again, Vladimir and Alice seemed to be sleeping. The twins were still breathing evenly, but the paraffin lamp was lit in the kitchen, the door of which was open. A smell of coffee, spiked with brandy, floated in. Two persons were talking in the kitchen in low voices.

Wasn't it like that in every home, in every house, in every family?

His grandmother had once remarked:

'Louis hardly ever talks. He must be a little backward.'

He did not remember who had answered:

'All the same, maybe he thinks about things. It's children like that who are often the most observant.'

168

He had paid no attention because he did not know what it meant, but for some reason or other the words had stuck in his mind. There were others too, and particularly images, for even if he really was dull-witted he had not lived till the age of four without seeing what was around him.

But it was rather as if he had wanted to limit the world to as narrow a space as possible.

'If he were allowed to do as he liked, that child would never go out of the house.'

Had he actually heard that comment or had it been repeated to him later? It's not easy to distinguish between what really happened at a particular time and what you were told later on.

He was sure that the hole in the hanging sheet and the business of Vladimir and his sister were a part of real life, despite the vague glimmer from outside. He had seen his brother and sister do the same thing at a later time, in broad daylight, without bothering about him.

There had been a father in the home, a man named Heurteau, Lambert Heurteau, whom he had never known, except for the lone photograph tacked on the wall of the room. He was oddly dressed and was standing next to the children's mother, who was wearing a white dress and a veil.

Lambert Heurteau was not the father of all of them. How old was Louis when he discovered that in most families the children all had the same father? Not in theirs. And not in others in the Rue Mouffetard, where they lived.

His mother's name was Gabrielle Heurteau. Her maiden name was Cuchas. As for the eldest, his real name was Joseph Heurteau, but Louis did not realize until much later, when he went to school, why he was called Vladimir.

Alice's name was also Heurteau.

'It's hard to know who she resembles. In any case, all you have to do is look at the eyes and that sharp nose of hers to tell that she'll go far.'

'Unless she runs a push-cart in the street like her mother and grandmother.'

The twins were Heurteau's too.

'They're the only ones he couldn't disown!'

Why hadn't Louis known the man in the photo and why was he himself called Cuchas? No one seemed to wonder about it, and for years he didn't either. Later, when he knew, he felt completely indifferent.

What mattered most, at first, was the two rooms in which they lived, more exactly the bedroom and the kitchen. During the day, the sheet which hung from copper curtain-rings was pulled back, revealing, on the left side of the window, a very high walnut bed, its two mattresses, its coverlet and the huge quilt.

The image was vague, but Louis would have sworn that he had seen his mother in that bed surrounded by other women, that she had screamed a lot while they kept him in the kitchen and that later they showed him an ugly baby and informed him that he had a new little sister.

His grandmother was present too. He saw her as a very fat old woman whom everyone called Ernestine.

Had he too been born in the walnut bed, and had he sucked his mother's breasts as he had seen Emilie do? Nobody called her Emilie. It was a long time before he knew her name. They simply said 'the little one', the way they said 'the twins'.

'You twins, let the little one alone! Go out and play.'

Much later, and only when he had become an adult, was Louis to remember other images that had not registered consciously and which, perhaps because they had to do with his daily life, had not struck him at the time.

The walls of the room had formerly been papered, but all that remained was patches on which there were still pictures of persons dressed as in the time of the kings. On one of the patches, near the door, was a young woman with very wide skirts who was on a swing. The rest of the wall was dirty, yellowish plaster on which were initials that had been carved with a knife and pictures representing genital organs which someone had tried to rub out. Who had drawn them? Who had tried to efface them?

Not his mother, in all likelihood. When the weather was warm, it didn't bother her in the least to walk around naked in the room and even in the kitchen. When she had not yet put up her big red bun, her hair hung down to her waist, and the bush

170

at the bottom of her slightly plump belly was very fine and fluffy, of the same light shade as Alice's hair.

She was cheerful and often sang while doing the housework, when she had time to do it.

The straw mattresses were covered with a thick, rough brown cloth, except Vladimir's which was bluish. The only sheets were on the wooden bed and the enamelled cot.

'Alice! Go and warm your sister's bottle.'

'Why is it always me?'

Who had given *him* the bottle?

The twins were only three years older than he, and he was four and a half years younger than Alice. Was Vladimir eight when Louis was born?

These questions did not yet occur to him, except a few, the simplest ones, which did not disturb him, because everything seemed natural. Later, much later, he was to wonder how such and such a thing had happened when he was a child in the Rue Mouffetard, but it was out of idle curiosity, a kind of amusement.

It was in 1897 or 1898 that he had observed what his sister was doing so docilely to Vladimir, though it did not interest him enough to prevent him from going back to sleep. It did not surprise him that his mother wore a high corset which left marks on her fine skin, soft skin, or to see some men wearing caps in the street, others bowlers, and others silk top hats. He had heard it said that the family was poor, but wasn't everyone in the building poor and almost everyone in the street, except the shopkeepers, such as his Uncle Hector who ran a butcher's shop at the corner of the Rue du Pot-de-Fer?

'If he hadn't been a fast talker and a good-looking boy, he wouldn't have got around the Lenain girl. Besides, the family let him have her only because she limped. All the Lenains have something wrong with them. The grandfather ended up in an asylum, and as for Azaïs's brother, God knows what he died of. It wouldn't surprise me to learn that Hector, even though he is my brother, had a hand in it . . .'

She laughed. His mother laughed as often as she sang. When she was in bed with a man she began by sighing and moaning, but it always ended with a burst of laughter.

171

She got up very early in the morning, at times, in summer, at three o'clock. She would wash her face in the kitchen, where there was a copper tap. In winter, she lit the fire before leaving. Louis would sometimes hear her. At other times, when he woke up he would see that she was no longer there.

He knew that she went to Les Halles, the central market, with her push-cart, which she had hired from a certain Mathias who had a yard full of them in the Rue Censier, to stock up with fruit and vegetables. At six o'clock she was on the pavement, facing the shoe shop, while his grandmother installed herself about a hundred yards lower down the street, near the Church of Saint Médard.

At the age of four or five, he was unaware of all that, or rather it was part of a world which was not his, which was only remotely connected with his daily reality.

For example, the stove was, for a long time, more important than his mother and was the focal point of his existence. He did not yet know how it was lighted, or by whom. All he remembered was that his mother, who would be out of breath from climbing the stairs, would cross the room with a bucket of coal whose weight tilted her to the right.

There was no door between the kitchen and the corridor. You had to go through the room. Louis did not mind the fact that their home had only one exit. It was reassuring, because he felt safely shut in, just as he was safe in the blanket at night when he wrapped it around his body.

The stove, which was next to the sink, filled a good part of the kitchen.

'We're lucky to have water on our landing. There aren't many people in this street, even those who are lots richer than us, who have water in their rooms. If only we had gas too . . .'

He knew what gas was, for in the evening he saw its pale illumination in the shops across the street and in certain houses. It was even installed in the yard of the building, or rather in the carpenter's shop.

From his mattress Louis could hear sulphur matches being struck. He liked the smell of them. Then, almost always, his mother would sigh and mutter words that he could not make out, and the smell of sulphur would be followed by that of paraffin,

172

which drowned it, and the new smell in turn was drowned by that of kindling wood and coal. He could have got up to take a look. He did later, around the age of six or seven. Until then, he preferred the mystery of the fire as it appeared to him from his bed, and since it was celebrated very early in the morning, almost always when it was still dark, he would fall asleep again before the end, before the jet of steam spurted from the kettle and the drops that fell one by one into the coffee-pot changed the smell of the room once again.

He was told later when they had tried to put him into a nursery school when he was two years old, that he had not cried but had struggled, and that when his mother had left he had escaped by the window. As he still did not know his house from the outside, he had wandered about among the push-carts and a policeman had finally gone up to him.

'What are you looking for, little boy?'

'I'm looking for Mama.'

'Where is your mama?'

'I don't know.'

'Have you lost her?'

'Yes.'

'What's your name?'

'I don't know.'

'You don't know your name? Don't you know where you live?'

'No.'

He was wearing a little smock, the kind worn at the time by boys his age, and his hair came down almost to his shoulders.

'You're not a girl by any chance, are you?'

'No. That's my sister.'

He had only one, for Emilie had not been born yet.

'What does your father do?'

'I don't have one. I want to go home.'

The policeman, it seems, had taken him from shop to shop.

'Do you know this boy?'

The shopkeepers examined him more or less closely and shook their heads.

'Do you live in the neighbourhood at least?'

'I don't know.'

173

Finally, he had caught sight of his mother behind the pile of vegetables in her push-cart. Or rather, as the story was told to him, his mother had caught sight of him walking hand in hand with the policeman.

'What are you doing here, Louis?'

'I don't know.'

'How'd you manage to get out of school?'

'I don't want to go to school any more.'

'Germaine, would you mind my cart for a moment?'

She had taken him back to the house where the twins were sitting on the kitchen floor playing with blocks. These were not memories of his own. He was unable to remember so far back.

'Even when you were six, they had a devil of a time keeping you in school. You refused to learn . . .'

Perhaps it was not so much that he refused to learn as that he refused to be taken away from the universe which he considered his own and in which he felt safe.

He liked the room that was divided in half by the sheet which hung from a rod, he liked the smell of the mattresses lined up side by side, the portrait of his mother in a white veil and of a man with a blond moustache, the patches of wallpaper, particularly the one with the girl on a swing. He liked, above all, the warmth that the stove gave off in waves, in blasts, the way it roared at times, the glowing ashes that suddenly collapsed into the drawer at the bottom.

'Your son doesn't talk much!'

What would he have said?

*

He must often have tried later, at different ages, to reconstitute the successive stages of that birth of the world around him. Not because he attached any importance to the matter. It was only a game, though a secret voluptuous game.

He never quite managed to link them up. Images were missing, particularly pictures of himself, for the only photograph he knew was the wedding photo of his mother and Lambert Heurteau that was on the wall. The latter had one hand on his wife's shoulder, and the other, which was gloved and holding

the other glove, rested on a pedestal table that fascinated Louis
for a long time, until the day he ventured beyond the neighbourhood and discovered an identical table in the shop of a second-
hand dealer.

Why did it seem to him, when he contemplated the ill-lit face
and pale blond, drooping moustache of that man he had never
seen, that he was dead?

'But he's not, idiot. If he were, Mama would be a widow and
we'd be orphans.'

'Me too?'

'Not you, since he's not your father.'

'Why?'

'Because he went away long before you were born.'

'Why?'

Perhaps because he had been fed up. Or because their mother
had been.

That conversation took place several years later, when he was
about eight or nine and dared ask Vladimir questions. Vladimir
continued to despise him, but now took the trouble to answer
him condescendingly.

'Did they fight?'

'When he drank, or when Mama drank. Haven't you ever
heard Mama fight with the others?'

'Did he beat her?'

'Sometimes. Mama was stronger than he and he always ended
by getting the worst of it.'

'How do you know?'

'Because I used to look through the hole, and I listened when
they drank in the kitchen.'

Vladimir had adopted a defiant attitude. He out-stared everybody and never gave in. He was the only dark-haired member
of the family and was taller and more nervous than the others.
His long eyelashes fluttered about his dark pupils.

'I don't give a damn ... He's not my father. Mama was pregnant before she knew him. My real father was a Russian and I
heard someone say he was an anarchist.'

'What did he do?'

'He prepared bombs and set them off.'

Before that, Louis must have discovered one of the two

monuments of their flat, the sink and tap, which were almost as important as the stove. On Sunday mornings their mother, who did not work that day, put water to heat in a huge laundry tub.

She had to ask Monsieur Kob, their neighbour, to help her set the tub of almost boiling water on the reddish tiles in the kitchen. Monsieur Kob did not have to be asked twice, for Gabrielle had nothing on under her dressing gown and generously displayed her breasts when she bent.

At that hour, on Sundays, he smelled of cosmetics and wore a gauze appliance to set his black moustache.

Alice, because she was a girl and was less dirty, got into the tub first. She was soaped from head to foot, with her hair hanging in wet locks on her cheeks and hunched shoulders.

Then it was Vladimir's turn. He insisted on washing himself without anyone's help.

'Don't forget to wash your ears.'

'I'll wash whatever I like.'

Then came the twins. At times it was one and at times the other who was first. In the street and at school they were called the redheads, and other children were afraid of them because they were always looking for a fight. At home, on the other hand, they seemed indifferent, as if they did not feel they were members of the family. They had violet-blue eyes and very pale skin, and almost every winter they caught flu together.

'Your turn, Louis.'

The water was already blue and slimy with soap. It did not disgust Louis to be fifth. He was never disgusted. Not by the smells either. Was anyone in the house or even in the street disgusted by smells?

There were no lavatories on the landing. And neither the arch nor the yard nor the stairway was lit up, so that the most important object in the room was a heavy white crockery chamber pot. Everyone used it, the mother first, and also the men who came to see her, who sometimes lived with them for a month, sometimes for a few days, sometimes only for a night.

'Hell! The damned chamber pot is full again!'

This one was a coachman who brought back two bottles of red wine in the pockets of his box-coat every evening. Gabrielle and he did not go to bed immediately. They would sit in the kitchen, which was lit by the paraffin lamp, and, with their elbows on the table, would talk in low voices as they drank their wine. When the mother started laughing, it meant that before long they would be going to bed.

She would lower the wick, which went out a minute or two later, and the room would be lit only by the street lamp opposite the window. Since they lived on the first floor and the Rue Mouffetard was not a wide street, it was rather light in the room. The man, in his shirt-tails and long underwear, would lift up the pot that the children had filled.

'Hell! This God-damned chamber pot . . .'

He would open the window and empty it on the pavement while Gabrielle howled with laughter. She herself poured it into the kitchen sink and then let the water run. The coachman had been with them for almost a month. One Sunday he piled them into his hackney and took them to the Bois de Boulogne. Emilie, who must have been a year old, sat on her mother's knee. Vladimir was perched on the high seat and before long was using the whip.

For years, it was their longest trip. Actually, they never took another one together.

Of course, Gabrielle left for Les Halles very early with her mother and other street-sellers, each pushing her cart. But when the local market began, at the kerb, she spent the rest of the day about a hundred yards from the house.

When Emilie was very little, Alice looked after her, and it was also she who filled the stove and stirred the fire. From time to time, their mother would ask a neighbour to mind her pushcart for a few minutes.

'Here! Put this meat to cook with onions and a dash of vinegar.'

The meat did not come from the shop of her brother, 'Hector the millionaire,' as she called him.

'Ever since that lousy pimp married his cripple and became a boss, he's forgotten that his family ever existed.'

At heart, she did not hold it against him. She was rather proud of him. Isn't that the way things always happen in families, and wouldn't she have done the same in his place?

177

She had another brother, Jean, who was a bit feeble-minded, a lamp-lighter who went by in the evening with a long pole at the end of which shone a small flame for lighting the gas lamps and who went by again early in the morning to put them out.

'A loafer's job. And yet he was the only one of us who went to school till he was fifteen.'

All of this had registered in bits and pieces. Louis never seemed to be listening. What he heard was always mingled with the hubbub of the street, especially in summer when the two windows were open, the one in the kitchen and the one in the room.

'That one's not interested in anything.'

Perhaps it was true. Nevertheless, certain phrases, certain intonations were filed away in his memory without his bothering to put them in order, to link them up, to try to understand.

'And yet he looks intelligent . . .'

Because of his smile, most probably. A gentle smile, without irony, without meanness, without aggressiveness, a smile that someone once compared to that of Saint Médard, whose church stood at the bottom of the street.

He was happy, he watched, he went from one discovery to another, but, unlike Vladimir, he made no effort to understand. He was content with contemplating a fly on the plaster wall or drops of water rolling down the window-pane.

Certain drops, for example, which were bigger and muddier, caught up with the others by taking a short cut instead of zig-zagging. At times, this went on for hours, against the background of the huge red boot with a gilt tuft that was the signboard of the shoe shop on the other side of the street.

The shopkeeper was Monsieur Stieb, and his name, which Louis was unable to read until much later, was elegantly written out in cursive style on the two windows that framed the narrow door. Louis could see people enter, especially women with one or more children, and it was fascinating to watch them gesticulate without hearing their words. Monsieur Stieb had a square beard and wore a detachable wing collar, a flowing purple necktie, and a frock-coat.

He invited the mothers and children to be seated, got down on his knees to remove the youngsters' shoes, and then began to play a game with boxes, which he went to take from the shelves and from which, with the gestures of a conjurer, he removed shoes of all shapes.

The mother, who held a shopping basket on her lap, would shake her head: no.

'Wait! Wait! I've got just the thing. How do you like these?'

'No . . . No . . .'

No patent leather. No kidskin. Good solid thick-soled shoes, preferably with hobnails!

At the left, in the semi-darkness, thin, severe-looking Madame Stieb would look on with an air of indifference. She was ugly. The redheads called her a sick hag.

She was buried a year or two later. Everyone in the Rue Mouffetard, including the street-sellers, went to the funeral. The shutters remained drawn for three days. When Monsieur Stieb reopened them, there was a saleswoman in the shop.

The shutters were fascinating too. Those of the shoe shop were lowered with a crank that fitted into a small hole in the shop front, and in summer another crank lowered a red-and-yellow-striped awning, the edge of which stopped just above the heads of the passers-by, so that the tall ones or those who wore a top hat had to stoop. Another awning, a solid grey one, obliged them to do the same in front of the tripe shop.

The shopkeepers did not all shut up shop at the same time, and the grocer, whose shop was long and narrow, having only one shop window, was the last to put up two wooden panels which he wedged with an iron bar and then locked before doing the same with the door, so that he had to leave by way of the blind alley.

Louis spent hours at the window, as he did in the yard watching the carpenter in his glass-fronted workshop. Monsieur Floquet was a tall thin man who stopped sawing or planing from time to time to roll a cigarette.

He was probably not rich enough to employ an apprentice, and when he needed someone to lend a hand in order to hold two pieces of wood together, he would call his neat and tidy wife, who emerged from the kitchen in a starched apron.

When, in spring or summer, part of the glass front was open, a pleasant smell of glue and fresh wood emanated from the

179

shop, though it was spoiled a little by that of the building's only lavatory, whose door, on which someone had sawed out a heart, was ajar day and night, revealing on the ground a dirty crockery slab with two places for the feet and a hole in the middle.

Beyond the yard opened still another world, for the building was very large. Though all the tenants were more or less poor, those whose windows overlooked the street were the privileged ones. Among them were even people like Monsieur Kob, who, when he went out, always wore a bowler, sometimes a top hat, and almost always a frock coat. People said he was a laboratory assistant at the medical school and that it was he who cut up the corpses which were not claimed by relatives.

Nevertheless, even in that part of the house there were more old people than young, widows and widowers, especially widows. Some of them received a little help from their children, some had savings, others were on outdoor relief, and at least three of the tenants on the upper floors could no longer manage to go down the stairs.

A kind of tunnel led to the second yard, where the rubbish-bins were lined up. At night, cats and, so it was said, rats too would knock down the not properly placed lids. A stairway, whose bottom steps were of stone, though the rest were wooden, led out to the right. The iron banister was supported by bars that were too far apart, and several children had been hurt. One of them had fallen down two or three flights and had died.

Not everyone spoke French. There were a little girl and her brother who had almond eyes. A tall, thick-lipped Negro lived with a tiny little woman whose skin was as pale as that of the twins. Louis would sit on a step and watch. He rarely asked questions. When his mother came home alone for a meal, she was too busy with the others, and almost every evening there was a man in the room, sometimes a stranger, most often someone who stayed rather long and did not mind playing with the children, as the coachman had done.

Vladimir was the only one who could have cleared up certain points, but he looked at his brother so haughtily and with such contempt that Louis preferred not to ask him anything.

Yet Louis could have denounced him. Vladimir had got into the habit of bringing home in the evening things that did not

180

belong to him, sweets and chocolate which he munched in bed before going to sleep, coins that he hid in his mattress, a penknife that shone as if it were made of silver, and even a lady's watch that he would sometimes put to his ear before going to sleep.

One day Alice discovered the watch, and when Vladimir got home she dangled it in front of his nose at the end of its chain.

'Where'd you get this, Vladimir?'

'Let me have it.'

'Only if you get another one for me.'

'I'm ordering you to let me have it.'

'And I'm warning you that if you don't give it to me, I'll tell Mama. And I'll also tell her that you look through the hole and make me do what she does.'

'She doesn't care. Let me have the watch.'

'I won't.'

'I promise you I'll give you another one.'

'When you do, I'll give this one back to you. Is it gold?'

'It's plated.'

'Is it fake?'

'It's not fake, it's plated. It's almost as good as gold. Listen Alice . . .'

'I won't.'

Vladimir then turned his rage on Louis.

'What are you doing here?'

'Nothing.'

'Were you listening?'

'I heard.'

Vladimir went to get the penknife, which he opened with a meaning gesture.

'If ever you make the mistake of talking about it to Mama or anyone else, I'll puncture you. You know what that means?'

'I do.'

'Come here.'

'No.'

'You'd better.'

Vladimir stepped forward, grabbed Louis's wrist, pulled up

181

his sleeve, and, with a quick stab, dug the point of the blade into his skin.

'Does it hurt?'

'It does.'

'Well, if I really stab you, it'll hurt even more, and they may have to take you to the hospital. Do you remember the man they found on the pavement last month with a knife in his belly?'

The people who got up early had seen him from their windows, for he had lain in the street more than an hour without help.

'All right! So keep your mouth shut. Understand?'

'I understand.'

And Louis walked away from his brother with a smile.

Chapter Two

Was his memory playing tricks, was it an optical illusion? He had the impression, later, that his childhood had been a succession of periods of discovery, of intense activity, and of periods of somnolence of which he had no recollection, except of a kind of general tonality, sometimes a greyness, sometimes a sort of luminous fog.

The same went for his contacts with people. Some of them seemed, for a time, to have disappeared from his life, though he had continued to see them every day, whereas others, for no apparent reason, entered the foreground, and in such minute detail that they seemed ridiculous.

Such was the case of Monsieur Stieb, whose gestures and facial expressions were so deeply engraved in his mind that he remembered when the shoe-seller had clipped his beard and when he had changed the style of his detachable collars.

Thus, from his first-floor window he followed, without trying to understand, goings-on which for him had no importance but which must have had an enormous amount for Monsieur Stieb. The new saleswoman was dark-haired, full-breasted, and broad-hipped, and she had a well-rounded behind. She dressed strictly in black, as if she too were in mourning. Was she a widow, or a member of the family, Madame Stieb's younger sister?

In the beginning, she served the customers and knelt in front of their stockinged feet, juggled cardboard boxes, climbed up the ladder that slid along the shelves.

Formerly, when there was no one to wait on, Monsieur Stieb would stand at the door of the shop and make pleasant remarks to the women who stopped in front of the shop windows.

But now, as soon as he had a free moment he would disappear with his saleswoman into the back of the shop until, a few weeks later, he started waiting on the customers as he had done before, while the buxom young woman sat in front of the cash register.

Louis did not remember the marriage, which must have taken place during one of his periods of apathy. Nor did he ever know whether Vladimir stole another watch for his sister. At the age of about five, there was a void of several months of which almost nothing remained, except an impression of sun and heat, of the smell of fish and other food that rose up from the street.

Vladimir, who was thirteen, would return from school with a school bag that he tossed into a corner, near Emilie's cot, but Louis never saw him open a textbook or notebook, nor heard him talk about his class or teacher or schoolmates, whereas the twins sometimes sat face to face at the kitchen table doing their homework and learning their lessons.

They were all different. Except for the fact that they lived under the same roof, usually ate together, slept on mattresses that lay side by side, and washed in the same water on Sunday, there were few contacts among them.

Vladimir had black hair, which was thick but fine, with a lock that fell over one eye.

The twins, who were more square-faced and bonier, had their red hair cropped close.

Alice was blonde and fragile-looking, and her chest was beginning to swell a little around the nipples.

Louis could not see himself. The only mirror hung too high on the wall for him and was used only by their mother when she put up her bun.

Louis was short, he knew it, shorter than the other boys his age, and his hair was even finer than his sister's.

As for Emilie, she was beginning to walk in a kind of pen that was set up for her during the day with the mattresses.

Why was Vladimir more present to his eyes than the twins, of whose doings over a long period he had no recollection at a later time?

That summer his mother cut his hair, and he was surprised to see her wrap one of the curly locks in a piece of tissue paper. But though he remembered the lock and the tissue paper, he had no memory of the operation itself and could not tell on what chair or where in the flat he had sat.

He was discovering the Rue Mouffetard, where he was beginning to walk around by himself, with his hands in his pockets. As he saw it, the street was divided into two distinct parts.

To the right of his house, on the way to the Place de la Contrescarpe, the shops were not so closely huddled together. There were fewer dark alleys between the houses and few push-carts along the kerb. It was a foreign world.

In the other direction, towards Saint Médard's, the street became denser, more swarming with people, full of noises and smells, of the cries of pedlars, of piles of food, and of refuse in the gutter.

He often went to see his mother, whose green push-cart he recognized from a distance. On sunny days, it was covered with a piece of canvas that was held up by two sticks and bits of cord.

'Take a look at my lovely peaches, Madame. . . . Don't be afraid. . . . There's none like them in the whole market . . .'

The stock changed every day: peaches, plums, lettuce, string beans.

'Monsieur, try my William pears. . . . Come! Don't be shy. . . . Your wife won't scold you . . .'

A slate was stuck at the top of the pyramid, and between the shafts of the cart was a small board that supported the scales and the metal container.

His mother hardly had time to talk to him. The members of the family never talked much.

'Is Alice with your little sister?'

He wondered whether Alice had ever been to school. His mother would give him a piece of fruit, in other seasons a stalk of tart rhubarb, a few thick-shelled, fuzzy beans, and sometimes a sou. He would walk down the street, jostled by the crowd, stopping at the fish market to look at the heaps of mussels and shrimps and green-eyed fish.

At times he would have to step over a man, unshaven and in rags, who lay sleeping across the pavement beside a pool of vomit.

He never went beyond the church, which was his frontier, and he took no interest in the carriages and omnibuses that rolled by with a clopping of horses' hoofs.

His only expedition beyond the neighbourhood, when the family had piled into the coachman's hackney, already seemed unreal to him. He had seen the Seine flowing, churches, huge buildings, wide streets with silent houses where there were no pedestrians, avenues, and carriages drawn by two and even four horses in which young women, dressed in white, toyed with their parasols. He had caught sight of horsemen in shiny boots, officers with gold epaulettes.

No doubt it was all very beautiful. His mother went into raptures.

'Her whole dress is real lace and she's wearing enough jewels to buy half the Rue Mouffetard ...'

He was unimpressed. For him, it was outside reality, and he had finally dozed off.

The Dorés, opposite the window, were more real and for a time played an important role in his life. They lived on the first floor, above Monsieur Stieb's shop, but their flat was not like his. It contained at least four rooms, maybe five or six, for Louis could only catch a glimpse when the door happened to be open.

The floors were so brightly waxed that the sun played on them as on a pane of glass, and in certain places they were covered with multicoloured rugs in which dark red predominated.

Madame Doré and her husband were old. They were at least fifty. In summer, their three windows stayed open all day, and a

185

young housemaid in a white apron and white cap would beat the rugs and carpets over the pavement.

Did other residents of the street have a maid? Madame Doré wore a corset which was so stiff that it made her look like a statue. Her tight bun, which was still black, had streaks of grey. She was never seen in house clothes. Her dresses, with wide leg-of-mutton sleeves, were of colours hard to describe, violet, for example with mauve glints, or oak-leaf brown or even lavender-blue.

The two front rooms were the dining-room and living-room, and when Madame Doré sat down to breakfast she was already fully rigged up, without a hair sticking out, wearing a white or black tucker that made her keep her head straight and hold up her chin.

Lots of little dishes and utensils with which Louis was unfamiliar lay on the white tablecloth, and almost every day Madame Doré shook a little bell to call in the maid and tell her to put such and such an object in its right place.

Monsier Doré was fat, had broad side-whiskers, and wore, at home, a snuff-coloured jacket with frogs and braiding.

They almost never seemed to talk. He would read his newspaper in a velvet armchair. His complexion was florid, and after every meal his wife would take a decanter from the sideboard and serve him a little glass from which he drank while smoking a cigar.

They were the landlords of Louis's house and also of the house in which they themselves lived, to say nothing, so people said, of four or five buildings on the street. In summer, when Monsieur Doré left the house he wore a pearl-grey frock coat and was very careful not to soil his patent-leather shoes by walking in the rubbish. He invariably carried an ivory-headed cane, and his eyes were always sad.

It was the Dorés who, in the past, had run the hardware shop a little farther down the street which had been established by Grandfather Doré, who had started as a blacksmith.

For Louis, the Dorés were linked up with his illness and that of his brothers and sisters. By cross-checking, he later established the fact that he was about five and a half at the time. It was after a hot summer, most of which he spent in the street.

After that, there had been a series of storms, one of which was more violent than the others and had transformed the sloping street into a torrent, and as the sewers had overflowed, the street had reeked with a foul stench for several days. Workmen and firemen had even come to dig a trench in order to repair the damage.

When the storms were over, the rain had persisted and got colder every day. He did not know whether it had been in October or November. In any case, they had started lighting the fire in the kitchen stove and the window-panes were covered with steam. He had made drawings on them with his fingers.

One night, Louis, had a stomach ache and went to the chamber pot twice. In the morning, he felt very warm and his eyes itched.

He had not spoken of it to anyone, because it was not unpleasant. He had even gone out for a moment in the morning and had seen Monsieur Doré, who was wearing an overcoat and carrying a rolled umbrella instead of his cane.

'Aren't you eating?'

'I'm not hungry.'

'Have you been on the pot yet this morning?'

'Once.'

'Was it liquid?'

'I don't know. No. Not too liquid . . .'

'If it continues I'll ask the chemist for a remedy.'

No doctor, as far as he knew, had ever set foot in their flat. He knew the one who treated almost the whole neighbourhood, for he had often seen him go by with his medical bag. The doctor was a round-shouldered man with a white goatee who was always dressed in black and dragged along as if he were dropping with fatigue.

The mother went, instead, to the chemist, who would ask her a few questions and sell her a syrup or a powder to be diluted in water or whitish pills that melted on the tongue when you couldn't swallow them and which then left a bitter taste.

'Louis, are you ill?'

Alice was minding the little girl. She never complained about all the things she was asked to do. Nor did she ever play. She

187

wasn't sad, but the expression on her face wasn't the same as that of other little girls.

'No. I only had a bellyache.'

'You're all red.'

He could feel that his skin was getting hotter and hotter, and he went to the window to cool his forehead against the pane. He felt hot and cold. It was both pleasant and unpleasant. He would have liked to lie down, but he didn't dare to, for if he were really ill he would be taken to the hospital. Though no one in the family had ever yet been there, he did occasionally hear it mentioned:

'You know the fishwoman's little boy is in the hospital.'

'What's the matter with him?'

'They don't know. It seems to be something in the head.'

From time to time, an ambulance would stop at the kerb. Men in white would enter a house carrying a stretcher and come out with someone on it, usually an old man or old woman. He had once seen a woman struggling to free herself and screaming:

'I don't want to go there . . . I won't. . . . Help! . . . Don't let them take me . . . Maria! . . . Hortense! . . . Help! . . . If I go, I'll never get out and I'd rather die at home . . .'

Louis had witnessed the scene without turning a hair. The only person who had commented on the incident was a little old woman.

'I understand her, poor thing. No doubt they take better care of you there, but I feel the same, I'd rather die in my own bed too . . .'

Louis did not want to go and die in the hospital and he said nothing that evening, though he had the impression a number of times that the walls were spinning around him. He had night-mares. He felt that he was huge, that he was getting huger and huger, as if he were being blown up, until he filled the room, and he floated.

He did not know how he had floated, but he had lost contact with the floor and was begging them to hold on to him, to help him get down.

When he woke up, his blanket was damp. He felt drained.

His mother had left for the market long before. It was broad daylight and no doubt she was already at her place beside the kerb with her push-cart. Alice, who was sitting on the mattress of one of the redheads with her chin in her hand, was looking at him in a way she had never done before.

'Am I red?' he asked anxiously.

'No. On the contrary. You're all white.'

She seemed sunk in thought and kept staring at him.

'Are you hungry?'

'No.'

'Would you like a bowl of coffee and milk?'

He didn't know. He didn't feel like having or doing anything. Or rather he would have liked to go back to sleep, for his eyelids were heavy and swollen, and he felt bone-weary.

'Do you want it or not?'

He nodded. He heard her moving about in the kitchen, while Emilie crawled on the floor, pushing a tin can. Alice came back with the bowl, helped him sit up, and, when he protested, said to him gravely:

'You've got to do as I say. I'm your nurse. If you don't obey me, you'll die.'

His throat was tight. He tried to drink, but before he had drunk half the bowl he squirted the liquid.

'You can see that you're very ill. If they took you to the hospital, they'd probably open your belly, the way they did to a little girl I know. They took out a lot of pus and then they sewed her up again. She showed me the scar. It's as long as that. It seems they've got a room there full of coffins for those who die . . .'

She suddenly seemed much older than he, and he did not doubt the truthfulness of what she was saying. She spoke with the detachment of someone who knows but can't do anything about it.

'I'm not ill.'

'You are! You're very ill.'

'It's not true.'

'It is. I'll take care of you.'

'What are you going to do to me?'

189

He already saw her opening his belly with a kitchen knife or a pair of scissors.

'I'll ask the chemist for some medicine.'

'You won't say anything to Mama?'

'Where'll I get the money?'

'There's probably some in Vladimir's mattress.'

'Do you like Vladimir?'

'I do.'

He liked everyone, even the twins, who never paid any attention to him except to make fun of him. They claimed he was too short, that he wouldn't grow up, that when he was old he'd be a tiny little man, maybe a dwarf, like those who lived in the Rue du Pot-de-Fer.

'I don't like him.'

She added, while removing, without surprise, coins and unexpected objects from her brother's mattress:

'He's cruel. Sometimes, instead of sucking me, he bites my pisser . . .'

He did not see her leave, did not remember what happened afterwards. When he opened his eyes again, his mother was in the kitchen. There was no man with her. The paraffin lamp was lit.

He felt he had a damp, warm dressing around his chest and stomach, and he had difficulty breathing, probably because the dressing was too tight. In spite of himself, he started groaning, and his mother knelt beside him while the others continued to sleep.

'Does it hurt?'

'No.'

He tried to push aside the dressing.

'I'm choking.'

'Don't touch it. It's good for you.'

She had put her cool hand on his forehead.

'You're already less warm. You're going to drink a little broth I've prepared for you.'

He wasn't hungry, only thirsty, thirsty for very cold water, but he was forced to drink the broth with a spoon. He was so tired that all he could think of was going back to sleep, but he had strength enough to ask:

'Why is everything wet?'

'Because you did it twice in your sheets and I had to wash your mattress.'

It lasted two days. He learned this only afterwards. His grandmother spent one of them in the house, and she too made him drink broth with a spoon. As soon as he opened his eyes, he made sure that he was in their room, still fearing they might have sent him to the hospital. He also made sure that the old doctor wasn't there. Once, he caught sight of Vladimir looking at him, somewhat the way Alice had done, as if he were expecting to see him die and were curious to know what would happen.

'Does it hurt?'

'No.'

'Are you cold?'

'I'm hot.'

'But yesterday you were shivering and your teeth were chattering.'

'Did the doctor come?'

'What for? Would you like a chocolate?'

'No.'

He added:

'Thanks.'

For it was the first time that Vladimir had ever offered him one of the sweets that he swiped from stands and of which he always kept a supply. He was filled with tenderness for Vladimir, for Alice, for the twins, for little Emilie whom he neither saw nor heard, as her cot had been transferred to the kitchen.

The others, the big ones, were strong enough to defend themselves against contagion. At one age or another they had all had the same thing, fever, stomach ache, diarrhoea.

'Thanks,' he repeated more gravely.

He would have liked his mother to be there too, and his grandmother, he would have liked them all to be around him, for it seemed to him that they formed a unit, that they were different from other people, that they alone, all together, had the power of defending one of their members.

He felt very small. The redheads were right. If he lived, if they helped him live, he would remain the smallest in the family.

He was only a child and he was almost frightened at the thought of being a grown-up some day. His mother would be old, as old as his grandmother. Perhaps she would even be dead.

As soon as Vladimir grew up, he would go away and they would never see him again. Then the twins would go away. Why did he think they would marry the same woman?

He himself could marry Alice, so that she would always stay with him. He was afraid of being left alone. If they left him alone, he would die.

People were talking in the kitchen as if he couldn't hear. There were the voices of his mother and of a neighbour, an old woman who lived in the next house. She was a cleaning woman and smelled bad.

'All that's necessary is to moisten his dressing, as warm as possible, every two hours, by diluting a soup-spoon of dry mustard and a handful of bran in a little water.'

Then his mother spoke:

'I've got to go back to work. What with the rain, I've hardly made anything all week. If something happens, Madame Gibelin, let me know right away.'

'You can rely on me, Madame Heurteau. Work is work, and I can understand you, I who've worked every day of my life.'

... If something happens. ... If something happens. ... If something happens ...

Maybe he was dying, since he no longer felt anything.

He never knew how long his illness had lasted, nor exactly what it had been, for it merged, not only in his own memory, but in that of his brother and sister, with the illness of the others. One day, Olivier, one of the twins, returned from school in the afternoon and complained of a headache. A little later he began vomiting. Gabrielle came home. She made him drink a cup of herb tea, which he threw up, and despite his pleading she wound a damp dressing around his torso.

It was midwinter, since, the next morning – Louis was sure of it – he was kneeling on a chair watching the snow fall, and on the other side of the street Madame Doré, whom he saw indistinctly in the light and shade, was pensively contemplating the same spectacle.

It was an extraordinary period, for while Louis was getting better and regaining his strength, Vladimir announced, with an evil look at his brother:

'That does it, you've passed it on to me too . . .'

Because the children were ill, Gabrielle overheated the flat, and the chamber pot was emptied into the lavatory in the yard ten times a day. Gabrielle was obliged to work, for, as she said, only rich people can buy bread on credit.

Madame Gibelin came for only two or three hours a day and spent most of her time looking after Emilie. Guy, the second redhead, joined his brother on the row of mattresses.

Louis could remember his mother leaving her push-cart for a moment, rushing up the stairs, feeling the children's foreheads, preparing a compress or distributing spoonfuls of a sticky syrup, and then going out again with her knitted woollen shawl tightly drawn over her chest.

'Louis, come and get me if anyone needs me.'

For he was now the healthiest of the lot. His hair, which was finer than ever, was more curly. He spent most of his time looking out of the window or watching the gleaming ashes drop into the drawer of the stove.

Alice was less ill than the others. She too shivered with fever, and at night she uttered moans, at times actual cries, and seemed to be trying to push someone away.

Little Emilie crawled about on all fours from one room to the other, playing with anything, sucking whatever she could lay her hands on. No one realized that she had fallen sick too. She did not look ill and did not complain. She was put to bed, as every evening, in her cot, and as she did not wake up in the morning, Gabrielle leaned over her and then realized she was dead.

Madame Gibelin, who arrived a little later, went to buy a bottle of cognac in the grocery shop three houses away to buck their mother up, and she herself drank quite a glassful.

'You have to notify the district office. They'll send the doctor.'

Louis did not cry and was not really sad. His main feeling was one of surprise.

It was he who had started the series, and it was the youngest of the children who died of the sickness.

The comings and goings that followed disturbed his tranquillity, and he was annoyed with the people who came in, looked at the little girl's white face, uttered laments, gave advice, related personal memories, and asked whether there would be a funeral service in the church.

The old doctor came too, for the first time, with his medical bag. What struck him most was the hanging sheet that isolated the wooden bed.

He sounded the chests of Alice and the twins, without knowing that Vladimir was hidden in the kitchen closet. He asked questions with an air of resignation, like a man who had seen and heard everything. How had it begun? . . . With Louis? . . . 'Is that Louis? . . . Stick out your tongue, my boy. . . . Don't be afraid. . . . So you were the one who was sick. . . . Did you have a stomach ache? . . . Did you have to move your bowels often? . . . What did you give him, Madame? . . . Did you put damp compresses on his chest? . . . Good. . . . Didn't he have headaches? . . . Did he recognize you? . . . Who had it next? . . . Your tongue. . . . Can you swallow easily? . . . Did you have a stomach ache too? . . . And then your brother? . . . Obviously. . . . Obviously. . . . These children ought to have been isolated the very first day. . . . I'm not blaming you. . . . In any case, there's no room in the hospital and they wouldn't have been able to admit them. . . . And you, little girl, do you feel better? . . . I bet you began by taking care of your brothers . . .'

He looked about for a table, something on which to write, and it was in the kitchen that he wrote out the death certificate and then, as a measure of precaution, a prescription.

'Isn't it you who sell vegetables on a push-cart a little way down the street? I've seen you before. You work in the neighbourhood, don't you? I think my wife often buys from you . . .'

When the body was put into the coffin, the children, whether ill or not, were locked up in the kitchen. Louis expected that there would be hammer strokes and was disappointed at hearing only the conversation between the carpenter and his assistant.

It wasn't the carpenter downstairs, but another one, a more important one, who made coffins only.

Had Emilie spent that night with them? He did not remember, just as he had no recollection of other things that were more important than those that had stuck in his memory. In any case, the funeral took place on a windy, freezing morning. The neighbours, who were waiting in the street, held their hats in their hands, and the women's skirts stuck to their legs on one side and waved like flags on the other.

Vladimir was well enough to go out, for he disappeared a little later and did not come back until it was dark. Gabrielle returned home slightly drunk, accompanied by her mother, who tried to force her to go to bed with a hot-water bottle.

'I'm so afraid you may have caught cold at the cemetery . . .'

'No, Mama, it's not on a day like today that I'm going to coddle myself.'

Madame Gibelin had prepared a stew, and everyone ate heartily, even the twins, who were still running a temperature.

'The thing that consoles me is that she didn't suffer, and maybe it's better for her that she was spared this bitch of a life.'

'Gabrielle!'

The grandmother was reprimanding her daughter, who, in order to pull herself together, was helping herself liberally to red wine.

'You're right, Mama. Why worry? Such is life, eh?'

It was not until much later that Louis learned these details, at second hand, from Vladimir, and perhaps Alice had not been wrong in claiming that Vladimir was cruel. One day, she too was to confide in Louis.

'You can't imagine what he forced me to do.'

'I saw it.'

'You mean when he looked through the hole and made me imitate Mama?'

'That's right,' he admitted, blushing.

'That's not all. It annoyed him not to be able to do it like the

195

men, you understand? So he hid a big carrot under his mattress and stuck it into me. I couldn't even scream because of Mama and the fellow who was with her. I don't know how many times I bled and I had a burning pain for several days.'

It would have been necessary to collate all the testimony. That was done, more or less, over the years, in bits and pieces, but Louis would merely listen half-heartedly, as if the truth about the others did not interest him.

He had not taken sides at that age either, when he was about six. His mother, who had once arrived unexpectedly during a fight between Vladimir and the redheads, had asked him:

'Louis, who started it?'

And he had answered quietly:

'I don't know, Mama. I wasn't looking.'

He looked at lots of people and things, but not those in which he was expected to be interested. That same winter, he entered elementary school, after the term had begun.

His first day in the classroom, which was a turning point in his life, ought to have left an impression. He had not the slightest memory of it, though he very clearly recalled trying on blue-checked pinafores at Lenain's, the clothing shop near which his mother set up her push-cart.

He remembered particularly the smell of the materials, the stiffness of the starched pinafore, and, a quarter of an hour later, the sight of Monsieur Stieb, at close range, trying to fit him with high laced shoes.

'They wear them out so fast, Monsieur Stieb! You'd swear they do it on purpose.'

At that moment, he himself had wondered:

'Are Monsieur Stieb and the lady smiling behind the cash register going to get married?'

They did get married, in the spring, discreetly, without a white gown and veil, and the shutters remained close for the three days of their honeymoon.

On the long grey wall was printed: POST NO BILLS. Then there was a building of the same grey, two floors of classrooms, a short flight of worn steps in front of the building, a green door. The pupils did not enter by that door but by a small one in the wall of the yard. In the middle, the ground had been hardened by trampling. A band of paving stones two or three yards wide ran around the yard, and on one side was a covered playground for rainy days.

His classroom was on the ground floor. From his seat in the first row he could see the dark trunks of four chestnut trees. He had been placed in front because he was the smallest in the class.

'Are you sure you're six years old?'

'Yes, sir.'

That wasn't the first day, but the second or third. On the first day he must have taken a seat anywhere, on an available bench. On the walls were a number of maps, though he did not know of what countries, for he had not yet learned to read, but he could contemplate the patches of different colours which were separated by sinuous lines, light blue, yellow, green, and particularly the purplish pink of the biggest patch.

There was a jumble of exciting lines on his desk too, the veins of the wood which stood out in spite of the black paint, and, in addition, the mysterious patterns that pupils had carved with pen-knives over the years.

'What are you looking at, Cuchas?'

'Nothing, sir.'

Whenever the teacher called him by name, some pupil would burst out laughing, as if it were extraordinary or comical.

'What was I saying?'

'I don't know, sir.'

For he had been taught to say 'sir' whenever the teacher addressed him. That was not hard for him, since he was naturally polite and deferential.

'Weren't you listening?'

'No, sir.'

'Why are you in school?'

'In order to learn.'

'What have I put on the blackboard?'

'Strokes, sir.'

'I want you to make the same strokes on your slate. Be sure that they're the same distance from each other.'

He got down to work. He did not rebel, like Vladimir, and

197

did not, like the twins, loathe school, where they were unable to let off steam except during break. The girls were on the other side of the buildings and had a smaller yard, without trees, for their recreation periods.

The big boys came running out at about ten o'clock and before seeing them he heard the clatter of their hobnailed shoes on the stairs. The twins had already thrown a red rubber ball which the others tried to get from them, and they defended themselves energetically, throwing it back and forth over the others' heads and elbowing and sometimes kicking those who were about to get hold of it.

Vladimir was one of the biggest and walked around the yard with a friend whom Louis knew by sight because he was the son of shopkeepers in the street.

He did not know their name. People said 'at the Spaniards' '. They had no shop window. Their shop was a kind of broad corridor, both sides of which were filled with displays of food, some of which Louis would often go to contemplate with even more admiration than envy.

For example, rough, hairy coconuts with a reddish tuft in the form of a goatee. Pomegranates, one of which was cut in two so that the customers could admire the colour of the delicate flesh surrounding the seeds.

He had never eaten coconuts or pomegranates or those tangerines which were preciously wrapped in silver paper.

The oranges were enveloped in crinkled tissue paper, and exotic-looking salamis, flat hams, and dates with plaited stems hung from the ceiling.

It all must have been good, tasty, different from what he ate at home, those little fish that were soaking in a tart sauce, those shrimp salads, those anchovies laid out in such neat circles in casks, the different kinds of nuts, the bottles surrounded with straw, the tin cans of all colours . . .

He was amazed to discover that his Vladimir was a friend of the Spaniards' son, of a boy who lived in the midst of so many good things and who no doubt ate them.

He too was dark-haired and had heavy eyebrows, and his lips were as red as those of a woman with make-up. The two boys kept apart from the turmoil of the others and seemed to be exchanging secrets. Louis could tell from the Spaniard's attitude that he admired and respected Vladimir.

'What are you thinking about, Cuchas?'

'I was looking at my brother, sir.'

'At home you'll have all the leisure you need to look at him. Here you're supposed to work.'

The young boys had break after the older ones. When he in turn was in the yard, he had no desire to play with his classmates or make their acquaintance. The boy who shared his desk, who was also short, barely taller than he, and had a big red pimple on his forehead, went up to him.

'Why do they call you Cuchas?'

'Because it's my name.'

'A name from what country?'

'I don't know.'

'Don't you know what country your father's from?'

'I haven't got one.'

'You haven't got a father?'

'No.'

'Is he dead?'

'I don't know.'

'Doesn't your mother know either?'

The question seemed to him so foolish that he shrugged. He had promised himself to go and look at the dark trunk of one of the trees which had a bump, like a big wart, and to run his hand over it. There were complicated patterns on the bark, like maps, but they were deeply carved and one could stick one's finger into them.

'Where do you live?'

'Rue Mouffetard.'

'What does your mother do?'

'She sells vegetables.'

'Does she have a shop?'

'No. From a push-cart.'

'Is your family poor?'

'I don't know.'

It was true. He had never wondered whether they were poor. Actually, everyone in the building was poor. Even Monsieur Kob, who dissected corpses and wore celluloid collars.

'Those people have to spend their money on clothes,' their mother would say, 'and I'm sure they don't eat as well as we do. Some of them try to act like ladies and gentlemen and then, after bargaining for a quarter of an hour, ask me if I haven't any leftovers.'

'My father works in a bank.'

This did not impress Louis, who did not know what a bank was.

'My mother doesn't work and we have a cleaning woman every Saturday. My two sisters go to a parish school. Are you so short because you don't eat enough?'

'I've always been the shortest.'

'Why?'

'I don't know.'

He never asked himself the question.

After all, if he was always so calm and had a serene smile, perhaps it was because he did not ask himself questions.

'Too bad, because if a big fellow hit you, you wouldn't be able to defend yourself.'

It was already time for the pupils to line up in front of the classroom, take their seats, and make pot-hooks.

Chapter Three

The teacher was a rather heavy-set, flabby, shapeless, colourless man named Monsieur Charles. That was his family name. He was twenty-eight years old and unmarried. For reasons of economy he boarded with a widow in the Rue Lhomond who mended his shirts and other clothes, which were never new. He had a child's mouth and almost no nose, and one could feel that he suffered from not being good-looking or able to aspire to a minimum of elegance.

From the very beginning, mysterious relations were established between him and Louis, as invisible, on the surface, as an electric current. It was a matter of neither sympathy nor antipathy. Perhaps, on the part of the teacher, whose only vanity, a rather naïve one, was to wear fancy waistcoats under his

200

ill-fitting, threadbare black jacket, it was mainly a matter of curiosity.

He taught two classes in the same room, the walls of which were pale green, and while the little ones were still making pot-hooks on their slates, the second group studied the multiplication table and the history of the Gauls.

Louis applied himself, but without eagerness or enthusiasm. He did correctly what he was told to do and when his neighbour, the son of the bank clerk, left in the middle of the term to enter a private school, the teacher said to him:

'Cuchas, from now on I'd like you to attend to the stove.'

The pupils all burst out laughing. Had the teacher done it on purpose? The stove, a big black cylinder six feet high, the pipe of which went through the ceiling, looked even more monumental when little Louis went to open its firebox and refill it.

Yet those were the best moments of the day. The school was not sparing of coal, as they were at home. Nor did it use little balls of greyish charcoal, but good shiny anthracite that burned with a clear bright flame. It was so beautiful, so fascinating, that Louis hesitated each time to close the cast-iron door.

In the yard, he did not play. He didn't feel like it. He stayed in a corner watching, or digging up pebbles encrusted in the hard ground. The others would jostle him on purpose as they ran by. He sometimes fell his full length, and he would pick himself up without protesting, with neither ill-humour nor rancour, but with a vague smile on his lips, a kind of inner light in his blue eyes.

The two years in Monsieur Charles's class went by so quickly that he was unable to tell later when he had begun to read and write.

For him, it was the trees and the yard that marked the flow of time. The trunks became less black, seemed less rough; then tight buds appeared at the ends of the branches. The sparrows chirped more often, and soon other unfamiliar birds appeared.

'What are you doing, Cuchas?'

The children had got into the habit of pronouncing his name with a stress that made it comical.

'I'm looking.'

'May I ask what you're looking at with such attention?'

'The cloud.'

A light pink and white cloud that remained suspended ʼn the pale blue sky, right above one of the chestnut trees.

'I suppose it's interesting.'

'It is, sir.'

The pupils burst out laughing. It had become a game in which Monsieur Charles participated by his unexpected questions, which he asked in a deliberately gentle, insidious voice.

'What is your slate used for?'

'For writing, sir.'

The incident of the marbles took place later, when the buds, after swelling, began to burst with the sprouting of the young leaves. Everyone had begun to play marbles during break, and Louis had some in his pocket which he fingered but, most of the time, dared not take out.

Most of them were fine-veined agates. Others had multi-coloured spirals inside the glass. He had not bought them. Vladimir, who now affected a protective air with him, had said one day, when he was feeling generous:

'You can take my marbles if you like. At my age, we no longer play kids' games.'

Sometimes, however, Louis would take his marbles from his pocket in a corner of the yard and make them shine in the sun.

'Where did you buy them?'

He was being questioned by one of the big boys, a fellow named Randal, who regarded himself as the leader of the main group.

'I didn't buy them.'

'You swiped them?'

Louis could feel that Randal was going to become menacing.

'I didn't. My big brother gave them to me.'

'Well, you're going to give me the yellow one and the blue one.'

'I won't.'

'You're going to give me the yellow one and the blue one.'

'I won't.'

They were surrounded by four or five boys in Randal's gang.

'Did you hear what I said?'

'Yes, I did.'

'You know what's going to happen?'

'No.'

The big boy, who was a head taller than Louis, winked at his friends and then dashed at him. With an instinctive movement of defence, Louis, who was squeezing the marbles, thrust his fist into his trouser pocket, and Randal twisted his arm to make him pull out his hand.

'And now?'

'No.'

They had rolled on the ground among the spectators' legs.

Randal punched and pulled and pushed. There was a ripping sound. The trousers, though they were of thick corduroy, had torn.

'You still refuse?'

'I do. They belong to me.'

'They don't. You stole them.'

One of the corners of Louis's lips was bleeding. Long black legs approached.

'What's going on here? Are you fighting?'

Randal sprang to his feet.

'No, sir. It's him.'

'You mean that Cuchas attacked you?'

Louis stood up too and, running his hand over his lips, drew it away spotted with blood.

'Why were the two of you fighting?'

'We weren't fighting. He stole two of my marbles, a yellow one and a blue one, and won't give them back to me.'

Monsieur Charles studied the faces around him. The spectators said nothing. One or two of them, however, friends of Randal, nodded their heads affirmatively.

'Is it true, Cuchas?'

Then Louis, instead of answering, took his hand out of his pocket, opened his fist, chose the two marbles that Randal had been hankering for, and handed them to his opponent. Randal was dumbfounded. He hesitated to take them. Was Monsieur Charles being taken in?

'Well, Randal, don't you want them any more?'

'I do, sir.'

'You see, there was no need to tear your classmate's trousers and scratch his face.'

'I apologize, sir.'

But everyone could see that Cuchas was smiling, with a smile that was barely perceptible, like the reflection of an inner joy.

'Don't let it happen again. If I catch anyone fighting, he'll stay in for two hours.'

From that day on, the evolution took place more rapidly, though it was barely visible, both among the students and in Louis's innermost heart.

Anyone could kick him as he went by without his hitting back or complaining to the teacher. When, on rare occasions, he brought a roll with a chocolate filling to eat during break, all one had to do was demand it in a certain way and he would give it.

After school, almost all the others would leave in small groups, while he would walk off alone, with his school bag on his back, to the corner of the Rue Mouffetard, looking at the house fronts, the sun or rain on the roofs, anything at all.

His smile was perhaps not a true smile but the reflection of a quiet and almost continuous satisfaction that could have been taken for placidness. Vladimir was not the only one who was irritated by this placidness. Smaller boys than Randal would attack Louis for the pleasure of feeling stronger than someone else.

'I bet if I slapped you, you wouldn't dare hit me back.'

What could he have answered? He took the blow, didn't cry, and even disdained to put his hand to his cheek.

'You don't happen to have a screw loose, do you? Maybe you're a little batty, eh?'

'It's not only that he's batty. Don't you realize he takes himself for a little saint? I bet he goes to mass every Sunday. Maybe he's a choirboy.'

He had never been to mass. Their mother never spoke to them about God except to exclaim, when a misfortune occurred:

'What have I done to that damned God?'

She had nevertheless married Heurteau in church, and there had been prayers of intercession for the dead before Emilie's body was taken to the cemetery.

Nor did he attend the course in religion which a priest came to give once a week after school.

'No!' she had yelled when he had brought home from school the note asking parents whether or not they wished their child to receive religious education. 'So he can talk to you about sin and make you start thinking I'm a bad woman! Religion's for the rich.'

The little saint. The expression had been tossed off during a recreation period and was to stick to him all his life.

'Come here, little saint. . . . You wouldn't happen to have a top in your pocket?'

For marble time was followed by top time. The chestnut trees were in bloom. They became fuller, with dark holes in their leaves. Monsieur Charles always observed Louis with amazement, and at the end of the school year Louis was surprised to learn that he was at the head of his class.

He did not have the impression of having studied. He was embarrassed by the mocking or envious way his classmates looked at him.

On his way home, as he threaded his way through the crowd in the Rue Mouffetard, the voice of a boy who was running and whom he did not have time to recognize cried out to him:

'Go away, little saint!'

He was not a saint. If he did not swipe things, like Vladimir, it was not out of honesty but because he felt no desire to, or perhaps lacked courage. Too many people might start chasing him, people who ran faster and were stronger than he. He would be taken to the police station, then to prison.

For a time, he was afraid that Vladimir would be locked up. It was after the holidays and during the winter, which was so cold that his mother and the other street-sellers were obliged to light a charcoal burner near their push-carts and keep warming their fingers which stuck out of their mittens.

One morning, when they were all in the kitchen sitting around the table, which was covered with oilcloth, someone knocked at the door. That was a bad sign, for the postman never went up to their flat and nobody came to see them.

'Go and open the door, Vladimir.'

He had to go through the room, since the kitchen did not open on the corridor. Vladimir's mouth was full. They heard him turn the knob.

'Does Madame Heurteau live here?'

The odd thing was that Vladimir, who was usually free with his tongue, did not say a word, and when he appeared in the doorway his face was livid with fear, his features were drawn, he had a shifty expression. Behind him they could see the uniform of a policeman with a weather-beaten face.

'Is your name Heurteau?'

He laboriously drew a piece of paper from his pocket. His hands were stiff with cold.

'Gabrielle Françoise Joséphine Heurteau, maiden name Cuchas . . .'

She was upset too, but not frightened, as Vladimir was.

'If you're from the neighbourhood, you must be new, because I've never seen you. The other policemen can tell you that my licence is in order, that I've never tampered with my weights or my scale, and that it's not like me to cause a disturbance in public.'

Whereupon she grabbed her bowl of coffee and began to drink.

'When did you last see your husband?'

She did not pretend to be dumbfounded. She really was dumbfounded by that sudden mention of her former husband.

'Lambert?'

He looked at his paper again.

'Lambert Xavier Marie Heurteau, born at Saint-Josephère, Nièvre, on . . .'

What struck Louis most was that one of the given names of the twins' father was Marie.

'Wait, let me work it out. Louis's nearly eight. Eight or seven?'

She counted on her fingers.

'He'll be eight next September. The twins are ten. Lambert

up and left one day between the two deliveries, ten or eleven months before Louis was born, so that I even wondered for a moment whether he wasn't his. How about a cup of coffee to warm you up?'

That permitted her to stand up, go to the cupboard for a bowl, and take the coffee-pot from the stove.

'Have a seat.'

There were only enough chairs for the members of the family, but Vladimir remained standing, distrustfully.

'You can see it was ages ago. Two lumps of sugar? Milk? To get back to Lambert, what's it all about?'

'Haven't you ever seen him again?'

'Never. Disappeared. Went off without leaving a trace, except debts in the bars which I had to pay. That seems to be the law.'

'He hasn't written to you?'

'In the first place, he wouldn't have been able to write. He could hardly sign his name.'

'It says here that he was a tile-setter by trade.'

'When he felt like working. I'd say that he was a loafer by trade. He'd hardly be on a job a week and right away he'd injure his hand or foot or get bronchitis – when he didn't argue with the foreman. Bear in mind, I don't hold it against him. He had a weak chest and he used to spit blood. Once a month he went for a check-up to the Cochin Hospital where they made them line up in the yard in the middle of winter. They told him he had to build himself up, that the climate was bad for him, that it would be better if he lived near Nice. Can you see us at Nice? So he didn't believe them. The first thing he'd do when he left the hospital was to go to a bar. When he came back, he was blind drunk and couldn't take his trousers off.'

'Did you argue?'

'Just look at me. Do I look like a woman who argues with people? Ask anyone in the whole street if Gabrielle ever argued in her life! Even with the grumpiest customers, I tell them what I think of them with a smile. He beat me occasionally, but I didn't defend myself, because it didn't hurt.'

'I have orders to take you with me.'

'To the police station?'

'To the mortuary. Some of the down-and-outs in the Place

Maubert have identified him but, since according to the record you're still his wife, you've got to come and identify him officially.'

'Lambert's dead?'

She did not speak in a tragic voice. She was barely astonished, without any sadness.

'Did they finally put him in a hospital? I'm idiotic! If he died in a hospital, you wouldn't be taking me to the mortuary, would you? Well, well! Children, who'd have expected such news when I lit the fire this morning? . . .'

The twins continued indifferently to eat their thick slices of bread and butter which they dipped into coffee and milk. It was about a father they had hardly known. Perhaps Alice remembered his face, his moustache which used to smell of wine or brandy.

Had he ever bounced them up and down on his knees or held their hands and taken them for a walk in the empty streets on Sunday? Did Heurteau even have a Sunday suit?

Alice was particularly interested in the young policeman's ruddy face, and Louis was fascinated by the silver buttons of his tunic, which he was seeing at such close range for the first time and which he would have liked to touch.

'As a matter of fact, how did he die?'

'He threw himself into the Seine from the Pont Marie at about eleven at night. Some tramps who had made a fire under the bridge and who knew him went to inform the river police, but it wasn't till two hours later that they fished out the body more than half a mile downstream. The only thing they found in his pockets was an old dirty military-service certificate.'

'Since we've got to go, let's get going.'

She was looking for her shawl and mittens. Alice asked, in the hollow voice she had got into the habit of assuming whenever she knew in advance that the answer would be no:

'Can I go with you?'

She was quite unmoved. Her face merely looked longer, her features sharper, and her nostrils more pinched. Her mother gave her a look that Louis had rarely seen in her eyes.

'Are you depraved or something? So you feel like taking a look at a corpse?'

He did not attend the funeral. He did not even know whether there was an actual funeral, a ceremony in church, a procession, a coffin that was lowered into the grave with ropes, in a cemetery.

He had once followed a hearse, out of curiosity, to know what it was like. He admired hearses, especially those of second-class funerals, with tassels and silver fringes, with horses attired in a kind of cloak.

He was also impressed by the women who were hardly recognizable behind their crepe veils and who held a handkerchief in their hand. The cemetery was beautiful. It was pleasant to walk in the lanes covered with dead leaves that made an odd sound beneath the soles of his shoes.

In any case, if they had been Catholics he would have liked to be the choirboy in a white surplice who walked in front of everybody and held a long black pole surmounted with a crucifix.

Heurteau was a pauper, a word Louis had often heard but the meaning of which he had only recently learned. Somewhere in the fabulous neighbourhood through which the coachman had driven them one Sunday lived the rich people who, for him, belonged to another species and whom one was not likely to meet in the Rue Mouffetard. Then came the bourgeois, about whom his mother sometimes spoke and who were located, in his mind, in wide, quiet streets and in avenues, such as the Avenue des Gobelins or the Boulevard du Port-Royal where they lived in grey stone houses.

There were also the landlords, for example those opposite, above Monsieur Stieb's shop, who did nothing but collect rent and evict tenants who didn't pay.

The shopkeepers, both the important ones and the less important, lived apart. Last came the mass of the poor, the majority of the people who lived in the street and in the neighbourhood.

The paupers did not have enough to eat every day. When they were ill, they were visited by persons from Public Assistance who gave them bread tickets so that they would not actually die, and some of them, when they were drunk, slept on the pavement with old newspapers under their coats instead of blankets.

Heurteau was a pauper, like the tenants at the back of the yard, like the one whom people had seen from their windows with a knife in his belly.

'What do they do with paupers when they die?'

'They're buried in the paupers' grave. Or else, if nobody claims them, Monsieur Kob attends to them.'

Had his mother claimed Heurteau? He wasn't sure. He dared not ask her. He preferred to imagine Monsieur Kob cutting him up on a big table and carefully laying out the pieces, as on the butcher's counter.

*

Gabrielle was receiving male visitors again. In fact, there were always such visitors, except during the weeks following Emilie's death. Their absence had been their mother's way of being in mourning.

She also spent a few nights alone after the death of her husband, about whom there had never been much talk in the family but who thereafter was never mentioned again. Nevertheless, the wedding photo in its black and gold frame remained in its place on the wall of the room.

Louis was beginning to be aware of his physical appearance. There was a mirror in the shop window that was full of hats with flowers on them, and he would sometimes look at himself in it. He was really short, much shorter than boys of his age, but his features were very fine. They were not the features of a baby or a little boy but already those of a man, and his bright eyes sparkled. His lips were more curved than those of his brothers and even of his sister. He blushed easily, especially when a passer-by, male or female, caught sight of him observing himself in the mirror. And yet he was not vain. Perhaps, had he been able to transform himself, he would have preferred to be a big, rough, jeering fellow like Vladimir. The day he received his school report, he had merely put it on the kitchen table, without saying anything, and forty-eight hours went by before his mother happened to open it and learn that he was at the head of his class.

'So,' she exclaimed in amazement, 'you're the most intelligent of the lot! It's the first time anyone in the family got first prize.'

Whereupon Vladimir had snapped bitterly and mockingly:

'He's the little saint!'

'What do you mean?'

'That's what his classmates call him. Because he lets himself get knocked around without defending himself. All he does is put up his arms to protect himself, and then he refuses to tell the teacher who hit him.'

'Is that true, Louis?'

'I'm the smallest '

He was lying, and the proof was that his cheeks turned pink. Even if he had been built like the twins, he probably would not have hit back. The blows didn't hurt much. After a few seconds, he didn't feel anything and there was no point getting involved in a fight. Some day they would tire of always picking on the same one and would let him daydream in his corner.

He didn't like people to bother about him, didn't like to be asked questions, to be torn from his thoughts of the moment. He had always been interested in the stove, the stairway, the yard, the carpenter's shop, the stalls in the street, but he was now becoming interested in people too, in his mother, in his brothers, in the faces he saw in the street. However, even with regard to his family he felt untouched, he remained apart, without suffering or rejoicing at anything whatever.

'Monsieur Pliska, a friend of mine.'

Their mother sometimes introduced those of her lovers who spent several nights or several weeks with them. They occasionally played with the children.

Monsieur Pliska, whom she called Stefan, lasted at least two months, which included the period of the Christmas holidays. He was a big fellow of not more than twenty-five, with a powerful build. When he stood in the kitchen, the room seemed too small for him, and the chairs creaked under his weight.

They did not know what he did for a living. When Gabrielle got up to go to Les Halles, he would stretch out on the bed and sleep late, until nine or ten o'clock. The noise did not waken him.

211

He was very fair, in fact his hair was almost white, and he had orange-coloured skin that was pitted in spots with smallpox marks. He spoke only a few words of French but tried to understand what was said. Without taking an interest in Vladimir or the twins, he had immediately singled out Louis, though he often paid compliments to Alice, whom he pretended to treat as a young lady. He even kissed her hand at times, though there was no telling whether he was being playful or serious.

'Pretty!' He would go into raptures. 'Much pretty!'

Nothing could prevent him from going down to the yard bare-chested, wearing only underpants and an overcoat thrown over his shoulders, and washing himself thoroughly at the tap. When he came up again, he glowed with satisfaction and would hum a Czech song, prepare his shaving brush and sharpen his razor, for he wore neither beard nor moustache.

'It's what?' he asked Louis, pointing to the only mirror in the flat.

'A mirror.'

'Mir-ro-ar . . .' he repeated painstakingly.

'Or a glass.'

'Glass? Why glass? Me drink from glass . . .'

Although he did not mind the cold, he nonetheless appreciated the pleasant warmth of the stove, near which he would sit with a pocket chess set on his knees.

'How you say . . . ?'

Those were his favourite words: How you say?

He outlined a crown on his head with his finger. 'Queen, yes? . . . Queen will take castle . . .'

It was so entrancing, thanks to his mimicry, that within two weeks Louis knew the chessmen, how they functioned, and a few of the standard moves.

'You play? Me give you queen and castles . . .'

It was the only Christmas that the family really celebrated. Other years, they contented themselves with eating forcemeat sausage. On the evening of December 24th, Monsieur Pliska returned with a three-foot Christmas tree which he set up in the middle of the table, and then placed packages on it; a jellied chicken, meat pie, ham, and a bottle of sparkling wine.

For Gabrielle he had bought an enamelled brooch in the

shape of a rose, for Vladimir a whistle that resembled a police whistle, for Alice a thimble which was so light that a needle would probably go through it. It was the intention that counted. The twins each received a top and Louis a box of coloured pencils.

Everyone could have some of the wine, and when he saw the bottle was almost empty he rushed out in his shirt sleeves and came back a minute later with a second bottle and a bag of biscuits.

Then he sang, and after that he insisted that Gabrielle sing too.

'She's woman of my life!' he cried in a burst of enthusiasm, turning to the children after she had sung a ballad of which she remembered only the first stanza and the end of the last.

The street was bright and noisy. The shops were all open, and all the windows were lit up. It was like a canal of light, and Louis went to the window several times to look out, for he was no longer hungry for the biscuits, and the sparkling wine had made him feel a little sick.

Monsieur Pliska's ideas always occurred to him abruptly. Suddenly he would stand up and dash to the corridor as if seized with an urgent need. This time he stayed out longer, so long that when he returned, triumphantly, the children were undressed. He brandished in triumph, while repeating a Czech word, a square bottle covered with unreadable signs and containing a yellowish liquor.

'For Christmas! ... Only Christmas! ... Health, woman my life ... My life always ...'

Gabrielle sipped it warily and remarked that it was strong, but she must have got used to it, for she remained in the kitchen part of the night drinking it. The children, who were over-excited, slept badly. At times they were awakened by Monsieur Pliska's singing, at times by his sobs, and finally by the clang of the bedsprings on which he and Gabrielle collapsed.

He usually disappeared in the afternoon and was away for part of the evening too.

'Me work.... Much work ...'

He would point to his head in order to explain that it was with his brain that he worked. He would also sulk at times,

213

would not say a word for two days, except to explain to Louis, who was definitely his favourite:

'Mother cruel. . . . All women cruel. . . . Men very unhappy. . . . Pliska unhappy . . .'

He had brought an odd-shaped case, with railway labels pasted on it, which remained for a long time in the corner of the room where Emilie's cot had been and in which he carefully arranged his clothes and other personal effects.

What, indeed, had become of the cot? It had disappeared almost at the same time as the little girl. No doubt it had ended up in a second-hand store.

Pliska in turn disappeared, as did his case. Gabrielle did not explain why. She never explained. Perhaps she did not try to explain the whys and wherefores of things even to herself.

For Louis, it was the winter of discoveries. The first of these hardly surprised him. One night when he had awakened with a start from a bad dream and the moon had kept him from falling asleep again, he had gone to the window and leaned against it quietly with his elbows. The big moon lit up the landscape more brightly than the lamp-post and made it look unreal. Four dust-bins, so full that the lids did not close, were lined up on the pavement just in front of the alley.

He had often seen rag-pickers poking about in dust-bins with their spiked sticks and thrusting whatever was still usable into the bag they carried on their back or into a pram.

That night, two people were rummaging in the dustbins opposite, a man and a woman, but they were not rag-pickers, and what they were looking for was crusts of bread, anything edible, which they immediately stuffed into their mouths.

They were not old. They were not wearing rags, like the tramps in the Place Maubert. They were younger than the children's mother, a bit older than Monsieur Pliska. So there existed a category below the paupers who received bread tickets or help from Public Assistance or who could get a bowl of soup at the Salvation Army. When they had finished going through the four bins, they started walking down the street. Without a word, without looking at each other.

The second discovery was more important. To begin with, he knew that Vladimir's friend, the Spaniard's son, was called

Ramon, for when he passed the shop one day he heard the boy's mother call him by name before yelling to him something that Louis did not understand.

Two or three times, while walking in the street after four o'clock, when the lights went on, he had noticed his brother and Ramon strolling along with a self-assumed air of animals on the alert. Not only was Vladimir the taller and more resolute of the two, but Louis could feel that he was the leader and that his companion was his slave.

It must have been a Saturday night, for there were more people than usual in the narrow street which was narrowed even more by the stands that overflowed the shops and by the carts of the street-sellers.

Louis had just spoken to his mother. He was on his way home when he saw Vladimir and Ramon standing on the kerb. They were talking in a low voice, with an expression of self-importance. Vladimir really looked like a leader, and even from a distance Louis could tell that he was giving an order.

Ramon, who was wearing a blue frieze overcoat with gilt buttons, was hesitating and making objections, and finally Vladimir simply shoved him off the pavement by poking him in the side with his knee.

Once again, in the middle of the street, Ramon turned around imploringly but encountered only the hard look on his friend's face. In front of him was a butcher's shop that specialized in poultry and game. A wild boar, which was partly cut up, was hanging from a hook near a garland of wild ducks and other birds that were unfamiliar to Louis, who had never seen them alive or eaten them.

On a stall lay plucked chickens that were marked with a label and, to the left of the door, unskinned wild rabbits.

Two women were waiting their turn. An old gentleman in a bowler hat was being shown some birds at which he kept sniffing.

Ramon waited for the moment when no one was looking in his direction, grabbed a rabbit, slipped it under his coat and started walking very fast while Vladimir, on the other pavement ambled up the street.

Louis followed them with his eyes. They got together in the

dimly lit Rue de l'Arbalète, where Ramon handed his friend the rabbit as if performing an act of homage or offering his tribute of loyalty.

Vladimir took it by the ears, swung it around two or three times and tossed it into the first alley they came to.

Louis then remembered the watch, sweets, and miscellaneous objects that his brother used to hide in his mattress. Did he still collect them? Louis had never since been curious enough to find out. He didn't care. The important thing was that Vladimir had been able to make Ramon steal. Was it actually the Spaniard who had swiped the watch? Probably not. He seemed to be a novice. He had implored Vladimir and had crossed the street reluctantly.

A rabbit that was good to eat was now lying in an alley where rats would soon be squabbling over it.

Louis said nothing about the matter to anyone. He never said anything.

One day he saw a gathering at the head of the street and had no difficulty worming his way up to the front. It was simply a crowd of onlookers surrounding a street-seller, a tall, bony, lantern-jawed fellow with an enormous nose who was contorting his face as if it were made of rubber.

'Now listen closely, ladies and gentlemen, and if the ladies are wise and their husbands have common sense, every family is going to gain a quarter of an hour a day, to say nothing of avoiding three or four fights every week.'

He was not wearing a detachable collar. From a small case, which he barely opened, as if it contained treasures, he took a very high collar with a double lining and, looking as if he were squirming in front of a mirror, attached it with two buttons.

'First and easiest operation, especially if your wife or girl friend lends a hand.'

Another dip into the suitcase, from which this time he withdrew an aggressively purple tie.

'And now for the second morning operation to which elegant men are condemned. Bear in mind that this tie is new and therefore easier to handle than an old one.'

Then followed a comedy which he played with his hands, eyes, neck, mouth, in fact with his whole body, twisting and turning in order to work the tie up between the two flaps of the starched collar.

After which, he gave up in exhaustion, wiped his forehead, and beckoned to a plump, jovial woman in the audience who had a shopping bag under her arm.

'So you, Madame, are willing to be my spouse for a moment. You've nothing to be afraid of. We're in public and I know how to behave. Be so good as to help me get this tie on.'

He had taken her shopping bag and slipped the tie into her pudgy fingers. As she was shorter than he, he leaned forward comically, acting as if he were half strangled each time she raised the flap of the collar.

'And *that*, ladies and gentlemen, is the cause of half – what am I saying? – of three-quarters of family fights, the other quarter being caused by our better half's corset. Unfortunately I don't go in for corsets because police headquarters forbids such demonstrations in public.'

All that remained for him to do was to take from the case a celluloid device to which the tie was attached in the twinkling of an eye. Two or three seconds later, it was set in the collar.

'Ladies and gentlemen, unfortunately not everybody will be able to take advantage of this work of genius which will ensure peace in the family and put valets out of work.'

The case was finally opened. Just as the sale was beginning, one of the spectators nudged his wife with his elbow and, pointing to Louis, who was still up in front, whispered:

'I've never seen such a shrewd look as on that child's face!'

Louis heard him and did not smile. He already knew, in a vague kind of way, that it was not true, that he was not shrewd at all, that he had simply been watching and taking in the spectacle and that every detail of the scene, the man's twisted mouth, the dumpy woman's black polka-dot dress, the wart on her cheek, the expression of the various spectators, was inside him.

He was not laughing at them. He did not think them ridiculous. He had never yet thought anything ridiculous or seen anything not worth watching with interest.

Chapter Four

Vladimir had stopped going to school. He had not succeeded in getting his diploma. Or rather, no doubt, though he did not bother to explain to anyone – except perhaps to Ramon – he had not wanted to get it, out of protest, out of defiance.

From the very beginning, he had made a point of being at the bottom of the class. He had always been big for his age, and at about fifteen he had suddenly grown almost four inches.

Not only were his clothes tight on him, but he was not used to his height and his movements were awkward. His gait was at times too manly and at times too childish. His face was covered with a dark fuzz that made him look unwashed, and Louis once caught him putting their mother's powder on his face to cover his pimples.

For two or three weeks, he had almost never been seen during the day. He did not wander along the Rue Mouffetard with his Spanish friend, who was now at a *lycée,* where he wore the school uniform. What did Vladimir do with his days? He would come home at night looking, at one and the same time, feverish, arrogant, and depressed.

'When are you going to make up your mind to work?' his mother would ask him.

He would answer like a man who was not obliged to account for what he does:

'You'll see.'

She was definitely worried when she saw him wearing a new suit for which she had not given him money, new shoes, a white shirt, and a wing collar.

'Starting Monday morning, I'll be working for Monsieur Brillanceau as an apprentice.'

'The locksmith on the Rue Tournefort? You want to become a locksmith?'

He had reached his decision alone and had not discussed the matter with anyone, and nobody ever knew by what process or after what experiences he had come to choose the locksmith's trade.

218

Louis knew the shop, which was not far from his school. It was at the corner of an alley, of which there were many in the neighbourhood, on the side of the street that did not get the sun, and the windows were so dirty, the walls so dark, with hundreds of keys and tools hanging from nails, that a gas lamp burned all day long.

Monsieur Brillanceau had the colour of his trade. He was grey and sad-eyed. A curved pipe, most of the time unlit, was always in his mouth, as if it had been dug into his grisly moustache.

Vladimir started work at seven in the morning. He took with him a canteen of coffee and slices of bread and butter in an old biscuit tin.

Life at home suddenly began to change quickly. Alice was thirteen and, though she was frail, looked older than she was. She had barely passed the examination for her diploma, but refused to continue her studies and stayed at home, where she did the housework and prepared the meals.

'What did you do when you were my age?'

To which Gabrielle replied frankly:

'I'd rather not tell you.'

At times, Alice would replace her mother at the push-cart for an hour. At times too, in the evening, she would disappear for rather a long time, and when she undressed before lying down on the mattress next to his, Louis would get a whiff of an odour foreign to the family, an odour of boy.

She was pale, but pretty enough for people to turn around to look at her as she went by. She was beginning to put on make-up, but ineptly, which gave her a dubious look. With her small pear-shaped breasts and the sparse, blonde down between her thighs, she would strut about nude in front of her brothers, dragging her clothes.

There was a feeling in the air that things were starting to go to pieces. There was no longer the old solidarity in the home, and one night there was a violent scene during which Louis saw his mother in a rage for the first time.

For the past few days she had been coming home with a middle-aged man she called Papa who spent the night with her behind the torn curtain. He was a huge, hairy-chested fellow with impressive hands. He probably worked at Les Halles, for he left with her in the morning, without bothering to wash his face. He had a strong smell and made love very fast, with strong thrusts that shook the floor, after which he crashed down on the bed and sank into sleep.

One night, the fourth or the fifth, Louis was awakened by Gabrielle's shrill voice.

'Let go of her, you son of a bitch!'

It was still dark. The sky was just beginning to turn greyish, vaguely lighting up the room, as did the gaslight from the lamp-post. Louis, without moving, half opened his eyes and saw the man's bulk on the bed of his sister, of whom all that was visible was her blonde hair.

'Let her alone, you hear, you pig?'

He kept breathing hard and emitting a kind of laugh. Perhaps Gabrielle and he had been drinking the night before, as she so often did with others.

She tried to pull him off the mattress.

'Get the hell away, you whore!'

Vladimir, who suddenly awoke, punched him on the back of his head with both fists, but the man didn't seem to feel anything. Then Gabrielle, who was in her shirt, ran into the kitchen, came back with the poker and started beating him with it, screaming with all her might:

'You bastard! You pig! You sex maniac!'

He began to groan and got down on all fours with a dazed look, uncovering the body of Alice, who put her hands to her face.

Gabrielle kept hitting him, and blood spurted at the base of his skull, while he staggered painfully to his feet.

The twins, who had not stirred, were surely awake. The scene wavered between the grotesque and the tragic. All the protagonists were in their shirts. For some reason or other, perhaps out of habit, the man had kept his socks on.

He looked like an ox that the killer in the abattoir had failed to knock out with his cleaver. Louis would have sworn, later, that the man's eyes had become red. He stood there with his huge hands open, hesitating to dash at Gabrielle, who was still holding the poker and standing up to him.

'Mama!' screamed one of the twins with terror as the man took a step towards her.

'Don't you worry about me! I'll attend to him!'

The poker rose and came down hard. Luckily it missed his head, grazed his cheek, and landed on his shoulder. There was a sound as of a bone cracking.

'And now, you swine, if you haven't had enough, say so!'

She turned around without hesitating, fearing nothing more from him, picked up the clothes that were piled on the floor, walked to the door and threw them into the corridor.

'Get the hell out of here if you don't want me to finish you off, you dirty rat!'

Then the big shoes were sent flying into the narrow hallway towards which the man she had called papa a few hours earlier was staggering.

Heedless of the neighbours, she slammed the door in his face and when she came back she was still so excited that she knocked over the chamber pot.

Standing in the middle of the room, she yelled at her daughter, who was hiding her face.

'And you, couldn't you scream, you little bitch? Admit you liked it!'

One shitting business, as Gabrielle would say with her fondness for expressive words, brings another. The following day, a letter arrived, something that almost never happened. The principal of the school 'requested Madame Heurteau to be so good as to come to his office regarding an important matter'.

Louis was expecting it. For some weeks he had been seeing the redheads less and less often at break. They left and returned with their school satchels at the usual time, but they did not go to school.

When Gabrielle got home, she was furious, though this time her fury was partly an act.

'You, the two of you, so you imagine I've got it too easy and you've got to complicate my life, is that it? I want to know where you go traipsing most days? You, Guy, answer me.'

He was the more vulnerable of the two, and though they were born the same day he looked younger than his brother.

'I don't know, Mama.'

'You don't know how you spend your time?'

Her hand became menacing and Olivier spoke up.

'We don't like school, Mama. They've got a grudge against us. We're blamed for everything. When someone talks in class, the teacher doesn't try to find out who it was. He says, "Redheads, be quiet!" He doesn't call us by our names, like the other boys. We're "the redheads". And we're always the ones, even when we haven't done anything, who have to stand in the corner. The boys keep away from us and claim we smell of rotten vegetables.'

'Who said that?'

'All of them. They're all against us.'

Because of the vegetables, solidarity was springing up again.

'Didn't you ask them what their mothers do?'

'No, Mama, we didn't.'

That was the twins' shrewd side.

'Some of them are in a dirtier trade than me and I know at least two who earn their living with their behinds. You can tell them that next time. But you've got to go to school, because it seems they've done some investigating, that I'm not a good mother, that I let you fool around and don't look after you. The pompous idiot I went to see who they call the principal threatened to send a report to the police asking that you be sent to an institution.'

'An institution?'

'I think that's the word he used. He meant a reformatory!'

Was there any connection between those events and the habit that Louis began to fall into shortly thereafter of accompanying his mother to Les Halles? He did not ask himself the question. As with many of his ways and acts which were to stand out in his memory, it simply happened one day, without his trying to know why.

One spring morning, very early, before sunrise, while his mother was dressing, he asked her in a humble tone as he lay on his mattress:

'Can I come with you?'

'To Les Halles?'

'That's right. I've felt like doing it for a long time.'

'You need sleep.'

'I won't fall asleep again anyway. Once, Mama! Just once!'

He was not pretending. His intention was to go with his mother just once.

He had already slipped on his trousers and he dressed more quickly than ever. Except in winter, when she lit the fire before leaving, their mother did not drink her coffee at home.

'Are you the one who's going to push the cart?' she joked as they went down the dark stairway where they had to run their hands along the wall so as not to miss a step.

'I'll try.'

It was an exciting experience. In the yard, he already smelled the odour of night, which is not the same as that of day, and he was surprised, as they walked up the street, to see a light. It lit up a narrow, shallow bar in which two dark tables stood near the horseshoe-shaped counter. The bald proprietor was wearing a very white shirt, the sleeves of which were rolled up, and a blue apron.

A woman with a shawl over her shoulders was leaning on the bar with her elbow and dipping her croissant into a cup of coffee and milk. It was a new smell, a new image too, and Louis was happy at the thought that almost everybody was still asleep at that hour.

'Hello, Céline! Ernest, two coffees.'

He placed two glasses, first one and then the other, under the percolator, which let out a jet of steam.

'With milk for the boy?'

'Do you want milk, Louis?'

'A little. Can I have a croissant?'

There was a basketful of them. They had just come out of the oven and were still warm and crisp, and he was allowed to eat four of them, which had never happened in his life.

The owner turned to a shelf and grabbed a bottle at the end of which was a long tin nozzle, and without asking, no doubt following a daily rite, he tossed a dash of liquor into the mother's coffee, which immediately gave off a different smell.

She too was eating croissants. She ordered a second cup, which received another dash.

'You on your way, Gabrielle? Did you sell out yesterday?'

'There was just about enough left to make soup with.'

Everything was different, the sound of footsteps on the pavement, the way the houses looked. Some were four storeys high, two or three with red brick fronts; another, which was painted white, adjoined houses that were only one storey high. An empty hackney went by with the coachman dozing on the seat.

They turned right at the Rue du Pot-de-Fer and entered a yard where they joined other women, among whom was the grandmother. A sleepy little man with a pot belly was in charge. Each of the women picked one of the push-carts lined up against a wall and then went to get her scale and weights in a dark shed.

'Where'd you spend the night, Henriette?'

They yelled to each other, laughed like little girls during break, teased each other, exchanged catty remarks that only they could understand. Some were young and some were old. Most of them were big women with blotchy faces, pudgy fingers, and swollen ankles.

Without waiting, they left the yard and went down the Rue Lhomond. When they passed the Pantheon, the sky was getting lighter, and in the Boulevard Saint-Michel an omnibus drawn by six horses with clopping shoes almost hit the push-cart as it went by.

'You and your hearse!' yelled his mother.

They crossed the Pont Saint-Michel, and Louis, who stayed at the right because Gabrielle wanted him to be nearer the pavement, pushed with all his might. He would have liked to be between the shafts and roll the cart by himself, but he dared not ask his mother to let him.

The Courthouse was dark and empty and only a yellowish-green light shone above the gate of the mortuary.

After the Pont au Change the streets began to get lively. Several omnibuses were waiting to leave. Then, in the Rue des Halles, there were all kinds of noises. He saw carts that were loaded with pyramids of cabbages and carrots, crates full of live chickens and rabbits.

The people there were wide-awake, because activity had started long before, for many of them even before midnight,

and beyond the gaslit warehouses, from which issued an un-
broken din, a continuous stamping and trampling, yells, calls,
oaths, and laughter, stood a little train of trucks behind its
engine, which was puffing peacefully.

'Do your feet hurt?'

'No, Mama.'

'Aren't you cold?'

His feet didn't hurt, he wasn't cold, and he was having the
greatest adventure of his life. His nostrils quivered without
managing to take in all the smells, for they changed every ten
yards.

There were vegetables, fruit, poultry, cases of eggs, everywhere, on the pavements, in the gutter, all over the warehouses,
and everything was moving, was heaped in one place and then
transported to another.

Figures were yelled. People were writing in black pads with
violet pencils. Market porters wearing big hats and carrying a
side of beef on their shoulder rushed through the streets. Tubs
were overflowing with guts. Women sitting on stools were
plucking poultry with the rapidity of magicians.

It all looked chaotic, but he would soon learn that, for all
the apparent disorder, every waggon, every crate, every cauli-
flower, every rabbit, every man had a definite place and precise
job.

He saw there people of a kind who hung around the Rue
Mouffetard, bearded old men in rags, with long hair down to
the back of their neck who were carrying crates that were too
heavy for them from a waggon to a warehouse while a young
man jotted down a check beside their name each time they
entered.

The grandmother went by, and Gabrielle yelled out to her:

'It's a good day for red cabbage.'

Why? He realized that she had seen everything, the price
marks on piles of merchandise, the vegetables that the other
street-sellers of the Rue Mouffetard were already loading on
their carts.

'Got to be shrewd in our line of work,' she explained to
Louis.

He was grateful to her for saying this, for it was the first time

225

she had ever spoken to him in confidence about her professional life.

'Some women buy anything just because it's cheap.'

She would listen to figures that were quoted as she went by. She stopped, tempted, in front of some crates of potatoes.

'How much?'

Then, without answering, she continued pushing her cart towards a street where the bustle continued, and entered a high-ceilinged shed. On a blackboard, next to the names of foods, were figures written in chalk which a man in a black smock kept changing constantly, the way the teacher did on the dais.

Clerks were working in a glass-enclosed cage. Everything went fast. You have to have your wits about you not to be knocked over by one of the porters, and Louis instinctively held on to an end of his mother's apron.

'Have you got any red cabbage, Samuel?'

'Did you see it on the board?'

'It's not there.'

'Go and ask François. There may be a few crates left.'

She did not change her mind easily, and Louis was pleased to see that everyone knew her and treated her with affectionate familiarity. She got her red cabbage and they started going back, but by other streets in order to avoid those that were too crowded to get through easily.

The sun was up. The windows of the houses were shining. The blues were bluer, the pinks pinker, the reds redder. He began to see cooks and even well-dressed women carrying shopping bags.

They passed three men in evening clothes and top hats coming out of a restaurant in the company of young women covered with frills and furbelows. One of the men who was a little the worse for drink wanted to hire a marketer's horse and waggon at any price in order to drive home.

Louis was pushing with all his might. He felt the resistance of every paving stone. His mother stopped before the Châtelet.

'Wait for me here.'

She entered a wine-shop where she was served a small glass as a matter of course. She tossed down her drink, took a coin from

226

the money-bag under her apron, and threw it on the bar. It was a glorious morning, bursting with life. Everything was alive. Everything was colourful. Everything smelled good and he drank the air rather than breathed it.

'Aren't you tired?'

'Not at all, Mama!'

'What are you going to do till it's time to go to school?'

For at half past six she was already setting up her push-cart in its usual place, opposite the fishmonger's, and she was not the first.

'Don't worry. I'll find something to do.'

His head was spinning, his legs were limp, he was full. He walked slowly up the dark stairway and opened the door of the room, where the twins were still sleeping. His sister was in the kitchen lighting wood for the coffee.

'Has Vladimir left?'

'Five minutes ago. Where have you been?'

'I went with Mama.'

'To Les Halles? She let you? Are you hungry?'

'I ate croissants.'

'Lucky you!'

He was tempted to stretch out on his mattress in order to digest in peace what he had just lived through. His cheeks were flushed, and he knew that if he let himself lie down he would sink into blissful slumber.

He made himself sit by the window and go over his home-work. Alice went to wake the twins with little kicks, and they groaned before getting up. They were in their shirts. Their hair was sticking up and their eyes were bleary.

'Hey, little saint, what are you doing?'

'I'm not doing anything.'

They were aggressive as soon as they awoke.

'He went to Les Halles with Mama.'

'What for?'

'Ask him.'

'Just to see,' said Louis casually.

He did not yet know that it would become a routine or that in the classroom he would relish the torpor that kept him suspended between dream and reality.

'Are you dreaming, Cuchas?'

'No, sir.'

'Twelve times twenty-seven?'

'Three hundred and twenty-four.'

A vague smile, which no one understood, would drift over his face.

*

The morning trip to the market behind his mother's push-cart was to play an important role in his memories and his life, but legends grew up around the experience and it became difficult, even for him, to distinguish clearly between truth, exaggeration, and falsehood.

People wrote, for example, that for several years, despite his age and weak constitution, he got up every night at three in the morning, winter and summer alike. But his mother did not always go out at three in the morning. It depended on the season. In the autumn, she would leave the Rue Mouffetard later, for there would have been no point in being at her post with her wares at six o'clock, when there was no one in the street and the lamp-posts were still lit.

There were also mornings when, depending on her companion, she would let herself sleep an extra hour or two.

In any case, Louis himself did not always wake up. It was true that often, as soon as his mother awoke, he did too, that he sometimes was up before her, but at times he would fall asleep again, unless it was a Thursday* or a holiday, or during the holidays.

People also said that the women of Les Halles were so amazed to see a child impose such discipline on himself in order to help his mother that they had nicknamed him the little saint. In what way could he help her, in the beginning, he with his skinny arms? It was for his own sake that he went, in order to renew the wonder of it, to complete his set of exciting images, for example, that of the Seine, which had hardly struck him the first time, of the tugboats that pulled their barges and disappeared for a moment beneath the arch of the bridge, of the

* French children do not go to school on Thursday, but do on Saturday —Translator's note.

horse-drawn canal boats which a carter followed slowly along the towpath. He was constantly discovering images, yellow and green house fronts, signboards, nooks crowded with barrels.

It was not the women of the market but his schoolmates who had nicknamed him the little saint. The term had reached the market by chance. A woman with whom his mother was bargaining over baskets of plums on the pavement had gone into raptures in his presence.

'What a pretty child! He's like a miniature!'

Though he no longer had long hair like a girl, it was still longer than that of most boys and, being very fine, tended to flutter about his face, which thereby seemed all the more delicately designed.

Gabrielle had replied:

'It would be better for him not to be a miniature but a brute like his brothers. The boys in school take advantage of his size and hit him, and since he won't tell who did it they call him the little saint.'

It was also related that he had acquired a passion for chess at the age of six because Monsieur Pliska had sat with him in front of the kitchen stove for a few days and shown him how the pieces moved.

But it was not until a year or two later, when he began to be given spending money for Sunday, that he saved up to buy a cheap pocket chess set, the pieces of which were made not of ivory or wood but cardboard.

When it rained, he would sometimes sit near the window bent over the black and white squares for an hour.

At about that time, the landlord, Monsieur Doré, decided to install gas in the house, and the paraffin lamp, which was no longer needed because of the incandescent gas-mantles that hung not only in the middle of the kitchen but in the middle of the room as well, ended up in a second-hand store, like Emilie's cot.

The mantles, which were delicately suspended from the end of the gas jet, were made of a fragile material and turned to dust as soon as anyone touched them or when they were shaken. They gave rise to a whole series of minor dramas, for on the floor above lived an Italian family from Piedmont with seven or eight children.

The father, a construction worker, wore heavy boots and kept them on when he got home in the evening. He would walk up and down the room, play with the children, and make the ceiling tremble, with the result that the mantles in the room had to be changed twice a week.

'I'm going upstairs to those brutes and tell them a thing or two!'

Gabrielle would go bravely up the stairs, which were now lit by a gas burner with a dancing flame that was at times white and at times yellow. She would knock on the door, and for a quarter of an hour there would be an exchange of insults in French and Italian.

The children would cry, their mother would yelp. Vladimir, if he was at home, would go to the rescue.

Other tenants, disturbed by the noise, would yell at everyone, and once, when Louis had gone upstairs to see what was going on, he discovered through the chink of a door a skeleton-like, glassy-eyed old woman who already belonged to another world and who was telling her beads.

Had it not been for that incident, he would never have known she existed, for she never left her room and it was not until six or seven months later that she was taken away very early one morning, on the sly, in a white pine coffin that resembled the crates in the market.

Vladimir was still working for Monsieur Brillanceau. He wore a cap and a pair of heavy blue overalls. He smoked cigarettes which he rolled and let droop from his lower lip in an affected way.

In the street, he walked with his hands in his pockets, rolling his shoulders with an air of disdain, as if everyone were watching him.

He was losing weight. His face was peaked and the rings under his eyes grew darker and darker. There were evenings when he did not get home until twelve o'clock, and one winter night, which Louis could not place exactly, he did not return until breakfast.

He had a new way of treating the men who spent the night with their mother. He would look them up and down mockingly and aggressively, as if challenging them to pick a fight with him.

One Sunday morning – it was still winter – a tall young man with the head of a musician was drinking his coffee and eating bread and butter with them when Vladimir, who almost always slept late on Sunday, entered the kitchen. His eyes were bleary.

'You're not satisfied with sleeping with my mother, but she has to support you as well.'

He was obviously in a bad temper, ready for anything, ready to bite.

'Keep quiet, Vladimir, and mind your own business. Don't get up, Philippe. Don't mind what he says. He's always like that in the morning and an hour later he forgets all about it.'

The musician nevertheless preferred to leave, and his departure took place amidst an awkward and painful silence. No sooner was the door closed than Vladimir attacked again. Pouring himself a bowl of coffee, he sat down, with his elbows on the table, and snapped at his mother:

'Do you make them pay or don't you?'

'If I made them pay I'd be a whore and your mother's not a whore.'

'Then you're just stupid.'

'I'm a woman, and that's that, and I can't help it if I need a man in my bed. I got married because I thought that was the most practical way. I happened to pick a half-impotent good-for-nothing who spent his time in bars and came home only to vomit.'

'That's no reason.'

'No reason for what?'

'Nothing.'

It was obvious that he had something on his mind, but he checked his anger and chewed away glumly.

'If you're not satisfied with your mother, go and get another one. Aren't you ashamed to talk the way you did in front of your sister?'

He looked at Alice and opened his mouth, but managed to control himself and said nothing. It was only as he left the kitchen that they heard him mutter:

'They're all whores, all of them!'

Twenty years later, Vladimir was to admit to Louis that the

night before that Sunday he had had his first disappointment in love, that he had found his girl, the one with whom he went out and on whom he spent his money, in a corner with a man who was making love to her standing up.

He had pulled away the man's overcoat, which was hiding them, and he had seen. He was determined to fight. The other fellow had run away as fast as his legs could carry him, and suddenly Vladimir, who was chasing him, had stopped hearing his footsteps. The man must have been hiding in the shadow of an alley, of which there were many in the neighbourhood. Perhaps he had rushed into the first house he came to and was sitting on the stairs waiting.

Vladimir had searched for a long time. The girl had gone home.

'I'd have killed him,' he admitted.

He also admitted that for the first time in his life he had cried, he who, as a child, had forbidden himself to shed tears, to let anyone hear him complain.

They got used to the new lighting, which was less intimate than that of the paraffin lamp. Instead of there being a limited circle of light surrounded by a zone of shadow, even the nooks and corners of the two rooms received the same white brightness, which revealed wounds.

They suddenly realized that the walls were dirty, that the mattresses had been patched many times, here and there with cloths of different colours. The ceiling was cracked, and a broad streak of bright white plaster showed where the gas pipe went.

Was it that winter? The following winter? Louis could not remember, not knowing whether he had been in the third or fourth form, for the teacher had changed classes at the same time as the pupils. Louis was always first, though he sat at his desk as dreamily as ever.

He had happened to find, quite by chance, the coloured pencils that the Czech had given him for Christmas and that he used to keep in his school satchel.

The teacher did not resemble the one he had had in the lower forms. He was thin and had a long, curled moustache and long, narrow goatee which he would tug at nervously. He had very beautiful long, white hands with carefully trimmed nails. He probably earned little money, like the other teachers, but nonetheless made an effort to be elegant. Though his tail coat was rather worn, it was well cut and did not come from a ready-made clothes shop. His collars and cuffs were almost always clean and his shoes were of fine leather.

Louis had at first annoyed him with his placidness, with his smile, which the teacher perhaps thought ironic. Then he began to observe him more closely. He would loom up behind Louis when he was writing a composition, would question him point-blank while pretending to look elsewhere.

It was as if Louis were a riddle to him and as if he made it a point of honour to solve that riddle. Perhaps he thought he had found the key to it that morning. It was a market day, and Louis, who was drowsy, was listening to the lesson while drawing one of the pear trees in the yard in black and violet.

He had not noticed that the voice of the teacher, whose name was Huguet, had changed its place, that it no longer came from the dais but from the back of the room. Suddenly a familiar hand seized the unfinished drawing.

The odd thing was that Monsieur Huguet did not say anything to him, did not punish him, but about ten days later, during break, he went over to Louis.

'What are you planning to do when you grow up, Cuchas?'

'I don't know, sir.'

'Isn't there anything that tempts you?'

He searched in his mind, trying hard to be sincere, as he always did.

'No sir,' he finally concluded in disappointment.

'Oh.'

That was all. At about the same time, a week or two later, his mother was summoned again by the principal. The twins had not set foot in school for three consecutive days. There was talk of the police, of the juvenile court.

In the evening, the redheads let the storm break, without flinching. The following noon, they were home for lunch as usual. They did not return in the afternoon. Twice, despite the bad weather, Gabrielle, wrapping her shawl around her, scoured the neighbourhood and questioned the shopkeepers.

The gas in the kitchen burned almost all night long. It was Vladimir who, before leaving for work in the morning, thought of the biscuit-tin. There were six of the tins, with different designs, on a shelf.

The one with a picture of a mill contained the flour, the one with Millet's 'Angelus' the sugar, and so on for the coffee and bags of spices, until the last one in the corner, the one painted all over with pompon roses.

That was the family safe. It contained Gabrielle's marriage licence, the children's birth certificates, a few yellowing papers that were perhaps old letters, the rent receipts, and now the gas receipts too. In short, that was where their mother kept the family treasures, and also a few dozen francs in a man's wallet and small change for purchases in the neighbourhood.

Gabrielle, who had not gone to Les Halles the night before, had already understood.

'Just as I thought. They took the money and left only the bronze coins.'

'Vladimir, what should I do?'

She was addressing him as a man for the first time, was asking him for advice as if he had suddenly become the head of the family.

'They won't get very far. Someone'll spot them and inform the police.'

'Unless they come back themselves, with the money spent. Where could they have slept in such weather? It isn't as if it were summer!'

'They won't come back by themselves.'

'How do you know?'

'I know them better than you. You'll have to report their disappearance to the police.'

'But then they won't give them back to me, especially after what the principal said. They'll be locked up in a reformatory. Vladimir, they're too young!'

Louis was unable to figure out later whether they were eleven or thirteen at the time.

'No hotel will take them without asking them questions. After all, they can't sleep under the bridges.'

She was crying, and Alice began crying too. She was the

closest to the twins in age, since she was only a year and a half older than they. They had played with her more than with the others and spoke freely in her presence, though they were secretive with the others, because she was a girl.

'It's time for me to go to work. Be sure to go to the police station, Mama. Otherwise you're the one who'll have to explain.'

'What do you mean?'

'Nothing. Just go! That's the only way to handle it.'

Vladimir had become a man overnight, and their mother felt it so strongly that she started dressing as soon as he left. She had a Sunday dress which she almost never wore and which lasted her three or four years, a lavender-blue silk gown with a yoke and a high lace collar that made her look like a girl, for her face was fresh, without wrinkles, and she was always ready to laugh.

Instead, she put on her everyday clothes and threw her black shawl around her shoulders.

'Don't forget to leave for school on time, Louis. If the principal asks you any questions, say that you don't know where your brothers are.'

She was still sniffling as she left the room, but her attitude was bolder, and in the street she held her head high as if she were already confronting the inspector. The principal did not send for Louis. Did he even know that young Cuchas and the Heurteau brothers were members of the same family? They were only names among others on his rolls, and he knew only the pupils whom he had to discipline.

It was cold. It was raining. Rubbish was flowing down both sides of the gutter when Louis got home for lunch. Perhaps there was just as much rubbish other days, but on that particular day he noticed it. For him, it was a colourless day, a tasteless day, a day without the usual sounds. He walked in a vacuum, and when he saw his mother and sister sit down at the table in the kitchen, he asked no questions, feeling that they had no good news to report.

'Did anyone say anything to you, Louis?'

'No, Mama.'

'I went to the police station.'

'I know.'

'They're going to try to find them. They were polite. They even offered me a seat. Here's Vladimir! Sit down and start eating.'

'I was telling your brother that they were polite and that the inspector asked me to sit down. He probably has children, because he understood right away and when I suddenly couldn't keep from crying, he came over and patted me on the shoulder.

'They're going to do what they can. It seems they won't find them in Paris. They're used to that kind of thing. Runaways, as they call them, are reported to them every week.

'They asked me if we'd ever lived in the country, if we went there on holiday or if we had relatives there, because that's where children almost always go when they run away from home. Most of them take the train, often a goods train.

'I asked him if they'd be locked up and he said he didn't think so, that I was known in the neighbourhood as an honest tradeswoman who's never violated police regulations.'

'You see!'

'I did the right thing in following your advice. There'll always be the inspector to defend us.'

'Didn't he talk to you about me?'

'Why? Do you know him?'

'Is he a stout man who has a watch chain with charms on it?'

'That's right. You mean you were taken to the police station, and you never told us?'

'I was a child. I was about Louis's age and a cop caught me swiping a handful of sweets from a stand. He picked me up like a rug and took me to the station. The inspector put on a gruff voice. I cried and begged him not to tell you because you had enough troubles without that.'

'Well I'll be damned!'

She was so dumbfounded that she forgot about the twins. It was not until two days later that they were brought back from Rouen, where they had been found huddled behind crates in a goods train. They had thought the train was going to Le Havre, where they were planning to stow away on a boat. They had picked the wrong truck, which had been disconnected at Rouen.

They gave no details about their adventure, spent an afternoon in the police station, and the wallet was put back in its place in the box with the pompon roses. Only two francs were missing.

Chapter Five

'Listen to me, Guy and Olivier. The rest of you too, because what concerns them concerns all of you.'

Gabrielle was weary. Although events usually left few traces on her and she quickly regained her good humour, the twins' escapade had left its mark on her. She was limp. The children could see, if not how discouraged she felt, at least how tired she was.

'I had another talk with the inspector today. I beg you, Guy, don't look off into space that way as if it didn't concern you. It's a matter of your future, and your brother's too. He's really taken your situation to heart. The school doesn't want to take you back.

'He thinks there's no point in sending you to another one. You'll soon be thirteen and you'll never get your diploma. I haven't got one either, neither has my mother, nor lots of boys who've made good. So, to avoid the reformatory, he advises me to apprentice you. He's found an employer who'll take you, Monsieur Cottin, the printer in the Rue Cardinal-Lemoine.'

That was beyond the Place de la Contrescarpe, Louis's frontier, in a world where he hardly ever ventured.

'I'm warning you that Monsieur is strict, but I've been told he's fair and that he's decent to his workmen. The inspector first thought of separating you. I begged him not to. I assured him you wouldn't be able to bear it. Do you want to become printers?'

They both shrugged.

'I think that's your best bet. Don't you agree, Vladimir?'

'It's certainly better than the reformatory.'

237

'Well, you start Monday morning. Tomorrow we'll go and buy the clothes you need.'

It seemed to Louis that there was a different atmosphere in the home that evening, a certain constraint, an emotion difficult to define. Was it perhaps the end of a certain kind of existence?

Until then they had lived with each other as in a burrow, sheltered from the outside world, and come what may, their mother was there to protect them. The mattresses, lined up against the wall, formed one big bed, and their mother, though there was usually a man with her, was separated from them only by a sheet that hung from a rod.

There was a beginning and an end, the wooden bed on one side and Emilie's little cot on the other, with the whole brood between the two.

The cot had disappeared at the same time as Emilie. Vladimir had become a man. He appeared at mealtimes only occasionally and led a life of his own about which they knew almost nothing.

Alice, who was fifteen, had already hinted a few times that she was bored being alone in the house for hours on end and that some day she would look for a job. She had become a young lady who went dancing in the evening and brought home foreign odours.

And when the twins started working for Monsieur Cottin, Louis would be the only one who went to school.

Oddly enough, he bore a grudge against the gas. It seemed to him that ever since that hard white light had been installed in the two rooms their life had changed and that part of their intimacy, of the warmth of the burrow, had disappeared. Even the god-stove, on which too much light fell, no longer had its good-natured animal look and one could barely perceive the sparkling of the ashes that fell through the grate from time to time in a fine rain.

Was that the thing that brought him closer to his mother, that impelled him to go to Les Halles with her more often, to spend a few moments near her push-cart when he got out of school? In the years that followed there were bonds between them that had not existed before.

He had become the last of the brood, the last little one. She said so implicitly one day when Vladimir asked why they didn't move to a more comfortable flat where he could have a room. He felt a need to have a room of his own. He did not even have a cupboard but shared the hanging wardrobe with his mother, brothers, and sister.

'What's the point?' Gabrielle had replied. 'You won't be staying with us much longer and you'll be called up for military service in a few years. Alice, I'm sure of it, will marry at the earliest opportunity. The twins are working and don't come home for lunch.'

Louis would often stop in front of the laundry with the pale blue front. Its door was always open, and from it there escaped a special smell, almost as agreeable as that of the bakery. Like most of the shops in the street, this had a narrow front but was very deep, and five or six women worked side by side ironing linen on a long table covered with white thick cotton. Behind them stood a special stove with sloping surfaces on which they heated their irons. Most of them were young, and in summer they probably wore nothing under their white smocks, for he could see their breasts swaying and their hips rolling freely with every movement.

He knew that the name of the woman who ran the laundry was Madame Antoine, that she had started as an apprentice, and that most of the time she stayed in a room at the back where she tagged the linen and made out bills.

The washing was done in the basement, in a cellar crowded with big tanks whose ventilators opened on the yard.

Towards the beginning of autumn, Alice decided to take a job in Madame Antoine's laundry.

From then on, there was no longer a particular time for meals. Had there ever really been one? They all came home at different times. They knew where the bread was. They found cheese, ham, or liver pâté in the larder, which was a crate that Vladimir had covered with wire screening and fixed outside, on the window sill.

On Sundays, Gabrielle continued to prepare a special dish, boiled beef, lamb stew, or more rarely, a chicken that she had managed to get cheap. Yet even on Sunday the whole family seldom ate together, especially if the weather was good.

Vladimir dressed like a man and had bought at the Samaritaine department store a fashionable black-and-white-checked suit with a short jacket which he wore with a stiff collar and a bow tie.

In summer, he sported a broad-brimmed straw hat, which he wore tilted, and for several months he could be seen twirling a cane.

His area of operation had been spreading for some time, and the Rue Mouffetard was now merely a dormitory for him. He would take the train to spend his days off on the banks of the Seine, at Saint-Cloud or Bougival, and spoke of buying a bicycle as soon as he had put enough money aside.

Alice also wore a straw hat, with a much broader brim and adorned with a red ribbon, the ends of which fell down her back.

'Children, where do you expect me to get all that money?'

There had never been so much talk of money before the older children started working. Alice had bought, for the summer, a white dress trimmed with English embroidery, and, as winter approached, she dreamed of a velvet dress that she had seen in the window of the shop run by the Pochon sisters.

On Saturday night, she would go with girl friends to Bullier's, a big dance hall at the far end of the Boulevard Saint-Michel, where she met students. The next day she always had a story to tell. She would be very excited and would mention names that meant nothing to the family: Valérie, Olga, Suzanne Eugène, Roland.

'Roland is the nicest of the lot. He's at the university, where he's studying to be a lawyer, like his father. His father's the one who defended the anarchists who threw a bomb in front of the Royal Tavern.'

There was a great deal of talk about anarchists and bombs, about the underground, a network of tunnels under the streets of Paris where there would be trains that were faster than the omnibuses. Nobody in the family read newspapers. Vladimir would occasionally bring home instalments of a kind of magazine entitled *Nick Carter*, the cover of which showed a square-jawed man threatening someone with his revolver or freeing a girl who was tied to a tree or the foot of a bed.

Opposite Saint Médard's was a newspaper kiosk around which other publications hung from clothes-pins, for example *Le Petite Parisien Illustré*, which described, with violently coloured illustrations, the crimes of the week, an old man strangled in the Rue Caulaincourt, the woman poisoner of the Ternes neighbourhood . . .

All this began to exist for Louis on the fringes of his life. Before that time, the world was limited to a closed space which had little by little expanded without his realizing it, somewhat as it had for the twins, who now spent almost all their Sundays on the ramparts.

This reminded him of one of his rare conversations with his mother, for when they went to Les Halles together they spoke very little, despite the fact that the market was a long way off. Louis had never wondered what his mother thought about, though he had noticed that she was not engrossed, as he was, in the spectacle of the street.

She would cross the Seine at the Pont Saint-Michel without being aware of the colour of the light that day or whether there was a current, and she had probably never really looked at the towers of Notre Dame.

She worked. All grown-ups worked, except landlords like Monsieur and Madame Doré or rich people who would go horse-riding, ride in carriages, go to the races in grey top hats, and dine in restaurants with velvet seats and crystal chandeliers.

It was only recently that he had begun to realize this, only since he had started going to the news-stand from time to time to look at the illustrated periodicals.

'What are you thinking about, Louis?'

'Nothing, Mama.'

She pushed the cart along a few more yards of pavement, looking straight ahead with her lovely blue eyes.

'You're an odd little fellow.'

There was an intimacy between them which was composed of a vague tenderness that never manifested itself in words or effusiveness but only in shy, furtive glances or certain intonations.

It was true that he had no recollection of having been cuddled in her arms, the way children were in the books he read.

241

Perhaps when he was a baby? He retained a vague image of his mother holding Emilie against her bosom, but it was in order to suckle her.

'Are you really thinking about nothing?'

'I don't know.'

'It seems one's always thinking about something, even when a person doesn't realize it. I don't remember who told me that, someone who'd been to school.'

They walked on a little. A red and yellow tram went by them with a clatter. Louis was fascinated by the trams, mainly because of their colours, which enlivened the streets, and also because of the tinkling bells with which they warned pedestrians and the blue sparks they sometimes threw off at the top of their current collectors.

He had recently begun to venture at nightfall as far as the Boulevard Saint-Michel just to watch them go by, for it was nicer in the darkness. All he could see of the people who rode in them was their top hats and heads, as in a Punch and Judy show. They sat silently in a row, side by side, with fixed stares, in the diffuse light of another world, and at every jolt the heads would all bend to the same side before slowly straightening up.

'When your brothers and sister were your age, and even long before, they never stopped asking questions. Don't you ask questions in school either?'

He had to think. The world of school was so far away from that of the market.

'No, Mama.'

'What about your friends?'

'I haven't any friends.'

'Don't you ever play with the other pupils?'

'No.'

'Is it that they don't want to play with you?'

He was embarrassed by her trying, for no apparent reason, to penetrate his secret world. It wasn't a world, but rather a picture book, perhaps a silly one, but he didn't feel like talking about it.

'Don't you like to play?'

'I do play.'

'All by yourself?'

'Sometimes I play chess.'

'That's no game for a young boy.'

'I've played marbles, I've played with my top, I've rolled a hoop.'

Not for very long, but he had played.

'You never laugh. Are you happy, Louis?'

'Very happy, Mama.'

'Wouldn't you rather have been born in another family? Isn't there anything you miss?'

'I've got you.'

She looked at him in amazement, her eyes shining.

'You really love me?'

'I do, Mama.'

If she had not had to push her cart and if they had not already entered the Rue des Halles, where it was impossible to stop in the midst of the traffic, she would probably have kissed him or hugged him to her beautiful bosom. She forced a laugh, a muffled laugh.

'You don't really mean that I'm enough for you?'

'You are, Mama.'

'You're the most charming boy in the world. If only you continue to be happy. If only I could guess what goes on in your mind! With Vladimir, with your sister, even with Guy and Olivier, however tight-lipped they are, I think I can work them out and I'm seldom wrong. But you, you're a mystery. And yet – I oughtn't to say so – you're the one I like best . . .'

She could not prevent herself from adding:

'Although Vladimir . . .'

As if Vladimir, for her, were in a class apart. He was born when she was very young, and she was pregnant with him when she married Heurteau. Vladimir belonged to another race, so much so that though the name on his birth certificate was Joseph, he was always called Vladimir. Was Vladimir the name of his real father? Was he a Russian? Had she loved him? Had he abandoned her?

Questions floated across his mind, as they also did in later years, but he did not really put them to himself. He considered them unimportant and never did anything to find an answer to them.

243

They had entered Samuel's huge shed, and his mother, who was looking up at the blackboard, seemed ashamed of their unusual conversation.

'What should I get today?'

The blackboard had become familiar to Louis. As soon as they entered the area of the market, his watchful eyes observed the piles of fruit and vegetables, his mind noted the prices written on the labels and those that were yelled out by the fiercely competitive vendors.

'Apples, Mama.'

'Why apples?'

'Because they're red, the kind that children like best. They're not expensive today.'

He did not add that he admired the crimson colour of the pippins, the golden, star-shaped designs that illuminated their skins, their slightly flattened shape.

'How much can I have the apples for, Samuel?'

'How many crates?'

'Enough to make a big pile on the cart. In the Rue Mouffetard, the more there are, the more they attract people. They think you're selling them cheap because you're afraid to have any left over.'

It was true. He had seen his mother waiting for hours trying to sell a few bunches of leeks that were left at the bottom of the push-cart, whereas when it was overflowing with them she didn't know where to turn first.

'If you knock off two sous, I'll take ten crates.'

He felt she wanted to please him and it bothered him all morning in school. At noon, he ran to find out how the apples were selling and was overjoyed to see from a distance that the pyramid had melted. His mother was very vivacious.

'You see, my boy, you've brought me luck. Here! Go and buy yourself a bar of chocolate.'

She gave him a sou, which he dared not refuse, but he was sorry to be rewarded, particularly since he didn't deserve to be, because it wasn't she he had thought of but the apples. He nevertheless bought the chocolate and licked it as he walked up the street. His sister's voice yelled out to him as he passed the laundry.

244

'Did Mama give you some money? Why?'

'Because I advised her to buy apples and she's sold almost all of them.'

It must have been autumn. The weather was almost as warm as in summer and there were broad rings of sweat under Alice's arms. Only the two of them would be home for lunch. When things were selling well, their mother preferred to get rid of the whole stock before going home and contented herself with a snack, a chunk of bread and a few slices of salami, plus two or three visits to the bar opposite to gulp down a glass of wine.

'Which would you rather have, Louis? Dutch cheese or camembert?'

'Isn't there anything else?'

'There's some currant jam left, but you know Mama doesn't like us to eat it at noon.'

'Then camembert.'

It was a coincidence. It was not a legend that he created later as others were to create legends about his childhood. The chocolate was a point of reference. Louis was not particularly fond of chocolate. It was Vladimir who, when he was Louis's age, had eaten it whenever he could treat himself. When his mother handed Louis the coin, she must have confused him with his brother. When he sat down to eat, he still had the taste of the chocolate in his mouth, so that the camembert seemed less good to him than usual.

His mother had almost indulged in confidences that morning, had displayed more tenderness to him than usual, and he had the impression that she loved him as if he were a warm, soft kitten that was still defenceless.

As they sat and ate face to face, his sister looked sometimes at the window and sometimes at her brother, with a hesitant air.

'Listen, Louis. I think you like me and that I've never done you any harm.'

She was nibbling without appetite and spoke in a forced manner.

'You're a nice boy, you can keep a secret. I've got to tell it to someone and I don't dare say a word to Vladimir or Mama. Vladimir would blow up. And as for Mama . . .'

245

He waited. He felt embarrassed by the role of confidant, just as he had felt that morning.

'Louis, I think I'm pregnant.'

She was surprised at his being unperturbed, as if there were nothing startling or dramatic about the news.

'Do you hear? Don't you realize what that means?'

'Of course I realize. You're going to have a child.'

'I wonder whether I ought to let it happen. I'm not quite sixteen.'

'Mama wasn't much older when she had Vladimir.'

'It's not the same.'

'Why?'

'I wouldn't even be able to tell who the father is. Sylvie, my girl friend at the laundry, has been pregnant twice. She went both times to see a midwife in the neighbourhood who got rid of it for her. She didn't suffer at all the first time and didn't miss a day's work. But the second time, she was so sick that she had to see a doctor who had to do a curettage. All the same, she advises me to go to the midwife. I'm scared, Louis! What would you do if you were in my boots?'

'Nothing.'

'You'd let it happen?'

'Of course.'

'Even if it meant messing up my life?'

He felt she was annoyed with him for his seeming indifference. What else could he have said to her? Alice would have a child, and that was that.

*

Time passed quickly during that period. He had known long periods, of endless weeks, winters that went on and on though people talked about spring and buds every day. He had known short spells that brought you back to school, which seemed only to have just ended.

This one was a very brief period, and the seasons were so mixed up that later he was unable to determine when things had happened.

He was to remember evenings he had spent waiting for his sister to talk to their mother finally about the child, for ever since she had let him in on the secret he could see that she was getting bigger, that her face was pale, that she had a resigned look.

At the same time he noticed that his mother was receiving fewer and fewer men. Perhaps she even no longer had regular lovers who lounged in bed in the morning, ate with them, and came back in the evening as if they were members of the family.

The twins would come home from work tired, with their finger-nails black and their clothes smelling of lead and printer's ink, and would go to bed early. They went to the shop regularly. Monsieur Cottin would not have tolerated absence. Their attitude nevertheless remained grim and they had a shifty look. They did what they had to do, because there was no getting around it, but they felt like prisoners and some day they would take their revenge.

'Aren't you sleepy, Louis?'

There were only three of them in the kitchen, his mother, his sister, and he. As he did not answer at once, Alice signalled to him and he understood. She was going to talk.

She closed the door behind him. He felt uneasy and did not fall asleep immediately. He expected to hear shouting.

The conversation began in a monotone. There were only some indistinct sounds, and he woke up in the morning without knowing anything of what had followed. He had not heard his mother get up, but she was no longer in bed. His three brothers, who started work at seven o'clock, had left. Alice began at half past six. So he was alone in the house, as often happened when he did not accompany his mother to Les Halles.

There was some coffee left in the flowered coffee-pot beside the fire. He ate quickly so as to have time to run down the street before going to school. He saw Alice ironing with the other girls. She was the third in line, and since he pressed his face against the window she finally caught sight of him. She smiled and nodded in a way that meant it's all right, that is, that the thing had gone off smoothly.

Almost immediately, or so it seemed to him, her pregnancy became obvious and he wondered whether she wasn't exaggerating it deliberately by tightening her dresses at the waist. She

247

walked with her head tilted slightly back, as if to resist the weight of her belly, which nevertheless was still quite small.

'Have you heard the news, Louis?' asked his mother when he went to see her at the push-cart after school.

'I have, Mama.'

'Are you glad you're going to be an uncle?'

'I am, Mama.'

Vladimir, knitting his thick black eyebrows, was the only one who displayed resentment towards his sister.

'You're stupid enough to have done it on purpose! You think you're playing with a doll.'

For Alice had bought wool, knitting needles, and a magazine with coloured illustrations entitled *Layettes* and had begun to knit in the evening, which did not prevent her from going dancing at Bullier's the next Saturday and the following Saturdays.

As for their mother, though she no longer received men, she began to go out at night, on Saturday too, so that Louis stayed home alone that day. She dressed up in a way that, in the past, she had done only on rare occasions. She would take her lavender-blue silk dress out of its cardboard box and iron it, and also her petticoats, and she wore a corset that Louis had to help her lace.

'I'm getting fat,' she remarked. 'If I continue, I'll be enormous. You'd think it was due to my work.'

She had partly unstitched the famous dress in order to let it out, and even then it was tight on her. After powdering her face, putting on make-up, and sprinkling herself with carnation perfume, she would kiss Louis on the forehead.

'Good night, my little man. You're nice, you know! I hope you won't think too badly of me when you're older.'

A few weeks later, Alice had time to explain to him, while knitting slippers that resembled doll's slippers:

'Mama was marvellous. I offered, for her sake and the whole family's, to go to the country and work on a farm or at an inn where they'd have surely taken me on for my board. She could have simply told people that I was tired and she had sent me to live with relatives out of town, or to a nursing-home. I'd have given birth and left the child at a baby farm and no one would have known anything. Mama said no right away, that I had nothing to be ashamed of, that all the shopkeepers in the street, including the most stuck-up, had their first child before they were married or only four or five months later.

'She said to me, "Daughter, look them straight in the face. Carry your egg in front of you like a real female and be sure not to lower your eyes." '

Public works were going on all over Paris and streets were being torn up. Electricity was being installed everywhere. One Saturday evening when his mother had not got dressed up, Louis asked her: 'May I go to the Belle Jardinière department store?'

'It's closed by now.'

'I know, but I'd like to see the arc lamps.'

They talked about the lights in school. They talked about lots of things that he didn't know, about the Eiffel Tower, for example, which he had seen only from a distance, though most of his classmates had been to the top of it.

In summer, many of them took the train to spend their holidays at the home of grandparents or aunts who lived in the country. At least two boys in his class had relatives in Caen and had seen the ocean.

He himself had not been on a tram. He was not bitter about it, was in no hurry to have new experiences, did not try to widen his universe. Perhaps everything outside that limited circle even frightened him. He let the world come to him, little by little, bit by bit.

'Would you like me to go with you?'

'I'd be pleased, but if you've got something to do I know the way.'

Whenever he went to Les Halles, he saw the department stores and, from a distance, the wax dummies frozen in strange postures.

It was an unforgettable evening.

'You want me to dress up?'

He dared not answer either yes or no. She dressed as carefully as she did when she went to meet someone, sprayed herself with the same carnation perfume, dabbed her face with the pink powder, and put on lipstick.

'Don't I look too old?'

'Oh no!' he exclaimed fervently.

She locked the door and put the key under the mat. In the street she suddenly said to him:

'Take my arm, as if you were my sweetheart.'

That had never happened to them. He made himself walk on tiptoe, for he had not grown much. If they had met Vladimir, he would have sniggered, whereas the redheads would have looked away.

'Shall we take the tram to the Châtelet?'

All the lights were dancing in his head. For the first time, he saw people sitting at lighted pavement cafés in the evening. In the tram, he held his breath so as not to lose the tiniest bit of his emotion, and he smiled vaguely at the lady in black who looked funny when the movement of the tram jolted her from side to side. At times she looked as if she were about to doze off and suddenly, just as her head grazed her neighbour's shoulder, she would open her eyes in astonishment.

He saw the famous arc lamps, big globes that shed a bright, bluish light that quivered and crackled. When you stared at one and then closed your eyes, you saw ten, twenty globes in your head and it took a long time for them to go out.

'In the spring, if all goes well, I'll buy you a suit like that one.'

A wax boy with painted hair was wearing a sailor suit with a big white-trimmed collar. He looked as if he were taking a step forward, with his hand out to receive something, and was wearing patent-leather shoes.

'Come. I'll treat you to a drink.'

His mother would occasionally buy him an ice-cream soda in the bars around Les Halles where she would have a glass of wine to buck herself up, but he had never set foot in a real café. There was one opposite the Châtelet with mirrors on the walls and tables with white marble tops. He looked at the crowd anxiously, wondering whether there would be room.

Lots of men stared at his mother as she went by and some of them threw her seductive smiles. She was resplendent. She seemed beautiful to him in the light of the chandeliers that livened her face and made her eyes sparkle and the silk of her dress shine.

'A grenadine syrup for my son and an apricot cordial for me.'

The words were also new to him. He realized that his mother, whom he usually saw pushing her cart, frequented such places. She was completely at ease.

Although she had almost reproached him for not asking questions, he did ask one. There was an object that fascinated him much more than the mirrors and the ceiling on which naked women were painted, much more than the long white and gold bar where the waiters went to pick up the drinks and where a cashier with a cameo on her black dress sat like a queen. The object was a big, bright metal globe at the end of a metal stem.

There was not only one but four of them, in different parts of the vast café.

'Mama, what are those globes for?'

Perhaps he was disappointed by her reply:

'For the dishcloths.'

He got his diploma. Instead of being first, as he had been the other years, he was only third. He had worked neither more nor less than usual. Perhaps he had been more fascinated by the outer world.

His sister, whose belly had grown bigger and whose features had become somewhat puffy, had stopped working on the layette.

'Actually it's cheaper to buy it in a shop.'

The truth was that she had acquired a taste for reading. She had discovered a bookshop in the Boulevard du Port-Royal which had stalls on the pavement, the kind one saw on the quays.

The cheap novels that she read had coloured covers, like the illustrated Sunday papers. They cost sixty-five centimes, and after reading them one could exchange them for others by paying an additional ten centimes. Most of them were dirty, dog-eared, and spotted with grease, but their coarse, yellowish paper had a good smell. She sometimes read as many as three a week, especially towards the end, when she could no longer stand on her feet and iron all day.

Occasionally, when her legs were very tired, she would ask Louis to go and exchange a book for her.

'What kind do you want?'

'You know, a sad one.'

She was not sad herself and was delighted at the idea of having her baby.

'I think Mama's right. If I keep it here, I won't be able to work any more or go out in the evening. I'm too young to live in two rooms with a baby and it's better for both the child and me to send it to a farm. To say nothing of the fact that the open air will be good for it and that I'll go to see it every Sunday.' There were some feverish days. They would buy the newspaper in order to see the classified advertisements and would discuss them in the evening.

'Meaux! It's nice, but it's too far from Paris. Imagine how far I'd have to go just to catch the train.'

They considered Sartrouville, Corbeil, and a village near Etampes, and finally chose a place run by a Madame Campois in Meudon. It was only a few minutes by train from the Montparnasse Station. Vladimir had a regular girl friend and did not go with them. Neither did the twins, who had organized a gang on the ramparts and attacked a rival gang every Sunday.

Their mother had put on her pretty dress. Alice, who was in blue, was wearing a broad straw hat with a ribbon attached under the chin to prevent it from being blown away by the wind. Louis rode in a tram for the second time, went through the gate of the station, and climbed into a third-class carriage filled with soldiers in red trousers.

In Clamart they had difficulty finding the way that Madame Campois had indicated in her letter, or rather in the letter she had asked a neighbour to write for her.

They first went in the wrong direction. The road was covered with a thick layer of dust into which their feet sank. The cornfields were dotted with poppies. The weather was warm. Their skin smelled good. Everything smelled good, the air, the meadows, the barns that they passed, the cows.

They stopped at a farm to ask directions and continued on their way, feeling weak in the knees and overcome by the sun. Finally they saw a man in leather boots and a brown corduroy outfit who was standing at the side of the road and seemed to be waiting.

'Madame Heurteau? Did you have much trouble finding us? It's because we're in an out-of-the-way spot here.'

He pointed down to a house with a pink roof and white-washed walls. The apple trees were laden with fruit. The grass was bright. Two goats came over to look at them before capering off, as if inviting them to play.

'Are they yours?' asked Alice excitedly.

'Yes, they are. We've got a few animals. After all, my wife has to keep busy.'

Chickens were foraging around the white house. There were also ducks and two big ungainly geese, and a few yards from the house was a pond covered with duckweed.

'Rosalie!' called the man.

She emerged from a low room, whitewashed like the rest of the house, and put on her nicest smile. She had a beaming face, enormous breasts, and hips that rolled when she started walking. In the kitchen was a youngster about a year and a half old who was sitting on the floor.

'He's my first. I nursed him at the same time as Doctor Dubois's grandson. My husband's the doctor's coachman. I had so much milk that I could have fed three. Come inside. Sit down and have something.'

The chairs were straw-bottomed. They did not see a stove, but there were ashes in the fireplace where an iron hook was hanging.

'When are you due?' asked Rosalie, looking at Alice's belly like a connoisseur.

'Probably in two weeks.'

'Well, if you ask me, it could happen tonight or tomorrow, or the day after tomorrow at the latest. Don't you think so, Léonard? Come take a look in here.'

Opening a door, she showed them a huge room with windows on both sides, a bed with a white coverlet, and two wicker cradles adorned with tulle flounces that seemed to be waiting. In the opposite corner, next to an enormous wardrobe, was the child's little bed.

'That way, you realize, I can always keep an eye on them. If we agree about terms, you can bring it to me whenever you like, and Doctor Dubois can tell you he'll be taken good care of.'

Léonard allowed Louis to pick apples from one of the trees in the orchard and pulled down a branch so that he could reach it.

'Take a lot of them. As many as you want. There's quite a crop this year. Would you like to see the rabbits?'

There was a hutch full of them and others too in a square of grass surrounded by wire netting where they sat motionless, except for the mechanical movement of their cheeks.

'Would you like to live in the country?'

'I don't know.'

'Do you prefer Paris?'

'I don't know.'

His mother was served a small glass of brandy. Alice dipped a lump of sugar into it. Louis was given a glass of cold water that was drawn from the well in a wooden bucket.

His mother woke him when the train reached the Montparnasse Station. His cheeks were burning and his eyes were feverish. It seemed to him that an important event had just occurred, that the protective cocoon in which he had been enveloped had suddenly cracked, and he felt both heavy-laden and light-hearted.

Part Two

The Little Boy in the
Rue de L'Abbé-de-L'Epée

Chapter One

Dates hardly mattered in the family. There was no calendar on the wall. They reckoned rather by season, Gabrielle by the fruits and vegetables that succeeded each other on the push-cart, cherries, strawberries, runner beans, and the first peas, peaches which were less expensive in midsummer, apples in the autumn, cabbages and salsify in winter.

The appearance or disappearance of charcoal burners on the pavement was also a sign, as were the days when there was no market because excessive cold, or fog, which remained a subject of conversation for a long time, or ice on the streets or a heavy snow would have made it impossible for the street-sellers to get their loaded carts back from the market and because, in addition, housewives did not go out in such weather.

Gabrielle could not have told the children's dates of birth without consulting the official papers that were yellowing in the biscuit tin, and in order to measure time they would refer to memorable events: the year when the Seine had frozen, the year of Emilie's death, the autumn when gas had been installed, the period in which Vladimir had started working as an apprentice for Monsieur Brillanceau.

Others were added as the children grew up. Some points of reference were common to all of them, others had special meaning for individual members of the family.

In the case of Louis, for example, it was not so much the birth of Alice's child that mattered as his first train trip. The things that constituted his discovery of life, Vladimir looking through the hole in the sheet, then his sister's blonde hair on her naked belly, were more important than Alice's marriage to a boy named Gaston Cottereau who worked in a delicatessen in the Rue de Rennes.

There was also the gap between the little ones and the big

ones and the one between the children and the mother, which had varied several times. For example, Vladimir had been a little one at a time when a certain man was living regularly in the flat, and he must have remembered it, whereas for Louis Vladimir had always been a big boy. He himself remembered only men who came and went, smells, voices, the different footsteps of those who stayed three days and those who stayed a month, of those who ate with them and those he saw only in the evening, so that Pliska, who was only a vague figure in the memory of Vladimir and Alice, remained an important personage for him.

Louis was perhaps the only one, in addition to his mother, for whom little Emilie, of whom they never spoke, had had a real existence, because at that time he spent the whole day at home.

Vladimir and Alice were the eldest. They understood each other and exchanged secrets. Then Vladimir had suddenly become a man whom his mother asked for advice, whereas Alice remained a girl for a while and the difference in age between her and the twins and then between her and Louis mattered less and less.

It wasn't his first day in school that counted but the first time he had been attacked there, when he had refused to give up his marbles. His school record no longer existed, though he could still see the hand of the teacher, whose name he had difficulty in remembering, suddenly coming down over his shoulder and seizing the drawing he had just made of one of the chestnut trees in the yard.

Was it Monsieur Charles? No. Monsieur Charles was the big fellow with the flabby mouth. It was Monsieur Huguet.

The twins' escapade, the first one, the one that had ended in Rouen, had no date, could not be placed. The discovery of Les Halles as he clung to his mother's apron strings was more precise in time and space.

Then there was the conversation with his mother on a bench in a little park where pigeons came begging for bread, which they had not thought of bringing.

Why had they been in a park around the middle of the afternoon? He would have been unable to tell, just as he could not remember the name of the park, which was not far from a hospital.

Yet he had not been a small child at the time. He recalled details of the period when he was six or seven, but certain details of this experience remained hazy.

'You're intelligent, Louis. You learn things easily. You're the only one of us who has a diploma. Tell me frankly, would you like to go on with your studies?'

'I don't think so, Mama.'

'Have you thought of what you want to do later on?'

'Not exactly.'

'What about now? You're less strong than your brothers. I can't see you working in a shop or on a scaffold. If you feel like continuing, don't worry about money. Your brothers are starting to earn wages. I've got good customers and I'm strong on my feet.'

'Thanks, Mama, but I don't feel like it.'

'You can't go on indefinitely following me to the market in the morning and daydreaming the rest of the day.'

'I'd like to work at the market. For Monsieur Samuel.'

'What would you do there?'

'Last year I saw a boy who carried slips of paper from one end of the shed to the other and did errands outside.'

'The Flea!'

'I could do the same thing.'

Monsieur Samuel never wore a jacket or a collar. He was stout and short-legged and his big belly overflowed his trousers, which were held up by pale blue braces. The number of folds of his chin varied, depending on whether he was looking up or down, and a tiny black cap sat perched on the top of his bald pate. With a pencil in his ear, he sat in state in the middle of his shed, the importance of which was not suspected by the people who walked up the Rue Coquillière during the day. To them it was only a porte-cochère.

At night, one noticed the glass vault, as in railway stations, piled-up cases, crates and bags. Three clerks, one of whom was a woman, worked without stop in the glass cage. Push-carts entered, threaded their way through the stock, and came out full, while figures were written on the blackboard.

For years, that warehouse, that little stock exchange for small shopkeepers and street-sellers which was on the margin of the big exchange, the central market of Paris, was going to be Louis's vital element, as water is the element of fish.

He no longer left with his mother between three and six in the morning, depending on the season. He started work at ten in the evening, when men in rags began wandering around looking for a job.

At that hour, the shed was almost empty. There was only the food that had been unsold the day before. Samuel, with his pencil in his ear, would wait for the first waggons, which were drawn by broken-down horses, to come in from the Argenteuil plain or some other rural area.

At first, the shed was lit by gas, but before long Samuel installed arc lamps which were as bright as the ones Louis had seen at the Belle Jardinière.

'No, Victor. I can't pay that price. You know my customers. They're not people that the sky's the limit for, who slip a rebate to the cook or head-waiter.'

He was a lachrymose type and always tried to play on his clients' feelings.

'I feed simple, ordinary people, people who work hard and who don't know that they owe it to Samuel that they've got peaches on the table, just like the bourgeois, instead of having to settle for bruised plums. You fellows from the country imagine there are only rich people in Paris.'

He had several refrains in his repertory which he recited without giving anyone time to interrupt.

'Hello, little one. Come and take a look here.'

For him, Louis was always 'the little one', with no other name.

'This little one, for example! I took him on out of charity, because his mother has God knows how many children and she'll be here tonight with her push-cart along with the others. The grandmother's been pushing hers for thirty years. Little one, go and ask in the office if Vacher phoned up about the leeks.'

It was true that Samuel did not sell to the stores in the smart neighbourhoods but to the vegetable dealers who had only a hole in the wall and a few baskets on the pavement and who stayed open until ten at night.

Louis would come back with a slip of paper. Everything was settled by means of slips that were torn from pads in which a sheet of carbon paper made a copy.

'That's another one who takes me for a philanthropist!'

He would pull his pencil from his ear, cross out a figure, and jot down another.

'Tell them they can take it or leave it!'

Louis would go off again to the paved shed where, when no people were around, his footsteps resounded as in a church. The warehousemen were beginning to receive merchandise. The telephone on the wall, in the glass cage, rang constantly and the clerk would yell into it so as to make himself heard.

'Run over to that robber Chailloux and tell him . . .'

The Rue Rambuteau, the Rue de la Ferronnerie, the Rue Sainte-Opportune, or one of those huge, spectral sheds. He would worm his way with a bill in his hand and find an agent or wholesaler as busy as Samuel.

They would spend two or three hours that way, buying from each other and keeping up to date on the prices, which varied according to what came in, and shortly thereafter the little train from Arpajon would arrive and stop in the street with its goods trucks that smelled of the country.

The shed would fill up with merchandise. They would take on a few down-and-outs to carry loads on their back.

The second year, Louis was already given the job of standing near the main door and checking what came in: so many cases of this, so many crates of that. And, of course, jotting down the names of the producers.

Some of the helpers who were taken on for two or three hours and then went to eat a bag of fried potatoes and a dried sausage at the corner of the Rue Montmartre were young men who had only recently arrived from a cosy house in the provinces and come up against a Paris that was hard and indifferent.

The others, the old ones, whom one saw staggering out of the bars after work, had no more illusions.

Women with big behinds walked back and forth on high

heels, and they would stop under the lighted globe at the door of a hotel.

At a given moment, the tide rose again. The figures that Monsieur Page chalked on the blackboard changed each time that Louis, who went back and forth between him and the glass cage, brought a new slip of paper. No sooner did the merchandise come in than it started going out, not by the cartload but a few cases at a time. He would recognize his mother among the purchasers and would find time to whisper to her as he rushed by:

'Wait a while and take carrots.'

At 8 a.m. the noise and bustle was over, and a man in a blue apron would wash the tiled floor of the shed with a hose.

'See you tonight, little one.'

Louis would go to a bar for a cup of coffee and croissants and would sometimes treat himself to a bag or two of fried potatoes.

When he got home the flat would be empty, and as soon as he undressed he would flop down on his mattress. The other mattresses had disappeared one by one as discreetly as Emilie's cot.

The first to go was that of Vladimir, who had left for Toulon to do his military service and never understood why he had been assigned to the Marines, since he had never seen the ocean except in photographs. He came home several times on leave, and his wide trousers, blue collar, and tufted cap were quite becoming to him.

He had to pass through Paris several times during his training period, but he did not always visit the flat in the Rue Mouffetard.

One spring, around the month of April, two more mattresses disappeared. The twins, who were about fifteen but as big and strong as boys of twenty, ran away from home for good. They left a note on the kitchen table:

'Don't bother informing the police. We won't be back. Goodbye to all of you.'

They had both signed it. There were four spelling mistakes in the note. This time they did not take the money from the tin but only their birth certificates and whatever linen and clothes they

262

had, which did not make up a bundle too heavy for their shoulders.

The room suddenly looked empty. The curtain was no longer in its place. One day when Gabrielle had been in bed with the 'flu, she remarked:

'I wonder why we keep that old sheet. It no longer serves any purpose. Louis, don't you think we ought to take it down?'

It was now he whom she asked for advice. He had taken it down, including, though not without difficulty, the rod, which was too firmly fixed.

'Good God, the room looks so big! I didn't remember it as big as this.'

No doubt she was imagining it as it had been in the days of her marriage with Heurteau, when there was only Vladimir, who slept on the cot.

In the evening, Alice stopped at the threshold, dumbfounded, and likewise exclaimed:

'It's so big!'

No sooner had she lain down than she murmured:

'Look, Mama, would you mind if I slept with you?'

'Aren't you afraid of catching my 'flu?'

'You forget that I had it first.'

The mattress remained unused for a few days, and one morning, when he got home from work, Louis took it and laid it on the dustbins in the yard, when the carpenter had been replaced by another one, for the former had committed suicide. He had been found hanging in the cellar after a two-day search, for he had never used it and, as it was summer, no one had gone down to it to get coal. There was a rumour that he had been neurasthenic. Another resident of the street, Ramon, the Spaniard's son, also disappeared. It was Alice who kept her brother informed of what went on, for he hardly spoke to anyone.

'Did you know he was almost thrown into gaol?'

Louis showed no surprise.

'Such a good-looking, elegant young man, always so well groomed. Well, he belonged to a small gang that snatched handbags from women who were alone. Two others were also arrested, but we don't know their names because it seems they come from good families. Their parents greased someone's palm and the thing's been hushed up. Ramon's been sent to an uncle in Spain, and his parents tell people that he wanted to enter an officers' training school.'

Everything was changing, quickly or gradually, depending on the particular period. Cars, which had been such a rarity that people had gone out of their way to see one, became more numerous than horse-drawn carriages and there were as many taxis in the streets as coaches. People no longer called the underground the Métropolitain, but the Métro, and at times one would see an aeroplane passing in the sky.

One of the women in high-heeled shoes who walked up and down the pavements of Les Halles was younger, smaller, and thinner than the others. She had dark hair and black eyes.

One winter morning, when he had finished working, she had called out to Louis:

'Have you ever tried it, boy?'

He had answered frankly that he hadn't. How had she guessed that he had been wanting to for some time?

'You want me to break you in?'

The expression had shocked him.

'I know how it's done.'

'But you still don't know how nice it is. Come along! I feel like doing it with you. You'll give me whatever you like.'

She had a room on the fourth floor of the hotel whose globe was always lit at night. It was about fifty yards from the shed.

'You're lucky! Since you're the last and I'm going to bed, you'll see me undressed.'

He watched her get ready but kept his clothes on. When she was naked, she lay down on the bed, the coverlet of which was partly protected by oilcloth.

'What are you waiting for? Come here. I'll help you. I bet you're ashamed to show me your tool.'

He shook his head hesitantly. He was keenly disappointed but would have liked not to make her feel bad, not to hurt her. A few moments before, when she was undressing, he had desired her. She had made a mistake in taking all her clothes off, in spreading her legs, in exhibiting a slot invaded by long black hairs.

His mother's was delicate, surrounded by a reddish moss

264

which stood out elegantly against the whiteness of her belly.

The other slot which he had often seen, and still saw occasionally, his sister's, was barely shaded with blonde down.

'What's happening to you?'

'I don't know.'

'Do I disgust you?'

'No.'

'Well, are you or aren't you?'

He shook his head as he stepped back towards the door and stammered:

'I apologize.'

'That's the limit. I make you a present because you've been eyeing me for months when I pass Samuel's place. And the one time I get undressed – which would give the other girls a laugh – I did it because you're a virgin and I thought it would help you. So the gentleman turns up his nose. Tell me, you undersized little runt, do you think you're . . .'

He didn't hear the rest of it. He tore down the stairs, frightened at the thought that she might run after him just as she was and keep screaming insults at him and that the doors of the other rooms might open one after the other.

When he got to the street, he walked away fast, and it was not until he reached the Châtelet, where he felt safe, that he remembered he had not eaten.

Standing at the bar of a café whose walls were covered with tiles, he dismally dipped his croissant into his coffee and, for the first time in his life, wondered whether he was like anyone else.

Would he have been able to go through with it if she hadn't had such dark hair and a bushy triangle that went up to her navel? She had pretty eyes. She had been nice, at first.

She had called him 'runt'. He had been called that by schoolmates and was used to it. But hadn't she given the expression a special meaning?

Perhaps he ought to have tried it the same day with a blonde or a redhead, to set his mind at ease. He remembered what a woman shopkeeper in their street had once said to his mother when he still wore his hair long:

'Is it a little boy or a little girl?'

It would be a long time before he tried again. He was afraid of discovering that he was impotent.

*

He saw no connection between that experience and the event, a much more important one, which took place a few weeks later. Yet the woman's image often came back to him. He dreamed about her several times in the room where he had had to put up a shade, since he slept there during the day.

He even recalled details which he did not remember having noticed, such as the brownness of her nipples and the wide pink band around them. Not only did she have hair high on her belly, but also very low down, on her thighs.

He had twenty-two francs in his pocket that afternoon. Later, in the case of other sums, he was often all at sea, for the value of money changed many times in the course of his life. He earned forty francs a month at Samuel's, which he would turn over to his mother, including the tips from the market gardeners, and Gabrielle would then give him pocket money for the week.

Twenty-two francs represented two months' savings. He had noted the shop at the lower end of the Rue de Richelieu, not far from the National Library. It was a big stationery firm with two shop windows, a whole section of which was reserved for artists' materials and which employed ten clerks in the shop alone.

He had often stopped in front of the display, looking at what he called the 'colours', for he had no idea of the various mediums, and everything fascinated him, the paints in the little white earthenware bowls lined up in iron boxes, the chalks of softer and gentler tones, the tubes in small chests, which had a palette that fitted into the cover.

It must have been five in the afternoon. He had two ways of spending his days, depending on the weather, how tired he was, his mood of the moment. There were times when he would return to the flat at about nine in the morning, go straight to bed and sleep until four or five in the afternoon. as he had done that day.

On other days, he preferred to roam about, sit on a bench, go walking in a new neighbourhood, then kiss his mother at the kerb, go home to eat, and sleep until evening.

The salesmen and saleswomen wore the same grey smocks.

There were three saleswomen, and he waited outside until they were busy with customers before entering the shop, then he went straight to the artists' counter.

'What would you like, young man?'

Because of his height everyone thought he was younger than he was, and people adopted a protective, almost gentle manner with him.

'I'd like some colours, sir.'

'Coloured pencils?'

'No. I've got some.'

He jealously preserved, without quite knowing why, the set that Pliska had once given him. He used them only on rare occasions.

'Water-colours, gouache?'

He hardly dared express his desire, fearing lest the salesman laugh at him.

'The brightest colours.'

And, after a hesitation and a furtive glance at the marvels on the shelves, he added:

'Pure colours.'

He had uttered the word 'pure' in such a tone, with such fervour, that the salesman, a middle-aged man, took an interest in him.

'If I gather correctly, you've never painted?'

'I've drawn at times with coloured pencils.'

'Has someone seen your drawings and advised you to paint?'

'No one.'

'Have you seen many paintings?'

'Never.'

He had occasionally stopped in front of picture galleries around the Rue de Seine. The paintings on display in the windows had not interested him. It had not occurred to him that one could enter, see the other paintings inside, and leave without buying anything.

'Lots of young people start with water-colours.'

He showed him an open box of them and picked up another.

'These are in tubes and those in bowls.'

'Do the colours stay just as bright?'

'Not quite. Gouache fades less.'

'Is it better?'

'It depends on what you want to do. Landscapes? Portraits?'

He dared not say 'Everything together', spots, streaks, colours next to each other, the way he saw them in the street, the kind his memory was full of.

'Of course, if you want real brilliance, the only thing is oil paint.'

He opened a chest of oils in which at least thirty tubes were set between two metal flasks.

'I don't like some of the colours.'

He pointed to them: that one ... that one ... that one ...

'Why don't you like them?' insisted the salesman, who was amused.

'They're dark and sad. They don't sparkle.'

'The simplest thing is to do what painters do. Buy an empty box and a palette, and choose your colours. Come over here and have a look.'

He took him to a glass-topped counter that Louis had not noticed, and it seemed to the boy that all the colours in the world were offering themselves to him under the glass.

'May I touch the tubes?'

'Of course.'

The salesman pulled back the pane and Louis took out a long, thin tube and read: Veronese green.

'Is that the greenest?'

'There are more than twenty kinds of green. Their brightness depends on the colours around them.'

'I understand.'

It was true. He had understood, and he spent a quarter of an hour examining the coloured circles that indicated the colour contained in each tube.

'Is it just the same inside?'

'Exactly the same. Of course, you can mix them on the palette.'

The names enchanted him. They were more evocative than the poems he had been taught at school: Naples yellow, burnt sienna, carmine lake, ultramarine . . .

He laid aside those that seemed to him essential, but he would have loved to buy everything in the trays.

'Do you think I have what I need?'

In my opinion, you need some browns, some dark yellows.'

'I don't like them.'

'You also need oil and turpentine, and also, of course, a palette.'

'Are they expensive?'

'Here are some inexpensive ones. The box and palette, with two flasks, cost only twelve francs. See whether the palette is right for your hand.'

He did not know how to use it, why there was a hole in it.

'Like that, you see? The hollow of the palette against your body, the curved part on the outside. It'll be easier when your hand gets bigger.'

'How much does it all come to?'

He was radiant. He fingered the coins in his pocket. The salesman looked at each label, wrote down the figures, and added them up rapidly.

'Thirty-four francs and sixty centimes.'

Louis would not have thought that such little tubes would cost so much. A big tube of blue was marked only two francs and contained ten times as much paint as the others. Without daring to ask for an explanation, he spluttered:

'I haven't enough money. I'll be back. Be sure to keep them for me. Until what time is the shop open?'

'Seven o'clock.'

The man must have thought he wouldn't come back, and there was a touch of melancholy in his eyes as he watched Louis walk out. However, when he saw him start running as soon as he reached the pavement, he smiled confidently. From there to the Rue Mouffetard Louis slowed up a bit not more than twice, in order to catch his breath. His mother was still at her post.

'Mama!'

'What's the matter with you?'

'Nothing. Listen. It's very important. You've absolutely got to lend me fifteen francs. I swear I'll give it back to you.'

'What do you intend to do with fifteen francs?'

'You'll see. I'll tell you later. I'm in a hurry.'

She had never seen him like that. It was the first time he had ever manifested keen, insistent passion.

'Here! But don't knock yourself out like that.'

He bought others, later on, from the same salesman, who had taken a liking to him. Neither knew the other's name, but there was a kind of secret bond between them.

'Someday you'll need an easel. What do you paint on?'

'On heavy paper.'

'You'll have to try canvas.'

He showed some prepared stretchers and explained the various sizes.

'After all, you can prepare the canvas yourself, with glue and zinc white. Lots of painters do.'

He dared not believe it and yet he now lived only for that, as if the years before had been only a secret preparation. He painted near the window when he returned from work in the morning, for that was when the light was best.

If anyone had spoken to him about models, he would have been thoroughly surprised. He did not look at anything, except at times the workmen who made a din with their pickaxes demolishing the fronts of Monsieur Stieb's shoe-shop and of the tripery next to it. Scaffolds were erected. The demolishers were followed by other workers, and one afternoon there came to life the smartest-looking shop in the street, with two all-glass shop windows and a glass entrance as well, and, inside, a big room furnished with mahogany armchairs and matching stools. There was a section for ladies at the left and for gentleman at the right, and at the back one could see a dapple-grey rocking-horse for children.

Monsieur Stieb took on saleswomen, whom he picked young and pretty. Alice, who had gone back to work in the laundry, applied for a job in the shoe-shop and was taken on. It was indirectly because of Monsieur Stieb, who dressed more and more elegantly, that she found a husband, for one afternoon she had to wait on a tall, dark, slightly awkward young man. The following day, he waited for her after work. They went dancing together on Saturdays. Three months later, Alice announced to her mother that she was getting married in the spring.

'His name is Gaston, Gaston Cottereau. He's twenty-five and works in a big delicatessen in the Rue de Rennes. If only you could see what there is in the window! They make lobster in scallop shells, shrimp salad, chicken croquettes . . .'

'Where does he live?'

'For the time being, he rents a room in his boss's flat, but we're looking for a place of our own in the neighbourhood.'

'What about François?'

'Gaston doesn't want me to work after we're married, and François will live with us.'

François was a big, rosy, pug-nosed boy who resembled nobody in the family and who was already walking on his big chubby legs.

Louis hardly remembered the marriage or the wedding dinner on the first floor of a restaurant. Strangers were present, Gaston's parents, who lived at Saint-Aubin, in Nièvre. They had ruddy faces that looked as if they had been carved in wood.

He tried the next day and the following days to paint portraits of them sitting stiffly in front of the white tablecloth, and, without knowing why, he included the body of a woman lying on the cloth, a nude body resembling his sister's. The head was only a blurred outline, as if it were unimportant.

He was unsatisfied with what he painted, because it remained muddy. He refused to let himself mix colours and found it hard to place faces and objects on different planes.

There were schools. His salesman in the Rue de Richelieu had asked him whether he would enter the School of Fine Arts when he was old enough, and Louis dared not admit to him that he had only his elementary school diploma and worked at Les Halles at night. He expected to work there all his life and to be promoted little by little, for Monsieur Samuel liked him.

'Look, little one. Climb up the step-ladder and try to write figures in the columns.'

Louis did not know that the man who had been writing prices on the blackboard for years had entered the hospital the day before and probably would not come out alive. He was to undergo an operation the next day or the following day, though he did not know for what.

'I can't reach the top, sir.'

'Write on the other lines.'

Samuel called out a few figures to him at random: The chalk grated on the blackboard, the way it used to do in school. Louis followed tensely, as if his life depended on it.

'Your figures are better than poor Albert's. I can read them without my glasses. Let's see your handwriting. Here goes! Cauliflowers. Carrots. Turnips. Not so fast! Best quality peaches. Cavaillon melons. All right! You can come down. I'll tell Michel to raise the step-ladder another foot. Starting Monday, I'll give you sixty francs a month and we'll see about a raise at the end of the year.'

It was wonderful! He didn't tell his mother because he wanted to surprise her when she came to stock up. The neighbourhood tradeswomen had recognized him.

'Gabrielle! Look up there . . .'

She waved to him in surprise, but he had no time to wave back. He was catching figures on the wing, rubbing out, writing, looking down at people's heads, which appeared to him in a different light.

His work thrilled him. The look of the shed changed every moment. He could have painted for ten years without exhausting the material he had before his eyes.

Alice and her husband had found a fourth-floor flat in the Rue des Ecoles, opposite the Sorbonne.

'We even have a balcony. So François can be out in the air when I do the housework.'

She often walked with her son, holding him by the hand, to the Rue Mouffetard and chatted with her mother, who would cram her shopping bag with vegetables, but she almost never went up to the flat where she had lived so long.

There were only two of them in it now, and it was all the more comfortable in that they were hardly ever there at the same time, except on Sunday.

Louis found a second-hand bed, which he put against the wall, in Emilie's old place. He bought a night table with a cracked marble top which he got for a song.

When his mother's bed was pulled over to the night table, there remained a big empty space on the window side, and one day he set up an easel there, a light, cheap, deal easel for which he had been hankering a long time.

He had perhaps found a way of thinning his paint, of keeping it from being pasty, what he called smeary, though he was not sure of the result. Instead of spreading it carefully, as on a wall or door, he used a fine brush and dabbed touches of pure tones on the cardboard. For he continued to be haunted by pure colours. He never felt they were limpid enough, vibrant enough. He would have liked to see them quiver.

He was not yet ready to use canvas and found all the cardboard cartons he wanted on top of dustbins. He prepared them as the salesman had advised him. It took a lot of time, but he had no sense of time. He had never had it; events that were years apart had no chronological order in his mind.

He was sleeping warmly and voluptuously one day when he felt someone touch his shoulder and then heard his mother's voice:

'Louis! Wake up!'

He was struck by the tone of it, for it was grave, tragic.

'What's the matter, Mama?'

She stared at him. She was pale and drawn and looked as if she had suddenly been frozen by fate.

'They've declared war, Louis.'

'Where?'

'Here. In France. The Germans have attacked us. There are posters up announcing a general mobilization.'

'Do you think the Germans'll get to Paris?'

'I hope we beat them. Men are leaving, regiments are parading . . .'

He had no reaction, and he thought he heard a tone of reproach in his mother's vooice when she added:

'Vladimir will be among the first to go.'

He hadn't thought of Vladimir. His first thought had been that he was only sixteen, that he was too short to be a soldier, and that since the Germans weren't near Paris life would continue as usual.

'If the twins are in France or in the colonies, they'll be mobilized too, because they're nearly nineteen.'

She was counting on her fingers and moving her lips.

'In fact they're over nineteen, since they were born in April. They'll be pulled in right away, and if they don't show up they'll be deserters.'

'I'm sorry, Mama.'

'It's only natural. And there's Alice's husband, who's in the cavalry of the line. They're the ones who ride out ahead of the lines. He once explained it to me without realizing it would soon be happening.'

She bent over and kissed him listlessly, with her mind elsewhere.

'I wonder if Vladimir will come to say good-bye to me.'

He came in the evening, in service uniform, with his pack on his back. He seemed unimpressed by the events.

'Hello, Mama. Hello, you.'

He kissed them on both cheeks.

'I've got to get going. Have to be at the Gare de l'Est. This is no day for missing the train. See you both soon. Don't worry, we'll beat them!'

A blonde woman, heavily made up and wearing high heels, was waiting for him in the street and took his arm. Shopkeepers brought him various things, one a cheese, another half a bottle of cognac, which he crammed into his pack.

The florist handed him a carnation, and Vladimir stuck it into the end of his rifle. When he disappeared at the foot of the street, Gabrielle left the window where she had been leaning her elbows and sat down at the table.

'Hand me the wine, will you, Louis?' she murmured.

That evening she got drunk alone, dismally drunk, while groups of young people paraded in the street screaming patriotic songs and drinking songs.

Chapter Two

The war left few traces on Louis, some memories relating mainly to his family. No one at home had ever read the papers, nor did they now, since only he and his mother were left in the

274

flat. He tried to read them, because he heard people talk about communiqués. He tried again later, when he was older, but never managed to be interested in the news. It was just words and phrases that had no effect on him. He couldn't feel or smell or touch them. There was no vibration.

Perhaps if he had been four or five inches taller in 1914, he would have been swept up in the general frenzy and have volunteered without waiting to be called up. Then, in the trenches, the war would have entered him, would have been part of his being and, as must have been the case of so many others, would have accompanied him throughout his life.

In the Rue Mouffetard, the frenzy, apart from some singing and a few bouts of drunkenness, was practically non-existent. It was a street in which people's main concern was to get enough to eat every day, and, for those who had children, to feed them.

At Les Halles, one saw fewer and fewer young men, then middle-aged men started leaving, but the rhythm remained the same, cabbages remained cabbages, poultry was still poultry, and one continued to see sides of beef hanging from hooks and the little train from Arpajon waiting by the sheds.

He was to retain only a confused memory of historic dates, of battles whose names would be carved in stone, and he mixed up the names of the generals.

His first real memory of war, apart from the general mobilization, which he had experienced only from his window, was his sister's arrival one evening while his mother and he were having dinner together in the kitchen. Her eyes were red and dazed, and he thought her gestures theatrical. She had rushed from the doorway straight to her mother, who had had just time enough to catch her in her arms.

'Mama! Oh, Mama! It's awful . . .'

It was false. His sister wasn't like that. His mother had also, on the first day, adopted a tragic attitude that didn't become her. Both of them were perhaps sincere, but they exaggerated their gestures, like people who made speeches.

Alice sobbed on a bosom where he had never seen her lay her head, and she sobbed without speaking. Finally she pulled away and held out an official-looking paper.

'It's to inform me that Gaston's dead. He was killed in a

275

forest near Charleroi, in Belgium, while he was on patrol.'

To Louis, this Gaston Cottereau was a stranger, and had he lived he would have remained on the fringes of the family, just like young François, who was his sister's son but did not resemble any of them physically.

He nevertheless became conscious that evening that war really killed. For him, this was the first casualty.

'My poor child! You married at the wrong time, but there was no way of knowing, nobody could have known. Where's François?'

'I left him with a neighbour, a woman whose husband's also at the front.'

'What are you going to do?'

'I don't know yet. It seems we'll be given help, a pension. We'd hardly finished setting up the flat.'

Then she became aware of her brother's presence.

'You, Louis, you're lucky!'

She had no need to be more precise. She was alluding not to his age but his shortness. He did not remain present at the whining of the two women, who were hardly sincere, in any case not Gabrielle, who had never liked either Gaston or his family.

He left for work. In Samuel's shed nothing had changed, except that an office clerk and two stock clerks had left and been replaced.

His colours, as he said, for he never uttered the word 'paint', remained his basic concern. The war was reflected in his work in the form of flags, bugles gleaming in the sun, soldiers in red trousers, shoulder braid. Later, when the uniforms were changed, he liked the blue, which he put into several pictures.

His sister did not stay in Paris long. Gaston's parents, still remembering perhaps the Franco-Prussian War of 1870, imagined that the capital was starving and the Parisians were eating rats. They had written to Alice from their village in Nièvre asking her to come to Saint-Aubin, where they had a farm and three or four cows and where the child would be sure of being properly fed.

'I've found someone who'll rent my flat, the wife of an English officer who has some post or other in Paris.'

276

After a little more than a year, Louis moved to the glass cage, for another employee had been mobilized. He was earning a hundred francs a month. His mother too was taking in more money than before the war, and they felt almost rich.

As their occupations obliged them to play hide-and-seek and one couldn't light a fire in midsummer just to prepare coffee or fry two eggs, they had a gas ring installed next to the old stove, which of course would be used in winter, and after a few weeks they were so used to it that they couldn't understand how they had ever been able to do without it.

When they had dinner together, Gabrielle would sometimes fall into a melancholy reverie. It was not the violent, spectacular grief of the early days, but it was more impressive.

'Vladimir doesn't write to us. Just two little notes, simply to say that he's well and that he's been made a corporal. I'm sure he writes to that girl, who he never bothered to introduce to us and whose name we don't even know.'

Nor did they know what Vladimir had lived on between the end of his military service and the declaration of war. When he returned from his long stay in Toulon, he was a different man. He was tanned, had new mannerisms, and made gestures he had never made before, and he looked more aggressive than ever.

'Are you going back to work for Monsieur Brillanceau? I met him two months ago, and he's ready to take you on again.'

'He's likely to wait a long time.'

His smile was derisive. He had always been derisive, but not in that casual way.

'What do you expect to do?'

'I don't know. I've rented a room and I'll see what comes up.'

He made no mention of the possibility of living at home again.

'You'll stay in the neighbourhood at least?'

'I've seen enough of the neighbourhood. I'm going to live in the Rue de Clichy.'

She was timid in his presence, as if she were afraid he would get angry and go away for good.

'Will you come to see us?'

'Of course.'

'Will you leave me your address?'

'When it's definite, I'll let you know. For the time being, I'm living in a hotel.'

'Isn't it very expensive?'

'I manage.'

All the same, he had dropped in for a moment to kiss her before leaving for the front, but not without accompanying the girl who was waiting for him on the pavement.

Two brief notes in more than a year! He must have had leave, like the others, and he had certainly been in Paris.

Of course, the family was not in the habit of being effusive, and Gabrielle had led her life her own way without bothering much about the children as soon as they were old enough to stand on their hind legs.

Louis discovered little by little that the bonds between Gabrielle and her children were stronger than he had thought. Her attitude did not resemble the mother love that he heard people talk about or that one learned about in school.

It was rather as if, without her realizing it, the umbilical cord that had connected her with her children had never been completely cut.

'It's funny, Louis, that you've started to paint.'

She rarely spoke to him about his pictures. He was sure she glanced at them when she got home, but they bore so little resemblance to her idea of what a painting was that she preferred to say nothing.

'Are you planning to make it your profession?'

'It's not a profession.'

'There are some people who make a living at it. I used to know an old fellow who wore a big hat and a flowing polka-dot tie. He was a specialist.

'If I remember right, that was before you were born. I wasn't bad-looking in those days. He claimed I was beautiful, that I could earn my living as a model just by lying naked and not moving.

'I once went to pose for him in his studio near Saint-Germain-des-Prés, and he didn't even touch me. He hardly talked to me. I felt like laughing all the time, I don't know

278

why. It seemed funny to me to be all naked for hours in front of a gentleman who didn't try to paw me. He gave me five francs and told me to come back whenever I wanted. He made a good living and had, in addition to the studio, a nice flat, well furnished, with a big balcony.'

She felt like adding: 'You ought to paint like him.'

He was already doing better work with his touches of pure colours, especially since he had begun painting on canvas. The difficulty was still to make things that seemed to have no relationship 'hang together'.

He did not try to copy reality, a chair, a street, a woman, a tram, except as an occasional exercise, and he succeeded fairly well. But that was a mere matter of images. What he would have liked to get down on canvas was reality itself, as he saw it, or rather as it composed itself spontaneously in his mind.

For example, he had put little François in the middle of the schoolyard, alone, unsteady on his chubby legs. It was a winter scene, since there was snow, but he wanted the sky to be a summer sky, and a red and yellow tram, full of faces pressed against the windows, was going by in front of the wall.

He could not have explained. It was too complicated. The salesman in the shop in the Rue de Richelieu had urged him so often that he finally went to the Rue du Faubourg-Saint-Honoré and the Rue La Boétie where there were several picture galleries.

'You'll see the best Impressionists, Cézanne, Renoir, Sisley, Pissarro. Not long ago, people made fun of them, and now you've got to be very rich to buy one of their paintings. You'll also see the Fauves, Vlaminck, Derain, and others whose names I've forgotten. One of them's an odd type, a half-tramp, who spends his life in the Montmartre bars. You can recognize his paintings a mile away.'

He had looked at the canvases exhibited in the windows and was annoyed with himself because they left him cold. They were good, of course. He felt crushed by the craftsmanship of those painters who knew where to put their spots of colour and how to give them their full value.

He was nevertheless disappointed. What he saw did not resemble what he was looking for. If he showed his paintings to the salesman, the latter would lose interest in him. Louis had finally learned his name because he had heard someone call him from the back of the shop: Monsieur Suard. He was a friend of a painter named Marquet and of another one who was younger, Othon Friesz.

'Some of them come from quite a distance to get their supplies in our shop because we have foreign brands, especially Dutch, which are hard to find in Paris.'

'Are they pure?'

'In my opinion, they fade less rapidly. The trouble with most paints is that they start getting dark, and present-day painters don't want to varnish their work. Besides, how can you varnish paint that's laid on thick?'

He was learning words, unsuspected techniques.

'Haven't you ever been tempted to work in a studio, Julian's, for example? They have good models and a teacher who gives advice.'

Monsieur Suard was as delighted by Louis's naïveté about painting as by his passion.

'It's not a matter of schools, like the Fine Arts. You go whenever you like. You bring your materials, set yourself up in front of an easel that's not being used, and you draw or paint the model. You pay by the hour.'

Louis had almost asked: 'What model?'

But remembering his mother and the painter with the big hat who specialized in street-sellers, he had understood.

'There's a studio not far from here, in the Rue du Faubourg-Montmartre.'

He had gone there one morning with his box. The light was as cold as at certain hours in Monsieur Samuel's shed, except that you never saw the light, because the place had a northern exposure. The silence was impressive, sinister. Thirty or forty people, men and women, especially girls and middle-aged men, stood or sat in front of the easels around a wooden stand on which a naked girl with skinny thighs stood with her hands clasped at the back of her neck.

Some were painting, others drawing, erasing, drawing again, while an old gentleman with pince-nez and a goatee planted himself silently behind each in turn.

Occasionally he would point, without saying a word, to a charcoal stroke. Or else he would grab a girl's brush and with two or three touches correct the movement of an arm or position of a leg.

'Do you want an easel?'

'No, sir. Thank you.'

He could not have worked in that atmosphere and had no need of the model. Some day perhaps, if he had the courage, he would talk to Monsieur Suard about what he had in mind, but it was impossible to explain if it wasn't down on canvas.

When he finished a picture, he would, in most cases, scrape it down with a palette knife, a smooth flexible instrument that was voluptuous to handle. After a few days of drying, he would spread a layer of zinc white and so have a new canvas, which saved him money.

'Louis, I wonder what's become of the twins.'

He too thought back to the past every now and then. At times he would conjure up the image of Emilie, of whom no one had spoken for years. His mother had precise memories about each of them, but they were not the same as his, so that when they had these conversations they did not echo each other.

'Do you remember the day when a distinguished-looking gentleman with a decoration in his lapel came in with Olivier in his arms? Olivier was unconscious. Guy and he had been playing. They'd been jumping over a bench with their feet together. Olivier missed and his head hit the pavement so hard that the gentleman, who was reading on the same bench and who might very well have been annoyed with them for disturbing him, thought he was dead.'

'Was I born then?'

'I think so. Of course! How stupid I am! You must have been at least six, since you were going to school.'

He had no recollection of the incident, any more than his mother remembered most of the events that, for him, constituted the history of the family.

'The thing that consoles me is knowing they weren't unhappy.'

He would look at her without understanding, disturbed at the fact that other memories were being mixed with his, for he no longer felt so sure of himself. They were like false notes.

'Have you forgotten that they ran away a first time and were found in a goods train, in Rouen?'

'I remember . . .'

'If the police inspector . . .'

He would listen abstractedly, irritated, unwilling to hear all the details again.

'The second time . . .'

'I know, Mama.'

She would glance at him reproachfully.

'I had to see a doctor last week because I had pains in my stomach. I didn't say anything to you about it so as not to worry you and because it was a woman's thing.'

He had heard allusions to venereal diseases and wondered whether his mother had one, which made him blush.

'It's unimportant. He was a very nice man, very understanding. He asked me questions about my life. I told him about the twins and admitted that what happened must have been my fault.

'He swore it wasn't, that neither I nor the kind of life we led had caused them to run away. Doctors know all about that kind of thing, and now I understand why the inspector was a little lenient with them.

'It's in their blood. They take after their father, who didn't get along anywhere and who ended up you know how.

'I'm sure those two were Heurteau's. I've every reason to think so. About Alice, I couldn't swear, but I'd rather she weren't.'

He was obliged to sit and listen. It made him uncomfortable. He was interested, of course, but he would have preferred that she should not speak of such things.

'There are children who run away five or six times a year. Even when they're locked up, they find a way of getting out and some get killed trying to escape by the window, like sleep-walkers. Did you know that?'

'No.'

'The thing that reassures me is that in most cases they get over it when they're older. It gives me hope of seeing them some

282

day. Don't forget they're over twenty. They ought to be in the army. I wonder why we've never had a notice from their draft board.'

'You know, Mama, all the red tape . . .'

'All the same, it's funny. When it comes to military service, they usually know how to find people. They have enough military police for that!'

That must have been in 1916. The war had been going on for two years and people were no longer surprised.

Had Gabrielle had a premonition? A few days after that conversation, she received an official paper, as had Alice two years before, informing her that her son, Sergeant Olivier Heurteau, had been killed in front of Fort Douaumont in the course of a dangerous operation for which he had volunteered and that he had been awarded the Distinguished Service Medal posthumously.

The personal effects that had been found on him would be sent to the family later.

What intrigued both of them was that the African Battalions had a bad reputation, or at least had had before the war, for they were composed of troublemakers, delinquents, pimps from the Porte Saint-Martin district, Montmartre and elsewhere, of boys who had been in reformatories and those who had had a police record before the age for military service.

It was also odd to have news of only one of the redheads, and Gabrielle would not have been surprised to learn that they had died at the same time.

Olivier's personal effects arrived shortly thereafter. He had been the leader of the pair, the one who looked older, whereas Guy, who was as tall as his twin and had the same build, seemed milder, hesitant, and followed his brother around like a shadow.

Gabrielle and Louis learned from the service certificate that Olivier had volunteered for the African Battalions long before the war, with his 'parents' consent', from which they inferred that he had faked his mother's handwriting.

His address was given as the Rue d'Oran and his occupation

283

as that of agriculturist. His effects included a switchblade knife with a horn handle. The blade had been sharpened often and he must have used it in North Africa and in the trenches. An old wallet, which had lain in the mud, contained only a few bank notes, some postage stamps – why stamps, since soldiers' letters were post free? – a postcard from Algeria to an address written in an almost illegible handwriting and signed with a name that was undecipherable. Above the signature were drawn a star, a heart, and an animal that could have been a goat as well as a horse.

A blurred photograph was perhaps the key to this message, for it showed a young Bedouin woman squatting on the ground next to a donkey that was loaded with two baskets.

She looked about thirteen or fourteen and had a tattoo mark in the middle of her forehead, unless it was only a stain on the print. Her big gaping eyes were looking straight ahead with an expression of adoration. 'Don't you think she's his girl friend?'

'I don't know, Mama.'

'I don't think they're allowed to marry there while they're still in the army, especially a native woman. Besides, if he were married, she's the one they'd have sent his things to.'

The remaining items were a pipe, a pig-bladder pouch in which there was still a little tobacco, and a tinder pipe-lighter.

'Guy must have joined up the same time as he, in the same regiment. I'm going to inquire at the War Department. I'll go myself, because if I write to them they won't answer.'

She spent a whole day there, not only at headquarters, but in the offices scattered all over Paris. When she got home, she was in a state of exhaustion but was still hopeful.

'I'll find the right door sooner or later. I've never seen so many women, young and old, queueing in yards and hallways. A lieutenant, who resembles the police inspector, promised me that within a week he'd have the list of those who volunteered for the African Battalions in 1912.'

She smiled, and there was a certain pride in her expression.

'You know, Louis, it was wrong of us to think there are only criminals in the African Battalions. I asked the lieutenant. He agreed that they were made up mainly of troublemakers and boys who'd been sentenced.

'But it's different in the case of those who sign up, boys attracted by adventure and a hard life around the desert and who sleep in a tent more often than in a barrack room. He said to me, "At the front, they're our best soldiers." He knew one personally who'd become a second lieutenant and after ten years of service became a priest.'

She did get a reply, not after a week but after about a month. It was brought by an orderly, as if mail from the Ministries was too important or confidential to be entrusted to the post office. The letter confirmed the fact that Olivier Heurteau had enlisted as a volunteer on 21 October 1912, but stated that there was no record of a Guy Heurteau in the African regiments for that year or the following years.

'Do you think that means he's dead?'

'I don't know, Mama. They might have separated. Maybe Guy fell in love with a girl and married her.'

'He couldn't have done that without my consent. He wasn't of age.'

'Olivier couldn't join up either. Maybe Guy went to live in another country, in South America, for example. When he lived here, he often talked about South America.'

She shook her head sceptically. It remained a mystery to her, and Louis could tell from certain silences and a certain vague look that would suddenly come over her face that the matter preyed on her mind.

Louis was becoming more and more friendly with Monsieur Suard, and he would sometimes drop into the stationery shop in the Rue de Richelieu when he saw that the salesman was not busy, just to chat with him, without buying a tube of paint.

'It's too bad I married so young and had children right away. I have three, one of them a girl your age.

'And even so. I'm glad she's a girl. Otherwise the draft board would soon be after her!

'Remember, I'm not complaining. I myself once dreamed of being a painter. That's why I asked to be assigned to this department.

'Later, who knows, I may even become a picture dealer, I may open a small gallery. Not with big names, because that requires too much capital and there's no merit in it. With young painters that I discover. I already have a few canvases that some customers let me have cheap . . .'

Was it out of graciousness, so as not to disturb Louis, that he added:

'When you're satisfied with what you're doing, I'd be glad to see one of your paintings.'

'I'll never be satisfied. You know well enough that I'm not a real painter.'

At the beginning of 1917 – at any rate, it was the winter when it was so cold and there was a shortage of coal, the winter too when there was talk of mutiny of troops and soldiers' being shot as an example – at the beginning of 1917, Gabrielle learned from a street-seller in the Rue Saint-Antoine who had formerly worked in the Rue Mouffetard that Vladimir was in Paris.

The woman claimed she had seen him in the boulevard, not far from the Rue Montmartre, where she had gone to visit her daughter who was a saleswoman.

'I swear to you, Gabrielle, I wasn't mistaken. Don't forget that I knew him when he was a tot and that later he used to swipe peaches from my cart. He was wearing a marine's uniform, with a beret, and he had a bandage on his head. People turned around to look at him and he seemed proud of it. I yelled out to him, "Hey Vladimir! Don't you recognize your friends any more?" And he yelled back, "Hello, Aunt Emma!" That's what he used to call me when you and I were always together, with our carts side by side.'

'And to think he didn't come to see me!'

'If he was wounded, he's on sick leave. He has all the time in the world.'

'Meanwhile he's living at that awful woman's place.'

'It's just as if he were married.'

'You're right. I'm getting jealous of my children. His sister hasn't written to us once in the last two months and we've received only a photograph of her son.'

Vladimir came and even presented his mother with an oriental jewel, a charm that probably was not made of gold but that she thereafter wore proudly on her neck. He spoke of the Balkans, of Constantinople, as if he were talking about Clignancourt or the Porte des Lilas.

'Have you heard that Olivier's dead?'

'No.'

'He was a sergeant and got the Distinguished Service Medal. I have it here. Do you want to see it?'

'I've seen so many of them! What about Guy? Dead too?'

'We have no news of Guy. Nobody knows what's become of him.'

He could have said of the dead what he had just said of Distinguished Service Medals: he had seen so many!

'What about you, with your wound, didn't they give you a decoration?'

Louis shuddered when he saw his brother's face and heard the sound of his cutting voice:

'I'm not the kind of man they give medals to. Even if I were dead, like Olivier.'

'Don't you want to let me have your address in Paris, in case I have news of Guy?'

He merely answered evasively:

'I'll be back to see you before I leave.'

'When are you going?'

'When the doctors decide.'

'Is it serious?'

'A hole in the skull. They removed what they could, but there's still a piece of shrapnel somewhere.'

'Do you still have pain?'

'Occasionally.'

One afternoon by pure chance, Louis ran into an old acquaintance on the Pont Saint-Michel: the huge, colossal Monsieur Pliska, who now had a beard and whose blond hair flowed down the back of his neck. Louis would not have been sure it was he if the Czech giant had not recognized him and crushed his hand.

'Little Louis, eh? What happening?'

His French was hardly better than in the past, and he still accompanied his words with gesticulations and questioning looks.

'Your mother, Gabrielle? Gabrielle, yes?'

He remembered the pretty redhead with whom he had lived for almost two months, but he was no longer sure of her name.

'Brother Vladimir. Little sister. Big girl now?'

'She's married and has a son.'

'Me, very hard, lots trouble, because me foreigner. Two years in camp concen . . . how you say? Hard word. Concentra . . .'

'Concentration.'

'In nice country. Sun. South France, but pointy wire.'

'Barbed wire.'

'Yes. Huts bad. Soup bad. Lots little bugs. Fleas, you say? And in hair?'

'Lice?'

'Everybody lice. Now over. Me studio. Come see studio. Heavy work. Sculpture. Dealers come see sculpture. Not buy, but come see.'

Louis went with him as much out of curiosity as out of fear of offending him. They went by tram to the Boulevard Montparnasse. Pliska took him to the Rue Campagne-Première, where they entered a rather recently built house.

'Here. Lift. You know?'

There was indeed a lift, which carried them to the top floor, the sixth, where Pliska took out a key and proudly opened his door.

'My studio.'

Louis was dazzled. The room was vast and was flooded with light that streamed in through a large window that separated it from the street. Part of the sloping roof was also glazed.

'Magnificent, is no? Me work.'

He took off his jacket, waistcoat, and tie with the air of a wrestler challenging spectators from the platform of a fair booth.

Louis's gaze was attracted by a big block of clay on a rotating pedestal in the middle of the room.

'See? When finished, terrific. Terrific one says?'

For the time being, it suggested a couple locked in embrace. Louis could recognize human shapes, but without being able to tell what was a leg or an arm. He was moved. He looked at it eagerly and was filled with a sweet feeling. There was, in particular, a rather heavy mass, a rump which was already definitely modelled and which gave him a deeper impression of sensuality than the rump of a live woman.

'To sculpt very hard. Very much hard. Here . . .'

On a plain wooden slab stood a horse and rider made of bits of iron that looked as if they had been picked up in a workshop.

'Don Quisote.'

'Don Quixote?'

'Yes. Funny. No. Not funny.'

He frowned. His limpid eyes clouded over.

'Dealers say funny. Me not funny. Me and dealers . . .'

He made a show of throwing them through the glass and into the street from his top floor.

'Much work. Much make love. Not much eat because not sell. So me carry beef.'

'At Les Halles?'

'Halles, yes. Know Halles?'

When he learned that Louis worked there too, he wanted to have a drink with him and opened a bottle whose shape and label recalled an old Christmas.

'Not drink?'

'No. Too young.'

'Me, drink too much. Not good.'

He beat his chest like a gorilla and burst out laughing.

'See you Halles. You come back. You see love finished.'

What he called love was the half-ton block of clay in the middle of the studio. Although they worked so near each other at night, it was a long time before they met again, for Les Halles had sharply defined areas and varied activities, and Pliska's working hours, for example, did not coincide with Louis's.

On being promoted and getting an increase, Louis had locked himself up in a glass cage and could no longer, as in the beginning, thread his way through the market carrying messages from Monsieur Samuel to the agents in the neighbouring streets or in the big sheds.

It was unquestionably as a result of his meeting with the Czech that the idea of a studio took root in him, and from then on, when he walked in the street, he would make sure whether or not there was a big glass window or, better still, a workshop at the back of a yard.

His turn came to receive an official paper. He had to report to the district office on March 12 with a copy of his birth certificate and appear before the draft board. He did not mention it to his mother, who had been out when he found the envelope under the door. He spent an anxious week, not in fear of being declared fit for service, but at the thought that he would have to appear naked in front of men.

He was the only one in the family who was modest. His mother and sister were not at all ashamed of their nakedness, which they exhibited with a casualness that was perhaps not unmingled with satisfaction. Vladimir had begun to hide his sex organs only when he was about thirteen, and as for the redheads, they had paid no attention to them at all.

Louis had never moved his bowels in the pot, except in very early childhood, of which he had no memory.

Even though it was freezing cold on the stairs in winter, even though it was menacingly dark, just as it was in the yard, he nevertheless would go down at night when he would start feeling sick as a result of holding it in.

And when he was bathed in the tub, he always held a flannel with which he hid his genitals as long as he was not sheltered by the soapy water.

There were at least forty of them gathered in a dusty room. There were no clothes-hooks, but they were none the less ordered to undress.

'Be quick about it, boys. Another batch is due at eleven.'

He was more embarrassed when he recognized former schoolmates, three or four of them, including the lawyer's son whose name he had forgotten, the one who had left the state school to enter a private one.

'Well, well!' he exclaimed. 'The little saint!'

A wag called out, after looking Louis up and down:

'Are you sure it's not a girl?'

'We used to take him for a boy, but he's had time to change. Let's see your tool, little saint, so we can tell what you really are.'

Covering himself with his hands, he tried to turn his back to them.

'He'll have to show it when he goes by. And you know what the medical officer's going to do? He'll yank your balls and if he doesn't like you, he'll stick a finger up your behind. Don't think

I'm making it up. My brother was called up last year and tipped me off. Why do they call you the little saint? Do you go to confession every morning? Do you want to stay a virgin till you're married?'

The door finally opened into a larger room where men were sitting at a table covered with a green cloth. He could not distinguish them from each other. Although he did not shut his eyes, he saw only shadows, silhouettes, two horizon-blue uniforms, and a line of naked bodies.

'Step up. Stand up straight. Straighter than that. What are your hands fiddling with?'

One of the men in uniform announced:

'Five feet, three-quarters of an inch.'

There was a roar of laughter.

'Come here,' ordered the doctor.

Perhaps at the rate men were being consumed at the front, height no longer mattered? He was not afraid of being hit by a bullet, of being killed by a shell. What frightened him was the brutality, the orders that were rapped out in a snarling voice, the obligation to do what was ordered, without discussion.

He had made up his mind that if he were given a gun he would never fire it, or fire only in the air.

The medical officer dug his fingers between Louis's ribs, between his shoulder blades, then, after feeling his muscles, declared:

'Unfit. Rejected.'

He was pushed out of the room.

'What are you waiting for, my boy? Didn't you hear the doctor? The country doesn't want you.'

He let three days go by before saying to his mother, at dinner, in an expressionless tone:

'You know, Mama, I've been rejected.'

'That's no misfortune. That way, I'm sure of having one of you.'

Louis looked at her with the vague smile that intrigued them all and that did not necessarily reflect joy or gaiety.

His war was over.

Chapter Three

His mother continued going to Les Halles every morning to stock up, but she was less often heard joking aloud in her clear, vibrant voice. He remembered the time when he would recognize its brightness amidst the hubbub in the glass-roofed warehouse, as one recognized from a distance the brightness of her hair.

His grandmother too continued pushing her cart through the dark streets in the early hours of the morning, but there were more and more days when she did not turn up and when Gabrielle, between clients, would go up to her room at the foot of the street, near Saint Médard's, to make sure she wasn't ill and didn't need anything.

Louis hardly knew that room. He had been in it two or three times, when he was little, and remembered it as being dark and crowded with furniture. There was a dining-room sideboard through whose upper doors, which were made of glass, he could see crockery. There were a table and chairs with fake-antique carvings, greenish velvet curtains with satin-stitch embroidery, and also knick-knacks, vases, statuettes, porcelain sweet dishes.

'Be careful, Louis. The last time your brother Vladimir came, he broke another saucer that I was very fond of. They're souvenirs.'

The smell of the room was different from the one at home, and he suspected the old woman of not liking to have visitors, not even her grandchildren. He had always considered her old, but she was not so very old, for the girls in the family had children early.

In the spring of 1919 Gabrielle must have been fifty-four. Her brother, the butcher, whom they pretended to ignore, though his shop was in their street, and who ignored them too, did not know that Louis was his nephew. He had been the old lady's first child. She had had him when she was about sixteen.

She had grown very thin and was becoming eccentric. Once,

292

when she had not turned up at Les Halles for a whole week, Gabrielle reassured Louis, who was worried.

'Don't be upset about Grandma. She could live on her savings. She's put aside quite a pile. She's never spent a penny. And she didn't help me in the beginning either, even when I was in a tight spot. She'd say to me, "Every man for himself! One brings up one's children until they're old enough to manage. After that, they can fend for themselves. I don't expect anything from anyone, and I have no desire when I'm old to sue you and your brother to make you give me an allowance." '

It was between eight and nine in the evening. Louis and his mother were both at home.

'What do you feel like eating, Louis? An omelette? A steak?'

'An omelette, Mama, with cheese, if there is any.'

They would sit at the table facing one another, and there would be long silences. One would have thought they were observing each other. Actually they were, or at least Louis was.

For years he had been seeing his mother with the same eyes, and she had always seemed to be the same age. Though she had hardly changed physically, for her body was still firm and her face unlined, he had the impression that a kind of greyness had invaded her.

In the past, she had never looked sad or preoccupied, and even the death of Emilie had dampened her spirits for only a few days. All in all, she had taken things as they came, enjoying what was good in life, contenting herself uncomplainingly with what was less good and ignoring the rest as if it had not existed.

Was it because her children were growing up and seeing her with new eyes that she had suddenly stopped receiving men? Yet she was still having them up when Vladimir was fifteen.

Her life had dimmed. To talk in terms of painting, like Monsieur Suard, shade was forming, dull spots on the canvas.

When Louis took her out from time to time on Saturday night, she no longer wore the lavender-blue dress which he had been so fond of. Fashion had changed with the war. Petticoats had little by little disappeared, as had heavy boned corsets, dresses that swept the ground, and shoes that were laced half-way up the leg.

Women displayed not only their ankles but half their calves and wore military-style jackets above their skirts. This caused so little astonishment that Louis had to make an effort to remember pre-war fashions.

She still undressed in his presence.

'You don't mind my going out?'

'Why, Mama?'

'You may think I'm too old.'

'You'll never be old.'

'Doesn't it bother you to see your mother running to dance halls like a bitch in heat?'

He smiled at her in a way that was meant to be reassuring.

'You, you never go out.'

'I go out during the day.'

'I've never seen you with a girl friend. Do you have one?'

'No, Mama.'

'Why not? A boy of nineteen needs women.'

He realized what was worrying her, and it reminded him of the jokes in the office of the draft board.

'Don't be afraid. I'm a man.'

She had not lost the habit of coming straight to the point.

'Do you do it?'

'Sometimes.'

'You could have it for nothing, as much as you want, especially as most men are at the front. If only you knew how women squabble over soldiers on leave!'

'It would take up too much of my time.'

That was not quite true, it expressed only part of a truth which was too complicated, which he was not sure he understood.

The memory of his impotence at the sight of a tangle of black hair had kept him for a long time from trying again. His appetite rarely had a keen enough edge to awaken his torment.

Erotic fantasies sometimes prevented him from falling asleep, as they did everyone, but he had found a method of making the physical need less acute. He made an effort at times to compose extravagant images, to see them as street scenes, as spots of colour, to surround them with other details, and to create in his mind a picture of which he could have reproduced every detail.

There was a picture which he had a desire to paint but which he could not work on at the time because his mother would see it and he was ashamed of it.

Its colours would be as gay and bright as those he ordinarily used and yet, in advance, he entitled the composition 'War'.

He would start on it as soon as he had a studio, especially since the picture would be rather big. The vista would be that of the Champs-Elysées, with the greenery of the rows of trees and with bright houses whose details need not be visible, except for a profusion of flags at the windows.

The crowd would be represented by black spots dotted with blue, white, and red.

The important thing was the parade. As for the title, he hesitated between 'War' and 'The Parade', waiting for the canvas to be painted before deciding.

Ranks of soldiers, bigger than the crowd. He did not mind disproportion in his works among the figures or objects.

Naked soldiers, some of them rosy, others ghastly pale, as at the draft board. Each of them would carry a rifle and a peaked cap or helmet – he didn't know yet.

An officer, also naked, resembling the doctor, would be caracoling on a horse in front of them. They would be marching towards the Arc de Triomphe, except that it would be replaced by the dark and monumental sex organ of a woman whose legs were spread.

It would be hard to achieve. He probably would never be able to bring it off. Yet he had succeeded with a painting almost as complicated which he called 'The Little Train from Arpajon' and which, in his mind, was meant to epitomize Les Halles.

He had spoken about 'The Little Train from Arpajon' to Monsieur Suard, who said he would like to see the painting.

'As soon as I find a studio.'

'There are some available ones in Montmartre.'

'That's too far away.'

Too far away from his mother, of course, for he would go to see his mother every day, most likely would have dinner with her. He did not know how the matter could be arranged, and he foresaw that it would be painful. The actual reason for his rejection of Montmartre was that he would feel he was in a foreign country there, far away from the images he had been collecting unwittingly for nineteen years.

When he left the stationery shop one warm, humid afternoon, he had happened to pass a woman, not very tall, not young either, but plump, and with a pretty, smiling face. She had looked at him with complicity as she went by. The look was unlike that of the women who accosted men in the street. He had wondered whether he had quite understood. When he had looked back, she had too, the very same instant, and he had turned around and gone up to her.

She was wearing a blue suit with gilt buttons, and an overseas cap of the same colour, which was in fashion at the moment, was set on her curly hair.

She had not waited for him to make the first advances.

'Will you come along with me? I live only five minutes away.'

He warned her honestly that he was not rich.

'That doesn't matter. We'll arrange things.'

She looked to him about thirty. One could have taken her for a saleswoman in a store in the Grands Boulevards, or for a typist. She slightly resembled Mademoiselle Blanche, who worked with him every night in the glass cage and to whom he had never dared make a proposition, despite his desire to.

She lived in a cozy flat in a street that ran along the Palais Royal behind the Comédie Française. At the window, a canary was hopping about in a cage. The furniture and waxed floor were clean and bright.

'Do you often pick up women in the street?'

'It's the first time.'

Or almost the first. The other one had called to him and all he had had to do was follow her.

'How old are you? Sixteen? Seventeen?'

'Nineteen. People think I'm younger because of my height.'

'And because of your pretty little monkey face, eh? Do you know you've got a roguish look?'

296

She had taken off her hat and was undressing. Through an open door he could see a small dining-room beyond which must have been a kitchen.

'Are you embarrassed?'

'I don't know. A little.'

'Haven't you ever undressed in front of a woman?'

'Not entirely, no.'

'Haven't you ever made love?'

She understood his silence.

'It's nothing to be ashamed of, you know. Everyone has had to start some day. At your age, it was the same with me. I finally made up my mind. I was pretty scared and you'd be amazed if you knew what I imagined it would be like.'

She had thus far uncovered only her bosom, which was as beautiful as Gabrielle's, except that it did not have his mother's pearly sheen.

'Come and sit here.'

He sat down beside her on a couch with a yellow cover that later appeared often in his paintings.

'Do you like breasts?'

'Yes, I do.'

'Is that what excites you in a woman?'

She was speaking to him amiably, as if they were good friends who had known each other a long time.

'Don't think I'm in the habit of walking the streets. It looks like it, but it's very different. Haven't you ever been to what's called a massage establishment in the newspaper advertisements? Most of the time they're flats.

'I'm at Madame Georgette's in the Rue Notre-Dame-de-Lorette. It's quiet and discreet. There are only three or four of us, rarely five, and the customers are well behaved. They visit us regularly. You ought to drop in. One of the girls, Arlette, is just twenty-one.'

He stroked her breasts while looking at the canary in the cage, and she did not rush him. She kept talking casually. She unbuttoned his clothes little by little and he did not feel ashamed of being naked with her on the couch.

He wondered whether he wasn't going to love her. Entering

297

her was an experience unlike what he had imagined. It was very smooth and a feeling of well-being flowed through his whole body.

'Stay like that for a moment,' she whispered to him, stroking his hair and looking into his face with tender curiosity.

He was surprised, afterwards, that she did not act as if it were over, and they remained lying side by side, looking up at the ceiling and chatting.

'What do you do? I bet you're a student.'

'I work at Les Halles.'

'You? At Les Halles?'

'Some day I'll be a painter. I've started, but my work is bad.'

Later, she did not get dressed but put on a dressing-gown of the same blue as his mother's old dress.

He anxiously slipped his hand into his pocket, frightened at the thought that he might have to run home to get money as he had had to do the first time he bought paints.

'No. Not today. I've got another idea. Go down to the bakery. It's at the left, in the Rue des Petits-Champs. Buy some cakes, whatever you like, except chocolate cake, because chocolate doesn't agree with me. There's a grocery opposite and if you have enough money left get a bottle of port. There's no point in buying the most expensive, because I wouldn't know the difference. To me, port is port.'

Did she wonder whether he would come back or did she trust him? He read the names of the streets on the blue signs, for he was not familiar with the neighbourhood. She lived in the Rue Montpensier, and in order to get to the Rue des Petits-Champs he had to go by way of the Rue de Beaujolais.

He found the bakery and the grocery. Her odour was still on his skin, and it seemed to him that the passers-by could tell that he had made love twice.

She was leaning on the window-sill with her elbows, near the canary, when he returned with his packages, and the door opened the moment he reached the landing.

'You're very nice.'

Oddly enough, her name was Louise and his Louis.

'At Madame Georgette's, they call me Loulou.'

'May I call you Louise?'

'Would you rather? They say it sounds romantic, because of an opera.'

'My name is Louis.'

'Louis what?'

'Cuchas.'

'Is it a foreign name?'

'I don't think so. It's my mother's and grandmother's name and they were both born, just as I was, in the Rue Mouffetard.'

'Uncork the bottle. There's a corkscrew in the sideboard.'

They had gone into the dining-room. The sky above the roofs of the Palais Royal was lovely, very gentle, in spite of the heat.

She filled the glasses and handed him one, and he looked into her eyes as he drank. He did not like alcohol of any kind. It immediately made him dizzy.

'May I come back?'

'You seem to have liked it.'

'I did. I . . .'

He was at a loss for words, he felt moved, was filled with a sentiment he had had only for his mother or sister and once or twice, when they were younger, for Vladimir. He would have liked her to remain happy and gay, he hoped nothing unpleasant would happen to her.

She refilled the glasses.

'Here's to you!'

He rather liked the taste, as he did the warmth he felt in his chest and then, later, in his head. His eyes must have been shining and his ears getting red.

'You know . . .'

'A little while ago you called me Louise . . .'

'You know, Louise . . .'

It was really too difficult to thank her as he would have liked, as she deserved, to make her understand the importance of what had just happened, of the wonderful gift she had just made him and which would last all his life, he was sure it would.

There was no way of her guessing it. He would also have liked to tell her that Madame Georgette's didn't matter to him, that she was . . .

He got muddled, he spluttered, he had to control himself so that tears would not come to his eyes.

'You're a nice boy, Louis, very very decent. I'd like very much to see you again too, but don't come at the same time as today. It was just by chance that I didn't go to work this afternoon, because I had to see someone.'

'Who?' he dared ask.

'Now don't be jealous! It would surprise you if I answered that it was my uncle who comes from Tours once a month and invites me out for lunch. He's a wine-grower. My father was a wine-grower too. He was one of the first killed in 1914.'

'Like my brother-in-law.'

'He was in the cavalry of the line.'

'So was my brother-in-law.'

'I usually work until seven or eight and, since I have dinner in a restaurant in the Place Saint-Georges, I'm hardly ever here before ten or so.'

'What about in the mornings?'

'I sleep late. Then I wash and dress and make up and after that I do my shopping, because I prepare my own lunch.'

'I start work at ten in the evening.'

'Every evening?'

'Except Sunday.'

'On Sunday I go to the country with girl friends.'

'So?'

'Come and knock at my door from time to time around ten in the morning. You're not sleeping then?'

'I sleep just as well in the afternoon.'

'It doesn't matter if you find me in bed tired-looking and with my face shiny. Might as well empty the bottle, don't you think?'

He drank a third glass and half of a fourth, and when she accompanied him to the landing he was very animated.

'It's a day that ... a day that I ... Don't you think I'm ridiculous?'

'No. But it's time you had dinner. Your mother's waiting for you.'

He did not remember having told her that.

'All right, now go!'

And she looked at him pensively as he walked down the first flight.

He saw Louise again only twice. Each time he came with little cakes and a bottle of port. There were mornings when he left Les Halles feeling so sleepy that all he thought of was dropping into bed and did not even bother to lower the blind.

At other times, he was so eager to work on a painting that he could not get home fast enough.

The last time he went to see her, he did not feel that he was in form. He was acting from conviction. He rang the bell and waited. At first, there was no answer, though he heard voices inside. He rang again and there were footsteps. The door opened slightly and he caught sight of a man who had hastily slipped on Louise's blue dressing-gown.

'What is it?'

'Nothing,' he answered without insisting.

Nevertheless, a few months later he painted a picture that he entitled 'Portrait of Louise'. There was neither a face nor a body in it, only a window, a canary in a hanging cage, and, above the roofs of the Palais Royal, a sky of the softest and most dazzling blue he had ever obtained.

In October, a month before the famous Armistice Day, he feverishly awaited the evening conversation with his mother at the dinner table. He had a bad conscience, he felt like an executioner, he was ready to give in even before starting.

'I've got something to tell you, Mama.'

'You getting married too?'

When he went away, Gabrielle would be the only one left in the flat which had once been so full that everyone had to fight to defend his place.

'I'm not getting married. I don't think I ever will. I've found a studio. Wait! That doesn't mean I'm leaving you. What is it like now? We're never at home together except for dinner. Your working hours aren't the same as mine and we don't sleep at the same time. The studio will be the place where I work, you understand, the way Vladimir worked at Monsieur Brillanceau's. Remember, Mama, you didn't spend any more time with Vladimir or the twins than you do with me.'

'Where will you sleep?'

He blushed.

'First of all, I promise to come and have dinner with you every day. I'll spend my Sundays with you, either here or in my studio, where it'll be a pleasure to see you.'

'Are you taking your bed?'

'If you don't mind. I feel like working more and more. I don't go to sleep until I'm knocked out.'

'Where is it?'

'Not far from here, in the Rue de l'Abbé-de-l'Epée.'

'Is it expensive?'

'Thirty francs a month, with a lavatory.'

'Have you signed the lease?'

'I'll sign it tomorrow morning, if you allow me to.'

'And what if I don't?' she exclaimed with a burst of laughter. 'But of course, my little chick, of course I allow you to! Your wings and hackles have grown without my realizing it. And you, at the age of twenty, you blush at asking me to be free!'

'It's because of my painting, you understand?'

'Of course! Of course! It's always because of something.'

She was not crying and did not seem sad.

'When are you moving?'

'Tomorrow I'll move my things, my painting material and my canvases.'

'With my cart?'

'When you've finished work. I'll sleep here, and the day after tomorrow ...'

He imagined how the room would look. His mother's bed in the middle of the big empty space would seem tiny. He did not yet realize how lucky he was. A month later, what with the return of the men who were still in the army, with the arrival of foreigners who were going to invade Paris and the painters who would congregate in Montparnasse, he would have found nothing equivalent to his studio without having to pay a small fortune.

It was in the yard of an old house, or rather an ancient house, not an old house like theirs. It must have been a private mansion in the past, and it had been kept in repair during its two or three centuries of existence. The walls were of stone. The spacious arch led to a cobbled yard in the middle of which stood a linden tree.

There were flats only in the front part of the building. They were occupied by middle-class people, civil servants, a dentist, a young couple, of whom the husband was a prisoner in Germany and whose three- or four-year-old son played alone in the yard.

The low part of the building, at the rear of the yard, had no doubt been a stable in the past. It had been transformed into a glass-enclosed workshop that had been occupied for fifty years by the same craftsman, a cabinet-maker, who had specialized in repairing old, precious furniture and whose clients had been the best antique dealers in the Rue du Bac, Rue de Seine, and Rue Jacob.

'He died exactly a month ago, sir. I've been in the house only ten years, but he'd already been working at the back of the yard fifty years before and maybe even earlier. People say he was married for fifteen years and that from the day he became a widower no woman was ever seen entering his place, even to do the cleaning, because he preferred to do it himself.'

The concierge spoke on in that vein as she showed him around.

'When I think that furniture was piled up to the ceiling and that now the place is empty.

'A nephew in the provinces, his only heir, didn't even bother coming to Paris for the funeral and had everything sent to the auction-rooms, including a stove the like of which I've never seen, enormous, with bronze decorations, there was always a pot of glue heating on it.

'Look! He himself built this wall. It makes a nice room. Behind it is the lavatory. He didn't call in workmen for that either.

'You're quiet, aren't you? You look as if you were. I wouldn't want one of those painters who invite friends and models at night and make a racket until dawn. You seem rather shy.'

'You know, Mama, it even has electricity!'

Even in his wildest dreams he would not have imagined such luck. The next day, radiant with joy, he took his mother's push-cart and moved out his personal belongings, which did not weigh much. The following day, he took his bed apart and tried to centre his mother's against the wall.

The concierge had given him an idea while chattering away. For several days he prowled around the rooms of the Paris auction-rooms, obviously not those in which valuable paintings, jewels, and antique furniture were sold, but the rooms containing odds and ends. He ended by unearthing a cylindrical cast-iron stove which had escaped from some provincial station and which he got for a song, and a low armchair, that had no style at all but in which he felt very comfortable.

He kept his promise to have dinner with his mother.

'You'll have to tell me how much I owe you for my meals.'

'Don't be silly, Louis. I realize why they called you the little saint. Did I make you pay for the milk that came from my body?'

'This is different. If you had to keep feeding all your children . . .'

He felt like biting his tongue off. He had just said 'all'. Only three of the five were left. Nothing was known of Guy. Vladimir merely dropped in on her every now and then for a few minutes, while the same woman waited for him in the street.

Alice had written that, after thinking it over, she did not plan to return to Paris after the war, that she had sold the furniture in her flat to her English sub-tenant, and that perhaps she would remarry in the near future. She did not send a photograph of her son François, about whom she merely said that he was in good health.

'Will you come on Sunday, Mama? There won't be much furniture. I've bought only the necessary pots and pans. The kitchen is small, a kind of cupboard, but it has a gas ring.'

She came, dressed in the clothes she wore when she went dancing on Saturday nights. She looked at everything, sniffed the smell of varnish and old wood that lingered in the studio.

'It's nice,' she admitted, more to say something pleasant than out of conviction.

'Did you see my linden tree?'

For he had incorporated it into his universe, without knowing that, like the old cabinet-maker, he would be living in its shade for fifty years and more.

'It looks big, but when I become a real painter I'll need room.'

'Why don't you hang your pictures?'

The few canvases he had kept without scraping them down so as to use them again were on the floor, facing the wall:

'Later. They're not good enough. If I saw them all the time, I'd tear them up and might never paint again.'

She went to the studio only rarely, not feeling at home there, even less than if Louis had been living with another woman. 'I'm having a visitor on Saturday night, a man who knows about painting. It's the one from whom I buy my colours, and he's given me advice. He's a friend of lots of painters and plans to set up as a picture dealer some day.'

He did not suspect that in talking that way, quietly and with a smile in spite of his inner excitement, he was moving farther away from Gabrielle than Vladimir and Alice had done.

Yet the studio was only a five-minute walk from the Rue Mouffetard. His new street had the same kind of shops as those in the one he had left. The Boulevard Saint-Michel, down which his mother pushed her cart every morning, was a few feet away, a few houses off. Just opposite were the trees, benches, and iron chairs of the Luxembourg Gardens.

'It's only nine o'clock, Mama. I have time to walk you home.'

'Why should I make you go out of your way?'

He insisted. He was wrong, for that Sunday evening, with the shops closed the windows of the flats opened and the people leaning on the window-sill and looking out, he in turn felt like an outsider. It was no longer the street whose image was fixed in his memory, an image he needed, which must not be stolen from him. He had promised his mother to go home and have dinner with her every evening and he suddenly wondered whether he would have the courage to keep his word.

All at once, things began to happen fast. It began with the visit of Monsieur Suard, who was not surprised to see paintings hanging on the walls.

'May I look?'

As chance would have it, he picked up 'The Little Train from Arpajon', and his first reaction was one of surprise, perhaps agreeable surprise, perhaps disagreeable. For several minutes he kept looking back and forth from Louis to the painting, as if he were examining the relationship between a portrait and its model.

'The fact is . . . No! . . . I was about to say something silly. . . . I'll put it in a different way. . . . I don't suppose you've tried to reproduce reality . . .'

'Why?' asked Louis simply, though he was disturbed.

'You've tried to give an impression of Les Halles, haven't you?'

'Why Les Halles?'

'The little train . . . the shed on the left and that side of beef as big as the shed . . . the cabbages in the foreground . . .'

'I didn't try to paint Les Halles.'

'Then what *did* you try to paint?'

'I don't know. I started with the little train. That's why I've called the picture "The Little Train from Arpajon". It might have been elsewhere, in a street, even in the Champs-Elyseés.'

'In a certain way, anything that's represented is real.'

'Everything is real.'

'Have you seen any of the work of Odilon Redon?'

'No.'

'He too thinks that he paints reality, and in a sense he does. Do you dream much?'

'Not when I sleep.'

'But you do dream?'

'I don't know. I walk. I sit down on a bench. I look.'

'Thinking about what?'

'About nothing.'

Was he going to reply, like Louis's first teacher, the one with the flabby mouth, that it was impossible to think about nothing?

'And this picture, this one here, what title have you given it?'

'You know, the titles I give my pictures, they're meant just for me. The way, at first, one gives one's children a name, or a nickname that changes later. This little canvas is called, in my mind, "Portrait of Louise".'

306

'Are you in love with her?'

'Not any more.'

'Did she play an important part in your life?'

'Maybe. I think so. What I can't manage to get is a certain sparkle that I'm after, the quivering space between objects. You understand?'

'I understand. Monet spent his life trying to do that.'

Louis felt a pang of disappointment. He would have liked to be the first to have had that ambition.

'But Monet tried to achieve that result with light. The object was unimportant.'

'My cabbages, my beef, my little train are *very* important.'

Monsieur Suard seemed to be musing.

'You're an odd man. I ought to say an odd young man, because you're under twenty.'

'I'll be twenty in December.'

'Does your work at Les Halles tire you?'

'It takes up my time and obliges me to sleep part of the day.'

'What's that picture, the one bigger than the others?'

'It's a painting I botched. A sketch. I intended to do it again, larger, like a fresco, when I had enough room and money.'

He turned it around reluctantly, and Monsieur Suard was even more surprised than at the sight of the first painting.

'Don't tell me the title. I want to guess. "War." Am I right?'

'I hesitated between "War" and "The Parade". I may try it again some day. The soldiers will remain naked, wearing helmets or peaked caps. I prefer the cap, because of the colour.'

'What will you substitute for the woman?'

So Monsieur Suard had guessed that it was the monstrous female sex organ that bothered him. Did he also guess why?

'I don't know yet. Maybe the Arc de Triomphe?'

'Do you need this one in order to start work on the other?'

'No. I'll work without looking at it. I know it by heart.'

'Listen, Louis. Do you mind my calling you that?'

A few months later, Monsieur Suard was to start addressing him by the familiar *tu*, but Louis never reciprocated and for

307

many many years continued to call him Monsieur Suard.

'Of course not. I'd be delighted.'

'I'd like to buy this painting that you pretend to reject, which some day perhaps you will reject, but which I consider very important.'

'Why?'

'You're an artist and you don't have to understand. Perhaps it's better for you not to understand too much. German Expressionists worked along the same lines. They were intellectuals who knew where they were going, who were trying to express an idea. Did you know, when you were painting the soldiers, that they would be marching towards a monumental sex organ?'

'No, I didn't.'

'In your mind, towards what were they marching?'

'I don't know. At the draft board, we were naked. I added the rifle and the cap and instead of making us parade by the medical officer, I put in a lot more, in ranks.'

'That woman . . . No! Don't answer. I'm not rich. I know painters who haven't exhibited yet. I buy a picture from them from time to time. Let me confess something. Just between you and me. I've stopped smoking and having apéritifs in order to buy another painting when the opportunity occurred. I offer you a hundred francs for it. Fifty this month and fifty next. If, let's say in five years, your paintings are worth more, I promise to pay you the difference.'

'That's too much. I want to give it to you.'

'I know what I'm doing. Here's fifty francs. Before coming here, I was sure I'd buy something from you, but I didn't suspect it would be such a painting.'

'Why?'

' "The Little Train from Arpajon" will have more success, not right away, but in a few years. You see, Louis, you're neither an Impressionist nor a Fauve nor a Cubist. You're not an amateur either. If, as I hope, you remain yourself, it'll be hard to classify you. I don't quite understand either, but you've got something.'

'I can't manage to get down on canvas what I'd like to. I don't think I'll ever be able to.'

'Have you a piece of paper? It's raining and I want very much to take this painting with me.'

One day, shortly thereafter, Louis was sleeping in broad daylight, as he was in the habit of doing. It would have cost too much to buy curtains for a glassed-in bay twenty-five feet long and twelve feet high.

Someone was pounding at his door, and he did not immediately enter the world of reality.

'Monsieur Cuchas! Monsieur Cuchas! Wake up!'

And the voice of the concierge literally screamed:

'The war's over!'

He thanked her without opening the door, for he was wearing only a shirt and underpants. An uproar, including singing and the blowing of instruments, could be heard coming from the Boulevard Saint-Michel. He hesitated for a moment, barefooted on the cold floor, then went back to bed and fell asleep.

In the evening, he had difficulty in getting to Les Halles, where couples were dancing in the markets. There was no dancing in the shed in the Rue Conquillière, and Monsieur Samuel, whose stomach overflowed his trousers as usual, did not say a single unnecessary word. His face was ashen. He had just learned that his son had died of Spanish influenza at a military hospital in Amiens.

Monsieur was to die later, in the midst of work, in the midst of the crowd, in the midst of the hubbub, of a stroke of apoplexy.

Former employees who had been demobilized were entitled to their old jobs. The firm had been bought by two partners who knew nothing about the business and who began by not allowing push-carts, which they considered a nuisance and unprofitable, to enter the shed.

The street-sellers of the Rue Mouffetard scattered and either chose another wholesaler or preferred to prowl about looking for bargains.

Gabrielle was among the latter, so Louis no longer saw her during the night or at dawn.

He had left the glass office and gone back to the blackboard. At times he was so tired as a result of painting most of the day that he would get mixed up in the figures that were called out to him.

One of the partners, who had made a lot of money in scrap metal, was particularly foul-mouthed and had picked Louis as scapegoat. His name was Smelke and it was hard to identify his foreign accent.

Monsieur Suard, who had paid the remainder of the hundred francs, had taken 'The Little Train from Arpajon' to show it to two or three collectors whom the painting might interest. He was beginning to build up a clientele, not of rich people who bought, in galleries, the works of established artists but of people who cared enough about painting to buy pictures with the little extra money they had, doctors, lawyers, shopkeepers, clerks.

'I'm ashamed to tell you, Louis. Among the people I know, there's only one who's interested, but he can't give more than eighty francs.'

'That's a lot, isn't it?'

'If I were you, I wouldn't accept.'

'What if it made it possible for me to leave my job at Les Halles?'

'Well in that case it's different.'

'The Little Train from Arpajon' also was gone. A time was to come when full-size reproductions of it could be bought in most bookshops, not only in France but in foreign countries as well, even in America. The exact price of the reproduction was eighty francs.

Chapter Four

How long did he continue having dinner at his mother's home almost every day? The answer to that question, as to many others, depended on the period in which he wondered about it, for time seemed longer to him at the age of forty than at sixty. Events were placed in such or such a period, but their chronological order would sometimes vary.

His mother, who was to live on until after the Second World

War, kept making a reproach which he felt he did not deserve.

'If you'd stayed with me, if you'd kept coming to see me, I wouldn't be here with that lunatic and would have stayed in the good old Rue Mouffetard just as my mother did until she died.'

In 1945 she was living in a smart-looking cottage at Joinville, on the bank of the Marne.

'Léon's getting more and more impossible. Imagine, at his age and mine, he's becoming jealous. When he goes fishing, he fishes from in front of the house so as to keep an eye on me.'

She was over seventy and the Léon in question, her second husband, was six or seven years older. He did not look his age. He stood as straight, his shoulders were as broad and his flesh as firm as when Louis had met him for the first time.

Like the twins in the past, he had a square face and his hair was closely cropped, but it was all white.

Louis was sure that he had continued to have dinner alone with his mother for a long time and he could see himself bringing, when he had a little money, a dish that they were not in the habit of eating, a lobster, scallops in a shell, which had simply to be reheated, a cold chicken, a bottle of good wine or a small tin of fat goose liver.

Guy's letter dated from late 1919 or early 1920, and Louis and his mother had been sitting at the table. Léon had not yet entered the picture when she had taken it out of her bag.

'It's strange, Louis. You'll see. It's not his hand-writing, but he signed it.'

On the envelope were several Ecuadorian stamps.

Dear Mama,
'I suppose that now the war has been over for some time, letters are no longer censored and I can write to you without getting you into trouble. You'll be surprised to receive this letter, which I hope finds you all in good health, Excuse me for not writing to you myself. You know I was never very good at spelling since I didn't spend much time in school.

I have no news of Olivier or anyone else. I don't know if Olivier married his little Bedouin and if he still lives in Oran. When I left him, he spoke of joining the Foreign Legion or the African Battalions. I hope he didn't do such a foolish thing.

Maybe you'll find the city of Guayaquil on a map of South America. It's almost opposite the Galápagos Islands. Do you remember that at home Olivier and I often used to talk about the Galápagos Islands and you didn't believe me when I said there were huge turtles hundreds of years old and so big that two persons could sit on them?

Well, they exist. Olivier and I left with the idea of living on a desert island. Unfortunately, the boat on which we stowed away put in at Algeria, where we were discovered. Then we dreamed of making enough money to leave from Dakar.

We worked as labourers and at other jobs. Olivier met a little girl who begged in the street.

I admit that, for a Bedouin, she was very beautiful. Those people generally live in the mountains and are very proud.

I wonder how that one landed in Oran and why she held out her hand in the street, with her eyes covered with flies.

Olivier didn't want to go on. We argued and I went away alone. I got to Panama, which is a funny country, where I got a job on a freighter going down the Pacific coast.

I won't go into detail because it would take time and I had lots of adventures and hardships. If I started telling my life history, poor Dorothy would never finish writing this letter that I'm dictating to her. She's very educated. She's English and was born in Quito, the capital of Ecuador, where her father was consul.

He made her go to school first in Quito, then in Panama, where there's an American school, and after that he sent her to England, where she studied the natural sciences.

She's begging me, while I'm dictating this letter, not to talk about her so much and I'm sure she's writing down everything I say. She even worked for quite a long time at the museum. When she came back here, she was on a kind of mission.

I was still trying to get to the Galápagos. I would have had to hire a boat and I hadn't sufficient money. I worked as a lift-boy in a hotel, because they built an eight-storey hotel. I managed to get along until I met Dorothy, who's eight years older than I.

We were married in a few minutes by an English clergyman, so I've become a Protestant, but it's of no importance to either Dorothy or me.

I still don't understand how she could have fallen in love with a big brute who can hardly write and whom she had to teach everything.

We now live in a bungalow, which means a wooden house, very comfortable, with all improvements, twenty miles out of town. Since the road doesn't go any farther we live right in the bush.

It's hotter than in Africa. Plants grow amazingly fast and you'll be surprised to hear that we earn our living hunting butterflies, hummingbirds, and egrets, which we send to New York and London where we sell them at very high prices.

There are also certain lizards and certain birds that we catch alive and that zoos fight to get.

Dorothy attends to the correspondence and goes with me into the bush, where you have to be very careful not only because of the jaguars but particularly the insects.

We have a comfortable life. Three half-breeds look after the bungalow and prepare our meals. I speak Spanish and English almost better than French. The thing that makes me sad is that I won't ever be able to go to see you in France, where I'd be arrested as a deserter.

I hesitated when I learned that war was declared. The consul would have paid my fare.. He was angry with me when he realized that I preferred to stay here, and for years he pretended not to recognize me.

He has forgotten about it by now, calls me Troublemaker, and only last week came to our house for whisky. Dorothy and I have no children. Let us have news about all of you. The address is at the bottom of the page. San José is the name of the nearest village.

I kiss you with all my love. Forgive me for having gone away. I couldn't help it.

Your loving son,
Guy

At the age of more than seventy-five, Gabrielle still kept the letter in the biscuit tin, which she had taken with her to Join-ville. The Léon incident had occurred later, Louis was sure of it, in 1921 or 1922. She was still going to Les Halles. He had gone to see her at home one Sunday morning, at about ten o'clock, for she did not like either his studio or his paintings. He had found her *en déshabille,* sitting opposite a man touched with grey who seemed to be quite at home.

'Don't go away, Louis. It's not what you think. I want you to meet Léon, Léon Hanet. He's a foreman in a big plumbing firm in the Boulevard Voltaire. He's been a widower for ten years

313

and has two married daughters. One of them's the wife of a doctor.'

The man was wearing only trousers, a white collarless shirt, and a pair of old shoes on his sockless feet.

Gabrielle laughed with embarrassment.

'Imagine, Léon has got it into his head that he wants to marry me. He makes a good living and wants me to give up my push-cart.'

She in turn was betraying the Rue Mouffetard, like the rest of the clan. The others had gone off, of course, but it had never occurred to Louis that she would not remain in their home.

'He has a nice flat in the Boulevard Richard-Lenoir. What do think of the idea? Even though I keep telling him that I'm too old . . .'

She had remarried, discreetly, without telling anyone, and their former home was invaded by a family of Poles.

Later on, newspaper articles and even biographies of him related that during the long years when his work had been un-appreciated he had never had enough to eat and that he had hunted for food in dustbins.

It was untrue. The legend grew out of the fact that he had once spoken of the couple he had seen from the window in the Rue Mouffetard. He had added that he had later been curious to know what edible food was to be found in dustbins and had opened two or three as he walked by.

As for hunger, he attached no importance to it. He had never been gluttonous. Even when he had money, he would be satisfied with milk, hard-boiled eggs, and cheese. There were times, it is true, when he had to do without. Not for years, but occasionally.

There was also a tendency to include him among what was called the Montparnasse painters, who had invaded the four-teenth *arrondissement* after the war and who could be seen and heard, talking all languages, first at the Rotonde and on the terrace of the Dôme and late at the Coupole.

These cafés were frequented not only by painters and sculp-tors in odd get-ups, men and women alike, but also by writers, poets and critics whom, before long, tourists came to gape at.

Louis had spent a few hours a day over a period of a month

in a corner of the Rotonde, sitting in front of a cup of coffee and milk without ever saying a word to anyone.

He had recognized well-known painters there, men who, especially towards the end, always arrived accompanied by a court of aesthetes and pretty girls. Some of them had conspicuous cars which would be surrounded by onlookers.

Louis had not been involved in any group. Nobody in Montparnasse knew his name. He was only a short, thin young man with tousled hair and a contented smile.

Monsieur Suard had left the stationery shop in the Rue de Richelieu too late or too soon. Too late because in 1923 or 1924 there were as many picture galleries as night clubs in Montparnasse, to say nothing of the larger and more luxurious ones that sprang up in the Rue du Faubourg-Saint-Honoré.

The value of money had changed. Formerly, when Louis lived with his mother, people counted by sous. Now they counted by hundreds and thousands of francs, and artists whom no one would mention in ten years were selling their paintings at prices higher than those paid for works by an Italian master of the Renaissance.

Monsieur Suard had also started too soon, because people had not yet begun, as was to happen later, to distinguish between what would last and what would end up at the Flea Market.

The Rue de Seine was not a bad location, but the narrow shop window with the dark green frame was stuck between a butcher's shop whose marble counters were covered with poultry and a modest fruit and vegetable shop whose baskets and crates extended, as in the Rue Mouffetard, to the middle of the pavement.

Passers-by did not notice that between the two was a picture gallery, especially since the paintings that were shown and the posters that occasionally announced an exhibition bore unknown names.

It was to that period that journalists and others alluded later when they wrote that Cuchas had lived in poverty for years.

As a matter of fact, it did go on for years, with ups and downs, until 1927 or 1928. In order to carry on, Monsieur Suard sold some of his furniture and moved from his flat at the Porte d'Orléans to a cheaper one.

When he saw Louis enter the gallery with a canvas under his arm, he was torn between enthusiasm and his despair at not having money to give him.

'Are you at the end of your tether?'

Louis would smile and shake his head.

'There's someone interested who's supposed to come back on Monday. I'm sure he'll be back. He's excited by one of your canvases, "The Baskets", but I refused to let him have it cheap. Now's the time we've got to establish your reputation, and if I sell you for less than the others no one will take you seriously.'

The bowl was full, half full, or empty, depending on the month or the week. It was a big ceramic bowl that had been used for God knows what. There was no way of telling what craftsman had fired it, in what kiln, and how he had obtained that bright metallic red which had caught Louis's eye at the Flea Market in Saint-Ouen, where he sometimes roamed about on Sundays.

He had placed it on a shelf, for the studio had gradually become cluttered with tables, stands, easels, objects that interested no one, glass paperweights in which one could see snow falling, odd-shaped bottles of all colours – in short, a collection of odds and ends, which he called his treasure.

The bowl in the studio played the role of his mother's biscuit tin. When he came home with a little money, Cuchas would put it into the bowl, whether it was in change or notes.

'See whether there's enough left in the bowl to buy some salami,' he would say, without stopping his painting.

There was often a woman with him. He had built, with his own hands, a narrow couch, for he hated to sleep with anyone.

He had never been able to say no and everyone regarded his smile, his way of tilting his head, as an acceptance.

'I bet you're a painter, aren't you?'

He wore the same suit for ten years. It was made of a kind of corduroy that had been used for labourers' trousers when he was a child. He had not chosen it in order to look like a painter but because he had always wanted such a suit. Otherwise, clothes did not matter to him and he sometimes wore the same shirt for two weeks.

'You have a look in your eyes that women must find attractive.'

He did not believe it. He didn't care. He let them have their way. They would follow him home. Three cats had taken refuge in his studio, and he accepted a woman's presence as he did theirs.

He rather liked seeing a naked body moving about in the light that streamed in through the big window. But because of the complaints of a tenant whose flat faced the yard, he had to have a curtain, and one day, when there was money in the bowl, he had one made of the cheapest material he could find, burlap.

He was neither poor nor rich. He spent his time painting, in quest of the sparkling space that he had been seeking so long and that he continued to seek all his life.

Some girl friends stayed two days, others a month or more. For a time, there were two Lesbians, one of them a Swede, who had no place to sleep. They were fond of him, especially the Swede, whom he seemed to fascinate and who compared him to a Scandinavian elf.

Why did Cuchas suddenly think of Pliska one day when Suard, who was discouraged, spoke of giving up his gallery? He had run into the Czech again a few nights before on the terrace of the Dôme amidst a group of people talking different languages. He was the biggest and strongest of the party and had such a booming voice that despite the noise in the street he could be heard at the other end of the terrace.

'You ask my first name? . . . No first name. . . . Only Pliska . . . Pliska. . . . You all hear . . .'

Though he was drunk, he nevertheless recognized Louis, to whom he called his audience's attention.

'Ask my friend. . . . Knew him child. . . . Him know Pliska great sculptor. . . . Greatest sculptor in world. . . . Him have seen "Couple". . . . No more "Couple". . . . Changed name. . . . "Procreation" . . . eh! . . . "Procreation". . . . Understand? . . .'

This 'Procreation', which was to make Pliska famous and

really launch the Suard Gallery, not in the Rue de Seine but in the Rue la Boétie, attracted the attention of an American art critic who had been commissioned by a Philadelphia millionaire to buy the best works of painting and sculpture he could find for the collector's private museum, which he intended to bequeath to his city.

That was how one of Cuchas's small canvases, entitled 'The Wedding', happened to cross the Atlantic on the same boat as the Czech's monument.

Around the age of thirty, Louis became plump, and his cheekbones filled out and slightly dulled his features. He ate almost every day at the Caves d'Anjou, a restaurant with a tin counter and cane-bottomed chairs that was frequented by truck drivers. He would always sit in the same corner, for he liked corners and felt too conspicuous or vulnerable in the middle of a room.

A glass of white wine, Monsieur Cuchas?'

The carroty cat would jump on his knees and he would stroke it mechanically. He drank little, two or three glasses of white wine a day, walked the streets, and would stop to look at a piece of wall or watch women on a scaffold. He liked benches, especially those in the little parks or small squares where there was almost never anyone and where he could sit for two hours without being aware of the passing of time.

Suard was beginning to get better prices for his paintings and the bowl was almost always full.

'Is that where you keep your money?'

'It's beautiful, isn't it? I've never managed to get the same red.'

'Anyone can dip into it.'

He shrugged. Money or no money, his life remained the same. At times when he prowled about the Rue Mouffetard, he looked as if he were walking around a magic circle.

For a long time he had been inside it and he seemed to hesitate to re-enter it. Hadn't he picked the Caves d'Anjou at the corner of the Rue Rataud because it was at the frontier of his former universe?

Vladimir was living between Marseilles and Toulon. He had a car that stopped at the studio two or three times. He was more

318

ironic and aggressive than in the past and there was a certain disquieting heaviness in his gaze.

'Have you seen Mama?'

'I have. I don't like her man.'

'They're married.'

'I know.'

'So is Alice. She married a cattle dealer and claims she's happy.'

She too came to see him, though without her husband or children, for she had had two more since her second marriage.

'Are you in Paris alone?'

'No, all five of us came for the Motor Show.'

She had put on weight. Her gaze was lustreless.

'We're building a new house, a villa, two miles from Nevers. My husband's buying up all the grassland he can find. It's the best investment. I'm going to see Mama tomorrow.'

'Have you got her address?'

'She sent it me on a postcard.'

'She's remarried.'

'It's funny, isn't it? I'd have been embarrassed at her age.'

He would sometimes work on a painting for five or six hours at a stretch and then toss away his brush and throw himself down on his bed to cry.

Pliska encouraged him. Every time he came he was accompanied by a new girl whom he ordered, as soon as she opened her mouth:

'You not talk. . . Not know. . . . Only screw . . .'

He would examine the paintings one by one, carefully, with his brows knit. He was deeply moved one day when he caught sight of the box of coloured pencils he had given little Louis one Christmas Day.

'You keep?'

They were almost intact, having been used only for drawing the tree in the schoolyard and for two or three childish sketches. The dark blue one was missing. His sister had taken it one evening to copy the pattern of a skirt from a fashion magazine.

Since then he had painted another tree, the linden in the yard, 'Mr Tree'.

'Why Mister?'

What could he answer? He smiled, slightly embarrassed.

'I don't know.'

It had been the same with cabbages. He had painted lots of cabbages. Most people eat vegetables without ever having watched a cabbage or leek or young carrot actually live.

'Do you find cabbages decorative?'

'No. Not decorative.'

Journalists began coming to question him.

'Is it a memory from the time when you worked at Les Halles?'

'I don't know.'

One day when he was attending the opening of another painter's exhibition at the Suard Gallery, a voice cried out:

'Well, what do you know! The little saint!'

A man put out his hand. Louis tried in vain to attach a name to the face, which he nevertheless knew very well.

'Don't you remember? Randal. Raoul Randal, the one who fought you over a yellow marble. Is this your exhibition?'

'No.'

'I was told you'd become a painter. How's it going?'

He looked him up and down as if to judge the degree of his success from his face and clothes.

'I'm working.'

'Do you sell?'

'Sometimes.'

'That's good. What does this bird do? I don't know anything about art. I received an invitation because I've put some money into a small weekly.'

A journalist who had heard the conversation came over.

'Why did you call him the little saint?'

'Cuchas? Because at school he let everyone hit him without complaining to the teacher.

'Or maybe because he used to help his mother push her cart to Les Halles and back at three in the morning. She was a street-seller. They were very poor. If I remember right, there were two twins, older than he. They were nasty little bastards.'

Louis did not protest. He kept smiling, as he had smiled in the past when he was slapped or kicked. The story appeared in an

320

evening paper, which the concierge brought him. She was all excited.

'Now I understand, those cats you keep, those girls who take whatever they want.'

The legend spread. Before the second war, many people were calling him the little saint and caricatures of him appeared with a halo around his head.

Until the age of forty-two he had never had any desire to travel and it was only when people began to leave Paris when the Germans were expected to arrive any hour, that he left for the south. One of his collectors, a doctor, drove him as far as Moulins but went no farther because his wife had relatives there and it was unthinkable that the Germans would get as far as that. Louis got a few lifts from lorry-drivers and also walked part of the way. In Lyons, after waiting on the platform a night and a day, he was able to get into a train that took him to Cannes, where he was unable to find a room.

The sight of the sea thrilled him. However, he was obliged to go a bit north, first to Mougins, then to Mouans-Sartoux, a real village without villas or hotels for tourists, a few miles from Grasse.

He spent the war years there. He no more read the papers than he had done during the first war. He rented a shanty which he used as a studio. Suard and his family had settled in Nice.

'Well, do you find the light bright enough and the colours pure enough?'

'I thought I did at first.'

For two years he had been trying to render the vividness of nature.

'You no longer think so?'

'The light eats everything up, it chokes everything. All that's left is a kind of mush. I'd have done better to stay in Paris.'

'We'll be there before long. Here, take this! I've brought you a bit of butter that some friends sent me.'

Before long. . . . No. . . . It lasted another three years. Suard was selling his paintings at such high prices that Louis did not know what to do with the money. People were afraid of a devaluation and were buying anything.

'Do you want me to keep it for you?'

'I don't care.'

He had his corner in the local inn, the smell of which delighted him. His stoutness had gone and never came back. In fact, when he returned to his studio in Paris, where he was surprised to find every object in its place, he began to get lean. His hair, which remained fine and loose, had turned grey. It flitted about his face and made him look thinner and more delicately modelled than when he was a child.

There were paintings of his in many museums. People were surprised to find him in that comfortless studio where he did not even want to have a telephone. He continued to wear corduroy suits, though he could no longer find the thick, warm, strong cloth of the old days.

His grandmother had died. His mother and her husband were still living in the cottage at Joinville. Nobody in the family was left in the Rue Mouffetard, and when he went back to it he recognized few faces. Monsieur Stieb was dead. So were the Dorés. The old house was still there, but a six-storey building was under construction next to it.

'You're Louis Cuchas, aren't you, the half-brother of a man named Joseph Heurteau?'

He almost said no, because of the unfamiliar 'Joseph'.

'Do you mean Vladimir?'

'So you know his nickname?'

'He was called that when I was born.'

'Why?'

'I don't know.'

That was in 1960. His hair was now white and his features had become so pure that it was as if he were disembodied and were only a limpid gaze, a gentle, disquieting smile.

Two men had come to his studio and shown him their police badges.

'How long is it since you've seen him?'

'The last time was in Cannes, during the war.'

'What was he doing?'

'I don't know.'

'Didn't you ask him what he lived on?'

'No.'

'Did he spend a lot of money?'

322

'I don't know.'

'Didn't you notice that he hung around with shady characters?'

'He was alone with his wife. I happened to run into him in a café.'

'Do you mind if we look around your studio?'

The searched everywhere, methodically. One of them admitted in discouragement:

'We didn't find anything at your mother's place either.'

'What are you looking for?'

'Drugs. Joseph Heurteau, known as Vladimir, is one of the top men in the drugs racket in France. He was run in for pimping, but now we want to give him the works.'

He heard nothing more about Vladimir for a year. He was almost at the point of making the objects on this canvas vibrate by surrounding them with air or light. Almost. Not quite. It would take years.

He learned from his mother that Vladimir had been sentenced to fifteen years hard labour.

He continued to paint all day long. In most of his paintings there were traces of his mother, his sister Alice, and even little Emilie. Nobody noticed it. The faces of the redheads also appeared several times, as did the stove, a yellow marble, the sheet with a hole in it that had separated the mattresses from Gabrielle's bed.

He would soon be seventy and walked with short steps, conscious of his fragility.

In the evening, he liked to sit in a local cinema amidst the warm crowd. When early films were shown he discovered the actors of the time when he was a young man and had hardly been aware of the existence of the cinema.

He had worked a great deal. He was still working. It would take him years more to render what he felt had always been in him.

'What exactly is your aim?'

'I don't know.'

That was the sentence that he had uttered most often in the course of his life and which he kept repeating.

Monsieur Suard was dead. His son, who had taken over the

gallery, called him Maître. Many people called him Maître.

He remembered the evening when he had thought he saw a slight cloud come over his mother's face, which had always been radiant. One of the twins was dead. Emilie was dead. Pretty Alice was fat and callous. She too was clouded over. And Vladimir had no chance of getting out of prison alive. Only one of them was left, far away, in Ecuador, and he had stopped writing. He was nearing seventy-five and his wife was over eighty. Were they still alive and were they still hunting for butterflies and birds of paradise?

At times he thought he could feel the cloud coming over him too. He would think of the mattresses, of Emilie's cot, of the Rue Mouffetard, of the push-carts arriving at Les Halles.

Had he not taken something from everything and everyone? Had he not used their substance?

He didn't know, he mustn't know, otherwise he would be unable to carry on to the end.

He continued to walk with little steps, to smile.

'May I ask you, Maître, how you see yourself?'

He did not reflect very long. His face lit up for a moment as he said, joyously, and modestly:

'As a small boy.'

Epalinges, 13 October 1964

MORE ABOUT PENGUINS, PELICANS AND PUFFINS

For further information about books available from Penguins please write to Dept EP, Penguin Books Ltd, Harmondsworth, Middlesex UB7 0DA.

In the U.S.A.: For a complete list of books available from Penguins in the United States write to Dept DG, Penguin Books, 299 Murray Hill Parkway, East Rutherford, New Jersey 07073.

In Canada: For a complete list of books available from Penguins in Canada write to Penguin Books Canada Limited, 2801 John Street, Markham, Ontario L3R 1B4.

In Australia: For a complete list of books available from Penguins in Australia write to the Marketing Department, Penguin Books Australia Ltd, P.O. Box 257, Ringwood, Victoria 3134.

In New Zealand: For a complete list of books available from Penguins in New Zealand write to the Marketing Department, Penguin Books (N.Z.) Ltd, Private Bag, Takapuna, Auckland 9.

In India: For a complete list of books available from Penguins in India write to Penguin Overseas Ltd, 706 Eros Apartments, 56 Nehru Place, New Delhi 110019.

PENGUIN OMNIBUSES

☐ *Life with Jeeves* **P. G. Wodehouse**   £3.95

Containing *Right Ho, Jeeves, The Inimitable Jeeves* and *Very Good, Jeeves!* in which Wodehouse lures us, once again, into the evergreen world of Bertie Wooster, his terrifying Aunt Agatha, his man Jeeves and other eggs, good and bad.

☐ *The Penguin Book of Ghost Stories*   £4.95

An anthology to set the spine tingling, including stories by Zola, Kleist, Sir Walter Scott, M. R. James, Elizabeth Bowen and A. S. Byatt.

☐ *The Penguin Book of Horror Stories*   £4.95

Including stories by Maupassant, Poe, Gautier, Conan Doyle, L. P. Hartley and Ray Bradbury, in a selection of the most horrifying horror from the eighteenth century to the present day.

☐ *The Penguin Complete Novels of Jane Austen*   £5.95

Containing the seven great novels: *Sense and Sensibility, Pride and Prejudice, Mansfield Park, Emma, Northanger Abbey, Persuasion* and *Lady Susan.*

☐ *Perfick, Perfick!* **H. E. Bates**   £4.95

The adventures of the irrepressible Larkin family, in four novels: *The Darling Buds of May, A Breath of French Air, When the Green Woods Laugh* and *Oh! To Be in England.*

☐ *Famous Trials*
  Harry Hodge and James H. Hodge   £3.95

From Madeleine Smith to Dr Crippen and Lord Haw-Haw, this volume contains the most sensational murder and treason trials, selected by John Mortimer from the classic Penguin Famous Trials series.

A CHOICE OF PENGUINS

☐ **_Further Chronicles of Fairacre_ 'Miss Read'** £3.95

Full of humour, warmth and charm, these four novels – _Miss Clare Remembers, Over the Gate, The Fairacre Festival_ and _Emily Davis_ – make up an unforgettable picture of English village life.

☐ **_Callanish_ William Horwood** £1.95

From the acclaimed author of _Duncton Wood_, this is the haunting story of Creggan, the captured golden eagle, and his struggle to be free.

☐ **_Act of Darkness_ Francis King** £2.50

Anglo-India in the 1930s, where a peculiarly vicious murder triggers 'A terrific mystery story . . . a darkly luminous parable about innocence and evil' – _The New York Times_. 'Brilliantly successful' – _Daily Mail_. 'Unputdownable' – _Standard_

☐ **_Death in Cyprus_ M. M. Kaye** £1.95

Holidaying on Aphrodite's beautiful island, Amanda finds herself caught up in a murder mystery in which no one, not even the attractive painter Steven Howard, is quite what they seem . . .

☐ **_Lace_ Shirley Conran** £2.95

Lace is, quite simply, a publishing sensation: the story of Judy, Kate, Pagan and Maxine; the bestselling novel that teaches men about women, and women about themselves. 'Riches, bitches, sex and jetsetters' locations – they're all there' – _Sunday Express_

A CHOICE OF PENGUINS

☐ *West of Sunset* **Dirk Bogarde** £1.95

'His virtues as a writer are precisely those which make him the most compelling screen actor of his generation,' is what *The Times* said about Bogarde's savage, funny, romantic novel set in the gaudy wastes of Los Angeles.

☐ *The Riverside Villas Murder* **Kingsley Amis** £1.95

Marital duplicity, sexual discovery and murder with a thirties back-cloth: 'Amis in top form' – *The Times*. 'Delectable from page to page . . . effortlessly witty' – C. P. Snow in the *Financial Times*

☐ *A Dark and Distant Shore* **Reay Tannahill** £3.95

Vilia is the unforgettable heroine, Kinveil Castle is her destiny, in this full-blooded saga spanning a century of Victoriana, empire, hatreds and love affairs. 'A marvellous blend of *Gone with the Wind* and *The Thorn Birds*. You will enjoy every page' – *Daily Mirror*

☐ *Kingsley's Touch* **John Collee** £1.95

'Gripping . . . I recommend this chilling and elegantly written medical thriller' – *Daily Express*. 'An absolutely outstanding storyteller' – *Daily Telegraph*

☐ *The Far Pavilions* **M. M. Kaye** £4.95

Holding all the romance and high adventure of nineteenth-century India, M. M. Kaye's magnificent, now famous, novel has at its heart the passionate love of an Englishman for Juli, his Indian princess. 'Wildly exciting' – *Daily Telegraph*

A CHOICE OF PENGUINS

☐ *Small World* **David Lodge** £2.50

A jet-propelled academic romance, sequel to *Changing Places*. 'A new comic débâcle on every page' – *The Times*. 'Here is everything one expects from Lodge but three times as entertaining as anything he has written before' – *Sunday Telegraph*

☐ *The Neverending Story* **Michael Ende** £3.95

The international bestseller, now a major film: 'A tale of magical adventure, pursuit and delay, danger, suspense, triumph' – *The Times Literary Supplement*

☐ *The Sword of Honour Trilogy* **Evelyn Waugh** £3.95

Containing *Men at Arms, Officers and Gentlemen* and *Unconditional Surrender*, the trilogy described by Cyril Connolly as 'unquestionably the finest novels to have come out of the war'.

☐ *The Honorary Consul* **Graham Greene** £2.50

In a provincial Argentinian town, a group of revolutionaries kidnap the wrong man . . . 'The tension never relaxes and one reads hungrily from page to page, dreading the moment it will all end' – Auberon Waugh in the *Evening Standard*

☐ *The First Rumpole Omnibus* **John Mortimer** £4.95

Containing *Rumpole of the Bailey*, *The Trials of Rumpole* and *Rumpole's Return*. 'A fruity, foxy masterpiece, defender of our wilting faith in mankind' – *Sunday Times*

☐ *Scandal* **A. N. Wilson** £2.25

Sexual peccadillos, treason and blackmail are all ingredients on the boil in A. N. Wilson's new, *cordon noir* comedy. 'Drily witty, deliciously nasty' – *Sunday Telegraph*

A CHOICE OF PENGUINS

☐ *Stanley and the Women* **Kingsley Amis** £2.50

'Very good, very powerful . . . beautifully written . . . This is Amis *père* at his best' – Anthony Burgess in the *Observer*. 'Everybody should read it' – *Daily Mail*

☐ *The Mysterious Mr Ripley* **Patricia Highsmith** £4.95

Containing *The Talented Mr Ripley*, *Ripley Underground* and *Ripley's Game*. 'Patricia Highsmith is the poet of apprehension' – Graham Greene. 'The Ripley books are marvellously, insanely readable' – *The Times*

☐ *Earthly Powers* **Anthony Burgess** £4.95

'Crowded, crammed, bursting with manic erudition, garlicky puns, omnilingual jokes . . . (a novel) which meshes the real and personalized history of the twentieth century' – Martin Amis

☐ *Life & Times of Michael K* **J. M. Coetzee** £2.95

The Booker Prize-winning novel: 'It is hard to convey . . . just what Coetzee's special quality is. His writing gives off whiffs of Conrad, of Nabokov, of Golding, of the Paul Theroux of *The Mosquito Coast*. But he is none of these, he is a harsh, compelling new voice' – Victoria Glendinning

☐ *The Stories of William Trevor* £5.95

'Trevor packs into each separate five or six thousand words more richness, more laughter, more ache, more multifarious human-ness than many good writers manage to get into a whole novel' – *Punch*

☐ *The Book of Laughter and Forgetting*
Milan Kundera £3.95

'A whirling dance of a book . . . a masterpiece full of angels, terror, ostriches and love . . . No question about it. The most important novel published in Britain this year' – Salman Rushdie

ENGLISH AND AMERICAN
LITERATURE IN PENGUINS

☐ *Emma* **Jane Austen**   £1.25

'I am going to take a heroine whom no one but myself will much like,'
declared Jane Austen of Emma, her most spirited and controversial
heroine in a comedy of self-deceit and self-discovery.

☐ *Tender is the Night* **F. Scott Fitzgerald**   £2.95

Fitzgerald worked on seventeen different versions of this novel, and
its obsessions – idealism, beauty, dissipation, alcohol and insanity –
were those that consumed his own marriage and his life.

☐ *The Life of Johnson* **James Boswell**   £2.95

Full of gusto, imagination, conversation and wit, Boswell's immortal
portrait of Johnson is as near a novel as a true biography can be, and
still regarded by many as the finest 'life' ever written. This shortened
version is based on the 1799 edition.

☐ *A House and its Head* **Ivy Compton-Burnett**   £4.95

In a novel 'as trim and tidy as a hand-grenade' (as Pamela Hansford
Johnson put it), Ivy Compton-Burnett penetrates the facade of a
conventional, upper-class Victorian family to uncover a chasm of
violent emotions – jealousy, pain, frustration and sexual passion.

☐ *The Trumpet Major* **Thomas Hardy**   £1.50

Although a vein of unhappy unrequited love runs through this novel,
Hardy also draws on his warmest sense of humour to portray
Wessex village life at the time of the Napoleonic wars.

☐ *The Complete Poems of Hugh MacDiarmid*

☐ Volume One   £8.95
☐ Volume Two   £8.95

The definitive edition of work by the greatest Scottish poet since
Robert Burns, edited by his son Michael Grieve, and W. R. Aitken.

ENGLISH AND AMERICAN
LITERATURE IN PENGUINS

☐ *Main Street* **Sinclair Lewis** £4.95

The novel that added an immortal chapter to the literature of America's Mid-West, *Main Street* contains the comic essence of Main Streets everywhere.

☐ *The Compleat Angler* **Izaak Walton** £2.50

A celebration of the countryside, and the superiority of those in 1653, as now, who love *quietnesse, vertue* and, above all, *Angling*. 'No fish, however coarse, could wish for a doughtier champion than Izaak Walton' – Lord Home

☐ *The Portrait of a Lady* **Henry James** £2.50

'One of the two most brilliant novels in the language', according to F. R. Leavis, James's masterpiece tells the story of a young American heiress, prey to fortune-hunters but not without a will of her own.

☐ *Hangover Square* **Patrick Hamilton** £3.95

Part love story, part thriller, and set in the publands of London's Earls Court, this novel caught the conversational tone of a whole generation in the uneasy months before the Second World War.

☐ *The Rainbow* **D. H. Lawrence** £2.50

Written between *Sons and Lovers* and *Women in Love*, *The Rainbow* covers three generations of Brangwens, a yeoman family living on the borders of Nottinghamshire.

☐ *Vindication of the Rights of Woman*
Mary Wollstonecraft £2.95

Although Walpole once called her 'a hyena in petticoats', Mary Wollstonecraft's vision was such that modern feminists continue to go back and debate the arguments so powerfully set down here.

KING PENGUIN

☐ *Selected Poems* **Tony Harrison** £3.95

Poetry Book Society Recommendation. 'One of the few modern poets who actually has the gift of composing poetry' – James Fenton in the *Sunday Times*

☐ *The Book of Laughter and Forgetting*
Milan Kundera £3.95

'A whirling dance of a book . . . a masterpiece full of angels, terror, ostriches and love . . . No question about it. The most important novel published in Britain this year' – Salman Rushdie in the *Sunday Times*

☐ *The Sea of Fertility* **Yukio Mishima** £9.95

Containing *Spring Snow, Runaway Horses, The Temple of Dawn* and *The Decay of the Angel*: 'These four remarkable novels are the most complete vision we have of Japan in the twentieth century' – Paul Theroux

☐ *The Hawthorne Goddess* **Glyn Hughes** £2.95

Set in eighteenth century Yorkshire where 'the heroine, Anne Wylde, represents the doom of nature and the land . . . Hughes has an arresting style, both rich and abrupt' – *The Times*

☐ *A Confederacy of Dunces* **John Kennedy Toole** £3.95

In this Pulitzer Prize-winning novel, in the bulky figure of Ignatius J. Reilly an immortal comic character is born. 'I succumbed, stunned and seduced . . . it is a masterwork of comedy' – *The New York Times*

☐ *The Last of the Just* **André Schwartz-Bart** £3.95

The story of Ernie Levy, the last of the just, who was killed at Auschwitz in 1943: 'An outstanding achievement, of an altogether different order from even the best of earlier novels which have attempted this theme' – John Gross in the *Sunday Telegraph*

KING PENGUIN

☐ **The White Hotel** D. M. Thomas £3.95

'A major artist has once more appeared', declared the *Spectator* on the publication of this acclaimed, now famous novel which recreates the imagined case history of one of Freud's woman patients.

☐ **Dangerous Play: Poems 1974–1984**
Andrew Motion £2.95

Winner of the John Llewelyn Rhys Memorial Prize. Poems and an autobiographical prose piece, *Skating*, by the poet acclaimed in the *TLS* as 'a natural heir to the tradition of Edward Thomas and Ivor Gurney'.

☐ **A Time to Dance** Bernard Mac Laverty £2.50

Ten stories, including 'My Dear Palestrina' and 'Phonefun Limited', by the author of *Cal*: 'A writer who has a real affinity with the short story form' – *The Times Literary Supplement*

☐ **Keepers of the House** Lisa St Aubin de Terán £2.95

Seventeen-year-old Lydia Sinclair marries Don Diego Beltrán and goes to live on his family's vast, decaying Andean farm. This exotic and flamboyant first novel won the Somerset Maugham Award.

☐ **The Deptford Trilogy** Robertson Davies £5.95

'Who killed Boy Staunton?' – around this central mystery is woven an exhilarating and cunningly contrived trilogy of novels: *Fifth Business, The Manticore* and *World of Wonders*.

☐ **The Stories of William Trevor** £5.95

'Trevor packs into each separate five or six thousand words more richness, more laughter, more ache, more multifarious human-ness than many good writers manage to get into a whole novel' – *Punch*. 'Classics of the genre' – Auberon Waugh